On Her Majesty's

BERLIN MISSION

****

An **Ian Black** *Novel*

Richard *and* Barbara Osborn

RICHARD AND BARBARA OSBORN

For our family members and friends who have put up with us
while we wrote this book

Thank You for your patience

The authors of this book would like to pay honour and
respect to all the military/intelligence personnel of the three
Western powers, who served in Berlin during the Cold War.

Britannia-American Books
ISBN-13: 978-0692780855
ISBN-10: 0692780858

BritanniaAmericanPublishing@yahoo.com

LIST OF ADDENDUMS

For those readers who desire information on locations, abbreviations and people, please refer to the following pages:

PROLOGUE

On the 7th of May 1945, General Alfred Jodl signed the instrument of surrender, on behalf of the German Government, which was headed by Admiral Karl Dönitz, and World War Two officially came to an end. Although this was an unconditional surrender, isolated units of the German Army kept fighting for a few days, mainly against the Russians. In the summer of 1945, a conference was held at Potsdam where the four major powers – United States, Great Britain, France and the Soviet Union – finalized an agreement for controlling Germany. The country, including Berlin, was divided into four sectors; one for each of the victors.

The major problem, caused by the division of Germany, was that Berlin lay over one hundred road miles inside the Russian sector.

In 1945, at the end of the war, the German city of Berlin, formerly the capital of Germany, was divided into four sectors. The three Western powers, France, Great Britain and the United States, combined their sectors into one, but the Russians would not allow the East Berliners to be part of the West.

In 1948 Joseph Stalin, the dictator of the Soviet Union, tried to starve the western part of Berlin into submission. However, the Western powers managed to create an airlift that supplied West Berlin with enough fuel, food and aid to survive. The blockade by Russia lasted from the 24th of June 1948 to the 12th of May 1949. During that time there were over two hundred thousand flights carried out by the West to help the Berliners. After the Berlin blockade was lifted, the situation in Berlin became fairly peaceful.

According to the legal theory followed by the Western Allies, the occupation of most of Germany ended in 1949, with the declaration of the Federal Republic of Germany on the 23rd of May 1949 and the German Democratic Republic on the 7th of October 1949. However, because the occupation of Berlin could only be ended by a quadripartite agreement, Berlin remained an occupied territory under the formal sovereignty of the allies. Hence, the *Grundgesetz*, or the constitution of the Federal Republic, was not fully applicable to West Berlin.

On the 16th of June 1953, East German workers started to riot against the East German plans to make the GDR a fully communist state. The Russians sent in tanks to quell the uprising, and the Eisenhower Administration shipped food to the East, where the people did not have enough to eat. This food relief program went on for about five months and then the Americans decided it wasn't having the required effect. The GDR government placed obstacles in front of the food shipments and many did not go to the people who needed them.

Seeing the plight of their country, the East Germans decided to vote with their feet. The brain drain from the East to the West became a torrent, and the East started to lose educators, scientists, engineers, lawyers, doctors and other professionals. In 1952, the GDR, along with Russia's help, had decided that they had to seal off East Germany from the West. They built a barbed wire fence, together with border posts, guards, mine fields and patrols, and this effectively stopped East Germans from fleeing to the West, except through Berlin. The twenty-seven mile border between East and West Berlin was still open, and the city became a magnet for East Germans, who wanted to flee.

From 1958-1960, the situation in Berlin went from bad to worse, until the East Germany leaders decided that they had to totally stop the brain drain. It is estimated that five thousand East Germans fled to the West every day and that East Germany had lost twenty percent of its population by 1960.

The British, French, Americans and West Germans built up listening posts, developed HUMINT, SIGINT and other forms of intelligence, even tapped into the Russian cables (Operation Gold or Stopwatch) and, for a short time, monitored communications between Berlin and Moscow. Berlin was crawling with agents from the CIA, MI6, KGB, GRU, BND and other spy agencies; in fact they were almost tripping over each other. After attending a Special Advanced Intelligence course for selected officers, Lieutenant Ian Black of the British Army Intelligence Corps was assigned to this chaotic situation.

This story is about one Englishman (half American) who had served two years in the Cyprus Emergency and was now going to be influential in making a difference for the British, by collecting intelligence on future Russian and GDR operations in Berlin and Germany. Specifically, he was On Her Majesty's Berlin Mission.

GERMANY – 1960s

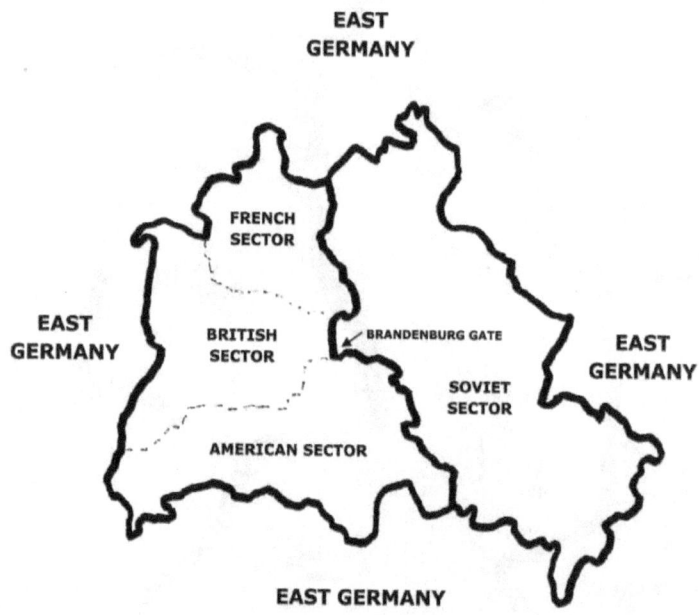

BERLIN - 1960s

1

Der Mauer

Ian Black, a first lieutenant stationed with the British Army Intelligence Corps in West Berlin, would remember this evening for the rest of his life. The date was Saturday, the 12th of August, 1961 and, at 1900 hours, the sky above Berlin was partially cloudy, with the sun heading down toward sunset, around one hour away. The temperature hovered around sixteen degrees Celsius and, since it wasn't raining, many Germans were strolling down the streets, looking in the shop windows. Others were in their favourite bar, drinking lager and having fun.

Ian left his flat and headed for his prearranged date with a young woman named Monika, at the Leuthen Club near the Brandenburg Gate, in the American zone of the city. She thought it would be safest if they met in the West. He was dressed in civvies and strolled along, trying to hide his military bearing. As he made his way to the meeting place, he thought about how he first met Monika and her unusual background. She had long black hair, an exquisite figure and was about five foot eight inches tall. Her eyes were blue, and they sent a sensuous message every time you looked into them. Overall, she reminded Ian of his lost

Cyprus love, Aphrodite Palas, who had been shot by an EOKA terrorist and died in his arms.

He first met Monika a few months ago at this same West Berlin Club, and since then, had a few dates with her. She had been somewhat secretive, but she did reveal a few facts of her background. Her real name was Ingrid Meyer, but she never told Ian that. He only found that out a few months later. She was a mistress of a key East German official; however Monika never told Ian the name of her benefactor. This politician had provided her with a better than average East German flat, and he made arrangements for it to be decorated with European made furniture. He also arranged to get her a steady job at the GDR Stellennachweise (Employment Agency). His wife never knew that he had given a young woman a place to live or at least gave no indication that she knew.

Ian, on the other hand, had told her his name was Kurt and that he worked for a large West German architectural firm designing new buildings, mainly in West Berlin. Monika never questioned Kurt about his job or the firm he worked for. Maybe she didn't want to find out it wasn't true or perhaps, she didn't want Kurt to ask too many questions about her situation. Anyway, they enjoyed each other's company.

Ian entered the night club and found a table that allowed him to keep an eye on the entrance. He ordered a beer and waited for Monika to appear through the dark, wooden door. He had only been there about ten minutes, enjoying his beer, when she walked in. She was wearing a colorful, summer dress and a light jacket, to keep the evening chill off her shoulders. Some of the males in the bar undressed her with their eyes and were disappointed, when she walked over to Kurt.

He stood up as she approached and said in German, "Monika, you look lovely tonight, as usual."

He pulled out a chair and she sat down saying, "It's great to see you again."

"What would you like to drink?" he asked.

"I think I'll have a Scotch and soda on ice," she responded, also in German.

Kurt never spoke to her in English, since he wanted her to know him as a West German citizen. In addition, he wasn't sure that she could speak English.

Ian called the waiter over and ordered Monika's cocktail.

"I'm glad you could make it this evening. It's been a while since we last met. I've been very busy on a new design project my company has a contract for," Kurt said to her.

"Is this project for West or East Berlin?" she asked.

"It's for West Berlin. We rarely receive a contract from the GDR, as they usually give them to an East German company."

"My friend Erich......" She stopped talking for a moment and then continued, hoping Kurt had not heard the name. "My friend has been very busy the last few weeks, which has allowed me to get into the West now and again. He has warned me, however, not to stay too long over there."

"Why don't you move to our side of the border? You would be a lot better off."

Monika replied, "My father is a party official in Leipzig and, if I left the German Democratic Republic, he would lose his job and maybe be sent to prison. Besides, my friend is very good to me and makes sure I'm well taken care of."

"Why did he warn you not to stay too long in the western sectors of Berlin?"

"He only warned me about this recently. Maybe the Stasi secret police are keeping a close eye on any person who visits there. Many doctors, lawyers, teachers and other professionals are fleeing to the Federal German Republic. My friend also told me that something had to be done about it or the GDR would not remain a viable country. In fact, our leader went to Moscow a couple of weeks ago, to meet with Khrushchev. What they talked about I don't know, but my friend became very agitated and preoccupied, when Herr Ulbricht returned. That was when my benefactor told me that he would be tied up for the next few weeks, on a crucial project. I believe that today he had to go to a major government meeting at Döllnsee. Of course, he didn't tell me the purpose of the get together, but it seemed to be very important."

While she was talking, Kurt absorbed all the details, including the first name she had let slip.

He thought, *"I bet the benefactor she's talking about could be Erich Honecker, who is about fifty years old. I wonder if they are getting close to building the Wall (Der Mauer). He had heard rumors from another source that it might be built in the middle of August."*

Ian had always guessed a barrier or wall would probably be built on an early Sunday morning, when most East Germans would be asleep.

"Monika, let's not discuss politics all evening. The weather is balmy and we should walk down the main shopping area and window shop. What do you think?"

"That's a great idea. Why don't we do that and then walk back to my flat for a nightcap. As I said earlier, we don't have to worry about him, since he'll be tied up for the next few weeks."

Ian thought for a moment and then replied, "Yes, that sounds like a great idea. If there's any problem in the East, I can quickly slip back to the West, since your flat is fairly close to the border."

"Don't worry Kurt, there shouldn't be any problem and with your Federal German Republic ID card you'll be able to just walk back into the West."

After Ian had paid the tab, they both rose from their chairs and walked out of the club, into the mild evening air. They strolled down a few streets looking in the shop windows, ending up on Ebertstrasse and headed for the Brandenburg Gate. At the Gate, they crossed over the border into East Berlin. There they were watched closely by some men, which Kurt suspected were East German plainclothes police. The men did not bother them, as they walked toward Schadowstrasse, where Monika's flat was located. It was in a fairly modern-looking, building compared to a lot of the common, drab East German tenements that had been built since World War Two ended.

Inside the building, they had to climb up three flights of stairs to her flat, as the lift was inoperable at the time. Monika opened her door and they both walked in. She then closed and locked the door behind them.

"Sorry about the lift. It's supposed to be repaired in a few days. How about if I rustle up some currywurst and pommes frites, while you go and open a bottle of wine to go with it?" she asked.

"That sounds great to me, "Kurt responded. "Where do you keep your wine?"

"You'll find a bottle of white wine in that small refrigerator over in the corner, and the corkscrew is in the third drawer down to the left of the fridge. We can watch the telly while we're eating. I believe the western show *Bonanza* will be on in a few minutes. Since I'm close to the border, I can pick up the West German channel ARD. However, it's illegal to watch ARD's *Das Erste* station, so we'll have to keep the sound down low. The English audio is dubbed into German, which sometimes is not too good."

"That sounds like a great idea. I've watched the programme a few times and I agree the audio could be better."

Soon, they were watching the western on her black and white television, eating the currywurst and washing it down with the wine.

"You're an excellent cook, Monika. That was the best currywurst I've ever tasted."

13

"I'm glad you enjoyed it, along with the television programme. Now it's time to pay for your dinner and the *Bonanza* show. Let me look at your hands, Kurt."

Kurt held them out to Monika, who took them into hers.

"They feel soft enough to me. They'll do quite well," Monika told Kurt, with a smile.

She crooked her finger saying, "Follow me."

She rose from the sofa and went into her bedroom, with Kurt walking right behind her. Once in the bedroom, she slowly removed each article of her clothing, while Kurt watched. She then lay face down on the bed.

Kurt looked at her soft, slim body and thought, "Boy *she's beautiful, sexy looking and her curves match her silky voice.*"

Turning her head to one side, she smiled at Kurt and said, "You can pay for your supper by rubbing lotion on my back. You'll find a bottle in the bathroom medicine cabinet."

Feeling a little nervous, Kurt asked, "Are you sure that your friend will not burst in on us?"

Shaking her head, she answered, "No, don't worry, as I mentioned he went to an important meeting at the Döllnsee, an old hunting estate of Hermann Goering and will probably be busy for the next couple of days."

Kurt went into the small bathroom, found the lotion and returned to the bedroom. He sat on the bed and prepared to massage her back. However, before he could open the lotion bottle, she sat up, slowly unbuttoned his shirt and slid it off his muscular shoulders.

Kurt stood up unzipped his trousers and let them fall to the floor. She looked at his trim body and watched as his member began to grow.

She took her hand and pulled him down to the bed. Kurt started to apply the lotion to her back and small, round, firm buttocks. She closed her eyes and moaned, in pleasure, as his firm soft hands rubbed her body, including her legs and feet. After about ten minutes, she rolled over on her back and Kurt applied lotion to her front. She lay there with her eyes closed, as he slowly and lightly massaged her firm breasts and flat stomach. He even rubbed the patch of dark hair at the spot where her long legs stretched from her body. All the time, she expressed her delight in what he was doing, with a sensual smile and low moans of pleasure. As he was rubbing her beautiful body, she opened her eyes slightly and looked at his member that had now grown hard and totally erect.

She thought, *"Tonight is going to be better than I thought it would be. I think he's about ready to take me."*

She fully opened her eyes and said to him, "Okay, it's time for me to reward you for all the hard work you've done."

She sat up on the bed and said, looking him straight in his eyes, "Now it's your turn to lie on the bed with your back to the sheet and looking straight at the ceiling."

Kurt did as he was told and as he lay on his back staring at the ceiling, she looked at his firm, large member pointing almost vertically from the junction, where his legs joined his body.

She smiled lustily to herself, as she looked at the trophy waiting for her. She straddled him with her honey pot entrance just inches from the top of his penis. Holding his throbbing member with one hand, she held it at the entrance to her vagina, and slowly lowered herself onto it. As it entered her body, Monika gave a moan of ecstasy.

She took hold of his hands, placed them on her buttocks and then slowly moved her body up and down. Kurt knew what she wanted, and he used his hands to help her get the correct pumping motion. Soon she was moving up and down faster and faster, until they both finally exploded with delight. He shot his fluid into her, while she went through a lustful orgasm. He felt some of his semen flow down his member, but that didn't bother him at all. She slowly lifted herself off his shrinking member and lay down beside him, giving him a sensuous kiss on his lips, muttering, "Thank you Kurt, that was heaven."

He thought to himself, *"I haven't felt this good since I was in Cyprus with Aphrodite, almost two years ago."*

They lay on the bed awake, stroking each other and making small talk. After about forty-five minutes, Kurt was ready to take Monika again. His member was not as hard as it had been, but her hand had caused it to firm up.

"Are you ready to try that again? Practice makes perfect, I believe," he said to her.

"Yes please," she replied.

Kurt spread her legs apart, climbed on top of her and slowly entered her honey pot. Again, as before, she groaned in ecstasy. Her vagina was very moist, partly from her fluids and also from his earlier eruption. He slowly moved in and out, and then increased the pace. Her hands were on his buttocks, making sure he had the right rhythm. Monika wanted to make certain that he didn't go too fast, as she wanted to make the experience last as long as possible.

Finally, when she knew her orgasm was coming close, she moved her hands causing him to go faster and faster; ultimately both of them came together at the same time.

"That was wonderful, Kurt. My whole body is throbbing. I never thought it could feel so good."

They lay together and slowly drifted off to sleep. The time was 23:30, on her twenty-four hour clock.

Kurt woke with a start, at thirty minutes after midnight, when he heard a low rumble in the distance. The sound got louder and louder as it approached. He climbed out of the bed and went to the window that allowed for a partial view of the Brandenburg Gate.

To his amazement, in the area of the Gate, he could see GDR army lorries and soldiers milling about, stretching barbed wire just inside the white line, which marked the border between East and West.

"Shit, this is it," he thought. *"They're finally sealing the border. The date in my intelligence report was only off by a week. All the rumours about Operation Rose were true. Der Mauer! I better get back to the West quickly, before I'm cut off."*

He shook Monika awake, who cried out, "What's wrong? We only just went to sleep."

"I have to go immediately. They're sealing off the border. It's happening; Der Mauer."

"Are you sure? I didn't think it was going to happen so soon," she said.

"I have to go now or I could be stuck in the East. Why don't you come with me?"

"I couldn't do that. As I told you before, my family is in Leipzig and they would be in danger, if I deserted the GDR."

Kurt quickly put his clothes on and gave Monika a kiss. "I'll call you soon to make sure you're okay. I'd like to see you again, if that'll be possible."

"Lock the door as you leave. I too hope I'll see you again; be careful," she said sleepily.

Kurt left her flat, making sure the door was locked behind him. He ran down the stairs to the complex main entrance. He exited the building and walked hurriedly away from the direction of the Gate. He hugged the wall of the buildings and tried to stay in the shadows.

As he walked down the street and came to the first road that led to the border, he saw an East German Bereitschaftspolizei (aka anti-riot policeman) standing guard. He assumed he was there to prevent anyone crossing the border. Kurt could see that he was armed with a PPsh-41 submachine gun.

He continued down the street until he came to a small narrow alley that looked like it also led to the white line dividing East and West. He turned into it and hurried towards the next street and the border. Halfway down the backstreet, an East German Bereitschaftspolizei stepped out of the shadows and blocked Kurt's way.

"What are you doing here?" said the soldier, who was also carrying a PPsh-41 submachine gun.

"I'm a West German and I need to get back home to my wife and children," Kurt lied.

"If I help you get across the border, will you take me with you?" the soldier asked Kurt, who was taken aback by the question.

"I don't want to stay in the East," he continued. "I have friends and relatives in Dusseldorf. Please help me. Don't be afraid, this gun is not loaded. In fact, they told us that we'll not be issued any ammunition for forty-eight hours. Authorities want to see what the reaction of the West will be to the sealing of the border. By the way, my name is Hermann."

"Well Hermann, my friends call me Kurt, and we'd better move quickly before we have to jump over the barbed wire. Follow me."

Kurt and Hermann ran down the alley toward the next cross street and the border that lay fifteen meters beyond it. As they reached the end of the alley, they looked out and saw another East German Bereitschaftspolizei standing with his PPsh-41, about one hundred meters away, at the end of another road.

Kurt turned and said to the soldier with him, "Let's hope he doesn't have any ammunition either. Are you ready to run?"

Hermann nodded and Kurt said, "Let's go."

They both sprinted across the road and the fifteen meters of gravel toward the white line, which marked the border. As they did so, the soldier at the next street shouted, "Halt or I'll shoot." Kurt and his new friend kept running. When they reached the white line, Hermann took off his gun and threw it as hard as he could back into East Berlin.

The soldier at the other street never fired a shot. Obviously, he hadn't been issued any ammunition either.

Kurt breathed a sigh of relief, because if he had been caught in the East, he would have been in major trouble. He turned to Hermann and thanked him for his help in crossing the border. He never told him that his real name was Ian Black and he was in the British Army Intelligence Corps.

Ian told Hermann to follow him and they found a taxi, which took them to the closest West German police station. They entered the building and found it was pandemonium in there. Officers were rushing in all directions. Obviously, they knew that the East Germans were sealing the border, and all available officers had been called in to work.

"Take a seat over there against the wall, while I go up and talk with the police officers," Ian told Hermann.

Hermann replied, "I'll do as you say. Am I in trouble with the West authorities?"

"No, you'll be fine. I won't leave until I have assurances from the police that you won't be harmed."

Ian went up to the counter and showed the officer his British military ID card, making sure that Hermann could not see it.

"Officer, I just returned from East Berlin ten minutes ago, and the East Germans were stringing barbed wire along the border."

"Yes sir, we've already received a report about that situation, as you can see by all the officers rushing around here."

"The East German Bereitschaftspolizei you see seated, over by the far wall, fled the East with me. He has relatives in Dusseldorf and he wants to reach them, so they can help him adapt to the West."

"We don't process anyone here at the station, other than criminals. He'll have to go to the Marienfelde refugee centre, in the south of Berlin. There they'll take care of him and help him reach his relatives in Dusseldorf."

19

"I'll go over and tell him the procedure. How will he get to Marienfelde?" Ian asked.

"As soon as I can free up a car and a driver, I'll have an officer take him down to the centre."

Ian walked over to Hermann and explained the situation about being processed for entry to West Berlin and West Germany.

"The police here will take you to the Marienfelde centre, as soon as they can spare a car and driver. You've nothing to fear. They'll not return you to the East. At the centre, they'll process you and help you get to Dusseldorf."

Hermann stood up and shook Ian's hand, saying "Thanks for everything, Kurt."

Ian then left the police station, found a phone booth and called Colonel Thurman at his home, to inform him of the sealing of the border.

"Colonel, I'm sorry to wake you up like this, but have to inform you Walter Ulbricht has got his way and is sealing the border with barbed wire. However, all the East German Bereitschaftspolizei, who carry guns, have not been issued any ammunition. Obviously, Khrushchev doesn't want to start a war. They want to see what the reaction is from the West. According to a soldier I met, they'll be issued bullets in forty-eight hours, if there's no response from the West."

"I'm glad you woke me up, Mr. Black. Your call is the first report I've had about the sealing of the border and I'll pass it up to my superiors."

"Goodnight, sir."

Ian walked back to the frontier near the Gate to see what was going on. East German soldiers and militia were everywhere stretching barbed wire, just on the East side of the white line boundary. There were armed guards spaced at most two meters apart, all armed with PPsh-41 submachine guns. It was strange because, although Walter Ulbricht had said the guards were there to prevent the West from invading the East, in fact, the guards faced into the

East and were aiming their guns at any East German, who tried to cross into the West. There were also water cannon vehicles everywhere, in case the citizens demonstrated about being cut off from the West.

Ian stood there for about thirty minutes surveying the scene and making mental notes of what was going on. This would allow him to provide details in his report, which he would file with his superiors, concerning the Berliner Mauer. Ian then found a taxi and returned to his flat in the British Zone, of West Berlin. There he went to bed and slept until about 1000 hours. After breakfast, he sat in his easy chair and thought about what had happened in the last eighteen months, to bring him to this eventful day.

2

Tricks Of The Trade

Friday, the 29th of January, 1960, was a cold, rainy day in England, with the temperature hovering around thirty-five degrees Fahrenheit and a strong wind blowing from the north. Today was the start of Ian Black's second assignment with the British Army Intelligence Corps; he was going to attend the Advanced Intelligence Academy. After eating his mother's home-cooked, full English breakfast, which she knew was his favourite, he finished packing his suitcase.

The door bell rang and his father, James Black, went to the front door to see who was there. He looked out and shouted back into the house, "Ian, your taxi is here." Ian picked up his luggage and walked toward the door, followed by his mother who looked very sad.

At the door, Ian turned toward his parents, "Mum and Dad, I love you both," he said, as he always did. "If the Academy allows it, I'll keep in touch with you regularly. After graduating from the Intelligence school in December, the army should give me some leave, before they send me to my next posting. I'll see you then. Perhaps you can come down for my graduation."

He gave his mother a hug and a kiss, and his father an embrace and a handshake.

Both of them said, almost in unison, "Take care son and do the best you can in the training. Of course, we'll be down for your graduation, if the army allows visitors."

Ian buttoned up his raincoat and walked briskly toward the taxi, parked at the kerb, just a few yards away. He quickly jumped into the rear of the cab, waved to his parents and closed the door. He looked out the rear window, waved one more time and then told the driver to take him to the Richmond station. After about a fifteen minute ride, the driver stopped in front of the station. Ian exited the taxi, after paying the fare and entered the Richmond Underground station.

Ian went to the ticket window and said, "One way ticket to Victoria station please."

"That'll be one shilling and sixpence," the man behind the window replied gruffly.

Ian handed the exact change to the man, who appeared to hate his job, and the ticket came out of the slot immediately. He picked it up and headed for platform one, where the train was waiting for passengers, since it was the end of the District line. He climbed on board and sat down in a seat close to the sliding doors. Soon they closed and the train headed for Victoria station, stopping along the way at Hammersmith and Earl's Court; twelve stations in all before it arrived at his stop.

At Victoria, he exited the Tube with his luggage and went up the escalators to the main train station. He walked up to the ticket window and asked, "How much is a one way, first class ticket to Uckfield?"

"Ten shillings and throop-ence, at this time of day," the pleasant, middle aged woman replied.

Ian handed the woman eleven shillings and asked, "What time is the next train?"

The woman took his money, gave him the change and shoved a ticket through the slot in the glass window. She

23

replied, "The next train leaves at 10:30 on platform ten and arrives in Uckfield at 11:46, if it's on time."

Since Ian had about thirty minutes before he needed to board the train, he went to the news theatre and watched a couple of cartoons and a Pathé newsreel. Upon exiting the theatre, he went to platform ten, showed his ticket to the guard and found a first class compartment, in the waiting train. He didn't have long to wait before the train started to move out of Victoria toward his destination.

In the compartment, there was one other man, dressed in a British Army uniform. As the train gathered speed and headed south over the Thames River, Ian looked at the other lieutenant and started a conversation.

"Lieutenant, I'm Ian Black. Are you going to Maresfield Park Camp, by any chance?"

"Glad to meet you, Lieutenant Black. My name's Robert Skinner but just call me Bob. In answer to your question, yes I'm going to Maresfield. Are you also?"

"Yes, would you like to share a taxi when we get to Uckfield? I believe Maresfield is only about one to two miles away from the Uckfield railway station. We could call for a ride from the camp, but it might be easier and quicker to take a cab."

"I agree. Let's do that."

Ian and Bob exchanged their family backgrounds and army experiences, and before long their train pulled into Uckfield station. No one else had come into their compartment during the trip, so they didn't have to keep quiet about where they were going.

They both got off the train onto the Uckfield platform and walked toward the exit with their bags. The rain had stopped, so they didn't get wet as they left the station, at the lower level. Just outside the railway station, they were lucky to find one taxi waiting in the assigned area,.

"Take us to Maresfield Park Camp." Ian told the driver, as he and Bob climbed into the back of the cab.

24

Since it was daytime and it was less than two miles from Uckfield to Maresfield, the ride only took about ten minutes, at most. As the taxi stopped outside the main gate of the camp, Ian paid the driver and both lieutenants exited the cab, with their baggage. They then walked up to the guard house and entered.

"Good morning, gentlemen," the sergeant on duty said, as he saluted both of them. "What can I do for you?"

"We're here for the training course," Ian said, as he gave his transfer paper and ID to the guard. Bob did likewise.

The sergeant looked at their papers and said, "Welcome to Maresfield Park Camp. I'll have Private Carnes here drive you to the camp headquarters. You must check in there and you'll be assigned your quarters."

"Private Carnes, place these gentlemen's luggage in the Land Rover and drive them to the HQ."

"Yes, sergeant, right away."

The private took their luggage and loaded it into the back of the vehicle.

"Thanks sergeant," Ian and Bob said, as they left the main gate guardhouse and climbed into the back seat of the Land Rover. Carnes drove them to the HQ in the middle of the camp and carried their luggage into the reception area. It was located in a fairly large house that obviously had been taken over by the military.

Lieutenants Black and Skinner walked into the main reception area and approached the duty officer, Lieutenant Blackman, who was seated at a desk reading an army manual. He looked up as they approached him and asked, "Are you here for the Advanced Intelligence Course?"

"Yes, we are," they both replied.

"May I see your transfer papers?"

Ian and Bob presented their papers and army identification cards. The duty officer looked at them and then picked up a roster on his desk. He found their names and made a check mark by them.

"You're the first ones here to check in. We expect a few more later today. The school starts promptly at 0800 on Monday, so you'll have the weekend to orient yourself with the camp. I'll have a driver take you to your quarters in Hut A-5, rooms 1 and 2, and drive you around the camp to show you the important buildings. Both of you are scheduled to meet with the CO tomorrow morning for an orientation. Lieutenant Black, you'll meet Colonel Hall at 1000, and, Lieutenant Skinner, you'll meet with him at 1100. The personal briefing will be held in office 2-A, upstairs in this building. Do you have any questions?"

"No, lieutenant," both replied.

"Good."

Looking over to the corner of the room, the duty officer said, "Private Giles, drive these gentlemen over to their quarters in Hut A-5 and, on the way, show them the camp including the dining hall, officers club, medical building and classrooms."

"Yes sir, I'll do it immediately," Private Giles said, as he picked up their bags and led them to a Land Rover, outside the HQ. The private drove them around the Camp, pointing out the main features and ended up at Hut A-5. He showed Lieutenant Black to Room 1 and Lieutenant Skinner to Room 2 and placed their bags in the appropriate rooms.

****

The next morning, after breakfast, Ian went to the HQ building for his orientation interview with Colonel Hall. He went up to the second floor of the building and found office 2-A. He knocked on the door and a voice inside said "Come in."

Ian entered the office, walked up to the desk and saluted Colonel Hall, the camp CO, who was seated behind it.

"Lieutenant Ian Black reporting as ordered, sir."

The colonel stood up, pointed at a chair and said, "Take a seat. Thank you for coming promptly, as I have other officers, like you, to talk to. You've been selected to attend this advanced intelligence course, upon the recommendation of your previous CO. In your case it was Colonel Baker in Cyprus. He expressed glowing admiration on how you handled yourself in several trying situations. However, I can assure you that you'll not be required to fly a four-engine Shackleton, while you're here at Maresfield.

The next forty-six weeks of training, which you and the other nine officers will undergo, is a major investment by the army, in all of you. The classes will be intensive and will require many hours of study to master the material. In your case, the language part may be the easiest for you, since you are fairly fluent already in German. However, we want you to end up being able to speak German better than a majority of Germans. You'll have to understand the different accents and from what parts of Germany they come from. Whether you're in East Germany or West Germany, you must sound like you belong there. You'll also have eight weeks of Russian language training, which although you will not leave here proficient in the language, you'll be able to handle yourself in any intense situation, if need be.

A daily PE class is required of all attendees, which will include going over or through different types of obstacles. In addition, you'll not only have to lead your team through them but also follow the lead of another officer.

There'll be a class in psychological training which will also cover stress, spotting possible turncoats and liars. Instruction will also include the use of radios, cameras and how to analyze troop movements of the enemy.

Here is a paper outlining the curriculum of this course."

Colonel Hall handed Ian a course outline covering the next forty-six weeks.

SPECIAL ADVANCED INTELLIGENCE COURSE	
Location	Maresfield, East Sussex, England
Course Start	1 February 1960
Course End	17 December 1960
Week	Monday-Friday 0800-1200, 1400-1700
German (oral and written	One hour per day
PE (+obstacle race training)	One hour per day

Weeks	Subjects
1-4	G, PE, Psychology, Handling Stress, Body language clues
5-8	G, PE, German history, geography, cultural, different German accents & words
9-12	G, PE, Intelligence operations, Dead drop, following people, spotting a tail
13-16	G, PE, Info from people, lying, personal habit detection – gambling, sex, money
17-20	G, PE, Berlin layout, landmarks, streets, transport, U-Bahn
21-24	G, PE, photography, cameras, first aid, communications – radio, other
25-28	G, PE, Analyze troop movements, aircraft and armoured vehicles, anticipate events
29-32	G, PE, Weapons training, ammunition - UK, US, German, Russian versions
33-36	G, PE, Russian Language, disguises, concealment
37-40	G, PE, Russian language, handle arrest and interrogation
41-44	G, PE, Driving skills, East/West politics, HUMINT and SIGINT in Germany
45-46	Recap and graduation

"Do you have any questions, Mr. Black?"

"Will we have any break, during the course, where we can visit home or have some visitors here?"

"No, I'm afraid not. However, at the end of the course, you'll be given two weeks of leave, before you'll have to report to your next posting, at the beginning of the New Year. If you have any questions, or want to talk about situations in the training, I have a basic open door policy. Within reason, you may come and discuss with me anything that concerns you, about the classes."

"Sir, I greatly appreciate the opportunity to attend this specialized course, and I hope that I'll not disappoint either you or Colonel Baker."

"Very well Mr. Black. I hope you have a good weekend, or what's left of it, and we'll see you tomorrow morning at 0800, for your first German class."

****

For the next eleven months, Ian went through the most intensive training he had ever faced in his life. He learned to speak and write German fluently; just like a native. In addition, he studied the art of intelligence gathering and developing contacts.

He passed all sections of the course and on the day before graduation was called to the CO's office.

"Mr. Black, I want to congratulate you on your performance here during the past eleven months. You're a credit to the Army and your former CO, Colonel Baker. I'll send him a letter stating such, in the near future. Tomorrow, we'll have the graduation ceremony and I understand your parents will be down here for it. I'm glad to say that all nine of your fellow officers have also passed and will be graduating with you. Your next assignment will be in Berlin, where the situation is heating up between the West and the East, thanks to Nikita Khrushchev. You'll have two weeks leave over the Christmas and New Year period. Then, you're due to fly to Berlin on the 3rd of January and will be required to wear a disguise, when getting off the plane at RAF Gatow, since there may be Russian cameras taking pictures of every one. We don't want your picture plastered all over the Stasi and KGB bulletin boards, before you even start your work there."

"Colonel, again thank you for giving me the opportunity to attend this course. As I perform my duties in Berlin, I hope that I'll be a credit to you and your staff."

Ian saluted the colonel and left his office. The next day, he was presented with a special pin and given his transfer papers for Berlin, together with instructions for his disguise. His parents were there to watch with pride, and afterwards Ian joined them on the ride back to Richmond, where he spent the two weeks of leave, over the Christmas holiday.

3

Guten Tag Berlin

After Ian spent the Christmas of 1960 and the 1961 New Year with his parents, he prepared to fly to his next posting, in West Berlin. Early Tuesday morning, the 3rd of January, 1961, his father drove him to RAF Station Northolt, near South Ruislip, after he had said a tearful goodbye to his mother. The trip from his parents' home took about thirty minutes, via Kew Road, Gunnersbury Avenue and Western Avenue. Since the traffic was not too heavy, they arrived around 0845, which meant Ian had plenty of time to spare, since the takeoff time was scheduled for 1000 hours.

As they came to the station main gate, Ian showed his ID card and his father presented his retired wing commanders identification card, to the guard. They were waved into the facility and Ian's father dropped him off outside the terminal building.

"Have a good trip son and write as much as you can, to your mother. She always worries about you and envisions all the potential problems, you could be getting into. Now you're going to Berlin, she'll be concerned that the Russians will arrest you or even worse."

Ian replied, "Don't worry Dad; I can take care of myself. Of course I'll write, as much as I can, and will also call occasionally. Hopefully, I'll receive some leave now and again, in which case I'll try to make it home to see both of you."

He gave his Dad a hug and shook his hand, as he picked up his bags and walked into the Northolt terminal. He stopped at the door, turned and waved to his father, one last time, before entering the building.

Ian went up to the departures desk, which was manned by a RAF lance corporal.

"Corporal, I'm on the flight to Berlin that leaves at 1000 hours. Where do I go to board it?"

"Sir, may I see your papers?"

He handed his transit papers to the corporal, who glanced at them and returned them to him.

"Thank you, sir. Your papers look in order, and you may proceed to the lounge, down the hallway to the left. If you want some refreshments, there is coffee and donuts, in there."

Ian walked down the hallway to the departure area, which already had a few officers waiting for the flight. He grabbed a cup of black coffee and a glazed donut, and sat down in a chair, close to the door leading to the plane.

While he sat there, he began to read a book about the Berlin airlift, written by a pilot involved in the strategy of breaking the Soviet blockade.

Thirty minutes before his flight was due to depart, Ian closed the book and looked around the departure area. Waiting in the embarkation lounge were ten officers, including Ian, for the flight to Berlin. They were from all branches of the British armed forces. Ian then got out his map of Berlin to refresh his memory of the various important sites.

As the time for them to board the DC-3 Dakota plane came closer, the pilot walked into the lounge to brief the passengers on the flight.

"Good morning, gentlemen. My name is Flight Lieutenant Chris Mullins and I'm your pilot for today's flight."

As he announced his name, Ian who was studying the map of Berlin, looked up in surprise.

Mullins continued, "The five hundred and eighty mile long flight today will take approximately three hours, and we'll be flying over the North Sea, toward Hanover, Germany." Suddenly Mullins stopped his announcement and looked over at Ian, in astonishment. He walked over to him and said, "Ian, I'm surprised to see you."

Ian replied, "It's great to see you again, Chris."

Mullins continued speaking to the passengers, "This officer here, Lieutenant Black, is the one that saved my life during the Cyprus Emergency, when the plane I was flying was shot at, by a gun-running ship. I hope he also does great things for the U.K. in Berlin."

Looking at Ian, he said, "Thanks again for saving my life, and my crew's life, during that ill-fated Shackleton flight."

Turning back to all of the passengers, he continued, "Gentlemen, once we're over Hanover, we'll start to fly through the Allied Access Route to Berlin and RAF Station Gatow. We'll be over East Germany for about 100 miles, before we reach West Berlin. Those of you who are able to look out of a window, you'll probably notice a huge difference in the buildings, once we cross the East German frontier; reconstruction has not come to many parts of the GDR.

For those of you who are concerned about being filmed by the Stasi or KGB, when you disembark at Gatow, we'll park the plane close to the terminal, so that your facial features will be blocked from the view of any long range cameras. Don't forget RAF Gatow Field perimeter borders right up against East Berlin.

We'll provide you with some refreshments and a snack while in flight, courtesy of the RAF. The weather is expected to be perfect for a January day on our flight path; sunny, dry and no turbulence. The ground staff is currently loading your baggage and some freight we have to take to Berlin. As soon as it's finished, you'll be allowed to board the plane and we'll take off. Are there any questions?"

None were forthcoming and Mullins ended his briefing by saying, "Thank you for your attention. If you do have any questions during the flight, please hand them to the flight attendant and I'll try to answer them."

Mullins then walked over to Ian, shook his hand and again thanked him for saving his life, more than two years ago.

"What are you flying nowadays?" Ian asked him.

"After the Cyprus Emergency ended, I was transferred to the RAF Air Transport Command. I now fly mainly Bristol Britannia four-engine transports, to wherever they send me. The pilot for today's flight called in sick, so I was volunteered to fly this Dakota to Berlin. Normally, I don't fly DC-3's anymore."

Ian responded, "Well I'm glad you're flying us to Berlin or we probably would not have met again. Hopefully, I'll have a chance to see you at the other end."

"I'm sure you will. I should have a few minutes to talk with you before I have to take the plane back to Northolt."

Mullins left to check out the plane with the co-pilot and in fifteen minutes the flight was called. After showing their identification cards again, the officers walked through the departure door and boarded the plane.

After all the passengers were on board and seated, the pilot started up the engines. He then got on the radio to the control tower, on a frequency of 122.1 Mcs., and requested permission to taxi, "Northolt, this is Ascot 1437 requesting permission to taxi to take off position."

"Ascot 1437, this is Northolt. You're cleared to taxi to the end of runway zero seven and perform your engine run up. Stop just short of the actual runway."

"Northolt, we're taxiing toward runway zero seven and will stop short."

The chocks were pulled away and the plane proceeded to taxi to the engine check out site, just short of the runway.

"Northolt, this is Ascot1437 ready for takeoff."

"Ascot 1437, you are cleared for takeoff on runway zero seven. The wind is out of the northeast, at ten miles per hour."

"Roger Northolt. This is Ascot 1437 turning onto runway zero seven for takeoff."

Flight Lieutenant Mullins moved the throttles forward slightly until the plane rolled onto the runway and was ready for takeoff. He pushed the controls way forward, and the aircraft proceeded to gather speed, as it went down the runway. Since the Dakota was a tail-dragger type aircraft, the pilot moved the controls so the rear wheel was off the surface first and then lifted the entire plane off the runway, as the specified takeoff speed was achieved.

Soon they were winging their way eastward over Essex, the North Sea, The Hague, Osnabrück, Hanover and into West Berlin. Since Ian had a window seat, he could see the transition from West Germany to East Germany. There were still many ruins in East Germany, caused by the allied bombing during World War Two. West Germany had completed a considerable amount of reconstruction of their bombed out cities.

As they flew over the border between West and East Germany, suddenly they were joined by two Soviet MiG-21 fighters; one on each side of the plane.

The pilot of the Dakota came on the speaker system, "Gentlemen, don't worry about the Soviet planes. They do this all the time, trying to intimidate us and checking to see if we have any special equipment for spying."

As they approached the West Berlin Border, the Soviet fighters peeled off and disappeared.

35

RICHARD AND BARBARA OSBORN

Flight Lieutenant Mullins got on the radio, "Gatow tower, this is Ascot 1437 fifty miles out to the west, requesting landing instructions."

"Ascot 1437, this is Gatow. There is no traffic at the moment, so you're cleared to land on runway zero eight left, with a straight in approach. Wind is five miles per hour out of the east."

"Roger, Gatow. This is Ascot 1437. We understand and we will land on runway zero eight left."

The Dakota pilot eased back on the throttles and the plane descended, toward the runway. Ian was looking out of his window and could see the "Iron Curtain" extending around West Berlin, as they crossed over it.

Soon they were on the ground at RAF Gatow and taxiing toward the terminal. As promised, Mullins parked the aircraft close to the terminal so that any prying eyes of the Stasi or KGB could not get a look of the officers' faces as they disembarked. This was critical for those officers involved with intelligence gathering.

The passengers walked into the terminal and waited for their bags to be unloaded.

Chris Mullins entered after a few minutes and walked up to Ian.

"Well Ian, I trust the flight was smooth enough for you. We're used to the Soviets pestering us with their fighters. They do it all the time. Again, it has been great seeing you. Maybe our paths will cross in the future."

Ian shook his hand and said, "Thanks for the smooth flight. I had an informative view of the East West boundary, out the window. Yes, I hope we do meet again someday."

Chris responded, "Well, I have to go now for a review of the outbound flight and get ready for the return trip to Northolt. Cheers."

He walked toward the door of the pilot brief room, turned and waved to Ian, as he vanished through it.

Ian collected his bags and went to the arrival help desk, where there was an RAF corporal, waiting to give assistance to anyone needing it.

"Corporal, I'm Lieutenant Black and need assistance to get to the Berlin Olympic Stadium Barracks. Will you arrange transportation for me?"

"May I see your transfer papers, sir?" replied the corporal.

"Thank you, sir." said the airman, as he handed the documentation back to Ian. "I've already called the Stadium Barracks for two other officers, who need to get there. Please take a seat over there with the other officers; the shuttle bus should be here soon. I'll let you know as soon as it arrives."

In about fifteen minutes, the corporal came over to where they were seated, "Gentlemen, your transportation for the Stadium Barracks has arrived. Please go out this door and you'll find it right outside."

Ian and the other two officers, a captain and a major, exited the terminal and found the shuttle bus waiting at the kerb. The ride to the Stadium Barracks, via Gatowstrasse and Heerstrasse, took no more than twenty minutes and the bus deposited the officers in front of the main building. A private came out, unloaded their bags and led them into the HQ.

Ian followed the major and captain inside and went up to the check in counter. After the other two officers had been taken care of, Ian presented his transfer papers. The sergeant behind the counter checked his name on the roster of incoming personnel. He found Lieutenant Black's name and made a check mark by it.

"Welcome to Berlin, lieutenant. We have you registered for the Officers Quarters in the London Block building 12, room C-4, under instructions of Colonel David Thurman. We have you down here for a three month stay. Let us know if you need the room longer."

37

"It'll all depend on my CO, Colonel Thurman, whom I will be meeting tomorrow. I'll certainly let you know, if I need the room for longer than that. Where is the Officers' Mess located?"

"It's right next door to your quarters. There is a large sign outside. I'll have a soldier drive you to your quarters."

"Private, take this lieutenant and his bags to Derbyshire, room C-4," the sergeant commanded to a soldier, sitting in a corner.

"Yes sergeant."

"Follow me, sir," the private said to Ian, as he picked up his bags.

The private drove Ian to the Officers' Quarters and led him to room C-4.

Ian unpacked his bags and then when to the Officers' Mess in search a sandwich or something, since it was 1430 hours and he had not had any lunch.

The rest of the day he relaxed and prepared for the meeting with his CO the next day, scheduled for 1000 hours. Colonel Thurman's office was located in the former Olympiastadion Administration Building, which was now the Headquarters for the Berlin Infantry Brigade Group.

4

Soviet Weapon Hunt

The next day, after he had gone to the Officers' Mess and had breakfast, Ian walked over to the Berlin Brigade Headquarters to report to his CO. As he entered the building, he heard a voice yell out, "Ian, what the hell are you doing here?"

Ian turned and saw a major walking toward the same building. He gave him a salute and then realized it was Clifford Phillips, from Cyprus, who must have received a promotion, during the past year. The last time he saw him, he only sported three Bath stars (pips) on his uniform; now he had a crown in place of the pips.

Major Phillips walked up to Ian and shook his hand, saying, "When I left Cyprus, Colonel Baker mentioned that you might be coming to Berlin, after you attended the Advanced Intelligence Course; and here you are."

"I see you've received a well earned promotion, since the Cyprus days."

"When did you arrive here in Berlin?" Phillips enquired.

"I just arrived yesterday and I'm on my way to meet my new CO, Colonel Thurman. Do you happen to know him?"

"Of course, I report to him also. I'm in charge of Counter Intelligence, which is part of the Intelligence and

Security Group, located here in West Berlin. You'll find the colonel is a fair chap and does not tolerate any BS. He reports to a Brigadier James Croxford, whose alias is Rex; my alias is Martin. We try to not use our real names most of the time, in order to confuse the enemy; the Russians and the GDR chaps. Well, you'd better go in before you're late Ian, as the colonel likes promptness."

"See you around, major," Ian responded, as he entered the headquarters building and went up to a sergeant seated behind a desk.

"I'm here to meet with Colonel Thurman. Where can I find him?"

"Go to the second floor, sir. He's in room 253."

Ian climbed up the stairs and soon found the colonel's office. As he opened the door marked 253, he found a secretary in the outer office, seated behind a desk, containing a typewriter, and name plate. Glancing at it, Ian gathered her name was Helga Jergens.

"Ms. Jergens, my name is Lieutenant Black and I've an appointment with Colonel Thurman at 1000 hours."

"Good morning, lieutenant. The colonel is expecting you," she replied in English.

She then suddenly switched to German and asked, "How was your trip over from England yesterday? Was it smooth and did you see the border, as you crossed over from West to East Germany?"

Ian replied in German, "We had a great trip over with very little turbulence. It was interesting to see the difference, when we passed over the border. The plane was piloted by an officer I met in Cyprus, so we reminisced about old times."

Helga and Ian continued speaking in German for a few minutes and then she switched back to English saying, "Please take a seat. The colonel will be free in a couple of minutes."

Helga picked up her phone and talked to the colonel in a low voice. Soon a buzzer sounded at her desk and, looking over at Ian, she said, "The colonel is free. You may go in now."

Ian went to the inner office door and knocked. A voice from inside barked, "Come in." He entered the office and found a curly haired officer with a moustache, who was fairly short in stature and seated behind a large oak desk. The colonel, who appeared to be about forty-five years old, did however radiate a sense of military professionalism. As Ian later learned, the colonel's father was a lieutenant in the "War to end all wars" and a very successful and courageous brigadier during World War Two.

Ian saluted Colonel David Thurman and said, "Lieutenant Ian Black reporting as ordered, sir."

The colonel smiled at Ian as he returned the salute and said, "Well Mr. Black, I'm glad you had a pleasant trip over from England, without any problems. Oh, by the way, my secretary tells me that you passed the first test."

Ian looked quizzically at the colonel and then, in a BFO, it dawned on him that Helga had been checking out his command of the German language.

"Welcome to West Berlin that is at the crossroads between the East and the West. We expect that conditions on the border will heat up over the next few months and maybe even years. You've been assigned to my small, effective and determined section of the Intelligence Corps, because of your past performance in Cyprus and your mastery of German. You are joining an elite group of intelligence professionals that report to me," continued Colonel Thurman.

"On the way to your office, I ran into Major Phillips who I understand reports to you, sir. In fact, I reported to him and Colonel Baker, while I was assigned to the intelligence corps on the island."

41

"Well good, I'm glad you met him. I'm relying on him, and his Counter Intelligence group, to keep me appraised on what the Soviet and Stasi intelligence groups are up to.

As to your first duty here in Berlin, I am assigning you to the Military Liaison Mission, under BRIXMIS (British Commanders'-in-Chief Mission to the Soviet Forces in Germany). Your fluency in German will come in very useful and hopefully you can pick up some worthwhile information. How's your Russian?"

"Well, sir, I wouldn't claim to be fluent in the language, but I'm able to understand and read it, if it's not spoken too quickly," Ian replied.

The colonel continued, "Good, you should do well in the MLM then. In case you are not aware, the MLM was established on the 16th of September, 1946, under an accord, with the Soviets, named the Robertson-Malinin Agreement. This is the reason I had you registered to stay in the London Block, rather than one of the other buildings that are all part of the Berlin Brigade. The MLM is a separate entity from the main British Military Force (BAOR) stationed in Berlin, and it's responsible for keeping surveillance on what the Soviets are doing in the East.

Please note that you must always be in uniform, when travelling through East Germany in the MLM vehicle. I would suggest that you replace your Intelligence Corps patches with Berlin Brigade patches, since you don't want to be identified as an intelligence officer. In addition, do not wear your green Corps beret, as it will also make you stand out. If you leave the car and want to disguise the fact that you are in the military, you may do so but, be forewarned, it could be dangerous, if you're picked up and taken to a komendatura (police station).

On a regular basis, for the next three to four months, you will drive around the Soviet sector of Berlin and Germany in a matte-olive-drab Opel Kapitän P, collecting intelligence on what the Warsaw Pact troops are doing.

Specifically, we're interested in the quantity, types and location of equipment in the Soviet and East German forces."

"Who'll be my CO, while I'm serving under BRIXMIS, and where's the mission actually located?"

"You will report to a Major Poole for the time you are in the MLM, and the location of the mission is at 34 Seestrasse in Potsdam. The *tours* into East Germany are anywhere from two to seven days in length, at the end of which you will write up a report and submit it to Major Poole. Every now and again, you will return here to your room in London Block and report to me on your progress. One other point I must emphasize is that the domestic staff at the Mission are all Soviet informers. They are handpicked by the KGB or GRU and you can be sure anything you say in the Mission will be reported to the Russians. Is this all understood?"

"Yes sir, but it would be helpful if there's a document, brochure or something, outlining the rules and background of the MLM."

The colonel pulled a document out of his desk and handed it to Ian.

"Here's a booklet on the MLM for you to read. Do not take it to the mission headquarters in Potsdam. Leave it in your room at London Block and return it to me at the end of your assignment to BRIXMIS. As far as rules go, there aren't any. Just use your common sense and don't be caught doing anything illegal. Also, and this is very important, do not violate the Permanent Restricted Areas (PRA) or Temporary Restricted Areas (TRA). They are marked on the maps provided by the Soviet Military and/or signposted in the areas. If you do breach these areas, it could become a major issue between the British and Soviet military, involving generals on both sides."

"When do I actually start on the MLM?"

"When you leave here, report directly to Major Poole, whose office is located in the London Block.

43

I believe that is all for now, Mr. Black. I have a meeting scheduled with Major Phillips. Don't forget to check in now and again with me, and let me know how you're progressing with your visits to East Germany."

As Ian saluted the colonel, he replied, "I'll do that as much as I can, sir. I appreciate this opportunity to see the East German countryside."

Ian walked out of the colonel's office into the outer office, where he found Major Phillips waiting. Ian walked over to him, shook his hand and said, "I'll see you around I suppose."

"You certainly will," Phillips replied, grinning.

Ian walked out of the Berlin Brigade Headquarters and headed for the London Block, to see Major Poole.

As he entered the building, Ian ran into a civilian whom he immediately recognized. It was John (Andrew Dinglefoot) from Cyprus who was in MI6 and, back on the island, was involved with the listening post at Ayios Nikolaos.

John smiled at Ian and said, "I'm glad to see you again. It's been awhile since you beat me at snooker. I heard you might be coming to Berlin. What are you going to be doing here?"

"I've been assigned to BRIXMIS for about three months and will be under Major Poole."

"He's a good man and he knows his stuff. He's firm but fair. You should get on well with him. After you've been on your first "tour", come and see me. You might be useful to our organization, since you'll be *touring* East Germany. For your ears only, the MI6 West Berlin Station is located in the London Block, on the top floor in a high security area. I work with Percival whom you met in Beirut, I believe."

"I'll do that. I'd like to see Percival again and thank him for his assistance in Lebanon."

Ian said goodbye to John and went to report to Major Poole to get instructions on how to join BRIXMIS in Potsdam.

He found the major in his office and saluted him as required, saying, "Lieutenant Black, reporting as ordered, sir."

"I'm glad you're here, Ian. Colonel Thurman has told me all about you. For the rest of the day, take some time off and prepare for tomorrows trip. You must gather some extra clothes and any personal necessities you'll need for making *tours*, lasting a few days at a time. We'll meet outside this building tomorrow morning, at 0800 hours, and then drive to the Mission. There I'll introduce you to the officer whom you'll be replacing, for the next few months. He'll be taking you on his next *tours* and show you the ropes, together with any problems that might crop up."

The next day, an army private drove Major Poole and Ian to the Mission House in Potsdam, in an olive-drab Opel car. The nineteen mile journey took them into East Germany, which proved to be no problem, after the major showed his Soviet issued pass to the Russian officer on duty. The private drove the car into the Mission compound on Seestrasse, where an East German guard across the street called in a report. The mission was a three story mansion that had a British sentry on duty at the front door and a flagpole atop the building, flying the Union Jack.

BRIXMIS Mission House, Seestrasse, Potsdam

Baltic Sea

Baltic Sea

• Schwerin

Fürstenberg
•

• Vogelsang

WEST
GERMANY

Gransee • • Zehdenick

Eberswalde •

POLAND

Potsdam •

| 1 | 2 |

| 1 West Berlin |
| 2 East Berlin |

•Haldensleben

• Magdeburg

EAST
GERMANY

Leipzig •

Dresden •

CZECHOSLOVAKIA

EAST GERMANY "TOURING" MAP

Major Poole and Ian entered the mansion and were greeted by a Lieutenant Giles who saluted the major saying, "Good morning major, I trust the Ruskies didn't give you any problem at the border."

"No thankfully, we were waved through by a very bored, Russian lieutenant. I'd like you to meet Mr. Black who'll be your replacement here, for about three months. The sooner he gets up to speed, the quicker you can have your well earned rest, at the Brigade Headquarters."

Lieutenant Giles shook Ian's hand, saying, "I'm glad you've come to relieve me for a few months."

Speaking to Mr. Giles, the major continued, "I want you to take him out to the Schwerin area on your *tour* starting tomorrow, in order to show him the ropes. Why don't you two get acquainted while I go to a planning meeting with Brigadier Dunn, who's in charge of this Mission."

Lieutenant Giles led Ian to the Officers' Mess in the Mission, where they sat down for a cup of tea and the lieutenant briefed Ian on the upcoming, three day *tour*. He only gave Ian some general information, since he didn't want the Mission staff to overhear any confidential intelligence data.

****

The next morning, Ian got up early and met Lieutenant Giles for breakfast. Afterward, they found an unoccupied office, where they could talk without being overheard by the Soviet provided staff.

Closing the door, Lieutenant Giles turned to Ian and said, "We'll be driving through East Germany to the Schwerin area, where the Soviet 2nd Shock Army HQ is located. The area also contains several Russian Rifle Corps, and we need to confirm the estimates of the size and actual locations of this infantry. Remember always write down anything of value, because it's easy to forget an issue, when you get around to filing the report."

"We can't actually go on the bases, can we?" Ian asked.

"No, they're a PRA, but you can go outside a base and count vehicles, men, weapons, etc. We'll talk more about it on the way to Schwerin."

After they gathered up their gear, they went out to the car park and found their Opel Kapitän, with an NCO and driver waiting. It had a Union Jack on the license plate indicating it was a BRIXMIS vehicle and the assigned number "7".

At around 0900 hours, the driver started up the Opel and pulled out of the Mission car park, with Lieutenants' Giles and Black in the rear, and the sergeant in the front passenger seat. They headed toward the Schwerin area, which was their intelligence target, for the next three days. The driver noticed that, as soon as they left the Mission, two nark Wartburg-311 cars started to follow them. He quickly gave them the slip; obviously, their drivers were not very experienced.

Ian had taken with him his ever-present swagger stick, in order to hopefully indicate authority, especially to the Russians and East Germans. Due to the possibility of an altercation with Soviet troops, it wasn't advisable to carry weapons on any of the *tours*, so he had left the British Army issued Browning automatic in his Olympic Stadium room.

For the next three days, they *toured* the area from Potsdam to Schwerin, making notes of any Warsaw Pact troop movements. The information included the number and type of vehicles, number and specifics on soldiers involved and where they were going from and to. They avoided the PRAs and TRAs in the Schwerin area and, as far as possible, made sure they lost any narks (Stasi agents) that tried to follow them.

At night, the officers slept in one-man tents while the driver slept in the car. They cooked their own food and were basically self-sufficient, during the entire time they were out of the Potsdam Mission.

On the second night, around a small campfire, Ian and Lieutenant Giles discussed what had transpired during the past two days.

"Have you ever covered up your uniform and gone into town, to talk with the local population?" Ian asked.

"Personally, I haven't," replied Giles. "I don't speak German very fluently. However, I know a few MLM officers who have done so, and they obtained some good information. One officer got caught and there was hell to pay trying to get him back. It involved British and Soviet generals who don't like to be caught up in such situations. If you decide to do it on one of your *tours*, be very careful and don't get caught. They'll take you to the komendatura for questioning and maybe even worse."

"Thanks for the warning. I do speak German fluently and know Russian fairly well. However, I understand the political issues involved, if one's caught." Ian responded.

"By the way, when we get back to the Mission in Potsdam tomorrow, we need to immediately write up a report of our *tour* and submit it up the chain of command. If you don't write it up promptly, you might forget something, unless you've made very good notes on the trip. Let's get some shut-eye now and we can talk more on the way back to the Mission."

The next morning, they lit a fire and the four of them cooked breakfast before setting out for the trip back to Potsdam and the Mission. On the way back, they passed a large convoy of Soviet trucks, loaded with soldiers, and armoured personnel carriers, heading from Schwerin toward Parchim. Giles and Ian made notes and took a few photos, with a hidden Polaroid Land camera, to include in their report.

Giles again emphasized to Ian the danger in violating the PRA and TRA zones, marked on the Soviet maps, and also stressed looking out for narks (Stasi) that might be tailing the MLM vehicle.

They arrived back at the Mission on Seestrasse in mid afternoon, and the driver and NCO unpacked the Opel, while Giles and Ian went in to start writing the *tour* report. They took turns typing it on a manual typewriter and included the photos they had taken. They finished it up the next day and submitted it to Major Poole for approval.

"This looks like an excellent report, Mr. Giles and Mr. Black," he said, as he scanned through it. "I'll forward it to Colonel Dunn."

Looking at Lieutenant Giles, the major said, "You can return with me to Berlin later today, for your well earned R&R."

Turning to Ian, the major asked, "Are you ready to go out on your own?"

"Yes sir. I certainly learned the ropes, thanks to Lieutenant Giles here."

"Very good, I've a new target for you to investigate on your next *tour*. It's a town named Zehdenick, in the Oberhavel district of Brandenburg, where we believe that there're some top secret, Soviet weapons being stored. On your way there, you'll travel near Eberswalde, which will also provide you with some Warsaw Pact troops to investigate. Incidentally, a man by the name of John asked me to remind you to stop by and see him, on the start of your next *tour*. I don't know who he is, but I can speculate, since he's on the top floor of the London Block."

"Yes, I do know John and I met him accidentally the other day. We became acquainted in Cyprus during my posting there. He was involved with the British listening post at Ayios Nikolaos. When do you want me to start this tour to the Zehdenick area?"

"Tomorrow, you can drive in to Berlin and stop at the Olympic Stadium, where you can sit down with me and discuss the plans for your trip. At the same time you can go see this John. On the following morning, you can drive from the Stadium up to your target area."

****

The next day, Ian had Corporal Barnet drive to the Berlin Brigade Headquarters at the Stadium, so he could stop by Major Poole's office and talk with him about the upcoming *tour*. Following this discussion, Ian went up to the top floor of the London Block, where he found two, tough looking MPs guarding the entrance, armed with Sterling submachine guns. After they asked Ian why he was there, they had him sign in and one of them placed a call to John.

In a few minutes, John came through the main door of the classified area, signed him in on the MPs log and led him to a conference room, just inside the secure area. Upon entering the room, Ian noticed that there was a large oak table, with Percival seated at one end.

He rose and came forward to shake Ian's hand, saying "It's been a long time since we met." Then, with a smile, continued, "I see you've totally recovered from your Beirut trip."

"Yes, thanks to you." Ian replied.

"Okay, let's get down to business," John said, as he indicated a chair to Ian.

They all sat down at one end of the table.

"Ian, anything we talk about is strictly secret and must not be repeated to anyone. You understand what I'm implying?"

"Yes, John, I completely grasp what you're saying. However, I will have to relay some information to the NCO going on the *tour*, in order for him to be of assistance to me."

"Okay, that's understandable. But only give him the necessary information, so he can be helpful on the "tour". There's a specific reason why we asked you to stop by here, after getting Major Poole's approval. We've been told that you'll be *touring* the Zehdenick area, starting tomorrow."

"That's true," Ian replied. "An NCO, a driver and I will be *touring* the area for up to five days. Stopping on the way, we'll get as close as we can to Eberswalde, without violating the PRA. I've been led to believe that there's a large Soviet base in the vicinity of the town."

"Good, we want you to help us track any Soviet weapons and/or vehicles that you come across during your *tour*."

"How can I do that?" Ian asked.

At that point, Percival produced a box from under the table and slid it toward Ian, saying "There are ten, specially coded, transistorized transmitters in this box, all with a magnetic contact for mounting to the target. Each one has a number on it, which to us indicates a specific frequency, and, by the way, they will all self destruct after a set period of time. This will make it unlikely that they will ever fall into enemy hands. We want you to turn each of them on, as you attach them to a Soviet vehicle, with the magnetic mount. You must keep a log as to the transmitter number, the type of vehicle you attach it to and where it was located in East Germany. We'll then monitor the location of the vehicles as they are moved around, either by a new monitoring station that is being built, or by air, using the RAF De Havilland Chipmunk T10 reconnaissance planes. John will be involved in the actual tracking of the signals."

"I believe that I can handle that task."

"Good, we figured that you'd be able to assist us in this critical intelligence. Just don't take too many risks and end up in an East German or Soviet jail; we may not be able to help you."

"Why are you so interested in the area that our *tour* will be visiting?"

John looked at Percival, who nodded approval.

"There've been previous reports that the Soviets built two major missile bases, one close to a village named Vogelsang and the other about twenty miles away at a place called Fürstenberg. According to these secret reports, the bases were built in the spring of 1959 and contained the Soviet R-5M nuclear missiles, with a range of 750 miles. They were hidden in wooded areas, which were hard to spot from the air, and no East Germans were even aware of their existence, or the nuclear warheads. In addition, newer reports indicate that the missiles were withdrawn by the end of 1959. We need to know if the missiles have actually been returned to Russia. Also, if they have been removed, what are the bases being used for now?" replied John.

"I'll do the best I can to ascertain the existence or non-existence of these missiles at Vogelsang. However, the Soviet maps mark the area east of Zehdenick as PRA, so I may not be able to get very close to Vogelsang, without a lot of risk."

"Ian, we know that you'll accomplish what you can, under the restrictions placed on the *tours*, by the Soviets."

Ian looked at John and Percival, asking, "Are there any specific types of vehicles you want me to place these transmitters on?"

"Mainly large transporters for tanks or missiles, rather than small army lorries," replied Percival.

As he talked, Percival produced another box from under the table. "One other point, here is a special camera for taking pictures in the dark. It includes a Zeiss telephoto lens and is already loaded with film, so all you have to do is point and "snap" the target. The Soviets move a lot of their hush-hush equipment around during the night. This camera uses infrared technology and, under no circumstances, must you allow it to fall into Soviet hands. I trust you know what I mean."

53

"I'll do what you ask, if I can, and I'll bring the log book back, together with the camera, when I return."

"Excellent, I'm glad we'll have your full cooperation. It's very important to Britain and the Western world. Thanks for coming in."

"Do you have any questions?" asked John.

"Yes, I have a request for you."

"What is it?" John answered quizzically.

"Do you know anyone that could provide me with an East German identity card?"

"I don't know, but I'll see if it can be obtained. No guarantees of course. What are the particulars you want on it?"

Ian replied, "I'd like to have it issued in the name of Kurt Engels, age twenty-two, brown hair, hazel eyes, weight 82.5 kilograms, height 185.4 centimeters and a domicile of Berlin. Here is a piece of paper with it all written down, together with a passport photo."

"If you don't mind me asking, why do you need an East German identity card? You have your British Army ID and you have a pass issued by the Soviets, for use on your MLM *tours*."

"If the opportunity arises, I may want to reconnoiter in mufti and obtain additional information, on what is going on in the Soviet zone. I realize it could be dangerous but, with my fluency in German, I believe I could handle any unforeseen situation."

"Well, I'll see if I can find someone to forge an identity card for you and I'll let you know when you come back in with the transmitter log. Okay?"

"That would be great, if you can help me," Continuing, Ian said with a smile as he stood up, "Well I guess we're now finished with this meeting."

Ian shook hands with Percival, and John led Ian out, carrying the box of transmitters and the camera, to the main door.

"Thanks for coming in and volunteering to install those transmitters. Again, it's very important to us and Britain. I'll let you know if an East German ID is feasible." John said

After John told one of the MPs, it was okay for Ian to leave with the boxes, he signed him out and Ian went down the stairs to his room, to get ready for the next day's *tour*.

****

The next morning, Ian headed out in the Opel from the Berlin Olympic Stadium, together with Sergeant Williams and the driver, Corporal Barnet. They drove into East Berlin and East Germany toward the Zehdenick area, approximately fifteen miles northwest of Eberswalde. As they entered East Berlin, they picked up some narks in a black Wartburg-311, which followed them from a distance.

Corporal Barnet pointed them out to Ian and said, "Lieutenant, I believe we are being tailed by at least one Stasi car. What do you want me to do?"

"Do you think you can shake them off our tail?"

"Certainly I can, lieutenant. They taught me how to do it, at the specialized driver's school I recently attended."

"Go ahead then, but try not to make it too obvious so that they call ahead."

Corporal Barnet drove quickly up and down some East Berlin side streets. He probably knew most of the roads better than the Stasi, who were following them. In about ten minutes, after what seemed like a roller coaster ride, he announced, "I believe we've lost them."

"Good, now head on the main road toward Szczecin for awhile, and then we will go onto some country roads toward Templin. This will bring us close to the PRA that surrounds our intended target but, if we are careful, we should be able to get a view of the railway line that goes through Templin to the hidden town of Vogelsang," Ian replied.

"How long will this take us?" asked the driver.

"It's about forty miles and could take us almost two hours to get there. We don't want to go too fast and attract attention. When you see a sign for Flieth-Stegelitz, get off the main highway there and go southwest toward Mimersdorf. It's not clear exactly where the PRA starts, but the Soviet map indicates it's close to Templin. We'll pull off before we get to Templin and hide in the woods, until dusk."

Corporal Barnet drove the Opel at below the posted speed limits and made the trip to the Flieth-Stegelitz turn off in little over an hour. The road here narrowed and so he had to drive the car slower, as he didn't want to get in an accident. There was not much traffic on the road anyway. Finally, as they came close to Templin, he pulled onto a dirt lane that led to a forested area and parked in a small glade, surrounded by trees.

"Good job, corporal," Ian said. "Let's camp out here until it gets almost dark, and then Sergeant Williams and I will walk toward where we believe the railway track is, which goes from Templin to Vogelsang and on to Fürstenberg. Most of the trains transporting Soviet equipment travel at night, to avoid detection from foreign agents or planes."

They stayed in the wooded area until sunset, which was around 1700 hours in this part of Germany.

"Corporal, while Sergeant Williams and I head for the railway track, stay here and be ready to take off as soon as we return, just in case we're being chased by the Ruskies or Stasi."

"I'll be ready, lieutenant."

Ian grabbed the box of transmitters, together with the special camera, and left with the sergeant in the direction of the railway line, running from Templin to Vogelsang. It took them about forty-five minutes, to find their way through the heavy forested area, thick with underbrush, until they finally located the railway. It was only about fifty feet from their hiding place. They settled down for a long wait, hoping a train would come by, before dawn arrived.

At around 2330, Ian and the sergeant heard a low rumbling noise coming from the north; they crept forward to get a little closer to the railway. The rumbling became louder and louder and, in about ten minutes, the light of the engine came round a curve, located at approximately one half mile from them. The train was going very slowly and, as if by a miracle, the center of it stopped almost in front of them. There didn't seem to be any guards on the rail cars, but there was a closed compartment at the end of the train that could be full of Russian soldiers.

The first five flatbed cars were loaded with what seemed to be the new Soviet T-55 battle tank. The next ten cars contained BTR-60 armoured personnel carriers, followed by eight BM-21 Grad Multiple Rocket Launchers on individual flatbeds. Finally, there were ten Ural-375 general purpose lorries and the compartment, probably carrying sleeping Soviet soldiers.

Ian opened up the box of transmitters Percival had given him, and turned them all on. He handed three of them to Sergeant Williams, saying "It looks like there are no guards watching the train. Go down and attach a transmitter to two of the eight multiple rocket launchers and the remaining one, on one of the lorries. In the meantime I will go and fasten a box to three of the tanks and three on the armoured personnel carriers. Be careful and keep your eyes open for anyone approaching."

After Ian had clamped his transmitters to the targeted vehicles, he crept back to their hiding place and grabbed the low-light camera. He went back to where he had a clear view of the train and, at that moment, it started to move again. The sergeant joined him just as he started to take pictures of every flatbed, while they rolled by.

When the closed compartment at the end of the train passed by, a Russian officer, who was having a cigarette on its rear platform, saw Ian in the moonlight and shouted out, in Russian, a warning to the others inside.

"Saboteurs are in the woods. Stop the train, six of you come with me and bring a dog."

The train came to a halt and the Russians jumped off the train, running toward the last spot where Ian had been sighted.

In the meantime, Ian had exclaimed, "Sarge, run, we've been spotted. We'd better get the hell out of here."

They both ran through the woods and underbrush, toward where they believed their car was located. In the background, they could hear the Russians shouting to each other and the dog barking.

Luckily for Ian and the sergeant, the partial moonlight allowed them to see where they were going, and they finally reached the car, after about thirty minutes of constant running. Breathless they jumped into the car, where the driver was waiting, as previously ordered. They could still hear the Russians and the dog coming in their direction. The dog had obviously picked up their scent.

"Start the engine and take off ASAP, back the way we came. Turn off the tail lights and just drive with the headlights," Ian ordered.

The driver headed back through Mimersdorf, toward the main road at Flieth-Stegelitz. Obviously, the Russians didn't have radio contact with the narks, as none were waiting for them when they turned onto the main road that led to the Eberswalde turnoff.

Proceeding down the road, Ian gave instructions to the driver. "When you get to the Eberswalde area, turn right on highway 167 and drive toward Löwenberg. We'll find a quiet secluded area in the vicinity of Liebenwalde, where we can stop for the night."

When they were close to Liebenwalde, Ian noticed a dirt road leading to wooded area on the approach to the small town.

"Turn right here and proceed slowly down this dirt road. Hopefully we'll see an isolated area in some trees where we can park."

Fairly soon, Corporal Barnet thought he saw an excellent place to stop and hide. "How about over there?" he pointed out to Ian.

"Yes, you're right that does look like a good spot. Back the car in there, and we will surround it with some brush, just in case some Ruskies or narks come looking for us. Corporal, you can sleep in the car, while Sergeant Williams and I camp out in the pup tents. However, before we sack out, I believe it would be a good idea, if we have a cold snack. I'm starved."

After they had eaten, all three of them went to sleep, listening to a few frogs croaking and some night owls hooting.

****

The next morning Ian woke up at around 0800, just as the sun rose above the trees, where they were hiding. He went to shake the sergeant in his tent and wake the corporal who was sprawled on the back seat of the car.

After they had eaten a cold breakfast from some British Army supplied tins, they drank some coffee brewed on a small fire that they had lit; making sure the smoke did not give them away. Then they cleaned up so that they looked fairly respectable, in case the Russians spotted them. At 1000, Ian suggested that they pack up and drive approximately thirty miles west through Löwenberg to a place named Dabergotz. This was a small municipality of about six hundred people, which was located on the main road from Berlin to Schwerin. From here they could watch the traffic on this highway, used extensively by the Warsaw Pact military.

They stayed for the rest of the day in a secluded wooded area, near Dabergotz, from which they could easily watch the main highway through binoculars. Then an hour before sunset, they packed up and got ready to move.

"Okay corporal, we need to drive back to Löwenberg, and then head up north to Gransee, which is on the southern edge of the PRA. Supposedly, there is a Soviet base a few miles further north, at a town named Fürstenberg, which is a key facility for storing battle tanks and armoured vehicles. The sergeant and I should have easy access to the Fürstenberg railway line, just one mile east of Gransee. We will not be violating any PRA or TRA as we drive up the road, so we shouldn't have any problems. Are you ready to go?"

"Yes lieutenant. Since there could be narks or Soviets on the road, I'll make sure I keep within the speed limit."

At dusk, they approached the outskirts of Gransee and Ian noticed a small road that led to a wooded area that appeared to be an ideal place to hide for the evening. At 2000 hours, Ian and the sergeant headed out for the railway line, if their maps were correct. As they left the car, Ian again told the driver to be ready, just in case they needed a quick exit.

Ian gave the special camera to Sergeant Williams saying, "Here, you had better keep this. You know how to use it, right? Take as many photos as you can. I have one transmitter left and I may have to run and board the train, if it doesn't stop."

The sergeant nodded, "Yes, I know how to use a camera. Be careful lieutenant, I would hate to see you fall off the train or get captured."

They plodded through the wooded area but, after about an hour, they still couldn't find the railway line. Then, they felt the ground shaking slightly and realized it was the vibration from a train. Soon, the sound of the engine reached them through the forest, and they now knew which way to find the railway. In actuality, it wasn't far from where they were standing, but it had been hard to find in the dark.

They quickly clambered through the underbrush, until they could see the track just a few yards away. The train seemed to be travelling at about one mile an hour and it contained several closed wagons. As it neared their location, they could see that there were actually seven covered transport cars, followed by a large open railway platform car, with a large object hidden under a tarpaulin. Following this strange looking car, there were ten more closed wagons and a passenger compartment, which they assumed contained soldiers. Again, there were no guards actually visible.

"Okay sergeant, take as many pictures as you can while I jump on that large open freight car and attach the transmitter to whatever is under the tarp."

Ian ran along the track and climbed onto the sixty-to-seventy foot special flatbed car. As he lifted the tarp slightly, he found what appeared to be a large missile underneath.

He thought to himself, *"Maybe, this is what John and Percival were looking for?"*

He quickly switched on the transmitter and attached it to one of the missile's fins. Then, realizing that the train was gathering speed, he jumped off it into some brush near the track. He stayed in the bushes, until the entire train had passed him by. He didn't want to be seen by anyone standing on the rear platform, this time.

After it gone around a curve, Ian jumped up and went to where the sergeant was waiting. Sergeant Williams returned the camera to Ian, and immediately the two of them set off back to their vehicle. They walked through the trees and underbrush, to where they had left the car; the driver was waiting for them, seated behind the wheel.

"Okay corporal, let's hit the road and return to the Löwenberg area. We'll find a quiet spot and spend the night there."

"Yes lieutenant. Did we get what we were looking for?"

"I believe so. That's correct, isn't it sergeant?"

Sergeant Williams nodded in agreement.

Corporal Barnet drove the Opel down the road toward Löwenberg and, when they were close, they found a quiet, secluded area in some trees, to spend the night.

They all slept well that night, considering the somewhat primitive conditions of camping out. The next morning they got up at 0900 and had another cold breakfast. They loaded up the car and headed back to the BRIXMIS Mission, at Potsdam.

Once there, they entered the building and Ian said, "I'm going to make myself presentable. Corporal, can you meet me down here in the main hall in about three hours? I need to go to the Olympic Stadium in Berlin, to meet with my CO and a couple of chaps."

"Yes sir. I'll see you at 1300."

Ian went up to his assigned room carrying the camera, so that the Soviet staff would not have an opportunity to steal it and turn it over to the KGB. After cleaning up, he created a log of the ten transmitters, as requested by John and Percival.

In little over three hours, Ian met the corporal downstairs and they drove over the Glienicke Bridge to West Berlin. At the Olympic Stadium, Ian went up to the top floor of the London Block with the camera, a transmitter log and a report of his tour.

Ian told the MPs at the door that he wanted to see John and Percival. One of them picked up a phone and talked to a secretary inside. Finally, John came to the door, signed him in and led him to the conference room. In a minute, Percival also entered the room.

John asked smiling, "Well, what do you have for us? Did you have some success on your vacation in East Germany?"

"Yes, I believe I did, but you are the ones who can tell me the answer to that question. Here's the log on the ten transmitters. The first nine were attached at about 2300 two nights ago and the last one was at 2100 last night," Ian replied, as he handed Percival a piece of paper indicating where he had planted the transmitters."

Trans. #	Target	Location	Going Toward
A150	T-55	South of Templin	Vogelsang
A151	T-55	South of Templin	Vogelsang
A152	T-55	South of Templin	Vogelsang
A153	BTR-60	South of Templin	Vogelsang
A154	BTR-60	South of Templin	Vogelsang
A155	BTR-60	South of Templin	Vogelsang
A156	BM-21	South of Templin	Vogelsang
A157	BM-21	South of Templin	Vogelsang
A158	Ural-375	South of Templin	Vogelsang
A159	R-5M?	Gransee	Oranienburg

"Also, here's the camera with photos taken of most of the weapon systems, loaded on the trains. I hope all this is satisfactory. We were spotted on the first night and chased by Russian soldiers and a dog. However, we managed to elude them."

"Good work Ian" said Percival. "We'll write a letter of appreciation to your CO."

"Let me know if you want any more help. I'll be *touring* for BRIXMIS, until the beginning of April," Ian replied.

"We hear there's a lot of Russian activity down near Magdeburg. You may want to make one of your *tours* in that area. However, be careful, it is shown as being a PRA on Russian maps." John suggested.

"Thanks for the tip and I'll consider it. I'd better leave now as I have to go and report to Major Poole."

As John led Ian out to the main door, he reached into his jacket pocket and pulled an envelope.

"I almost forgot to give you this," he remarked, as he handed it to Ian. "You must remember that I did not give it to you, and I know nothing about it; just be careful using it."

Before Ian could respond, they reach the main door and the MPs on guard. John signed him out in the visitor log, submitted by one of the MPs, and vanished back inside the large complex. As Ian then went down to the second floor to meet with Major Poole, he opened the envelope and discovered an East German identity card, in the name of Kurt Engels. He reported to the major and gave him the report on his *tour* in the Vogelsang area.

****

For the next three months, Ian, together with Sergeant Williams and Corporal Barnet, made several *tours*, each lasting from two to five days, of selected East German areas, conducting intelligence on Russian and Warsaw Pact troop movements. Since it was still in winter, snow and rain accompanied them on most of their *tours*, making for some uncomfortable times.

Then, toward the end of March, 1961, they travelled to the Magdeburg area that straddled the main highway from Helmstedt, in West Germany, to West Berlin. This city, which was on the edge of a PRA, had a population of approximately two hundred and sixty thousand and was only twenty-five miles inside East Germany. The headquarters for the Russian 3rd Shock Army was located nearby, which placed their troops close to the West German border, in case of a new war.

As they left the Mission in Potsdam, they picked up a nark car that followed them down the main East/West highway. Ian decided to let them tail them for a while. There was no urgency to shake them off.

As they passed the Magdeburg cutoff, Ian remarked, "Okay Barnet, it's time to shake those bastards off our tail. You know these roads better than them, since you have toured this area for the last year with Lieutenant Giles. Let's see what you can do."

"Right lieutenant, it won't take long."

The corporal drove like a madman up and down the country roads west of Magdeburg and finally announced to Ian, "Lieutenant, I've lost them."

"Well done corporal, you deserve a gold star. Let's head towards Seehausen, where there's a wooded area from which we can hide and spot any Russian troop movements, on the road that passes through there."

Eventually Ian and the sergeant recovered from the bouncing around, they had suffered, during Barnet's erratic driving. For the next three days, they drove around the area covering from Magdeburg to the West German border and north/south from Flechtingen to Oschersleben. They were always on the lookout for troop movements and equipment storage areas. At nights they parked their car in a clearing, surrounded by trees and bushes, if they could find one.

On the afternoon of the fourth day, they drove northeast to Haldensleben, a town situated on the Ohre River and at the edge of a PRA. They found a good wooded spot to camp out for the night, just southwest of the town, and within one half mile of the town centre.

Early in the evening, at around 1800 hours, Ian got dressed in some civvies, all with East German labels, and prepared to walk to town, for some intelligence gathering. He sat down with Sergeant Williams and Corporal Barnet to eat some British Army canned food.

Speaking to both of them, he said, "I'm going to walk to Haldensleben in order to visit a couple of cafés and bars for the purpose of getting some intelligence on the PRA east of town. If for some reason I get caught and don't return here, tomorrow morning, I want you to pack up and head back to the Mission at Potsdam without me. Is this clear?"

Sergeant Williams replied, "We'll do what you just ordered us to do, but are you sure you should be going into town, out of uniform, sir?"

"I agree it's risky, but I'm fluent in German and the danger is minimal, compared to the value of the intelligence I could obtain. On top of that, I do have an East German ID card that should get me out of any scrapes with the police."

"Lieutenant, may I ask how you obtained the identification card?"

"Sergeant, you may ask, but I'll not give you an answer. I'm going to leave now and should be back in a couple of hours."

"Good luck sir," the sergeant and corporal said in unison.

Ian walked the half mile distance to the centre of Haldensleben and, in doing so, crossed over the Mittelland canal that passed just west of the town. As he entered the town centre, he slowed his walk down, so as not to look like a military person. He entered a tavern on the main street, sat down at the bar next to a small, mustached, balding man and ordered a beer.

Ian struck up a conversation with him, "How are you doing tonight? Did you have a hard day at work, like I did?"

"Yes, you might say that. The Russians are not easy to work for," the man said, as he looked around to make sure no one was listening.

"I know what you mean. I've problems working with them also, but they're in charge here. Where do you work?" Ian replied in a soft voice.

"I'm a mechanic and work on the Soviet tanks at the base in the woods, east of here. Please don't tell anyone I told you so. I don't want to lose my job, as it pays fairly well."

The man then related to Ian facts about the base that would be very useful in his report to Major Poole.

"Don't worry, I won't tell a soul. I have to leave now and return to my hotel. Maybe I'll see you some other time when I come through Haldsensleben, on my way to Berlin. It's been nice talking with you."

Ian rose from his stool, walked out of the tavern and went to a café two streets away. He entered the establishment and sat down next to a tall, young man seated at the counter.

The waiter came over and Ian ordered a cup of coffee, together with a roll and a bockwurst.

"Man, you're someone looking for punishment ordering one of those," said the man, seated next to Ian.

"You're probably right," Ian replied, as he looked over at him. It was then that Ian noticed the man's hands were all bloody and raw. "What happened to your hands? They don't look so good," he asked him.

"I was unloading large rolls of barbed wire at a warehouse and didn't have any gloves. There were truckloads of the stuff, which had been shipped in from different companies, many out of the West. I needed the job so I had no choice. I don't quite understand it, but the supervisor there told me that these shipments just appeared in recent days. In fact, he said that he had been told barbed wire was being stored all over East Germany, much of it in Berlin."

Ian heard all this and stored it in his memory, so he could write it down in his report.

"You need to get your hands looked at before they become infected."

The waiter brought him his coffee and sausage roll. The coffee was worse than the British Army brew, but the bockwurst tasted okay.

The man replied, "I should get them looked at. I can't keep doing this type of work without gloves. Tomorrow, I'll try and find a good pair."

"I have to go now. Maybe we'll meet again." Ian said. He rose from the counter and walked out of the café, after paying the bill. As he walked down the street, toward the turning to cross over the canal, he noticed a dark Wartburg car sitting between two buildings. To Ian, it "smelt" like a

Stasi car. He turned around and walked down another street, looking over his shoulder. The car was not following him. He worked his way over the canal and back to where he had left the sergeant and corporal.

"We're glad you made it back okay. Did you have any problems?" the sergeant asked.

"I thought that I saw a Stasi car in the town, but I managed to avoid it, without attracting their attention. Let's get some sleep and we'll head back to Potsdam tomorrow."

The corporal sacked out in the back seat of the car while Ian and Sergeant Williams slept in their pup tents. The next morning, after they had eaten their army rations, they packed up the car and drove into Haldensleben to get some fuel. They had to drive all over town before they could find a "Minol" station that was open and had some petrol.

They pulled in and the sergeant got out to fill up the tank, while Ian and Corporal Barnet sat in the car. Suddenly, the sergeant came to the rear car window and banged on it.

Ian opened it a crack and the sergeant said, "I think you'd better get out lieutenant, there's a Russian coming toward us."

Ian jumped out of the car and told the sergeant to get in and lock the doors. He walked up to the Russian lieutenant, who had parked his four-wheel drive UAZ-69 behind their car, and asked in halting Russian, "May I help you?" Ian didn't want the Russian to know that he spoke the language fairly well.

The Russian replied, "You're in a PRA and that's illegal under the rules. Hand me your papers and accompany me to the komendatura."

Ian replied, "The maps provided by your government do not show this area as a PRA. It is one mile east of here." Ian produced the map and pointed out to the Russian where they were. The Russian shook his head, again asking for his pass and ordering Ian to get in his UAZ-69.

Ian went over to his car and told Sergeant Williams to follow them, keeping all the doors locked. He then went back to the Russian's vehicle and climbed into a rear passenger seat, behind the lieutenant. They took off, followed by Ian's car and ended up at the komendatura. Ian and the Russian went inside, while Sergeant Williams and Corporal Barnet remained outside in the Opel.

Inside the komendatura, the Russian lieutenant led Ian to a stark bare room, furnished with just a table, two chairs and a telephone. Obviously, it was an interrogation room which was intended to intimidate the prisoner. The lieutenant left the room for a minute and then came back in with a Russian captain.

The captain spoke some English and he started to interrogate Ian.

"Why were you in the PRA? Are you a spy? The British Military Liaison Mission is not allowed in a PRA or TRA."

Ian stood up and took his map to the table, placed it in front of the captain and pointed with his finger. "The petrol station is located here and that is where we were. According to this map provided by your government, we were one mile outside the PRA."

The captain looked at the lieutenant and, in Russian, stated, "I think this Englishman is correct. It looks like you made a stupid mistake. This could be embarrassing for us. Let's hold him here for fifteen minutes and then let him go." All the time, they didn't know that Ian understood what the captain was saying.

"You must stay here while we go and talk with headquarters," the captain told Ian. Both Russians left the room and Ian smiled to himself thinking, *They're about to let me go."*

In a few minutes, the captain came back in and said, "In the spirit of friendship and goodwill between our two countries, it's been decided to let you go with a warning. Do not enter a PRA again or it could be bad for you."

Ian thanked the captain and said that he would be careful in the future. He went outside the komendatura and climbed into their car.

"Let's get out of here, finish filling the tank and head back to Potsdam, before they change their minds."

Sergeant Williams laughingly remarked to Ian "Well sir, you've survived your first clobber."

They found the petrol station, filled up and made it back to the Mission in Potsdam before dark. There they cleaned up and had the first decent meal in five days. Ian spent the evening writing up his final BRIXMIS report, which he would submit to Major Poole tomorrow in Berlin.

The next morning, Ian packed his bags, said goodbye to Sergeant Williams and had Corporal Barnet drive him to the Olympic Stadium. Ian's BRIXMIS assignment was over, but he had enjoyed every minute of it.

5

MI6 Berlin

At the Olympiastadion, Ian met with Lieutenant Giles briefly and informed him that Corporal Barnet was waiting outside, to take him back to the Mission.

"Did you have a good R&R break these last three months?" Ian asked Giles.

"Yes, it certainly was a change to get away from those *tours*, although I did miss the excitement of them. See you around, I hope."

Ian walked into the London Block and went to Major Poole's office on the second floor, where he handed in his last *tour* report.

"Well Mr. Black, I trust you learned a thing or two about the Russians and East Germany. It's been a pleasure to have you on board these past three months."

"Yes sir, it's certainly been very instructional; especially how to jump off a train, as it's moving. In addition, I managed to survive my first and only clobber."

"I've sent a report on your performance to your permanent CO, Colonel Thurman, and I believe he is expecting you to report to his office today, in order to receive your new assignment. Again, thanks for your dedication to BRIXMIS and its intelligence gathering mission. Maybe our paths will cross again."

Ian gave the major a salute, turned and walked out of the office. As Ian left the outer office, where the major's secretary kept watch, he thought, *"The major is a great Army officer and, since he's still fairly young, he should go a long way in this Army. I wouldn't mind serving under him again, if I have the opportunity."*

He went to room 253, Colonel Thurman's office, in the Berlin Brigade headquarters building and entered the outer office, where his CO's gate keeper, Helga Jergens, sat behind her desk, which contained an Underwood typewriter and phone.

She smiled at Ian, as he entered and said in German, "Guten morgen Lieutenant Black, Colonel Thurman is expecting you. Please take a seat and I'll let him know you're here."

"Guten morgen Helga, it's been three months since you and I talked. As you probably know, I've been busy *touring* the East for BRIXMIS."

Helga nodded, pushed the buzzer on the intercom and, after the colonel answered, she spoke softly into it, using English, "Lieutenant Black is here to see you sir."

After she received the expected response from Colonel Thurman, she turned to Ian and said, "You can go in now."

Ian went to the colonel's door, knocked softly and entered. He walked up to about three feet from the front of the colonel's desk and gave him a salute.

He returned the salute saying, "Please sit down Mr. Black," indicating the chair in front of his desk.

He removed some papers from a file on his desk and scanned them. "I see you had a fairly successful time *touring* East Germany for BRIXMIS. I hope you discovered some of the capabilities of our potential enemy. Major Poole highly recommends you, based on your performance during the past three months," the colonel said.

"I did the best I could, sir. I did get clobbered one time, but I managed to convince the Russians that I was right and they were incorrect. By the way, sir, I discovered during an outing into Haldensleben, dressed as a German civilian, that the East is buying and storing a considerable amount of barbed wire. What it means I'm not sure, but I'd like the opportunity to find out."

"Mr. Black, I'm very concerned about your travelling around as a German civilian. You know if you get caught, it'll be embarrassing for Her Majesty's Government, and we may not be able to do anything to help you. I've also heard an unsubstantiated rumour that you may have obtained an East German identification card with your picture on it, but in a German name. I'll not bring this up again, but I must stress that you have to be very careful in this divided city. It's starting to heat up with Khrushchev flexing the Soviet might, and the United States having a new, young, inexperienced president."

"Sir, the rumour is true, but I only aim to use it in dire situations, where I've no alternatives. I've no intention of causing problems for the British Army, the Government or Her Majesty."

"Good, we'll not talk of it again. As you know I run a small, tight organization, where we have a lot of latitude, as long as we produce results. Since you have contacts in the organization on the top floor of the London Block, I and my corresponding number in that organization have decided to make you the liaison between us. Although this is the Army and I can order you to perform in this role, I'm giving you the opportunity to decline it. I want to be sure that you'll interface with them for the betterment of both organizations and develop far reaching, forward looking intelligence. We need to know ahead of time what the Warsaw Pact and the Russians, in particular, might do in the future."

"I appreciate this opportunity and will conduct myself in a professional manner. In addition, I realize I may become privy to confidential and secret intelligence that must not be divulged, except to the appropriate people. I accept this assignment without equivocation."

"Good, I'm glad you have accepted this assignment and you'll report directly to me. For the next three months, you'll remain lodged in the London Block after which time you may, at your discretion, obtain lodging outside the Army facilities. Of course, this assumes you can afford it on your measly Army pay. You'll attend my weekly, Monday morning, staff meetings and be prepared to inform my small team on any activities, you feel appropriate. Incidentally, at the next meeting, the Director of the Intelligence Corps, Brigadier Croxford who is also known as Rex, will be in attendance."

"I believe I've met him one time, while I was attending the Intelligence Academy at Maresfield Park."

"Excellent, then you know what kind of officer he is and what he expects. As I believe you're aware, there're three groups under my command: Intelligence and Security Company, including the Operational Intelligence, Protective Security and Counter Intelligence. You're already acquainted with Major Phillips who's in charge of the Counter Intelligence. You'll meet the officers in charge of the other two groups at our next meeting. Unless you have some questions, that's all I have for now. I'll see you at the next staff meeting."

"Are there any specific guidelines for my position as liaison to MI6?"

"No, you'll work with the organization and report to me any requirements they have of the Intelligence Corps. At all times you'll be on the lookout for any troop movements or other unusual actions by the East, and develop a scenario, as to what the future implications could be. One area I suggest you look into is what is the East planning to do with the stored barbed wire you found out about on your *tour*. I've made arrangements with the local MI6 director for you to be supplied with a special pass that will allow you to enter their facility. I suggest that you take a few days off, view the Berlin sights and then attend next Monday's staff meeting. By then I should have the pass ready for you. Make sure you treasure it with your life. Since George Blake betrayed the Operation Stopwatch tunnel, MI6 has been very skittish. That's all for now, I have another visitor waiting to see me. Good day Mr. Black and I'll see you at the next Monday staff meeting."

As Ian left the room, he noticed a tall, U.S. Army captain, waiting in the outer office. He bid farewell to Helga and headed back to his room in the London Block, speculating if the American was from the 513th Military Intelligence Group.

He took the colonel's advice and spent the next few days viewing the sights and sounds of Berlin.

****

The next Monday, Ian went to his CO's conference room in the Olympic Stadium Administration Building, for the weekly meeting. As he walked in, he recognized John from MI6 and Major Phillips. The other two officers he didn't know, but Phillips quickly introduced them to him.

"Mr. Black, I'd like you to meet Captain Bolton, who is in charge of Security Group."

"Glad to meet you, captain," Ian said.

"Likewise," the captain replied.

Phillips then similarly introduced him to Major Peters, the officer that ran the Interrogation Group.

At this point, Colonel Thurman entered the room, followed by a man, with a medium build and sporting a short croppy moustache, and who exuded authority and toughness. Since he had met him briefly before at the Intelligence Academy, Ian realized he was Brigadier James Croxford.

75

Colonel Thurman started out saying, "I believe all of you know Brigadier Croxford, since he's the Director of the Intelligence Corps. Of course, I don't think I have to remind you that if you ever refer to the Director to outside personnel, just use the codename "Rex". I assume you have, by now, met Lieutenant Ian Black who joined the group three months ago, but he has been *touring* East Germany on vacation, through BRIXMIS."

All the attendees laughed when the colonel mentioned the word "vacation".

Ian replied, "Sir, I hope you don't mind me interrupting but, it wasn't much of a holiday, camping out in thirty degree weather, in the snow or rain."

"Well, I'm glad you're still in good health," replied the colonel smiling. "Incidentally, Mr. Black will be our liaison with the folks at the top of the London Block. He's already well acquainted with two members of the group. If any of you need assistance from MI6 and want to provide information to them, please use Mr. Black as your conduit. Let's go around the room and each of you provide me with an update from the previous meeting."

Each officer gave a report about their group's work for the past seven days. Ian gave a summary of the *tours* he went on, for the past three months.

After everyone had finished, the colonel said, "Our director would like to say a few words before we disband for today."

As he looked around the table at each officer, Brigadier Croxford said, "Gentlemen, we are facing a challenging time here in Berlin. As you're probably aware, there'll be a June summit meeting in Vienna, between President Kennedy and Nikita Khrushchev. At this get together, we can expect Khrushchev to be very tough and push for a peace treaty, with East Germany, that will end the four power rights. In addition, East Germans and other nationalities are fleeing the East through Berlin. The East German government is

76

threatening to stop this outflow by force. Whatever that means! Therefore, I want all of you to be "on your toes" and report anything that appears to be out of the norm."

Everyone in the room nodded and said, "Yes sir."

The brigadier smiled saying, "Thank you all for your dedication to the Intelligence Corps."

Then Colonel Thurman said, "That's it for today. I'll see you all next Monday, same place and time. Mr. Black, will you please stay behind for a moment. The rest of you may depart and get back to work."

After the attendees had left, except for the colonel and brigadier, Ian's CO reached into his pocket, pulled out an ID card and handed it to Ian, saying "Here is the identification card that will allow you into the MI6 area. Guard it with your life. It mustn't fall into the wrong hands. There's an experimental card reader at the door, but it doesn't always work. Occasionally, you might have to show it to the MPs guarding the door."

"Thank you sir, I look forward to this assignment as the liaison."

Brigadier Croxford commented, "Mr. Black, I've heard good things about you and you should do well in the Army, if you decide to stay in for the long term."

"Thank you, sir. At the moment I have no plans of getting out and facing tough civilian life."

All three of them smiled and laughed at this.

"That'll be all Ian. I'll see you at the meeting next Monday," replied the colonel.

Ian rose, gave both of them a salute and left the conference room, carrying the ID card with him.

He returned to the London Block, visited the Officers' Mess for lunch and then went up to the fourth floor.

There he approached the stern looking, heavily armed MP's, one of whom, a sergeant, asked him, "What's the purpose of your visit, sir? This is a secure area and you must leave immediately, unless you're authorized."

Ian pulled out the ID from his pocket and placed it around his neck with the attached cord.

"Sergeant, I believe this will allow me to enter," he replied, as he held out the identification."

"Sorry sir, I didn't know you." He looked down at a list he had on the desk and found Lieutenant Black's name. "Please try your card in the card reader. It's experimental and it doesn't always work."

Ian walked up to the card reader next to the main door and inserted his ID. About three seconds later, there was a loud click behind the door.

The MP sergeant said, "I believe the door is unlocked, sir. You may enter."

Ian turned the door handle and the door opened. He thought to himself, *This modern technology is amazing. On my trip to Beirut two years ago, Percival loaned me those new transistorized pagers."*

Ian entered the MI6 inner sanctum and found a secretary seated close by, behind a desk.

"I'd like to talk to Percival and John, if they're available."

She smiled at Ian, as he used their codenames instead of their real names. "Let me see if they're in," she replied, as she picked up the phone.

She talked softly into the phone, hung it up and turned to Ian. "John will be out in a moment. Percival isn't present at the moment, but he should return from lunch within the half hour."

Ian looked down the hallway to his left and saw John walking toward him.

"Glad to see you again, although it was just this morning, that we met at the staff meeting," John said. "Let's go into a conference room. I've left word for Percival to join us as soon as he returns from lunch."

John led Ian down the hallway to a small room, close to where several men and a few women were seated working, behind partitions.

"I'm glad you were selected to be the liaison between us and the Intelligence Corps. That's as long as I don't have to play you at billiards," John said smiling, as he remembered the game in Cyprus where Ian trounced him.

"Was the information from my BRIXMIS *tours* any good to you? Did the transmitters work okay and did the low-light level pictures come out?"

"Percival can answer about the transmitters. The pictures taken, with the special camera, were excellent and we were able to identify every military target in them. It appears that the Russians are moving up some new weapon systems, into the forward areas. This could be bothersome with the summit meeting, coming up in June. On the other hand, it may be they're trying to pressure Kennedy into making some concessions."

"I'm glad to hear the pictures came out okay. As far as the missile issue is concerned, we only saw that one on a train leaving the Fürstenberg area, where one of the missile bases was supposed to be. I managed to place the last transmitter on one of its fins, as the train was moving. I had to jump off at the last moment before it gathered speed. Did you see in my report about the worker I met in a bar, who had bloody hands? He had been unloading barbed wire for the East German government and he saw rolls of the stuff stored in a large warehouse."

"Yes, I did see your report. We're still trying to find out if that was an isolated case or something larger."

The door to the room opened and in walked Percival. He had received John's message about the meeting.

"How're you doing Ian?" he asked.

"Great, I enjoyed *touring* the East, even though the weather did not cooperate. How's the tracking of the transmitters gone?

"We've been able to track all ten transmitters, mainly with the help of the RAF who use the de Havilland Chipmunk light aircraft, to pick up the signals. It appears the tanks, armoured personnel carriers, multiple rocket launchers and trucks were headed for Vogelsang. It must be a major base for armoured vehicles and the R-5M missiles have been withdrawn. The one R-5M that you placed a transmitter on was tracked as far as the Polish border."

"What's the battery life of the transmitters?" Ian asked.

"Approximately three months and then they fade fairly rapidly," Percival responded. "We appreciate the help you gave us in this matter.

"Do you have any intelligence on why the East Germans might be storing huge quantities of barbed wire?" Ian queried.

"No, we don't at this time. If you find out anything more about this matter, please let us know."

"Perhaps I'll go and apply for a job with the East German government, as a labourer, and see what I find out," Ian responded.

"That could be dangerous. I personally wouldn't advise it," John offered in response.

"Yes, you're probably correct. Anyway I'll keep you informed as to what else I find out. Thanks for your time and I'm glad at least part of my time with BRIXMIS was useful. See you chaps later."

All three rose and Ian shook hands with them, leaving the facility through the main door. He waved at the MPs, who saluted him, as he walked out. He didn't notice but one of them placed an exit time by his name on the visitor list. Everyone was being very careful after the George Blake traitorous incident.

6

Monika

One Friday night, toward the end of April 1961, Ian decided to don his mufti and go to the Leuthen Club, near the Brandenburg Gate. He had heard it was a lively establishment from several officers in the Berlin Brigade, with live music on Friday and Saturday nights. It was supposed to be a popular place for West Berliners and even some East Berliners, who could afford it. As a light rain was starting to descend upon the city, Ian decided to hail a taxi and take it to the club. By the time the cab arrived there, the rain had almost stopped and stars were starting to appear in the sky.

Ian walked into the club and the six-piece band was playing a slow dance that he recognized as *Unchained Melody*. There were three couples on the dance floor, moving to the music. He found a spot at the bar with an empty stool on each side. It was still fairly early and he expected that the place would fill up, as the evening progressed. In German, he ordered one half liter of Paulaner Salvator. The man behind the bar quickly poured the beer and placed it in front of Ian.

"Danke", he said, as he planned to speak German all evening, to anyone who struck up a conversation with him.

81

His pseudonym was Kurt Beck and he lived in West Berlin, where he worked for an architectural firm. Since he spoke German fluently, without a foreign accent, the chance of anyone seeing through his persona was slim to none.

As he sat at the bar nursing his beer, the club started to fill up and the stools at the bar ended up being completely occupied, except for one to the right of him.

As he continued to sip his beer, suddenly a soft voiced cooed at him "Is this seat taken, by any chance?"

Kurt turned and saw a woman who reminded him of his lost Cyprus love, Aphrodite. She was fairly tall, about five foot eight inches, with long black hair and blue eyes. He also noted, as any man would do, that she had an excellent figure dressed in a smart looking, cocktail dress, with a matching jacket. Additionally, like any young, virile male, he noticed that her breasts were not too large; just about right to fill a champagne glass or a man's hand.

"No," Ian replied smiling, as he pulled the stool out for her.

"Thanks," she said.

"My name's Kurt. May I buy you a drink?" he asked.

"Sure, that would be nice. Thank you," she purred. "My name's Monika."

"What would you like?"

"A Mai Tai, if they serve it here. I've heard it's a great, new cocktail that came out of the Far East."

At that moment, the bartender approached and queried Monika, "What can I get for you, Fräulein?"

Kurt replied, "She would like a Mai Tai."

"Of course, no problem," he muttered, as he walked away to make the drink.

The more Ian looked at her, the more she reminded him of Aphrodite Palas, the Cypriot girl he was going to marry, until she was gunned down by an EOKA terrorist and died in his arms.

The bartender returned with the Mai Tai, set it in front of Monika and walked off, leaving them to continue conversing.

After talking about the weather and other such mundane subjects, Kurt noticed that there was a table available in a quiet corner, as a couple left the club.

"Would you like to move over to that table, it'll be more comfortable?" Ian asked Monika.

"Yes that would be nice and maybe we can hear each other, over the music from the club band."

They picked up their drinks and walked quickly over to the table, before someone else took it.

"Do you come here often?" Kurt asked.

"No, this is the first time I've been here. I've heard about it from someone at work. Do you live in West Berlin?"

Kurt responded, "Yes, I live in the British sector of Berlin, and work for a large West German architectural firm, as a civil engineer, mainly in the western part of the city. It's hard for our company to obtain contracts from the East German authorities, as they give the work to East German organizations. How about you, Monika? Where do you work?"

"A good friend of mine obtained me a job at the GDR employment agency, where I assist people to find work. It's a good steady job and it pays fairly well, considering the general economic conditions in the GDR. I live in the East Berlin fairly close to the Brandenburg Gate, in a flat that this friend helped me qualify for."

"This friend of yours must be a fairly influential person to do all of this for you."

After she looked around to see if anyone was listening, Monika whispered, "Yes, he is. Actually he's a politician high up in the government, but I can't say much more, otherwise I could lose everything."

"*Hmm,*" Kurt thought. "*Maybe I can get out of her who the "friend" is and, in addition, I might be able to find out some information on what's going on in the East German*

83

government circles. But I have to be careful. Perhaps she's a Stasi agent and comes to the West to plant false information."

Then he asked, "Have you ever thought about coming to the West? You know you could probably double or triple your pay and not have to look over your shoulder all the time."

"Oh, I couldn't do that. My family lives in the East and they could be in jeopardy, if I deserted the GDR. In fact, when I come into the West, I sometimes disguise myself with a wig. This way, I don't always look the same as I cross the border and don't create problems for my friend."

Kurt thought, *"Monika could be a good contact for intelligence, especially with her political friend. I wonder what his name is. Perhaps she's his mistress or just a family acquaintance."* He felt a little guilty thinking about this, since he was also attracted to her. In addition, he hadn't told her the truth about who he was. Then he thought again, *"Possibly she hasn't told me everything either."*

At that point, the band started to play another slow dance; it was a current, popular waltz.

"Would you like to dance?" Kurt asked Monika.

"I thought you'd never ask," she replied.

They both rose and walked over to the dance floor, where they glided to the waltz, for the next few minutes.

When they returned to their table, the waitress appeared and Kurt ordered another beer and Mai Tai.

For the next couple of hours, they danced and chatted about non-political matters, including the mild spring weather, popular music and the latest films. The band played current music from the 1940's and 1950's, which were great to dance to.

As they danced, he mused, *"She's a great dancer. She is so much like Aphrodite, it's scary."*

Finally, at around 2200 hours, Monika whispered, "I have to leave now, so I can go back across the border with a crowd. This way I won't be so visible to the police."

"Can I see you again? Perhaps go to a movie, dinner or something?" Kurt asked.

"Yes, I'd like that. I'll be tied up with my friend for the next few weeks but, starting sometime in June, he tells me that he'll be occupied on a major project, which will leave me free. In addition my job, right now, is becoming hectic, as I have to find men to help in the GDR warehouses, for a project the East is working on. It's critical that I find some labourers, otherwise my friend may not be too happy.

Here's my phone number, but when you call me, please call from a phone booth. I'll answer just for a moment to find out who it is, and then I'll go to a booth and call you back at your public phone. One has to be very guarded and, again, I don't want to cause problems for my friend."

"I understand the situation and I'll be careful. May I walk you part of the way to the Gate?"

"I'd certainly appreciate it, just as long as we don't get too close to it, together."

Kurt paid the tab for their drinks and they left the Club going into the night, and walked down the well lit street, toward the line that marked the West from the East.

As they approached the Gate, Monika turned toward Kurt and said, "This is as far as you should come. I'll wait for your call."

Continuing she said, "Thank you for a lovely evening. I enjoyed it. It was the best time I've had in quite a while."

He held her in his arms for a few seconds and whispered, "It's been fun and, by the way, you're a wonderful dancer. I wish I could dance as well as you. I'm glad you came to the Club, otherwise I'd have probably never got to meet you."

Moving away from him, she started to walk toward the East, saying "Again thanks, I hope to hear from you soon."

She walked down the street that led to the white dividing line and vanished into the night.

Ian thought, as he walked towards a taxi stand, *"I hope I see her again. Maybe she'll vanish into the communist controlled East and never reappear. I wonder who her friend is and what control he has over her."*

He found a vacant cab and told the driver to take him to an area near the Stadium. For security reasons, he didn't want any West German taxi driver to see exactly where he was going.

****

At the next Intelligence Corps staff meeting, Colonel Thurman went through some staff matters and outlined the upcoming Summit Meeting, between Khrushchev and Kennedy.

"From information I've received, this summit could be a contentious meeting, out of which the Berlin issue could heat up. Khrushchev appears to want a separate peace treaty with East Germany, which would have ramifications for the rights of the three Western powers. There's considerable pressure from Walter Ulbricht to stop the flow of intellectuals, engineers, doctors and teachers that are coming west. Keep this in mind as you conduct your surveillance activities."

Continuing, the colonel said, "Okay, let's go round the table. Ian, you go first and give us a report on what you've been up to."

"Well, I've been patrolling the East trying to find out who is ordering the barbed wire and building material that I heard about during my BRIXMIS **tours**. So far I haven't found out very much. I'm thinking of trying to get a one day job, helping to unload at the warehouses to see if I can discover anything. I know it'll be risky, but with my East German ID card, I should be able to pull it off.

In addition, I've met this Fräulein who seems to have a very influential, political friend in the GDR government. Of course, she could actually be a Stasi plant, so I'm being very careful about what I tell her. In fact, she knows me only as Kurt and that I work as a civil engineer, for a West German architectural company. The name she gave me was Monika, but that may not be her real name. She did tell me she lived in East Berlin and would not think of coming over to the West. Her family lives in the East and she's afraid that they might be victimized, if she ever came over."

"That's very interesting Mr. Black," replied the colonel. "Just be extremely careful in what you tell her. She must never know that you'll in the British Army. Also, if you get caught using that ID card, we may not be able to help you much. You understand what I'm saying."

"Yes sir. Whenever I go out after duty hours, I always speak German and wear German clothes. I'll be extremely careful and will only do it, if I've no alternative.

As far as Monika is concerned, I plan to meet her again in about a month and will try to find out more information, including who her friend is. However, I believe she will be hesitant to give me that detail."

John of MI6 looked at Ian and said, "We've also been hearing rumours about the East purchasing and storing building material, but we've no indication as to the purpose. Try and find out as much as you can, so we can verify our information."

The other members of the group gave their reports, and then the colonel concluded the meeting by saying, "Before we end this session, I want to inform you that we'll soon have a new member of the group. As you're all aware, Mr. Black here can speak German fluently and some Russian. However, I believe it's imperative that we also have someone who can speak and understand Russian fluently, without any foreign accent. I am searching for such a person who also meets our overall security concerns. We don't want any more George Blake's betraying us. Thank you all for coming and we'll meet again next Monday, at the same time. Mr. Black, I'd like you to stay behind as I need to talk to you."

The attendees left the room and the last one closed the door behind them.

"Ian, I've three issues that I'd like to briefly discuss with you. First, I'm concerned about any relationship you have with this woman, named Monika. If she is indeed connected to a high up East German official, she could be under surveillance, at all times by the Stasi. You could then be identified and checked out by them. I want you to be extremely careful and only meet her in the West. On the other hand, as you pointed out, she could well turn out to be an excellent source of information. Second, you mentioned about trying to get a one day job at a warehouse, in order to find out what is going on. As I mentioned earlier, using a false East German ID card could be dangerous, so if you do, I suggest that you don't let the ID out of your sight, in case some official tries to confirm your identity with the Stasi.

Finally, you're currently staying in the London Block at the Stadium. As you'll have been here for six months in Berlin, by the end of June, you'll be allowed to find a flat out in the city, if you can afford it. The Army will give you an extra allowance for providing lodging and food, but it generally is not enough to cover it all."

"Sir, I totally understand the first two issues and will be extremely careful. In addition, I'll report on my progress and problems at each staff meeting. As far as the lodging matter is concerned, I appreciate the opportunity to get closer to the German public in general. If the extra pay by the Army is not sufficient, my father will hopefully make up the difference."

"Very good, Ian, that will be all. I'll see you next week."

Ian stood up, saluted the colonel and left the conference room.

7

Teacher Versus Student

For the next three weeks, Ian travelled around East and West Berlin looking for any signs of troop buildups by the Warsaw Pact. In addition, he scouted out warehouses in the East, where barbed wire and building materials could be stored incognito. He did find a few warehouses, where there were lines of day workers waiting to go in, and lorries coming and going into the facilities. He made a note of their location and thought, *"Next time I meet Monika I must try to find out how intensive a background check is made, before the labourers are hired."*

On the 3rd of June, 1961, a two-day summit meeting commenced between the American president, John F Kennedy, and the leader of the Soviet Union, Nikita Khrushchev. Khrushchev came well prepared, with a list of demands, to this meeting with a leader that he considered a neophyte and novice politician. It appears that there was no set agenda and both participants came with their own set of issues, they wanted discussed.

On the first day they met at the American Ambassador's residence in Vienna, ending with no real accomplishments. On the second and final day, the session was held at the Soviet Embassy, and again Khrushchev stressed the need for a peace treaty covering all Germany. The Soviet leader left the summit with the idea that Kennedy and the US would acquiesce on the issue of a permanent division of Berlin, in preference to war. Overall the summit was a win for Khrushchev and a failure for Kennedy. It was rumoured that Kennedy was annoyed with himself, for letting the Soviet leader browbeat and lecture him, as a teacher to a student.

On the following Tuesday, Ian placed a call, from his room in the London Block, to John of MI6.

When John answered, Ian asked, "Do you have time to see me today? I need to come and discuss with you the results of the recent summit meeting."

John replied, "How about at 2:00 pm? I'll see if Percival and a chap named Chetwyn will also be available. Chetwyn is our expert on political matters, affecting the East and the West."

"I'll be there at two o'clock," Ian replied. He then decided he was getting hungry and went to the Officers' Mess for lunch. There he met Major Phillips again and they chatted about the old times; when they were in Cyprus, trying to catch Colonel Grivas.

The lunch was typical army food and reminded him of the great food he had on the HMS Agincourt. Navy food always seemed better than army chow.

After he parted ways with the major, Ian went to the top floor of London Block to discuss with John, the situation in Berlin and the result of the Vienna summit meeting. At exactly on time, he approached the MPs, who were guarding the main door. They saluted him as he ran his pass through the card reader. After a few seconds, there was a click behind the door, Ian entered the "inner sanctum" of MI6 and closed the door behind him. He went down the hallway to John's office, knocked and, after hearing "Enter", opened the door.

"Hi, John, is this still a convenient time to meet? Will Percival and Chetwyn be able to join us?"

"Yes to both questions, Ian. Let's go down to the conference room, where there's more room and privacy. They'll be joining us shortly."

They walked down the hallway to a large conference room that contained a long oak table. There was one window that overlooked the Olympiastadion and to the south, about one mile away, a high hill was visible. This artificial knoll contained rubble from the bombed out buildings of West Berlin.

Ian and John entered the room and sat down at the table, making small talk, as they waited for Percival and Chetwyn to join them.

After they were all seated, Ian started the conversation off. "As we're all aware, including the East German government, approximately seven thousand East Europeans, mainly Germans, are crossing into West Berlin every week. Obviously, this situation is unacceptable to the Soviets and East Germans, and I'm sure they're making plans to stem the tide. Did anything come out of the summit meeting that would give any hint, as to what the Soviets plan to do about it?"

John responded, "We've intercepted increased coded traffic going back and forth between East Berlin and Moscow. So far, we haven't been able to decode it. Obviously, since the treachery of George Blake and the leaking of the tunnel in Operation Stopwatch, our intelligence on the communications traffic is limited. What all this increased traffic means we have no idea, until it can be decoded."

Chetwyn then chimed in, "What we do know is, at the summit, Khrushchev pushed Kennedy for a German peace treaty, which the president did decline. However, he did express sympathy to the East's plight of a brain drain and gave the impression to the Soviet leader that some kind of control would be acceptable. Kennedy expressed his opinion that some control of the East/West Berlin dividing line was obviously preferable to another armed conflict in Europe."

91

Percival added, "The Soviets and East Germans control the entire border between East and West German with watch towers, mine fields, etc. This is except for the twenty-seven mile border in Berlin. It is self-evident that one would require at least twenty-seven miles of barbed wire to create a rudimentary barrier on the *white line*. Is this why they are stockpiling building materials? Of course, we don't know, but the outcome of the summit seems to indicate that they might try to somehow control this flow of refugees."

"The problem for the East Bloc, in general, is that the West might retaliate with economic sanctions and withdrawal of trade agreements. This would have serious repercussions on the economies of the Eastern countries that already are shaky at best," Chetwyn pointed out. "Instability of all the Eastern European countries must be of great concern to the Soviet Union."

Ian then asked, "If some kind of border was created through Berlin, when would be the ideal time for the Ruskies to risk it? If I was in charge of such an operation, I'd pick a weekend; late Saturday night or early Sunday morning. At that time, many people are half drunk with great German beer, and they're fast asleep in their beds. I'd also pick some date in the summer, when many people are on their summer holiday. Again, this is what I'd do if I was in charge of the GDR."

"That's not a bad analysis, Ian. Let's hope you're not selected by Khrushchev to run the GDR," John responded half laughing. "Of course, this is no laughing matter. We've heard a rumour that a Warsaw Pact summit will take place in Moscow, at the beginning of August. Maybe a major decision will be made about this issue of a Berlin border. So far, we haven't received any intelligence of Soviet troop movements above the normal operations and training exercises."

Percival commented, "We've picked up hints from unverified sources that the KGB is preparing plans for increased subversion in various parts of the world, in order to distract the Americans from any events in Germany and Berlin. They also seem to be readying some misinformation, in order to confuse us. Again, all this has not been vetted yet and may all be rumours to confuse us. They're good at that."

"If you're all agreeable, why don't we meet again in about three weeks to discuss these issues further," Ian suggested. "In the meantime, I will try and hunt down exactly where and how much construction material is being stored. Hopefully, I'm going to meet Monika again next weekend and I'll attempt to carefully obtain more information about her friend. In addition, I'll see if I can find out more about the project he's working on. Perhaps, it's something to do with the border between East and West Germany, in general."

John rose and went to the window and asked Ian to join him. "You see that hill over there in the distance. It's called Teufelsberg, in English it is known as Devil's Mountain, and it stands approximately two hundred and sixty feet above the Berlin landscape. Starting in July we, together with our American cousins, plan to have a mobile listening post on top of it. It's an ideal location to intercept radio communications traffic between Berlin and Moscow. Obviously this information is not to be disseminated to anyone."

Ian responded, "Thanks for the info. Of course, I won't divulge it to a soul. Do you all agree it'll be worthwhile to meet again in three weeks?"

All three nodded and replied in the affirmative. They then all left the conference room and returned to their offices. Ian bade farewell to John and left the MI6 quarters through the main door and past the MPs, who checked him out on their roster.

8

The Teufel Club

On Wednesday, Lieutenant Black walked out of the Olympiastadion and took a taxi to the main Spandau shopping area, where small stores lined the street. There he found a public telephone and tried to place a call to the Berlin number, Monika had given to him. He attempted to dial her phone several times, before he finally got through. It seemed the connection between East and West Berlin was not very reliable.

It rang four times and then a female voice answered, "Hello?"

"Are you the Fräulein I met at the Leuthen Club a month ago?" Kurt asked.

"Yes. What's the phone number?"

Kurt gave her the number of the phone from which he was dialing and then hung up. It seemed like forever, but finally the phone rang and he answered.

"Hello." Kurt said, sounding furtively.

"It's been a long time since we met at the Club," Monika responded. "I didn't think you were going to call."

"I've tried to call you several times in the past two weeks, but could never seem to get through. How are you?"

"I'm doing fine, busy as usual at work. How've you been?"

"Well, I've also been tied up at work. I have a free weekend coming up and was wondering if you would like to go out this coming Saturday. We could go to a night club for dinner and dancing. I've heard about a great place, in the American sector, but it's not too far from the Gate. I'll tell you about it when we meet on Saturday. Okay?"

"I'm free then, I'd love to. At what time do you want to meet and where?"

"Great. How about at six o'clock? You'll find me at the edge of the Tiergarten under some trees, northwest of the junction where Behrenstrasse and Ebertstrasse meet. I'll be wearing a navy blue blazer, with a white handkerchief in the pocket and a fake, black moustache. When you approach me, use my name and ask, *Is there a Red Moon tonight*?" I'll reply: *"No, and I'll use your name, I think it's a month from now."* This is just in case we don't recognize each other and also as a security precaution. You can't be too careful in today's political environment."

"I understand. I'm looking forward to seeing you again. Incidentally I'll be wearing an auburn wig. The idea of using a code is an excellent idea. See you soon. Bye." Monika said softy into the phone, as she hung up. Looking around, she didn't observe anyone who looked like a member of the Stasi, but one never knew in East Germany.

****

The following Saturday at around five o'clock in the afternoon, Ian left this room at the Olympic Stadium, dressed in civvies and a navy blue blazer. He walked to the nearest taxi stand, where luckily there were several cabs waiting. He climbed into the lead car and directed the driver to go to the Brandenburg Gate.

It wasn't long before they were close to the Berlin landmark and Ian spoke to the driver, as he pointed out a good place to wait.

"Park by the trees, over there, and wait until I return. I'll pay for your waiting time."

He got out of the cab and walked over to a nearby clump of trees. The time was five minutes to six; the time they had agreed to meet. Ian waited for what seemed an interminable long time, and he started to worry that she wouldn't appear.

He was about to give up, when he heard footsteps behind him; he turned and saw a gorgeous woman, with auburn hair, approaching. She was wearing a pale green, flowered, summer dress that matched her eyes.

She said softly to him, "Kurt, is there a red moon tonight?"

Realizing it was Monika, he answered, "No, Monika, I think it's a month from now." He had trouble recognizing her momentarily, since her hair was black the first time he met her.

"Hello, Kurt, it's good to see you again. It's been a while."

"Well, I've been extremely busy at work and I haven't had much time off. How did you get here? I thought you would come through the Gate."

"As I approached it, there appeared to be a lot of security, so I went through some back streets and alleys that I know about. Luckily, there were no Volkspolizei officers around, so I was able to cross the *white line*, without any trouble or an identification check. I have to be very careful so as not to embarrass or cause problems for my friend."

"Well, I'm glad you're here. I understand about your need for secrecy. I've a taxi waiting over there that will take us to *The Teufel Club*. It was recommended to me, by a friend at work, and supposedly it has great food and a band that plays all kinds of music. It's not too far from here, and I think you'll like it."

"I've never heard of it, but it sounds great," Monika replied.

They walked to the taxi that Kurt had waiting and got in. Kurt said to the driver, "Please take us to *The Teufel Club* in the American zone. Do you know where it is?"

"Yes sir, I'm familiar with it. Many young Germans and foreigners go there on a Saturday night."

The driver went down several side streets in West Berlin and, after about fifteen minutes, arrived at *The Teufel Club*. It was lit up with a large neon sign, and there was a crowd of young people waiting to go in. It was obviously a very popular place, especially on Saturday nights.

Kurt and Monika got out of the cab, and he paid the driver, giving him a good tip. Kurt took Monika's arm and they walked up to the man standing guard at the main door. He looked like he was a combination of a bouncer and a doorman.

"We have a booking for six-thirty."

"What's your name?"

"Kurt Beck."

The man looked at his list and responded, "You may go in. Your table should be available, sir."

The bouncer opened the door and let them in, ahead of the crowd of people waiting to enter. There was grumbling among some of them, as they saw Monika and Kurt enter the Club, without having to wait.

Kurt gave his name to the maitre'd inside.

The man looked at his list and then said, "Follow me please." He led them to a table, fairly close to the dance floor, and stated "Your waiter will be here shortly."

The waiter soon appeared carrying menus, which he handed to Kurt and Monika, as he said, "My name is Hans. I'll be your waiter this evening. Would you like to order a drink?"

"Yes, but we haven't decided yet. Could you drop back in a couple of minutes?" Kurt replied.

"Of course"

"By the way, when does the band start to play?" Kurt asked him.

"They set up at seven-fifteen and start playing around seven-thirty. I'll come back soon and take your drink orders."

"Great," Kurt replied.

As the waiter walked away, Kurt asked Monika, "What would you like to drink?"

"I think I'd like a Greyhound. It's a fairly new cocktail and I've heard it tastes great."

"Well, I think I'll order a Vodka Martini." Kurt responded

As promised, the waiter returned in about five minutes.

"May I take your drink orders now?" he asked.

"Yes," Kurt answered. "The Fräulein will have a Greyhound and I'll have a Vodka Martini."

After Hans, the waiter, had gone to order their drinks from the bar, they both scanned the menus.

"Do you see anything you'd like, Monika?"

"Yes," she replied. "I think I'll have the Rahmschnitzel."

"Okay, would you like some wine with our dinner?"

"I'd love some."

The waiter returned to their table and said, "Your drinks will be here momentarily. Are you ready to order, sir?"

"Yes, my friend would like the Rahmschnitzel and I'll take the Münchner Schnitzel."

"Both meals come with one side, sir. Which ones would you like?"

Kurt looked at Monika and she replied, "I'll have the spicy Brussels sprouts and carrots."

"I'll have the creamed spinach," Kurt told the waiter. We'll also like to have a bottle of the Robert König spätburgunder, with our dinner."

"Yes, sir, I'll go to the kitchen and place the order for your food right away," the waiter responded, as he left their table and went to the kitchen. Soon he returned with their cocktails and placed the drinks in front of them, saying, "I'll serve your food as soon as it's ready, together with the wine.

They sat and sipped their cocktails, as they talked about their jobs and families.

"Have you been busy at work?" Monika asked.

"Yes, we have a new project we're working on. It's kind of complicated and I've had to put in some long hours, as we have a deadline coming up soon," Kurt answered. "We've had some problems getting enough day labourers. A lot of them that do apply don't have the right documentation. Since you work in the GDR Employment Agency, do you have the same problems in East Berlin?"

"At the moment, we have a major problem getting enough workers for the government warehouses. Nobody seems to know when the shipments will be coming in. Then, at the last moment, they ask us to find men to help unload the material. Normally, we do an extensive background check on any workers. However, since the need for workers is urgent, we only ask them to show us their GDR ID card. We don't have time to forward the information to Stasi and other organizations, so they can fully investigate every applicant."

"Well that sound almost the same as our problem," Kurt replied.

Just as they finished their cocktails, the waiter appeared with their meals and placed the plates on the table, in front of them. The server opened the wine and allowed Kurt to sniff the cork. He then poured a small amount into his glass, whereupon Kurt tasted it and nodded his approval. The waiter proceeded to pour both of them a full glass. After he placed the bottle on their table, he left to wait on other customers.

The food looked delicious and tasted even better. The recommendations Kurt had been given about this club were right on.

Kurt picked up his glass and toasted Monika by saying, "Here's to a beautiful Fräulein and a new friend."

She smiled and clinked her glass against his. *"I'm beginning to really like this guy,"* she thought. Then remembering her benefactor, she thought anew, *"I'd better be careful. I could lose everything, including my family."*

She was suddenly brought back to reality, when Kurt said, "How do you like the red wine, Monika?"

"Its smells great and it tastes even better. You made a good choice, Kurt."

After they had finished eating, the band came on stage and started to warm up. Kurt and Monika continued to sip their wine and talk.

"Have you always lived in Berlin?" Monika asked.

"Well not entirely. I was born in Magdeburg, three years before the war started. Later, after my mother received a promotion at work, we moved to Spandau, so she could be closer to her job."

"How about your father, what does he do?"

"Unfortunately, my father was conscripted into the Wehrmacht in 1939 and first fought in the West, during the blitzkrieg of Belgium and France. He was wounded and, after he recovered from his wounds, he was sent to the Russian front in early 1942. We never saw him again, as he died in the siege of Stalingrad."

"How sad, I'm sorry for you and your family. Do you remember him at all?"

"Not really, I was only five years old the last time he was at home."

"Do you have any brothers or sisters?" Monika asked.

"I had one sister who was a few years older than me. When the Russians entered the Magdeburg area in 1945, a group of soldiers found my mother and sister hiding in the basement of our home. They raped both of them and carried off my sister. We never saw her again."

"It must have been terrible for them and for you to be nearby."

"It was. My mother, who is a strong woman, finally recovered from her ordeal and we moved to Spandau. I ended up going to the Free University in Berlin and graduated in Civil Engineering."

"Is your mother still living?"

"Yes, she still works and has a fairly comfortable life. However, I don't think she's ever totally recovered from the loss of her daughter and husband."

"What about you, Monika? Last time we met you mentioned that your family lives in Leipzig."

"My family lived in Naumberg, which is about fifty kilometers from downtown Leipzig, and I was born there four years before the war started. Besides my parents, I have two brothers and one sister."

"Are they all still alive?"

"Oh yes. They all live in the Leipzig area. My father is a doctor, who had a practice in Naumberg. Just before the war started, he opened up another practice in the southwest suburbs of Leipzig, but he attended his existing patients in Naumberg, as much as he could. Luckily, he wasn't drafted into the Wehrmacht, due to a minor medical condition and the fact that he was needed as a doctor in Leipzig."

"I understand the bombing of Leipzig was very destructive. How did all of you manage to escape being killed or injured?"

"Most of the bombing went after the factories and military installations. Since we lived in southwest Leipzig, we escaped the worst of it. However, we did live in the basement of our house a considerable amount of the time, after the windows upstairs were blown out. When the Soviet forces entered the city, my father welcomed them with somewhat open arms. He had always been anti-Nazi and harbored some feelings toward communism. This fact helped save our entire family from any Russian atrocities, carried out against the German civilians. Later on, my father was appointed to a high position in the local communist government. My brothers, who attended Leipzig University and graduated as engineers, both have good jobs in the area."

"I can see why you don't want to go to the West. How did you end up in Berlin?"

Just then the band started to play *Moonlight Serenade* and Monika replied, "I'll tell you that story another time. How about a dance? I like this music."

"Sure."

They stood up and walked onto the dance floor. Monika was an excellent dancer and as they danced away, onlookers would have thought they had danced together many times before.

The band played for the next two hours, mixing fast and slow music, and took requests now and again.

After a couple of hours, Monika whispered to Kurt, "I need to go back to the East now, before it's too late. Most East Berliners will be crossing back before midnight, and I don't want to draw attention to myself."

"Sure," Kurt replied. "I'll just pay the bill and we'll go."

He called the waiter over and paid him.

They walked outside the Club to look for a taxi. As they strolled down the street, Kurt turned to Monika and said "I have to go to Munich for a few days, and then I will be tied up with a major building project in West Berlin, so I won't be able to see you for two to three weeks."

"I'm going to be busy also and I have to be careful not to be seen going to the West too often, if you know what I mean."

"How about if we get together around the middle of July?" he responded. There's a great cinema called the *Zoo Palast* in Charlottenburg, and they always show the latest and best films. We could have dinner before, if you'd like."

"Sounds great, I'll wait for your call. As before, call me from a public phone and I'll call you right back."

"I'll do that and we can meet just west of PotsdamerPlatz, on Alte Potsdamerstrasse. This is close to the *white line* and you can get there, using side streets and not having to go through the Gate."

A taxi was travelling slowly down the road looking for a fare and Kurt flagged it down. He helped Monika into the rear of the cab and told the driver to proceed toward the Gate.

"Why don't you direct the driver exactly where to go and to drop you off?" Kurt suggested to Monika.

"That's a good idea. I don't want to be seen getting out right by the Gate and it will allow me to use some back streets to get home."

Monika gave instructions to the cab driver and, fairly soon, he stopped close to the *white line*, but hidden from the border, by a partially constructed building.

She turned to Kurt, gave him a short kiss on his cheek and said, "Thanks for a great evening. I really enjoyed it; especially the dancing. I'll wait for your call."

She then got out of the taxi and, with a wave to him, headed down a narrow street toward the border.

Kurt told the driver to take him close to an area near the Olympic Stadium.

As he walked back to the London Block, Ian reminisced about the evening and what a great time he had with Monika. His only regret was that it was necessary to tell her the lie about his family and what happened to them. However, it was crucial to keep up his German persona.

9

East Germany Day Labourer

After getting off duty on Thursday, the 15th of June, Lieutenant Black went to the Officers' Mess in the London Block, to watch the six o'clock news on ARD's *Das Erste* television station in West Berlin. The Mess only had a black-and-white, fifteen inch television that showed the one German station. Now and again, the *Central Europe* channel, run by the American Air Force Television from Ramstein Air Base, was available at certain hours. Most officers did not watch *Das Erste,* since many of them were not fluent in German.

As Ian entered the room, he saw John playing pool with an infantry officer. After turning on the television, Ian sat down to watch the German news broadcast. There was a replay of an International Press conference that took place earlier in the day, at the House of Ministries in East Berlin. The Berlin station broadcast the conference in German only, and there was no English dubbing available. This was not a problem for Ian, since he was fluent in German. Additionally, RIAS (Rundfunk im americkanischen Sektor) broadcast Ulbricht's remarks on the radio to West Germany.

Ulbricht gave a speech to the press about the need for normalization of the borders in Europe, and then opened it up for a few questions. Toward the end of the meeting, Annamarie Doherr, a reporter from the "Frankfurter Rundschau" newspaper, asked an additional question of Walter Ulbricht, "Mr. Chairman, do you mean by stating the formation of a Free City that a border will be built at the Brandenburg Gate? Are you determined to take into account all the possible consequences?"

Walter Ulbricht replied, "I understand your question that some people in West Germany believing that we want to mobilize construction workers in the DDR capital, to erect a wall. I have never considered having such an idea. The construction workers of our capital deal mainly with housing, and their labor is fully employed. No one has any intention of building a wall. As I have said before, we are for contractual arrangements and relations between West Berlin and the Government of the German Democratic Republic. There is an easy and most natural way to decide on these issues."

Walter Ulbricht went on further to talk about the need to normalize relations between East and West. In his opinion, this meant that East Germany would be recognized, by the West, as the lawful government and that West Berlin would be integrated into East Germany. All foreign troops would be removed. This was the same issue that Khrushchev brought up at the summit meeting with Kennedy, two weeks before.

Ian heard all this and thought, "*It's strange that he even mentioned building a wall. It has never been brought up before. Is there something sinister behind Ulbricht's statement?*"

John finished up playing pool with the officer, after he had beaten him handily.

Ian called over to him, "John, if you have time, may I talk with you for a moment?"

John nodded, walked over to where Ian was sitting and sat down beside him.

"What can I do for you, Ian? Are you ready to play pool? You promised me a rematch, when you beat me in Cyprus, three years ago."

"I want to discuss with you the statement made by Ulbricht earlier today. I was just watching it on German television. Have you heard or seen a transcript of what he said?"

"No, I haven't. What did he say?"

"Well, he said a lot of things about normalizing the situation in Berlin. In other words, he wants the West to give up West Berlin and allow it to be integrated into East Germany. It's the same old issue that's been around since the end of the war. What's new, however, is that he said, and I quote, *No one has any intention of building a wall.* Why would he say that, if it hasn't been considered? Just the mention of a wall means they are considering one. With the flood of refugees increasing every day, if I was in charge of East Germany, I would consider closing the border. The only way to permanently close the border, between East and West Berlin, is to build a wall. What do you think?"

"It sounds like double talk to me. We need to find out if they're amassing material to build a wall," John replied. "It would take a lot of blocks, cement and labour, among other things, to build a twenty-seven mile wall, along the *white line* border. It would have to be at least ten feet high and topped with barbed wire, to make it difficult to climb over."

"We need to find out if they have or are storing material, to build some kind of wall. Back in April, if you recall, I met a man at a café in Haldensleben, who had blooded his hands unloading barbed wire, at a warehouse. He said there was a lot of barbed wire at the building," Ian responded. "In order to quickly seal off the East from the West, they would probably string barbed wire and then build a solid fence, interlaced with buildings already astride the border."

"We need to talk about this tomorrow," John answered. "Why don't you come up to the fourth floor tomorrow at

1000 hours, for a meeting. I'll have Percival and Chetwyn join us. Maybe they'll have some suggestions as to how we can find out, what is really going to happen. This Berlin issue is heating up, and I've an uncomfortable feeling about all of this."

"I'll see you tomorrow at ten o'clock. By the way, I'm ready for that pool rematch any time," Ian said with a smile, as he rose from the sofa and went to his room.

****

The next morning, Ian went up to the MI6 office and entered, after being cleared by the MP's guarding the door. He went to John's office and, after knocking, entered to find him studying some paperwork.

John looked up and with a smile said, "Ah, just on time. Let's go down to the conference room. Percival and Chetwyn will be there momentarily."

They walked down the hallway and entered the room. Before they could close the door, Percival and Chetwyn came in and shaking Ian's hand said, "Glad to see you again."

They all sat down around the table, and John started off the discussion.

"As we deliberated at our last get together, right after the recent summit meeting, it appears that the GDR is planning some action to stem the stream of refugees, into the West. Obviously, they can't allow it to continue going on or East Germany will be depopulated.

Yesterday, Walter Ulbricht mentioned, for the first time, the word "Wall" at an International Press Conference. That he used the word "Wall" at all, implied they may be actually considering one. Regardless, Ulbricht denied they are thinking about one."

"We've heard rumors for a few weeks that the East is stocking up on building material," Percival responded. "Yes, some could be used for new building construction to replace war damaged facilities. However, some of it would not be useful for that application. We need more intelligence, if we can get it. I'll see if our agents can find out the quantity and type of material actually being stored in the East's warehouses."

Chetwyn joined in, "The number of refugees coming to the West is increasing every day. I agree the East has to do something about it, or it will collapse economically. In addition, I have received some intelligence from friendly sources that, in the next month or so, President Kennedy will announce a ramp up in the U.S. armed forces. He is going to ask Congress for more money, delay deactivation of the B-47 bomber and call up reservists. All indications are that the U.S. will not allow West Berlin to be taken over by the Soviets or the East Germans."

"This is could be very serious, if the situation continues. If the East does build a fence or a wall, what will be the response from the United States, Britain and France? From the summit, it appeared that the U.S. acquiesced, as long as they could remain in West Berlin," Ian responded. "If the East takes any action, it would probably be on a weekend and in the summer; some time in August maybe, when a lot of Europeans are on vacation. I'll try and find out from my East Berlin friend if she has access to any more details. If so, they would come from her benefactor and pillow talk. When I leave this meeting, I'm going to attempt to visit my CO and get permission to go into the East. The purpose will be to find out what is being stored at the warehouses, and if anyone there knows when the material will be used."

"Is there anything else, anyone wants to add?" John asked.

"Yes," Ian said. "Percival, if I get a one day job at a warehouse in East Berlin, would you be in a position to provide me with a vibrating pager; like the one you loaned me in Cyprus? In addition, I would need one of your agents, with a pager transmitter to keep a look out for me, in case a truck load of soldiers or police pull up outside the warehouse. This would give me time to possibly get out of there, without getting caught. I know it's risky but, with my East German ID card that John thankfully got for me, I should be able to pull it off."

"I believe that I'll be able to provide both," Percival replied. "Just let me know when you need them, and I'll arrange for an agent, together with a set of pagers."

"Okay, that's all for today. Keep us informed Ian, as to any action you're going to take," John said, as he ended the meeting.

Ian left the MI6 complex and went downstairs to see if he could have a meeting with Colonel Thurman.

He entered the outer office and asked the colonel's secretary, in German, "Helga, is he available? I don't have an appointment, but it's important."

"It's great to see you again, lieutenant. Let me check," she replied, as she picked up her phone and buzzed his office.

"Yes, he'll see you now. You may go right in."

Ian knocked on the door and, after the colonel answered "Come In", he entered, saluted and approached his desk.

"Take a seat," he said. "What can I do for you, Mr. Black?"

"Well sir, I have two matters to discuss with you. First, I've just come from a meeting with John, Percival and Chetwyn, at which we talked about recent events, in East Berlin. In our discussion, I proposed that I visit a few bars in the East to determine which warehouses will need day labourers, to unload and stock building materials. According to my East German friend, whom I have mentioned previously, there is no major check on applicants. All one has to do is show their East German ID card for a day job. She said the requests for workers come at the last moment, and there is no time to put applicants through a major identity check. Anyway, once I've determined which warehouse requires workers, I'll apply for one of the jobs, at the local employment agency. I realize it is risky but the reward for getting information on the inside is immeasurable."

Colonel Thurman didn't answer for a few seconds, then looking sternly at Ian, he said, "What you are asking, Mr. Black, is strictly against any Army regulations. You could not only end up in an East German jail, but it would also end your Army career. I've read your file and you always seem to be pushing the envelope. If you get caught, there's no way I, the British Army or Government could help you. You understand what I'm saying?"

"Yes sir, I'll certainly take your comments into consideration, before acting."

"What is the other matter you wish to discuss?"

"Earlier, you said that I could find myself a flat in the city, after the 1st of July. Does this offer still stand?"

"Yes, you may, if you are not ensconced in a small East German cell. As far as the first subject is concerned, we've never discussed it. You understand my point," Colonel Thurman said. Smiling he continued, "Good luck with your flat hunting and the day job. I hope to see you again soon, as I would hate to lose a good officer."

Ian rose, saluted and then said, as he turned to leave, "Thank you for your trust in me, sir. I won't let you down."

Ian left the inner office and gave a wave to Helga, as he walked out and went back to his room. There he sat down and considered what the colonel had told him.

****

Next Tuesday evening, Ian dressed in civvies and walked into East Berlin, staying to the side streets. He didn't encounter any Bereitschaftspolizei and made it to the first pub without having to show any ID. He entered the bar, sat down at the counter and ordered a beer. On the stool, next to him, was a German who appeared to be in his forties and was employed by a state building contractor. Unfortunately, he helped build apartment complexes, to house other government workers. He knew nothing about the warehouse, where the state stored the actual building materials.

For the next two hours, Ian went "pub crawling" hoping to find a worker in one of them that had knowledge about the availability of day jobs. He had almost given up for the evening, but thought he would try one last time. He entered a small pub called *Marx* on Dorotheenstrasse, obviously named after Karl Marx. He sat down at the bar, next to an unshaven, disheveled, dirty man who appeared to be in his early thirties, ordered a beer and started to talk to him.

"Hello, my name's Kurt. You look like you've had a rough day at work."

"You're right about that. I worked all day unloading supplies at a warehouse, and all for a pittance. They don't pay very well. My friends call me Otto, but my real name's Rudolf. Why they call me Otto I'm not sure, because I'm certainly not wealthy." Then, looking around for any possible plain clothed Stasi man, he whispered, "If I had a friend in the West, I would go there to work. The pay is a lot better. Where do you work, Kurt?"

"I used to work in construction, but lost my job recently, due to an economic slowdown. Now, I'm looking for any work, to tide me over, until I can find a new permanent position."

"I know of a day job coming up on Thursday, which you might be interested in. It'll be hard work, unloading supplies at a warehouse on Jägerstrasse."

"I'll certainly consider it. If I decide to do it, where do I go to sign up and when?" Kurt asked.

"I'll tell you what. Meet me at the DDR State Employment Agency near the junction of Franz Strasse and Friedrichstrasse on Thursday, at 0800 sharp. We can go in together, and I'll introduce you to Bertha. She's an older, friendly woman, who is responsible for obtaining workers for this warehouse. All you have to do is show her your ID card, and she will give you a paper to take to the warehouse. The manager there will put you to work and pay you at the end of the day. That's all there is to it. Again, it's hard work, so be prepared to bring some work gloves with you and wear old clothes."

"Thanks for the tip. I'll probably see you there. I've got to go now and get home. Nice meeting you, Rudolf," Ian replied.

He paid for his beer and walked out of the bar. As he did he spotted a man sitting in a corner. He was dressed in a dark suit and didn't appear to have a drink. Ian thought, *"Maybe he's Stasi. I better be careful and make sure he doesn't follow me."* As he walked toward the border, he kept looking over his shoulder and stopped a couple of times, to look in a window. He thought he saw someone dart into a doorway, whenever he stopped but maybe it was his imagination. Each time he did stop, he had the feeling that someone was back there. Soon, however, he crossed the *white line* and breathed a sigh of relief. He found a taxi and returned to the Olympic Stadium area.

The next morning he placed a phone call to MI6, and Percival answered immediately.

"This is Ian. Yesterday evening, I did some pub crawling in the East and met this chap who was extremely helpful. I'm not sure if he was Stasi. However, when I returned to the West, I thought I was being followed. I took several precautions and finally shook him off my tail, if he was following me. Anyway, I have found a way to obtain a day job tomorrow, unloading material at a state warehouse located on Jägerstrasse. I have to be at the employment agency on Franz Strasse, near Friedrichstrasse, at eight o'clock sharp. Can you provide me with the vibrating pager system and an agent to watch out for me?"

"Come upstairs this afternoon around 1500 hours and hopefully I'll have the pager ready for you. As far as an agent being available, I can't make a promise this morning, but I'll see what can be arranged."

They both hung up and Ian went to find some clothes he could wear for tomorrow's job. He found in the bottom of his kit bag an old pair of pants and a grungy shirt, which hadn't been washed yet. He laid them out to wear the next day.

Around three o'clock, he went up to the fourth floor and entered the MI6 facility, after being checked in by the MP's. He walked down the aisle, past several doors, until he found Percival's office. He knocked and entered, after hearing him shout: "enter."

"Ah, Ian, you're in luck. I have the receiver of the paging system here. I know you're aware how it basically works, since you used one in Cyprus. This is an improved model from that one, but operates in basically the same way. This model is difficult for any foreign agency to pick up its signal. In addition, I have been able to make arrangements for an agent to watch out for you. You will never see him, but he will start tailing you outside the state employment agency. If he spots any danger, he will turn on his pager transmitter, and you will feel the vibration. Other than that, my friend, you'll be on your own. Good Luck."

"Percival, I knew I could count on you. This venture is worth the risk, since we'll hopefully find out what is stored in at least one GDR state warehouse. On Friday morning, I'll let you know what I've found out. Thanks again for your help."

****

The next morning, Ian rose early and went to the Officers' Mess, for an early breakfast. He then returned to his room and dressed in his old clothes. He placed a soft cloth hat on his head and made sure he had the DDR ID card in his pocket. He left anything that identified him as being a member of the British Army, behind in his room. He found a taxi that took him close toward East Berlin, and then he walked down some side streets to the border. He crossed the *white line* and, without any challenges, went to the state employment agency, Rudolf had told him about.

He was waiting outside and Kurt walked up to him, "Morning Rudolf, I managed to make it on time."

He replied, "Kurt, I didn't recognize you in those old clothes and the hat. Those are just what you need to do the job today. Let's go in and find Bertha."

Kurt didn't notice him but, across the street, was an MI6 agent that Percival had promised would be there.

They both entered the office and Rudolf led Ian up to the employment desk.

"Bertha, we're both here for that day job at the warehouse on Jägerstrasse, if it's still available. This is my friend Kurt, who needs to make some money."

"Yes, the jobs are still available. I thought you were going to bring me five people. The request from the head office was for five labourers." Turning to Kurt, she said, "Welcome Kurt, we need all the help we can get, right now. What's your last name?"

"My name is Kurt Engels and here is my ID card," he responded, as he showed her his identity.

She didn't take the document out of his hand, but just jotted down his name and ID number on a roster, she had on her desk.

Turning back to Rudolf, she said, "If you find any more chaps that want a day job, please send them my way. A boss from the headquarters is here talking to the head of this office, about the lack of workers."

As she said that, Kurt looked at a line of offices, not too far away, and became concerned, when he saw Monika talking to a man, in one of them.

Kurt quickly turned sideways so she couldn't see his face. He hadn't counted on this.

He asked Bertha, "Is that the boss from the headquarters in that office over there?"

"Yes. Her name is Ingrid Meyer and she is chewing out our manager about the lack of workers."

Kurt had finally found out Monika's real name.

"You had better get going to the warehouse. Here are your papers to give to the manager. At the end of the day he'll pay you. We'll need more workers next Tuesday, please come back and I'll fix you up," Bertha said, with a smile, as she handed them the papers.

They walked out of the office and headed for the warehouse, which was about three blocks away. Kurt was thankful that Monika had not seen him, since it would have ruined everything. In addition, it could have been dangerous, since he had no idea what she would have done.

They walked the few blocks to the warehouse and entered the office, in the front. There they found the manager, and they presented the papers Bertha had given them. He looked at the paperwork and then told them to report to the unloading supervisor, in the dock area.

Rudolf and Kurt walked out to the loading platform and found the foreman with two other workers. He was a tall, heavily built man who looked like he would take no guff from anyone. The type of man you wouldn't want to meet in a dark alley.

"There'll be two lorries arriving momentarily and I need you to unload them, as soon as possible. Two more vehicles will arrive in three hours, and they will need emptying also. After those we expect more all day and we may need you until about 2030. You will get well paid."

"That sounds great. I could do with the money. Where do you want us to stack the material?" Rudolf asked.

"Follow me and I'll show you," replied the supervisor.

He took them into the main part of the warehouse, where there was already some building material stacked in huge heaps.

"We expect loads of concrete, cement, building blocks and barbed wire to arrive today. As you can see, we already have some of each. When the new supplies come in, just stack them with the others already here. Do you understand?"

Kurt, Rudolf and the other two men all nodded and said, "Yes."

In thirty minutes, the first two lorries arrived and the four men started to unload them. This procedure continued all day and Kurt found it was back breaking work. He had never worked so hard in his life. In all, they unloaded eight truckloads of building material and stacked it in the warehouse. Kurt heard from one of the other men that this had been going on for eight weeks, at the other government warehouses. He had managed to obtain work at five of them, over the past month.

At around eight-fifteen, as they were in the middle of unloading the last lorry, Kurt felt the page vibrator go off in his pocket. *"Oh my gosh!"* he thought. *"I've got to get out of here."* In less than a minute, he saw two men in black suits enter the manager's office. Then the supervisor, who was also in the office at the time, came out and went over to the closest labourer. Ian couldn't hear what was said, but he saw the man pull his ID card out of his pocket and give it to the supervisor.

"What's going on?" Ian asked Rudolf.

"I'm not sure, but it may be Stasi is checking up on us, to insure we authorized DDR workers."

Then the supervisor went to the next laborer and took his ID. Fortunately for Ian, both Rudolf and he happened to be in the back of the warehouse.

Ian said to Rudolf, "I have to go to the toilet. Tell the supervisor that I'll be back in a minute, if he asks for me."

"I'll do that, but don't be long or you might get into trouble."

Ian walked quickly round a pile of building supplies and looked for a way out. He knew he was in deep trouble, if the Stasi guys got hold of his ID and thoroughly checked it out. Suddenly in the corner of the warehouse, he spotted a small door. He ran towards it and found it opened into a courtyard behind the warehouse. He quickly went out and closed the door.

The sun was just setting on Berlin, since the government hadn't instituted daylight savings time.

He ran over to a low five foot wall, climbed over it and found himself in an alley. He raced down the alley and, at the end, it turned into a small street. As he walked swiftly down this street, a man with a beard and moustache came out of a doorway, carrying a coat and a hat..

"Kurt, put this coat and hat on, and follow me."

"Who are you?" Ian asked.

"No questions. Just do as I say, pronto," the man responded.

At that moment, Ian realized it must be the agent Percival had promised would be there, to keep an eye on things. He quickly put on the coat and hat, as instructed, and followed the agent down the street. They saw headlights in the distance coming toward them, and the agent dragged Ian into a building that was in need of repair. It must have been a residence that had been partially bombed during the war and had not yet been totally repaired.

Luckily, the car sped by and they walked through the building and exited the ruins into another alley in the rear.

117

"I'm going to leave you now. I have done what I was instructed to do by Percival. Do you know how to get back to the West from here?"

"Yes, I have a good sense for direction and have been in East Berlin quite a few times."

"Good. I'll bid you goodbye and good luck. Be careful, as I don't want to hear you got caught by the Stasi."

The agent shook his hand and vanished down the alley, into the shadows. Kurt never found out his name, but that was probably for the best, in case he did get caught.

Ian went down the alley in the opposite direction that the agent had gone. As he went, he hugged any doorways available, just in case the Stasi came looking for him. By now, they had probably figured that he wasn't legit and that he was a spy from the West. They would certainly try to find him and increase the number of men watching the *white line*. Since it was twenty-seven miles long, he had a good chance of making it.

He slowly worked his way toward the border, avoiding the main streets and watching for anyone in uniform. He used the night sky as a compass. The lights from the West lit up the dark sky over Berlin; whereas in the East, the sky was not reflective of many street lights. As the sky got brighter and brighter, he knew he was approaching the border.

He came down a very narrow road and, at the end, he could see the border, about one hundred feet away. He stopped and looked both ways, for the presence of an East German Bereitschaftspolizei. He spotted one coming toward him, as the soldier marched down the road that paralleled the border. Kurt quickly jumped back into the shadow of a doorway and waited for him to pass. After he had gone by and was at least three hundred meters from him, Kurt decided it was safe to make a run for it.

On the other side, he saw a West German policeman just standing there, watching the border. Kurt appeared from the doorway and ran, as fast as he could, for the white line. He had won a medal at Harrow, for winning the hundred yard dash. As he crossed the line, he heard the East German shout, "stop". It was too late for the Bereitschaftspolizei to do anything, as Ian was already over the line.

The West Berlin policeman, who was a few feet from the border, walked over to him and asked, "Do you need any assistance, sir?"

In English, Ian replied breathing heavily, "No thanks. I just made it back without a hitch. Have a good evening."

Ian flagged down a taxi and had it take him close to the Olympic Stadium. He then hurriedly walked into the Stadium grounds and headed toward the London Block, where his room was. He had made it back and escaped a potential East German cell.

10

Cinema Evening

At the next staff meeting, Colonel Thurman walked in, looked around the room and counted heads.

"I see we're all here today. I was afraid we might be missing one. I'm glad you made it on time, Mr. Black," he said smiling, as he looked at him. "Let's get down to business."

"First, I'd like to introduce Captain Alexander Swiderski, who is joining our intelligence team, since he's fluent in Russian. As you can probably guess, he's of Polish extraction."

They all walked over to the newest member and shook his hand, saying, "Welcome."

After they had all sat down again, the colonel then made several other announcements and talked about the need for more intelligence on Soviet troop movements.

"Brigadier Croxford who, I believe you all met at a previous meeting, is breathing down my neck, wanting to know about any unusual movements of troops near the border, between East and West. He's received intelligence from other sources that the Berlin situation will be coming to a head, in the next three to four months."

Major Phillips, in charge of counter intelligence, responded, "Sir, my group picked up two individuals who recently had come over from the East and seemed suspicious. We turned them over to Major Peters for interrogation."

"We put them through the *ringer*, but it was determined that they were only minor former East German government officials, who'd fled to the West," Major Peters added. "They didn't know anything about troop movements or any other security issues."

"Very well, let's go round the table," Colonel Thurman responded.

"Colonel, if I may, I'll go first," John of MI6 responded. "We've received a report, from a reliable source, that Erich Honecker and Paul Verner are scheduled to visit Moscow, early next month, to discuss the brain drain from the East and the proposed German peace treaty. This treaty is a favorite idea of Khrushchev's, and he raised it at the recent summit. Another subject will be the possibility of economic sanctions being imposed, on all East European countries, if the East Germans somehow stem the flow of refugees crossing the *white line* in Berlin. In addition, we've also heard that there's going to be a major Warsaw Pact meeting in Moscow, on the third of August, and it's expected to last three days. All this seems to suggest that the East Germans are building up to some kind of action, and it'll probably take place in August. We don't know, at this point, what it will be? It would only be a pure guess at this juncture."

Each of the other attendees gave their report and Ian was the last one to speak.

"A few days ago, I did some pub crawling in East Berlin and, at one pub named *Marx*, I found a chap, who said his name was Rudolf. He mentioned he had been working at some warehouses, where they were unloading and storing building material. Also, he told me that he had a contact at one of the employment bureaus, named Bertha, and she had told him there would be another job available in two days. Rudolf suggested that I meet him at the employment office,

121

at the junction of Friedrichstrasse and Franz. Strasse., and we could both go in and talk to Bertha.

While I'll was at this office, I notice a woman talking to the manager, and there seemed to be a heated argument. Bertha told me it was the boss from the main office. Anyway, I looked over at this woman and it dawned on me that it was Monika, the Fräulein I have had a date with a couple of times. Bertha told us her name was Ingrid Meyer."

"Let me write her name down" John said. "I'll check into this woman and see if we can find out who her important political benefactor is? Please continue Ian."

"Luckily, I had discussed the potential of a job at a warehouse with Percival and he loaned me a special pager, which would warn me if there was trouble approaching. He also arranged for an agent outside the warehouse to trigger this pager. The long and the short of it is, I did obtain some work for one day at this warehouse and had to get out of there in a hurry, after two Stasi chaps came in to check identifications. They're storing barbed wire, concrete, building blocks and other miscellaneous material, which would not be too useful for erecting office buildings. However, it could be useful for sealing off the Berlin border, if they decide to do so."

"Thank you for that report and I'm glad you made it out okay," the colonel said. "John, if you can find out who this Ingrid Meyer really is, it might be useful. Ian, as I've said before, you must be very careful on how you communicate and act with this woman. She could be dangerous, if you know what I mean."

"I'm planning another date with her in a week or so, but it'll be in the West. There shouldn't be any danger for me, but there might be for her."

"Just be careful and give us a report on any critical information you may obtain from her," the colonel continued.

"Yes, sir," Ian replied.

"That'll be all for today, unless somebody has something else to add to this discussion. Again, we're glad to welcome our Russian expert; Captain Alexander Swiderski."

As they filed out of the conference room, Ian went up to John and gave him the pager, saying "Will you please return this to Percival and thank him for me. It saved me from going to an East German prison."

"Certainly Ian, personally I'm glad we don't have to find a way to get you out of a Stasi dungeon. It's not easy, you know."

Ian then went and found the colonel on his way back to his office.

"Sir, as we agreed, I've found a small flat in the British sector and I moved in there a few days ago. I've kept my office in the London Block and will keep most of my uniforms there. I didn't think it's wise to be seen entering and leaving this flat, in uniform."

"That's good thinking Ian. Thanks for letting me know. You carried out some good intelligence work the other day, even though it was extremely risky."

****

On Tuesday, the 10th of July, Kurt walked out of his office at the Olympic Stadium complex, went to a public phone booth and dialed Monika's number.

"Hello" she answered.

"Are you ready to go to a cinema?" Kurt asked.

"Maybe, what's the number?"

He gave her the number of the public phone and, in a few minutes, she called him back.

Kurt answered, "Hello, is this the sultry Fräulein that I danced with at the Teufel Club?"

"Yes, it is," she said with a smile. "But don't tell anyone I'm sultry. They may get the wrong idea. In fact, please don't tell anyone about me."

"Are you still free this coming Saturday evening to get something to eat and then go to see a film?"

"Yes, I am. What are we going to see?"

"If you remember, I mentioned going to the *Zoo Palast* in Charlottenburg. This weekend, the main attraction is "Elmer Gentry" starring Burt Lancaster. In addition, they'll probably be showing a newsreel and a short cartoon like "RoadRunner". All together, the programme should last just under three hours, and it's scheduled to start at seven p.m."

"I've heard of that film. It's supposed to be very good. Since the dialog is in English, will it have German subtitles?"

"Yes, I understand it will. Can we meet at six o'clock, so we can get a bite to eat? Nothing fancy, but I've been told about a small café close to the cinema. Let's meet at the location we talked about, the last time we met; just west of PotsdamerPlatz on Alte Potsdamerstrasse."

"I'll be there at six o'clock, as you suggest. See you then. Bye."

****

On the next Saturday, since it was fairly warm on that July day in Berlin, Kurt, who was dressed only in a light blue shirt and a pair of dark brown slacks, left his flat in Spandau and hailed a passing taxi. He wore a brown, peaked beret hat on his head that matched his pants and carried a light tan jacket, in case it became chilly later on in the evening.

"Take me to the corner of Alte Potsdamerstrasse and the PotsdamerPlatz," Kurt told the driver.

The taxi arrived at around just before six o'clock and, since there were plenty of cabs around, he didn't ask the driver to wait. He got out, walked to a lamp post at the end of the street and waited for Monika.

Soon, he spotted her in the distance, as she neared the border. When she almost reached the *white line* marking it, a Bereitschaftspolizei came out of a dim doorway and approached her.

"Let me see your papers," he commanded.

She handed them to him and, after he saw the special stamped pass that her benefactor had arranged for her, he saluted and said, "I'm sorry ma'am. You may proceed."

She crossed over the border into West Berlin and headed for Alte Potsdamerstrasse. As she neared the arranged meeting point, where Kurt was standing, he noticed that she was wearing a white blouse together with a white polka dot, navy blue skirt and a red belt. Her blue shoes matched the skirt, and she had a red ribbon in her hair.

"Monika, you look stunning. I'm glad you could make it. Did you have any problem coming over the border?"

"Thank you. Yes, I was stopped but, after the policeman looked at my pass, he waved me through."

"Let's flag down a taxi and go to this café, I've heard about, that's close to the cinema. The food is supposed to be good and the service is quick. The show starts at seven o'clock and the main feature starts at around seven-thirty."

A cab came by and screeched to a halt, when the driver saw Kurt hailing him. They climbed into the rear and Ian told the driver to take them to the *Guten Appetit Café* that was near the *Zoo Palast* cinema.

They entered the café, seated themselves and found a couple of menus on the table. After they had studied them for a few minutes, a waitress came over to their table and took their orders.

While they waited for their food, they chatted about mundane things; the movie Elmer Gantry and the stars in it, the weather, sports, work, etc. Then Monika mentioned something that caused Kurt some concern.

"You know Kurt, a funny thing happened the other day. I was in an office talking to a manager, when I looked out of his window and in the outer office I thought I saw someone who looked just like you. Do you happen to have a twin brother?"

"No, I don't have a twin that I know of and I certainly wasn't there, so it must have been someone who looked very similar." Kurt hated to lie to her, but obviously he couldn't admit it was him. He thought *"I've got to be more careful in future, or I might blow my cover."*

"Yes, you're probably correct; it must have been a look alike. I've been under considerable stress recently, because of the demands at work. In addition, my friend had to go on an important trip to Moscow."

Kurt's ears picked up on this and he thought, *"I wonder if her friend is Erich Honecker or Paul Verner."*

"I'm sorry to hear you are under pressure at work," Ian replied. "I know how that is, since on some days, I have to work for up to twelve hours, in order to accomplish the assigned tasks."

At that moment, the waitress arrived with their food, which they quickly ate and then exited the café, after Kurt paid the bill. They walked down the street to the cinema and luckily found the queue wasn't too long. Kurt bought the tickets for the balcony area and they entered just in time; the lights dimmed and the cartoon started, followed by the Universal Newsreel.

During the main film, Elmer Gantry, there were a couple of brief funny parts that the German subtitles did not show what the actors were saying. However, Kurt laughed at them, since he heard the actors talking in English. When he laughed, Monika looked over at him and wondered why he was laughing. She thought, *"I wonder if he knows some English. He has never mentioned it before."*

When the show ended, they walked out of the cinema and Kurt hailed a cab to take them back to the end of Alte Potsdamerstrasse. As the cabbie drove them to their destination, they discussed the film and how good Burt Lancaster and Jean Simmons were.

Then Kurt asked Monika, "Would you like to meet at the Leuthen Club on the evening of the 12th of August? We haven't been there for a few months."

"What day of the week is the 12th?"

"It's a Saturday. Is that a problem?"

"No, I don't think so. My friend has been so tied up lately that I don't get to see him much."

"Well, here's the phone number for my flat. You can ring me if something comes up. If not, I'll see you then." Kurt handed her a card with his number on it.

Then she caught him by surprise with a question. "By the way Kurt, do you know some English? I saw you laughing a couple of times during the film, but there was nothing funny written with the subtitles."

"When I went to University I took a couple of classes in English. So yes, I do understand a little of the language," Ian responded. Then he thought *I've got to be very careful with her. She's smart as a whip.*

The taxi pulled over to the kerb, near the end of Alte Potsdamerstrasse, and the driver said, "Here we are, sir."

After he had paid the driver, Kurt and Monika got out of the cab.

He walked with her a few meters.

She then turned and gave him a kiss on the cheek saying, "Thank you for a great evening. I really enjoyed it."

Kurt took and held her in his arms, and gave her a kiss on her lips saying, "I've wanted to kiss you for a long time."

She returned his kiss and responded, "I have to go now. It's getting late. I'll see you on the 12th of August at the Leuthen Club. My friend and benefactor has told me he will be attending a major meeting scheduled for that afternoon and evening, so I'll be free for sure. He didn't tell me what it was about, of course, but it sounded very important. He did say it was called by his boss who told all the people, directly under him, to attend."

She walked across the PotsdamerPlatz, over the white line and vanished into East Berlin. As she did so, she thought *"I like Kurt, but there is something about him that doesn't quite ring true. If he knows that I won't move to the West and I have a male friend in high places, why does he frequently want to see me? Somehow it doesn't seem to add up. Well, as planned, I guess I'll see him at the Leuthen Club on the 12th."*

Ian took a cab back to his flat thinking about what she had said. He thought, *"If her benefactor has a meeting on that day, just ten days after a rumoured, Warsaw Pact meeting scheduled in Moscow, something major is surely going to happen in August or early September. I need to see if I can find out what it'll be."*

11

Intelligence Review

At the 24th of July staff meeting, Colonel Thurman glanced around the table with a frown on his face and, looking at all attendees said, "Gentlemen, Brigadier Croxford, whom you all met a few weeks ago at this gathering, has information from other sources that speculates some action is imminent in Berlin. Just as I mentioned at a previous staff meeting, he wants to know what we've discovered in our day-to-day intelligence work. He's getting impatient and wants to see some results from us, not from other agencies."

John responded, "Colonel, we've written several reports about what we believe is going on behind the closed doors, in East Berlin and Moscow. They have been forwarded up our chain of command. What MI6 high command does with them we don't know, since we've received no feedback? We'd hope that they reach the PM's desk, but we never hear anything. We did obtain some intelligence the other day which suggests Paul Verner and Erich Honecker came back from their recent visit to Moscow, with a note expressing the Soviet concerns about closing the Berlin border. In addition, we know Walter Ulbricht has a one-on-one scheduled with Nikita Khrushchev, before the start of the Warsaw Pact meeting, at the beginning of August."

"John, that's all good information, but the question my boss wants answered, is: *Are they going to seal off the border between East and West Berlin, when and how will they accomplish it?*"

Major Phillips of counter intelligence commented, "We are interrogating every suspect we pick up in the British sector, to the fullest extent we are permitted, and we have found out that there is a belief among East German officials that the border will be sealed at some point. They had no information as to when or how. It seems to be a well kept secret among the highest levels of the GDR government. Paul Verner and Erich Honecker seem to be involved with some of the details."

Major Peters, of the interrogation group, followed up Major Phillips remarks saying, "As soon as Major Phillips turns over any suspects to us, we interrogate them with all kinds of methods to get as much information as possible from them. What Phillips has said is true. No one we've questioned seems to have any details about possible action in sealing the border. They all say the brain drain cannot continue indefinitely."

After the other attendees had made a few brief comments, the one remaining person around the table was Lieutenant Ian Black.

Ian spoke, looking directly at the colonel, "Sir, I'm writing a full intelligence report, and it'll be on your desk by the end of this week. This report will be the result of the intelligence work I've done, while on my BRIXMIS tour and subsequent visits to East Berlin, under cover. In addition, it will include what information I've gleaned from Ingrid Meyer, aka Monika. At the end of the report, I'll give my calculated opinion on if a border will be built, when and how. One point I'm not sure about, at this juncture, is the identity of Monika's influential friend in the GDR government?"

John spoke up, "I believe I can possibly provide an answer to that question. According to our information from agents in the East, it appears that Ingrid Meyer's friend could be Erich Honecker. We're not positive at this point, but anything Mr. Black can get out of Monika, on this score, could be useful in fully identifying him."

"Okay, Mr. Black. I look forward to receiving your report this Friday," said the colonel. "Please don't disseminate it to anyone, until I have reviewed it. After that, I'll let you know to whom you may send it. Is this clear?"

"Yes, colonel," Ian responded.

"Good, that's all for today. Everybody, since we seem to be approaching some climax, we'll meet every Monday for the next month, without any exception."

"Yes, sir, they all responded," as they rose and left the meeting room.

Ian raced after John of MI6, as he started to go up to the fourth floor.

"Are you sure that Ingrid Meyer (aka Monika) is an acquaintance and friend of Erich Honecker?" Ian asked him. "How did you obtain that information?"

"We're fairly sure that it's correct. We inquired an unnamed agent in the East and that is what he told us. We know of no reason why he would give us misinformation," John responded. "Of course, no one is sure one hundred percent about anything in this city. Spies are everywhere and the KGB is spreading disinformation all the time."

"Well I guess, if she's a friend of his, she's probably also his mistress, although I've never detected any nuance about their relationship. However, I have to assume it's true, for safety's sake. I've arranged to meet her next time at the Teufel Club on Saturday, the 12th of August. I'll see if I can obtain anything from her, without raising her suspicions of me."

"Just be careful, my friend," John replied.

Ian returned to his office in the same building and started work on his intelligence report, using an IBM model C electric typewriter he had checked out from stores.

SECRET

British Army Military Intelligence Corps
Berlin Brigade Headquarters
Olympic Stadium, Berlin
27 July 1961; 1700 hours GMT+1

Notice: This document is covered under the Official Secrets Act.
Intelligence Assessment No: IC/IB/19617X2

1. MISSION
To determine the response of the East Germans and Soviets to the refugee outflow to the West, from East European countries under Soviet control.

2. ISSUES FOR SOVIETS & EAST GERMANS
   a. Soviets: They do not desire to start WWIII, but they do want to drive the Western powers out of West Berlin and neutralize the entire city. They also desire to create a "firewall" against any attack upon Eastern Europe. An economic boycott by the West is also a concern for them.

   b. East Germans: They want to stop the brain drain from the GDR to the West. If they don't, the country will collapse economically. Also, they don't want to be a conduit for émigrés from other East European countries, using the Berlin open border.

3. INTELLIGENCE SOURCES
   a. 30 MAR 1961. KB met man in Haldensleben café (name not given) who had been unloading rolls of barbed wire at a DDR warehouse.

b. 29 APR 1961. KB met a girl at the Leuthen Club. Her name is Ingrid Meyer (aka Monika) and she has a friend high up in political circles of the DDR. She works in the DDR Employment Agency as a manager.

c. 10 JUN 1961. KB met Monika at the Teufel Club. She explained that they are having trouble getting enough workers to unload material at warehouses, across the entire DDR.

d. 20 JUN 1961. KB met man named Rudolf (aka Otto) at the Marx café in East Berlin. He had lost his construction job and was getting day jobs unloading building material at DDR warehouses. He gave KB tip on a day job coming up in two days.

e. 22 JUN 1961. KB goes to DDR employment office and gets day job unloading barbed wire and other construction material at a DDR warehouse on Jägerstrasse. There he sees stocks of barbed wire rolls, concrete pillars, mesh wire and other building material. Hearing workers talk, it appears warehouses across DDR are storing the same material. Looking at labels on the material, it appears it was purchased from various sources in the East and West; probably so as to not raise any suspicions.

f. 15 JUL 1961. KB meets Monika again and takes her to Zoo Palast cinema. At a café before the film, Monika informs KB that her influential friend was in Moscow recently. He is very busy and under a lot of stress, therefore he will not be able to see her for a few weeks.

4. SITUATION ANALYSIS

From various sources of intelligence, it appears the DDR has been buying up and storing rolls of barbed wire, concrete, blocks and other building material. An analysis of this material indicates that it is probably not for building apartments or offices, but rather for the construction of a wall. The DDR has purposely been buying this material from various companies throughout Europe so as not to highlight what is has been doing. By storing it in warehouses across the DDR, the leadership helped hide their true intentions.

5. TIMETABLE FOR POSSIBLE ACTION

a. 0100 hours on the 20th appears to be the prime time and date for the East Germans to seal the border. Other possible dates are the nights of the 13th or the 6th, with the time still being 0100 hours.

b. In order to close the border quickly, it appears the East Germans plan to string barbed wire along the twenty-eight mile border. In addition they will stage troops along the entire length, armed with unloaded PPsh-41. They will probably face into East Berlin in order to scare residents away from the border. Also, they will probably station truck mounted water cannons to disperse possibly angry crowds and rioters. They don't want a repeat of the 1953 East German riots caused by anti-communist workers.

c. If the West does nothing about the barbed wire fence within the first 48-72 hours, they will distribute ammunition to the troops and commence building a permanent fence, made of concrete and blocks.

6. CONCLUSION

a. East Germans will install a barbed wire fence, just inside the *white line,* the entire twenty-seven mile length of the East/West Berlin border. Thus, in no way, will they encroach into the Western Sectors of the city.

b. If the West does nothing about the barbed wire fence, the East Germans will replace it with a permanent block and concrete wall.

c. The barbed wire fence will be quickly built and fortified with troops. Since the East Germans stored enough material to accomplish this, they should be able to erect the initial fence within twelve hours.

d. The anticipated date, for the fence to be put in place, is the weekend of the 19th/20th of August 1961. Early Sunday morning will be the ideal time, since most Germans will be fast asleep, after a night on the town. Also, August is typically a holiday time in Europe, and many people, including politicians, will be away for the month. It could be built a weekend or two before this date, but it would take a considerable amount of organization to accomplish it.

INTELLIGENCE ESTIMATE by
Lieutenant Ian Black (aka Kurt Beck)
Intelligence Corps
British Army on the Rhine

SECRET

135

On Friday, the 28th of July, Ian went to Colonel Thurman's office to present his intelligence report. As he entered the outer office, guarded by Helga Jergens, he noticed an American captain seated along the wall, obviously waiting to see the colonel. Ian sat down by him and introduced himself.

"Good morning captain, I'm Lieutenant Black of the Intelligence Corps."

"Pleased to meet you lieutenant, my name's Patrick Silverman and I'm with the 513th Military Intelligence Group. I won't be long in there as I just have to talk with Colonel Thurman, for a couple of minutes. I assume you're waiting to see him also."

At that moment, Helga said, "You may go in now Captain Silverman."

He rose, smiled at Ian and said, "I won't be in there very long, lieutenant."

In a few minutes the captain came out, said goodbye to Helga and walked out of the office.

Helga said, "You can go in now lieutenant."

He rose from the chair, walked to the door and tapped gently.

"Come in." the colonel responded.

Ian entered, saluted him and stood in front of his desk.

"Reporting with my Intelligence Assessment as promised, sir."

"Sit down, Ian. We don't have to be always so formal, especially in private. Now let me see what you've been working on."

Ian handed him the original copy of the report. He had made four carbon copies, which he had placed in a secure filing cabinet.

The colonel scanned through it and said, "This looks very detailed. Give me today and the weekend to digest it, and I'll get back to you on Monday."

Ian left the colonel sitting at his desk, studying some papers and went into the outer office, where he wished Helga a great weekend.

****

On Monday, Ian received a call from Helga who told him the colonel wanted to see him immediately. He went straight away to the colonel's office and entered after knocking.

"Sit down Mr. Black," the colonel said, in a commanding voice.

Ian sat down in front of his desk and faced the colonel.

"I've studied your intelligence assessment and analysis document in detail, and I must say I'm very impressed with your work. I gather that you believe the East/West Berlin border will be created by the East Germans just after midnight on the 20th of August. Is that correct?"

"Yes sir, that's right. Since the Warsaw Pact meeting takes place the 3rd to the 5th of August, it might be a push for them to build the border, before my estimated date. However, I must stress I might be wrong, but I don't see how they could do it before the 13th of August time frame, for sure."

"I assume you have made some copies of this report. If so, I want you to install a SECRET cover on top of each copy, including this original. Keep this original in a safe place and take one copy to MI6 and another to the U.S. Army 513th Military Intelligence Corps Group, which is located at the US Army Clay Headquarters Compound at Clayallee, in the American sector. The contacts there are Captain Silverman and Major Vass. Also, bring me a copy so I can forward it to Brigadier Croxford. Make sure all the copies are marked with a copy number."

"Yes sir, I'll bring your copy within 30 minutes and will contact MI6 and the US Army to make arrangements for a meeting."

Ian left the colonel and went back to his own office, where he called John of MI6 and arranged a meeting with him and Percival, for later that morning. He then called Captain Silverman of the 513th, in the Clay Headquarters compound, and arranged for a meeting in the afternoon at 1500 hours.

At 1030 that same morning, Ian took a copy of the assessment to the colonel's office and then went up to the MI6 facility on the top floor. He checked in with the MPs, guarding the door, and entered using his special pass. He walked down the hallway until he reached John's office.

"Ah, I've been waiting for you Ian. Let's go to the conference room."

On the way they picked up Percival and Chetwyn, and they all entered the room, closing the door.

"Okay Ian, what's all this about?" asked Percival.

"Gentlemen, here is my Assessment on the East Berlin situation, and the case for a GDR border fence to divide the city. Basically, it lays out why it's necessary and that it will be built, starting immediately after midnight on the 20th of August. It's all laid out in this secret document, which is a carbon copy of the original."

"How can you be sure of this, Ian?" asked John.

"The East Germans are losing 1000 doctors, lawyers, teachers, engineers and others every day this month. They have to stop the flood, and the only way is to build a fence or wall. The best time to build it is on the weekend, especially in the holiday month of August. They've been stockpiling building material for many months all over East Germany. All Ulbricht needs is the okay from Nikita Khrushchev, which he'll probably obtain at the Warsaw Pact meeting, in early August."

"We'll look at this Assessment; it probably will tie in with intelligence we've been getting," replied Percival.

"Let's wrap this up. Ian, I'll get back to you on this Assessment, after we've read it in detail. Thanks for coming," John said, as they all got up and left the room.

Later that day, Ian checked out an army Land Rover and drove to the U.S. Army Headquarters, in the American sector of West Berlin. As he pulled in up to the guard gate, a sergeant came out.

"May I see your ID, sir? Who are going to visit?"

Ian handed him his British Army card and said, "I'm here to see Captain Silverman."

The guard looked at his list and said, "You may go right in, sir. He's waiting for you in room 21, on the ground floor."

"Thank you, sergeant. By the way, you don't happen to be from Tennessee, do you?"

"No sir, I come from Palms Springs, California."

Right on time at 1500 hours, he knocked on Captain Silverman's door and entered after hearing "come in".

"Great to see you again, lieutenant, I'd like you to meet Major Vass, who's also in the 513th Intelligence Corps Group. What can we do for you?"

Just as he did in the morning meeting, Ian handed them a copy of the Assessment and laid out the basic details which were included in it.

"We've received some intelligence of our own which somewhat supports the scenario you outline," said Major Vass. "Of course, we'll have to study it in detail and get back to you. Is that acceptable and may we keep this copy?"

"Of course, this document is classified Secret by the British Army, so I trust you will treat it as you would one of your own secret papers."

"You can count on us, lieutenant," replied Captain Silverman. "Thanks for coming and we'll be in touch."

Ian drove back to the Olympic Stadium and turned in the Land Rover. On the way, he thought, *"I hope the date listed in the Assessment turns out to be true. I'd hate to be off a month or two. It might damage my reputation and my career, let alone being promoted to captain."*

12

The Dictators Meet

On the 31st of July, 1961, Walter Ulbricht boarded a plane, for the one thousand mile flight to Moscow. He was the first Secretary of the Socialist Unity Party (SED) and Chairman of the State Council; in other words the East German Head of State. There, on the following day, he held a one-on-one meeting with Nikita Khrushchev, concerning the state of affairs in Berlin.

During the private get together, the DDR leader informed the Soviet leader that, in July alone, over one thousand people a day fled East Germany, for the West. If the flood of refugees was not halted, the DDR would not be a viable country for very long.

Two days later, the Warsaw Pact nations held a conference in Moscow, to discuss East European economic and military issues. In addition, the subject of the Berlin escape route for East Europeans was discussed in detail. Many of the nations were concerned that the West might impose economic sanctions, if the free border was closed.

On Monday the 7th of August, after the weekly staff meeting was over, Ian followed John to the MI6 facility, for a discussion on his Intelligence Report. They picked up Percival and Chetwyn as they proceeded to the conference room, which had just been swept for bugging devices.

141

Since the Blake tunnel incident, precautions were constantly carried out, in order to prevent any bugs being planted by spies.

"Ian, we've read your Assessment and agree in principle to most of the points you've laid out," Chetwyn said. "However, we disagree on the date that you anticipate major action by the East Germans. We believe the date of the 13th of August is more likely, since the GDR can't wait any longer, than necessary, to stop the flow of émigrés."

"Do you have any intelligence that backs up your date, versus mine?" Ian asked. "In the scheme of things, I'm not sure one week makes much difference. Either way, the West must be ready to respond to any action the Soviets and the GDR take."

"Ian, do you remember standing at this conference room window a few weeks ago, and I showed you Teufelsberg hill?" John queried.

"Yes?"

"Well, we've just installed a mobile listening post on the top of it, in conjunction with our American cousins. We've already picked up and deciphered some communications, between East Berlin and the other East European governments. In addition, we've received some HUMINT from an agent, about the recent Warsaw Pact meeting"

"That sounds great. What have you learned?"

"First, we understand that Ulbricht convinced Khrushchev to let East Germans install a permanent border, to separate East Berlin from the West. Khrushchev was concerned about starting a general war with the West. He told Ulbricht there were two conditions attached to his approval. First, there could be no air blockade of West Berlin. Second, there should initially be a barbed wire fence, to see how the West responded. If there was no military reaction forthcoming, then the DDR could commence with the construction of a permanent barrier."

"Have you obtained any information as to what was discussed at the Warsaw Pact meeting?" Ian asked.

"After the meeting concluded, the Teufelsberg listening post did pick up transmissions, between East Berlin and the other East European capitals, which indicated there was general accord, between all the parties. It was agreed, without any dissent, that East Germany had to seal the East/West border sometime in August, and the sooner the better," John replied. "Additionally, we've heard that there will be a meeting today of the Socialist Unity Party (SED), then the Volkskammer (Peoples Chamber) will convene on Friday. Finally next Saturday, the GDR top political leaders will gather at an estate in Döllnsee. It seems the situation is coming to a climax very quickly."

"I've a date planned with Monika on the 12th of August, at the Teufel Club in West Berlin. I'll see if she gives me any hints about what's going on," Ian responded.

"You'd better be careful because, if we're right and you end up in East Berlin at her place, you could find yourself trapped," John warned him.

"I still believe the fence won't be built until the 20th. However, I'll take your advice about being vigilant and, if I happen to go to her place in the East, close to the Gate, I'll check to see if there's any additional security at the *white line*." If there is, I'll not cross the border and enter the East."

"Ian, the bottom line is we like your Assessment. It's well done. Let us know if you find out anything from this Fräulein of yours."

"I certainly will."

They then exited the conference room, and Ian went back to his office. As he entered, the phone began to ring.

"Hello, Lieutenant Black speaking."

"Lieutenant, this is Captain Silverman of the 513th."

"Yes captain, what can I do for you?"

"Are you free this afternoon to come to our headquarters? Let's say around 1430."

"Yes, I certainly am. I'll see you then, captain."

In the afternoon, Ian checked out a Land Rover and drove to the Clay Headquarters Compound on Clayallee. As before, when he pulled up at the main gate, an MP Corporal came out and said, "Your ID sir, please."

Ian showed it to him and asked, "Do you happen to be from Tennessee?

"Why yes sir, I'm from Chattanooga."

"Hey, that's great. My mother was born in the Nashville area and moved to England in the 1930s."

"You must be a dual citizen then."

"Well, I guess I am."

The MP returned his ID and said, "You may go in, sir. You're expected in room 15."

Ian parked in a visitor spot and entered the headquarters. He found room 15 and knocked. Major Vass answered with "enter".

Ian walked in and found three officers seated around a table.

"Come in lieutenant and take a seat," the major requested. "I'd like you to meet Colonel Tracy Haga, who is from the United States Air Force Intelligence Group, here in Berlin. You already know Captain Silverman, I believe."

"It's a pleasure to meet you, colonel."

"Same here, lieutenant. We've all read your Intelligence Assessment and are extremely impressed. Based on our own intelligence, we actually agree with your prediction that the fence will probably be installed on the 20th of August. By the way, would you mind telling us who is KB, listed as one of the sources in your document?" asked the colonel.

Ian answered sheepishly, and looking at the colonel with a slight grin, "Yes sir, KB stands for Kurt Beck, who is my pseudonym. Monika knows me by that name. As far as my phony East German ID, I use the name Kurt Engels. This

ID allowed me to get a day job in East Berlin. Incidentally, MI6 believes the installation date will be the 13th of August."

"I take it that you are fluent in German, in order to take a risk by pub crawling, and working in East Germany," queried Captain Silverman.

"Yes captain, I studied German at the Harrow Public School and at the British Army Intelligence Academy. Most Germans, whom I come in contact with, believe that I am a German. Monika has never questioned if I'm German. I have made a couple of slight missteps. She spotted me, or my twin, for a second in the East German Employment Office. However, I convinced her it must have been a look alike, or my twin.

The other time I made a slight mistake was at a film where the audio was in English with German subtitles printed below. I laughed at something that was said in English, but was not printed in German. I told her that I took some English classes at University. This seemed to satisfy her."

"What is your actual relationship with this Fräulein?" asked the major.

"Well sir, initially it was just an intelligence source that I met in a Club, a few months ago. To be honest, I've come to like her. I know I have to be careful. My CO has even warned me about her. I'm afraid once the fence or wall is installed, I won't be able to see her again. I have a rendezvous scheduled with her on the 12th, at the Teufel Club. I just hope that it's not the night the GDR installs the fence."

"Thank you for coming, lieutenant," said Captain Silverman. "We ask that you keep in touch and communicate any new information to us. Colonel Thurman has already approved that you are to be the liaison between your group and the 513th."

After Ian said goodbye to the colonel and major, Captain Silverman escorted him to the main door. There he said, "Thanks again for coming."

Ian jumped into the Land Rover and headed back to the Olympic Stadium, waving at the MP from Chattanooga, as he sped out onto Clayallee.

13

A Garden Party

At 1400 hours, on Saturday, the 12th of August, 1961, the leaders of East Germany assembled for a garden party, held at the former Nazi Hermann Göring's Döllnsee estate, about fifty miles north of Berlin. The meeting had been called by Walter Ulbricht and was attended by Erich Honecker, Paul Verner, plus other members of the Council of Ministers.

After the party had started, Ulbricht rose to speak to the attendees. It should be noted that he had been classified as dull and devoid of personality. Even Laventry Beria, the former NKVD leader described him as the "greatest idiot" that he had ever met. In his squeaky, Saxon accent, he started to go into a dull oration.

"Comrades, I've gathered you here to announce that we are finally going to stop the flood of émigrés, leaving our great, socialist country. We are also going to prevent spies and infiltrators from the West coming here, causing unrest amongst our hard working people."

Actually, he was a hypocrite, since he had no empathy for the working masses of East Germany.

"At midnight tonight, we will start installing a barbed wire fence, just inside the *white line* border between East and West Berlin. In case any of you have not heard of this

147

project, it's named **Operation Rose** and the planning was started some time ago, by our comrade Erich Honecker. For the past few months, under his direction, we've been secretly purchasing and storing building material, such as barbed wire, concrete pillars, steel rods and concrete, in our government warehouses. Initially, this Berliner Mauer will be constructed of barbed wire and, after forty-eight hours, we will start construction of a permanent concrete barrier. There'll be only a few checkpoints that will permit people to enter and leave East Berlin.

As the barrier is being erected, we'll have the entire forty-three kilometer border manned by police, soldiers and worker militias, armed with weapons, to put down any unrest, by our people. The Soviet army will be ready in the background, just in case we need assistance in putting down possible riots, or if the West tries to destroy the barrier.

Comrade Khrushchev doesn't want to start World War Three on this Berlin issue, but he does agree that we must stabilize the situation here. We have his complete agreement in this matter, as well as the support of our other Warsaw Pact comrades. There's concern that the West might boycott us economically, but over time we will gain economically rather than lose. Western nations always want to trade, and any sanctions will be short lived. Berlin Radio, at 0100 hours tomorrow morning, will start broadcasting warnings to East Berliners that this Berliner Mauer is for their protection from Western trouble makers. These broadcasts will also ask all Easterners to stay home, until the situation has been normalized.

Comrade Shelepin of the KGB has prepared a plan to plant disinformation about destabilizing activities in several parts of the world, so that the Americans' attention is taken away from Berlin. He wants the inexperienced American president to be concerned about starting a war.

At this moment I will sign the directive that will place Operation Rose into action."

148

Walter Ulbricht then went over to a desk and signed the document authorizing the start of the operation.

While this garden party was going on at Döllnsee, Kurt Beck was getting ready to go to the Teufel Club to meet Monika, for the fourth time. He was looking forward to seeing her again, as he was getting attached to her. Little did he know that this evening would be the start of something major in Berlin. As he danced with Monika at the Club, the East German elite were celebrating the start of Operation Rose with food and beer, provided by their great leader, Walter Ulbricht. They disregarded the fact that Ulbricht fancied himself as a German Lenin and grew facial hair, to simulate the late Bolshevik's look.

14

Sunday, The 13th of August, 1961

At 1130 hours, Lieutenant Ian Black finally awoke from his trancelike daydream and fixed himself a light lunch. As he ate it, he listened alternatively to the West Berlin and East Berlin radio stations; Sender Freies Berlin (SFB) and Rundfunk der DDR. It was like listening to someone telling different versions of the same story.

SFB commentator: *"Today, at 0100, the East German government started to seal off the border running through Berlin. The purpose is to prevent its citizens from emigrating to the West, where life is free and economically sound. The DDR is imprisoning its own population, so it can justify the existence of the Socialist regime."*

Rundfunk der DDR spokesman: *"Today, at 0100, our government took the necessary steps to prevent West German militarists, spies and trouble makers from infiltrating our beloved city. The West is planning a revanchist war that will be in complete violation of the Potsdam Agreement, signed by the Western powers. Our brave leaders decided with our Soviet comrades, to seal off East Berlin from the West, until it can be neutralized by an overall peace treaty."*

So it went on, all the time over the radio; two totally different descriptions about the same actions, being taken by the East Germans.

After Ian finished his lunch, he took a taxi to the Western side of the Brandenburg Gate, to see what was going on. There were crowds of West Berliners shouting insults at the East German guards, who were facing into the East, holding their PPsh-41 submachine gun at the ready. Obviously, they were there to prevent East Germans from crossing over into the West, not to stop Western infiltrators entering the East.

West Berlin police were there, trying to keep the crowd reaction from getting out of hand. West Berlin relatives of family members, who lived in the East, were waving handkerchiefs, trying to catch their attention. The East German lorries, with water cannons, were arrayed along the *white line* facing into the East, ready to quell any major disturbance.

After standing near the Gate and watching what was going on, Ian decided to follow the *white line* and walk toward the American sector. After he had gone about half a mile, he heard a voice behind him shout "Kurt", where upon he turned around to see John from MI6.

"What are you doing here, John?" he asked.

"I came to see the East Germans install the barbed wire fence. It looks like they're well prepared to do Ulbricht's, and the Soviets, bidding. By the way, you owe me ten pounds. Today is the thirteenth of August, not the twentieth. I hope you remember our bet the other day."

"I don't recall the bet, but I'll pay you anyway. I was lucky not to be caught in East Berlin. I was over at Monika's place around midnight, when I heard a great commotion. I looked out of her flat window that faces the Gate, and saw all these lorries, filled with construction material, which men were unloading. There were scores of soldiers standing around, holding PPsh-41s. I decided I had to get out of

151

there and get back to the West. On the way, I happened to pick up an East German Bereitschaftspolizei, who wanted my assistance to help him defect."

"Well, I'm glad you were able to make it out of there. I assume you were in mufti which would have been a problem for you, if you'd been caught."

"Yes, it would have been. By the way, I found out from the Bereitschaftspolizei defector that the police and soldiers had been issued PPsh-41s, but no ammunition. They were told by their superiors that they would be issued new loaded magazines, after forty-eight hours. To me it says that, if the West does something about the fence in the first few hours, they will probably back down. Do you know if the British military plans to do anything about the border fence?"

"My understanding is that the PM has told the British Army not to move, until the Americans take some action. The problem appears to be that the East Germans are building the fence on their side of the *white line* and therefore is not infringing on the Western powers rights to be in Berlin. If the West decides to knock the fence down, they would, in effect, be invading the Soviet sector of Berlin. This could trigger a clash, and maybe a new European war. It seems President Kennedy isn't experienced in playing international political games, while Khrushchev, who has lived under Stalin and survived, is used to dealing in high stakes, competitive brinkmanship."

As Kurt and John walked the border to see what was going on, now and again they would see an East German trying to jump over the barbed wire into the West. Sometimes they would make it and sometimes they wouldn't. The soldiers shouted at them to halt or they would be shot. However, they never fired their weapons; probably since they had not been issued magazines loaded with bullets. What the defecting Bereitschaftspolizei had told Kurt, earlier that day, seemed to be true. After they had strolled another half mile, Kurt and John reached Friedrichstrasse where there was a huge crowd of West and East Germans, watching the soldiers and workers installing the barrier. Kurt was looking into the East and spotted someone who looked like Monika.

"Monika, Monika," he shouted, as he waved his hands. To Kurt, it appeared that Monika looked his way, then turned around, without responding and walked back up the street into East Berlin. He was disappointed and thought, *"Either she didn't see me, or thought it would be dangerous to respond. Either way, he considered his affair with her was probably over. It was a pity, because he had become enamoured with her."*

"Was that your girlfriend who you were shouting at?" John asked. "It looked like she didn't see or hear you; or didn't want to."

"Yes, I'm sure that was Monika. I believe she heard me, but didn't want to cause any trouble, for herself, family and benefactor, by recognizing me."

"Well, it's probably for the best, Kurt. With the border being installed, it would be difficult for you to have any kind of relationship with her."

"I guess you're right, John."

As they walked more of the *white line* to see what was going on, Kurt felt some sadness coming over him.

"I've seen enough for today, John. Let's go back to the Gate."

"That's a good idea," John replied, as they turned around and started to retrace the way they had come.

As they passed a tall building that was obviously a residence, they saw some of the West Berlin Fire Brigade holding a life safety net, as a woman jumped from the third floor window. Obviously, she didn't believe the lies of Rundfunk der DDR and didn't want to live under communism. Before she jumped, she threw some belongings and an eight year old daughter down to the firemen.

153

Ian returned to his flat in Spandau and prepared for Colonel Thurman's staff meeting.

****

The next day, Ian entered the conference room with the usual attendees. He walked over to John, gave him ten pounds, in one pound notes, and said, "Here it is, John. I hope you'll give me a chance to get it back, by playing pool one of these days."

"Certainly, any time, but be forewarned I'm a lot better now than I was in Cyprus."

At that moment, the colonel walked in and they all sat down.

"This will be a brief meeting today, as I have to go to a senior officers meeting, concerning the East German fence.

As you all know, they started to build the fence yesterday morning at 0100 hours, and already they have sealed off many avenues of escape for the East Germans. I'm sure many of you want to know what the response will be by the three Western powers. I've been informed by my superiors that Harold MacMillan, our Prime Minister, has given orders for the British military to do nothing, at this point. It appears everyone is waiting for the Americans to do something, and it seems no one is willing to start World War Three, over a barbed wire fence. Do you have any comments or questions?"

"Yes sir, it's my understanding the East Germans have been told by the Soviets that, if the Western powers take some action within forty-eight hours, they are not to fight back. This time limit will be up at 0100 hours tomorrow morning, can we expect any American action by then?" Ian asked.

"It's very doubtful, Mr. Black. I wouldn't hold your breath! The American president has his hands full with Cuba and other world trouble spots. Thank you all for coming. We'll meet again next Monday."

15

Escapes from East Berlin

In the first twenty-four hours, the GDR built a barbed wire fence along most of the entire length of the twenty-seven mile border, between East and West Berlin. Erich Honecker, Monika's benefactor, had done an excellent job for Walter Ulbricht. Since the West did nothing about it, the GDR then started to construct the permanent wall out of concrete pillars and panels. Sections of the wall connected to buildings, which ran along the border. Some residents of these buildings jumped to freedom, and the GDR authorities slowly cleared any East Germans out of these tenements.

A week later, at the next staff meeting, the colonel stated the obvious.

"Gentlemen, I'm sure you're all aware by now that the West isn't going to react to the East Germans building the wall, except to build up our military forces facing the East. The Americans are moving more troops to West Germany and sending additional fighter aircraft to existing airfields. In addition, the president is sending the US congress an appropriations bill, which will allow the increase of troops and arms. In conjunction with this American buildup, our PM has also ordered additional Army and RAF to be fielded in West Germany. Since the four power agreements, signed at the end of the war, is still in effect, the military forces of the three Western powers have the right to enter East Berlin and to be only checked by the Russians. The East Germans have no right to check our papers. Please remember this right does not extend to visiting East Germany. Only the city of Berlin is considered open to any official member of the four powers; travelling into East Germany is covered under the Military Liaison Mission agreement."

"We've received reports that the East German guards now have instructions to shoot any person trying to flee the East. If we are personally close to the border and see this happen, what are our options?" asked Captain Alexander Swiderski, the Russian expert.

"You must not fire your weapons into the East, and you cannot enter the East to help the poor victim. However, if the potential émigré, wounded or not, manages to make it to the *white line*, then it is acceptable for you to help them."

"Over the next few months, is there anything special that we are expected to do, other than to collect data on Russian and East German troop movements?" queried Ian. "Are we allowed to go into East Berlin to observe any unusual activities by the communists?"

"Again, under the terms of the four power agreement at the end of World War Two, Berlin is a city divided into four sectors, and soldiers from any sector can visit any of the other sectors. East Berlin police or soldiers are not entitled to ask for and/or see your papers. Only Russian authorities have the power to do that. Since Mr. Black is fluent in German and Captain Swiderski is fluent in Russian, I expect the two of you to visit East Berlin, on a frequent basis, in a British Army vehicle with military license plates. Is this understood?"

"Yes sir," Ian and Alexander replied.

"If no one has anything to add, we will meet here next week, at the normal time."

During the next few weeks, Lieutenant Black visited the wall to see the construction first hand. He watched as East Germans tried to escape their communist prison. Some made it and some didn't. Those escapees that made it to the British sector of Berlin were interrogated by Captain Phillips's group, to obtain information as to what was happening in the East. A few of the refugees were members of the East German military and the Stasi, and they provided some excellent intelligence on what was happening over the wall.

On one of the East Berlin forays, suggested by Colonel Thurman, Lieutenant Black and Captain Swiderski teamed up and drove into East Berlin, in an Opel with British military license plates. They agreed to call each other Ian and Alex, contrary to military etiquette, as long as they were alone. The purpose of the tour was to visit the Russian sector of Berlin, observe any troop movements and watch for other activities that looked suspicious. As they approached one of the thirteen remaining entry points, an East German guard approached their car.

"Let me see your papers," the East German soldier ordered gruffly.

Ian, who was driving the car, got out of the vehicle, approached the man, stared at the Gefreiter (Private First Class) and, in his excellent German said, "Under the four power Agreement with the Russians, we are only required to show our papers to them, not to any German."

The soldier was taken aback by Ian's Berlin accent and hurried to the guard house to get an officer. In a short time, an Oberleutnant (first lieutenant) came towards Ian followed by the Gefreiter.

"What's all this about? You cannot enter this sector, unless you show your papers," the Oberleutnant ordered.

"Under the terms of the Agreement, signed by the Soviets who control their Berlin sector, we do not have to show you anything," Ian replied. "I suggest that you go and get a Russian officer. We will then show him our papers."

The East German officer looked very annoyed, especially when Ian mentioned the Soviets control their sector. The Oberleutnant turned and stomped off to the guard house at the checkpoint. Ian could see him pick up a telephone and talk for a short time, to someone at the other end. He then hung up looking very agitated. In a few minutes, a Soviet officer drove up in a UAZ-69 jeep type vehicle, got out and approached Ian's car. Ian signaled for Alex to get out of their vehicle, since he spoke perfect Russian. He exited the Opel and stood by Ian. While all this was going on, traffic was beginning to line up behind them, and the drivers were getting upset at the delay.

The Russian captain walked up to them and said, with a loud voice in Russian, "You have caused enough trouble already. Look at the vehicles behind you, waiting for clearance. Let me see your papers." Since it was around lunchtime, Ian surmised that the Soviet was peeved at having his meal interrupted.

Alex answered him in Russian, "Here are our papers. If your East German comrades had obeyed the Agreement signed by your illustrious leaders in the first place, the long line would not be there."

The Russian captain, who was taken aback by the British captain's command of the Russian language, looked at the papers, and asked in a normal voice, "What is the purpose for your visit to East Berlin?"

Alex answered firmly, "We are here to make sure that there are no violations of the Agreement and to make sure no troop movements threaten our rights in West Berlin."

The Russian responded apologetically, "You are free to proceed. I'm sorry about the trouble our naïve German comrades have caused you."

158

ON HER MAJESTY'S BERLIN MISSION

Ian and Alex got back into their car, as the East German soldier raised the gate, and they entered East Berlin.

After they left the checkpoint, Ian looked in the rearview mirror and noted that a black Wartburg-311 was behind them. Ian knew that the Stasi drove such a vehicle. In order to check if they were being followed by this car, Ian drove through some side roads, turning frequently. The black car followed them wherever he drove.

"Alex, I think we're being tailed by Stasi. Hold on, I'm going to try and lose them. Get the Berlin street map out, just in case I need help."

Ian had a good sense of direction and had studied the East Berlin street map, in his spare time. He was well acquainted with most of the side streets and alleys.

He drove like a mad man, while Alex held on, and after a few minutes, announced, "I think I've lost them."

"Well done, Ian. However, if you'd continued for much longer, I might have lost my lunch."

For the next two hours, they drove the streets of East Berlin, looking for any unusual activity. Ian was tempted to ask Alex to visit Monika's flat complex, to determine if she was still there, but he thought better of it.

After they had completed their tour, they started to head back to the same checkpoint they came through. As they did so, they saw an English MGA driving ahead of them. It looked slightly strange, since it seemed to have no windscreen, or it was somehow folded down. Ian gave the car plenty of distance, because he was sure that they would be stopped, if they did actually go to the checkpoint on the border of East and West Berlin. One other fact, he noticed about the MGA, was that it appeared all of the tyres were low on pressure. A couple of streets before the checkpoint, the MGA stopped and the driver got out. He walked to the rear, lifted up the boot lid and, after a few seconds, closed it again.

Ian turned to Alex and commented, "Did you see that? I wonder what he was doing in the boot. The cars windscreen is missing and the tyres appear flat."

"Yes, it does look a little strange. Don't get too close to the car."

They proceeded toward the checkpoint giving the car ahead, plenty of leeway. As they neared the border, the MGA picked up speed and raced under the crossing barrier, with inches to spare. The guards took their PPsh-41s and aimed to shoot at the rear of the car. However, they were so taken by surprise, they didn't have time to get off a shot, before the car was over the *white line* and into West Berlin. Bells and sirens started to sound, and troops stationed nearby raced to the East German checkpoint; but it was all too late.

Ian drove up to the border and the same German guard, who had tried to check them through two hours earlier, was still on duty. He took one look at Ian and recognized him. The soldier turned to another one at the barrier and told him to lift it. Ian drove the military car through the border and reached West Berlin, without another incident. As they entered the West, they spotted the MGA a few hundred yards from the border. It had been stopped by the West German police. The driver had got out and was opening the boot lid, as Ian drove up to see if he could help. The driver was assisting two woman out of the boot.

Ian asked the MGA driver, "Can we be of any assistance? We followed you a few streets from the border and wondered what you were doing."

"Thanks for your offer, but I think we're okay. I was smuggling my wife and her mother into the West. It's lucky they didn't shoot at the boot or me."

A West Berlin policeman told Ian that they had to be taken away for questioning, and then they would be taken to Marienfelde, the main refugee camp for processing. Once Ian was assured the Germans would not be returned to the

East, they drove back to the Olympic Stadium, where the car was returned to the transportation department.

****

Toward the end of September, after a staff meeting, Ian met with Colonel Thurman, about the living accommodations in his Spandau flat.

"Sir, I've been staying at the flat in Spandau, for the past three months, and have now found one in another location for less money. It has two bedrooms, one of which I can use as an office/storage area. It happens to be in the American sector which will make it convenient for me to visit the American 513th Intelligence Corps, when necessary. Is this acceptable?"

"Normally, we expect officers to stay in the British sector but, given that you are a liaison with the 513th I will allow it. Just make sure that you're on time every day and that you do not store any classified documents there, except overnight when you're going to discuss matters with the Americans. Incidentally, where is this flat?"

"It's on Machonstrasse in the Mariendorf District and it's very close to the Westphalweg U-Bahn station. I can take the U6 line to Hallesches Tor and change to the U1 line, which will bring me right to the Olympia-Stadion."

"That sounds alright to me. Please make sure Helga has your address and phone number. Also, make sure that you keep your British Army involvement as low as possible. There are spies everywhere in Berlin, as you know."

Having received approval, Ian moved into this new flat in Mariendorf on the first of October. It was a lot quieter and saved him some money, which was welcome on his limited British Army pay. He hated to ask his father for financial help on a regular basis.

****

At the end of October, the colonel held his usual Monday morning staff meeting and John, from MI6, gave an update on some of the escapes made through the Berlin Wall.

"The number of refugees making it over, through or around the Wall has been slowly dwindling, since the middle of August. Our new, mobile listening post on Teufelsberg has picked up some transmissions that indicate Walter Ulbricht is satisfied with the results of the border control. Many of the escapees are men who have the opportunity to make it over the Wall. Specifically, we've received reports from the West German police that, for the last three months, the East Germans have been losing quite a few soldiers and policemen, on a daily basis. Since they're supposedly watching for people trying to jump over the barbed wire, they actually have the opportunity to escape themselves. Obviously the border guards don't want to live under communism, anymore than the general population."

"Do have anything else to add about the escapes?" asked the colonel.

"Yes, according to our information, up till now, three escapees have been shot and killed trying to escape; two in August and one in October," John continued. "One was killed swimming in Humboldt Harbour, one trying to swim the Teltow Canal and one was shot in the Spree. These shootings were authorized by the East German National Defence Council (DDR-NVR) and Walter Ulbricht is the head of this Council. From our reports, Erich Honecker was the person who actually issued the order to shoot, based on the request of Walter Ulbricht. Obviously, the policy is to instill fear into the general population, so that they will stop trying to escape."

"Thank you, John. That was good information. It seems the Berlin Wall is fairly effective in stemming the flow of refugees. It's important that we continue to monitor the situation and debrief any escapee that we come into contact with," the colonel commented. "Major Phillips, your Interrogation Group will be instrumental in this matter and any possible informant should be directed to his organization. Is this understood?"

Everyone nodded.

"Good. Mr. Black, I've been contacted by the American 513th and they want you down at their headquarters tomorrow at 1000 hours, for a meeting. Can you make it?"

"Yes sir, I certainly can."

"Good, that's all for today. We'll meet next Monday as normal."

The next morning, Ian took the U-Bahn from the station close to his flat and went to his office in the Olympic Stadium, where he changed into his uniform. He then checked out a Land Rover and drove down to the Clay Headquarters Compound, in the American sector, for the meeting scheduled with the 513th Intelligence Group.

As Ian (aka Kurt) entered the conference room, he noticed that there were two civilians, besides three US Army personnel, whom he had already met.

"Glad you could make it, Kurt," said Major Vass, as he shook his hand. "I'd like you to meet two men who are also here in attendance, for this important meeting."

A tall slender man in his forties stood up and shook Kurt's hand and said "I'm known around here as Wally and I come from a three lettered agency of the US government."

Kurt thought, *"Probably the CIA working here at the US Embassy and the Teufelsberg Listening Post."* "Great to meet you, Wally," Kurt responded.

Then the major introduced him to a fairly young man in his early thirties, with a thick moustache. "This is Franz from the German Government."

"It's a pleasure, Franz," Ian said in fluent German, which surprised him.

Franz replied," It's great to find someone who speaks German better than I do. We'll have to talk later about how you know the language so well."

"Okay, now we have all become acquainted, let's get down to business," said the major. "We have much to discuss. As you are all aware, last Friday and Saturday we had a crisis at Checkpoint Charlie, which could have blown into a major clash, between the US and the Soviets.

Just in case you are not aware, a little over a week ago, a senior US diplomat was stopped at the border and turned around by East German police. This was in clear violation of the four power agreement at the 1945 Potsdam Conference. Former General Lucius Clay sent another diplomat to test the border, backed up by armed Military Police. This time they got through.

Then last Friday, the same diplomat, Albert Hemsing, decided to again go into East Berlin. Clay sent some American tanks to Tempelhof airfield, just in case there was serious trouble with the Soviets. The diplomat proceeded into the East without any issue, and the US tanks were withdrawn.

However, the Soviets had discovered the US tanks and thought they were still on the ready at Tempelhof. So they moved thirty-three Soviet T55 tanks to the Brandenburg Gate, as a show of force. The Soviets claimed that they were East German tanks, not Soviet. This was proved to be false, when a Lieutenant Pike went, where they were parked unattended, and found a Red Army newspaper in one of them. Ten of these Russian tanks proceeded to move to Friedrichstrasse and stopped just short of the US Checkpoint Charlie.

On seeing this movement of Russian tanks, Clay moved ten American M48 tanks also to the checkpoint and faced the Russians off. Both sides had loaded their tanks with live ammunition. Finally, using a channel of communication, Kennedy and Khrushchev agreed to withdraw the tanks.

One Soviet tank moved back fifteen feet and then an American M48 moved back an equal distance. In the end both sides moved their tanks away from the border and the tense situation died down.

Kennedy has been quoted as saying: *It's not a very nice solution, but a wall is a hell of a lot better than a war.*

General Clay however, thought that he had an opportunity to knock parts of the Wall down, with the tanks. As is usual in cases like this, politics overrules the military."

When Major Vass said this, Ian thought, *"It's just like the time when we nearly caught the terrorist Grivas, in Cyprus. The politicians countermanded the military plans."*

"The bottom line is that the East Germans cannot deny our military personnel access to East Berlin, and we do not have to show them our papers. Only the Soviets have the right to inspect our documents." The major concluded his review of the tense situation in Berlin.

"Gentlemen, we all have to be extremely careful when dealing with the Russians and East Germans. One slight misunderstanding could set off an armed clash," warned Colonel Haga. "The 1945 Potsdam Agreement allows us to visit East Berlin, without any impediment. Whenever possible, it would be wise to have at least one person in the vehicle being fluent in German or Russian. Obviously, it would be ideal if someone could speak both languages."

"On a trip into East Germany, by two of us from the British Intelligence Corps, we had no problem since I speak German fairly well and my partner speaks Russian," Ian said. "Our fluency in the languages came in useful, since initially we were stopped by an East German guard. It was all straightened out quickly, when they realized that we could understand them, and they couldn't pull anything over on us."

"Communications between the East Germans and Moscow, which we picked up at Teufelsberg, indicates that Khrushchev was extremely concerned about an armed clash.

He figures that the Soviets will win around the world, without going to war. The KGB is spreading misinformation, so as to tie down American forces worldwide," commented Wally.

Colonel Haga then suggested they meet at least once a month, to consider the latest developments in the Berlin crisis.

The meeting broke up and Kurt left the room, followed by Franz. Outside the building, they started to chat in German and got into a brief discussion, about their backgrounds and the conditions in East Berlin.

"I received quite a lot of information about the Wall, from a Fräulein named Ingrid Meyer (aka Monika)," Kurt informed Franz. "I'm not sure what happened to her after the wall was erected. Her family lives in Leipzig and she doesn't want to move to the West, since her father is fairly high up in the local communist party there. She has a benefactor whom I believe is probably Erich Honecker, although she never told me his name."

"If you give me her address, I'll see if I can find out if she still lives there."

Kurt wrote down the address, as best as he remembered it, and gave it to Franz, saying, "She works at the main East Berlin Employment Office, as a manager."

"How did you learn to speak German, like a Berliner?"

"When I went to school in England, I took German classes. Then, before coming to Berlin, the Army sent me to the Intelligence Academy, where they drilled into me the art of speaking German, as someone from Berlin would do."

"That's great, they did a good job. If I didn't know you were English, I would've believed you were a German."

"I hate to say it, because I really liked her. However, I even fooled Monika into believing I was from West Berlin."

"By the way, when I was introduced to you, the major never stated what organization you were from. Can I assume you're from BND?"

Franz looked at Kurt and whispered, "You're correct, but my real name is not Franz. Just as I assume your name isn't actually Kurt. Let's meet again sometime to discuss the situation in Germany and the West. If you give me your telephone number, I'll give you a call."

Kurt wrote down his flat's phone number on a piece of paper and handed to Franz, saying, "Call me at this number after 1800 hours. I'm generally there by then. It's been great to meet you, Franz."

They shook hands and they parted, going to their vehicles, which happened to be parked in two adjacent spots.

Ian drove back to the Olympic Stadium and reported to Colonel Thurman about what had been discussed in the 513th Intelligence meeting, at Clay Headquarters.

Later, he went up to the MI6 facility, on the fourth floor of the London Block, to see John, Percival and Chetwyn. There he also briefed them on what was discussed at the United States Army meeting that morning.

****

For the next three months, Lieutenant Black and Captain Swiderski made frequent trips into East Berlin, to monitor Soviet troop movements. Most of the time, they were uneventful, except for a few arguments at the border crossings, when the East Germans demanded to see their papers. Ian and Alex used their proficiency, in the two languages, to persuade the authorities that they were in opposition to the Potsdam Agreement. In addition, they were creating problems, which their superiors might not appreciate. The Soviet military and diplomats also had the right to visit West Berlin, under the Agreement

On one of the visits, in early December 1961, they ran into Soviet and East German forces rushing to a border point, where a train track, no longer in use, ran from East to

West. It turned out that an East German, with his family, had managed to obtain a locomotive, run it on this unused track and crash through the border fence into West Berlin. In order to prevent any additional escape on this track, the East German authorities tore up all the rails.

In January 1962, Ian walked part of West Berlin, adjacent to the wall, to see what was going on. He noted that the construction of the first wall was proceeding very well, and very few East Berliners were able to escape.

As he observed the workers laying blocks, while being guarded by gun toting soldiers, he heard a voice behind him, speaking in German.

"Kurt, I'm glad to see you again. It's been awhile."

Kurt turned to see who it was and looked into the face of Franz, from BND.

"It's a pleasure Franz. What are you doing here? Have you come to watch the show?"

Before he could answer, the East German guards started to blow whistles and yell. It appeared one of the guards, a few meters away, had decided he'd had enough of communism and climbed over the partially finished wall. He ended up over the *white line,* before the other guards could shoot him.

Kurt and Franz walked over to the escapee and together said, "Welcome to West Berlin."

The man smiled and said, "Thank you, I'm glad to be here. I was afraid I'd be shot, but it was worth it, in order to get away from the prison."

Franz said to Kurt, "This is a fairly common occurrence now, but I'm afraid it will be rare when they build the second wall, behind this first one. It's been great to see you again, other than at the monthly 513th meetings. Maybe I'll call you soon."

They shook hands and parted. Lieutenant Black returned to his office, to write his weekly report.

16

Trouble at Friedrichstrasse

On Sunday, the 18th of February, Ian's telephone rang and he picked up the receiver.

"Hello?"

"Kurt, this is Franz."

"Oh hello, Franz, I didn't answer with a name, since I'm never sure who is calling. What can I do for you?"

"Can you meet me tomorrow night at around 1900 hours? I have an important matter to discuss with you."

"Yes, certainly Franz, where do you want to meet?"

"There's a small restaurant called the Café Mollwitz, on Bernauerstrasse, in the northwest part of Berlin. It's close to the Holzhauserstrasse station, on the U6 U-Bahn line. I don't believe spies or Stasi agents frequent the establishment."

"I'll be there by 1900, at the latest," Ian replied, as he hung up the phone. He then retrieved the U-Bahn map from his desk drawer, to determine exactly where Holzhauserstrasse was.

At 1800 hours, on the next day, Ian walked out of the ground floor of the tall, apartment building, located on Machonstraße and closed the main entrance door behind him. He started to walk down the street, which was almost deserted, due to the weather, toward the Westphalweg U-Bahn station. He wore typical German civilian clothes and was wrapped up in a heavy overcoat, wearing a soft peaked, wool cap. It was a bitterly cold evening with snow flurries, and the temperature hovered around minus twelve degrees Celsius. He briskly walked the two blocks, to get out of the cold and freezing temperature. It had been just six months since Walter Ulbricht, the GDR president, had ordered the Berlin Wall to be built, with Nikita Khrushchev's blessing.

He descended the stairs at the U-Bahn station which was on the U6 line, to wait for the next train. It soon pulled into the Westphalweg station, and Ian entered one of the carriages, settling into a corner seat. The compartment was almost empty, due to the weather and the fact that the rush hour was over. As the train took off from the station, he started to daydream about his life, and how he had ended up in the middle of the Berlin crisis.

Ian was born in England just before the World War Two, to an English father and an American mother. His father was an RAF Spitfire and a P-51 Mustang pilot, during the war, protecting British and American bombers on their way to Germany. After Ian had left Harrow public school, he had been drafted into the British Army in the fall of 1957 and ended up with a commission, as a second lieutenant.

His first assignment was in Cyprus, as OIC of a small radar site on the coast. Later, he was selected to join the Intelligence Corps, due to his command of the Greek language, and promoted to first lieutenant. In this intelligence role, he helped track the EOKA terrorist Grivas to a house in Limassol, where they were going to arrest him. However, at the last moment, politics trumped the military, and Grivas was allowed to leave the island, after a treaty was signed. Upon leaving the island in 1960, Ian went to an advanced intelligence school and ended up going to Berlin, six months before the Wall went up.

As the U6 train pulled into the Friedrichstrasse station in East Berlin, Ian awoke from his daydreaming. There were DDR security guards everywhere, armed with PPsh-41 submachine guns, alert and watching for people trying to jump on the train, to escape the East. Since the Berliner Wall had been erected, this was the only station on the U-6 line that allowed passengers to get on and off in East Berlin. The doors opened, however no one got off the train to visit East Berlin. The train remained in the station for about a minute, with all doors open.

Then, as the train conductor announced the doors were about to close, two men, one, who looked like he was in his twenties, and the other in his late forties, ran from a corner of the station, toward the train with its still open doors. A young, East German guard, on the platform, quickly took his PPsh-41 off his shoulder and aimed it at the two men, running for the train. He shouted at them in German "Halt or I'll shoot." The two men kept sprinting toward the carriage, and the guard opened fire, hitting both of the men.

The younger runner, in front, turned and grabbed his friend, dragging him the last few feet. At this point, Ian took his Browning automatic out of its holster, from under his coat, cocked it and went to the train doorway.

He stood there, with his Browning aimed at the guard, and shouted like a drill sergeant, "You idiot, drop your weapon. You're shooting one of ours."

The inexperienced guard was so taken aback by Ian, shouting in perfect German as he aimed his pistol at him, that he stopped shooting and lowered his gun.

Both of the escapees fell into the train, just as the doors closed.   Soon, it picked up speed again and proceeded to the north. Ian turned and went to assist the two men. The older man died in Ian's arms but, before he succumbed, he uttered *"Es gibt einen Wellenbrecher im West-berliner mit dem Decknamen Drache, Bri..............."* (in English it translated to: (There's a mole in West Berlin with a codename of Dragon, Bri...............").. It was then that Ian realized the two men were Germans. The younger man was not critically wounded, and Ian helped him bind his wounds. It wasn't long before the train carried Ian, together with the Germans, out of communist controlled East Berlin and back into the Western part.

The younger German turned to Ian, saying, "This is my father, and he worked for the Stasi for several years. However, he became disillusioned with what he was ordered to do and decided to flee to the West."

At the first West Berlin station, the West German police, with a medic, entered the carriage and gave emergency care to the survivor. As soon as the ambulance arrived, they took them both to a nearby hospital. Obviously, the engineer/driver of the train had called ahead, to warn the authorities about the shooting.

They questioned Ian for a few minutes about his involvement. After he had shown them his British Army ID card and explained what had happened, they did not detain him. He never told them that he aimed a gun at the East German; otherwise it might have been very awkward to explain why he was carrying a weapon in civilian clothes.

The train started up again, and finally it pulled into the Holzhauserstrasse station, where Ian got off. He went up the stairs to the street above, finding that the wind and snow were still blowing, as hard as ever. He walked down Bernauerstrasse, heading into the bitterly, cold wind, and ultimately arrived at his destination; the Café Mollwitz.

Ian entered it and sat down at an empty table, to wait for Franz. A waiter came up to his table to take his order.

Ian said in English, slowly, "I'll have one half liter of Paulaner Salvator, please. I'm waiting for a friend who should be here any minute."

The waiter responded in broken English, "Ein *gross* of Paulaner Salvator will come right up."

As Ian sat there waiting for his beer, he heard two men behind him, talking softly in German. He had very good hearing and his German was excellent. In fact, most of his acquaintances actually thought he was German, when they first met him. Finally, the waiter brought his beer to the table.

The two men behind him seemed to be discussing a newly, formed group that was planning to manipulate the Italian government, the Lira exchange rate and the financial markets in Italy. One of the men talking was a German named Lutz Schiller, and the other identified himself as Borge Ekstrom, from Stockholm. It seemed this group was trying to control events in Italy, so they could benefit financially from the chaos. Already, since World War II, the Italians had voted in approximately fifteen different governments, in seventeen years; most of them were coalitions of various parties.

Lutz and Borge did not realize that Ian could speak and understand German fluently, since he only spoke to the waiter in English. They kept talking about the group they were in and their plans for making money, by controlling events in Italy. Eventually, the two men left the restaurant and headed down Bernauerstrasse.

Soon after they left, Franz, his contact in the BND (Bundesnachrichtendienst), walked into the café. He shook Kurt's hand and then sat down at the table. The same waiter came over and took Franz's order. He ordered a *gross* Warsteiner Premiun Verum.

"How are you doing my friend?" asked Franz

Before Kurt (aka Ian) could answer, the waiter brought Franz his Warsteiner. The waiter then turned around and went back to the bar area.

Kurt replied, "I'm doing well considering what happened on the U-Bahn. I look a little disheveled and have some blood on my sleeves, because there was some shooting at the Friedrichstrasse station, while I was sitting my compartment. Two East Germans were trying to escape to the West and rushed the train."

Ian related to Franz exactly what happened and then added, "The older of the two Germans died in my arms but, before he expired, he whispered something that I believe was extremely important. He told me that there's a mole somewhere in West Berlin, by the codename Dragon. He then started to tell me the mole's name or organization, I believe, but he succumbed before he completed it. He did have time to softly whisper "Bri" before he died. It could have been for Brigitte or some other name, starting with the letter *B*. Anyhow, what can I do for you?"

In a low voice, Franz answered, "I'm glad you're okay. This goes on all the time, with East Germans trying to get into the West. Thanks for the tip about the potential mole. I'll mention it to my superiors and put it in my next report. The reason I wanted to see you is that we need to get a scientist, by the name of Manfred Ebner, out of the East. Unfortunately, it's becoming harder and harder every day, since the Wall went up. This rocket engineer is very important, because he worked on the German V-2 program and has, since the end of the war, been forced to work for the Russians, on their R-7 missile program. He and his family are being watched constantly, so it's going to be very difficult to get them out. Can you, or your organization, help us out? Do you have any ideas for getting him over, under or through the Wall?"

Ian responded, "I don't know. Let me check with my peers and superiors. There must be something we can do to help. Maybe, we could create a diversion or something. My organization is very sympathetic about the needs of the BND. I'm sure we'll do what we can to assist you. We're both on the same side. How about your cousins in the CIA and MI6? Perhaps they would be able to help. Anyway, I'll get back to you, within a few days."

"Good, I'll await your call," Franz said.

Ian then asked Franz, "Have you ever heard of a group that is trying to manipulate the Italian Government, exchange rate and financial markets? There were two men, one German and one Swede, here a few minutes ago, talking about such a group."

Franz replied, "Yes, I have heard mention of such a group in intelligence briefings, but there are very few details and the subject is low on the list of priorities for the BND."

Ian responded, "If you hear anything more about this group, could you please let me know?"

"Sure," Franz replied. "By the way, I have some news about your girl friend, Ingrid Meyer (aka Monika). One of our agents checked on the address you gave me and it appears that she still lives there. Also, we do have information that her benefactor, is in fact Erich Honecker, and he planned the installation of the Berlin Wall, with the surrounding security."

"Well, I'm glad to hear that she hasn't been shipped off to some gulag or concentration camp. Thanks for the information. I had a hunch Erich Honecker was probably her friend, based on a few hints she dropped accidentally."

"I have to leave now, but I hope to hear some good news from you in a few days, about helping the scientist to escape." With that Franz got up and left the Café.

Ian beckoned the waiter over and said, "*zahlen, bitte*." The waiter handed him the bill and he paid it in D-Marks.

He waited a couple of minutes, and then he also left the restaurant, in the opposite direction. As he walked down the street, he thought about what the two European men, in the bar, were discussing and put it in his memory for future reference.

He decided to take a taxi back to his flat, even though it would be more expensive. He didn't want to be on a train in Friedrichstrasse, this soon after the incident. As he rode in the cab back to the American sector, he thought, "*I have two important matters to attend to. First, determine if there is any method by which we can help getting this scientist to freedom. Second, try to find out who this mole is, either in the West Berlin Government or in some military organization."*

****

The next day, Ian called Colonel Thurman' office and asked Helga to transfer his call to him.

"Colonel, this is Lieutenant Black. I know we had a staff meeting yesterday, but I want to request another one for this afternoon."

"Why do we need an additional one, Mr. Black?"

"Well sir, yesterday I was on the U-Bahn and there was an incident at the Friedrichstrasse station, in which I was partially involved. Also, I met yesterday evening with a member of the BND, who had a request. I believe both issues are important, requiring discussion and resolution, as soon as possible."

"Who do you suggest we have in attendance for this special meeting?"

"I think all of your staff and the MI6 personnel, including John, Percival and Chetwyn, should be in attendance."

"Very well, Ian, I'll have Helga contact everyone and schedule the meeting for 1400 hours, in our usual room. See you then."

At 1355, Ian entered the conference room, to find some of the attendees were already there.   Soon, the rest of them came in and sat down. Promptly, at 1400, Colonel Thurman strode into the room and called the meeting to order.

"This conference was called at the request of Mr. Black, so I'll let him lead it off."

"Gentlemen, there're two issues that need to be discussed and, if possible, resolved.

"Yesterday, I was travelling north on the U6 line, and there was a problem at the Friedrichstrasse station. Just before the doors started to close, two men ran from the shadows, toward the carriage I was in. Before they could reach the safety of the train, a young East German guard shot at both of them, fatally wounding the older one and injuring the younger man. Before the older German died in my arms, he whispered, *"There's a mole in West Berlin with the codename Dragon."* The young man told me that his father was in the Stasi and he wanted to get out. At the first station in West Berlin, the police came on board and took them both away.

The important point of this story is that there appears to be an East German spy, either in Willy Brandt's mayoral government or in one of the military organizations. What do we do about that? Should we be trying to find out who it is on our own or should we mention it to the mayor's office, and leave it up to them, to see if they have a mole?"

"I'm of the opinion that the MI6 should place a couple of agents on this and compile a list of people in the mayor's office or the American, French and British military organizations, with the first or last name beginning with "Bri". What do you think, Percival?" asked Colonel Thurman.

"That's a good idea colonel, but I believe, if at some point we find a suspect in the mayor's office, we need to turn the information over to their security department. MI6 has enough problems on its hands, keeping track of Soviet troop and armor movements, as well as Soviet agents infiltrating the West. If however, it appears that the mole may be at the British Brigade headquarters here or at the American forces Clay Headquarters compound, then we may need to take more action to unmask the Dragon.

Also, it might be a good idea, if Captain Phillips' organization interrogates the young man who escaped from the East. Since the West Berlin police took him off the train, with the dead man, they should know where he can be located."

"Yes, I agree Percival. Major Peters, as OIC in charge of the Interrogation group, take it as an action item to find and interrogate this young East German. Major Phillips, maybe you could provide assistance in this interrogation, since you're in charge of the Counter Intelligence group."

"Of course, colonel," replied Peters and Phillips in unison.

"Mr. Black, I want to thank you for bringing this matter to our attention. Now, what's the other issue you wish to discuss?"

"Last evening, I met with a BND agent named Franz, who needs some assistance in getting a rocket scientist, by the name of Manfred Ebner, and his family, out of the East. He told me that Ebner was involved with the V-2 development and, since the war, has been forced to work for the Soviets. When a considerable number of Wernher von Braun's team escaped and went to America, he was somehow left behind. I told Franz that I would have to check with my superiors.

The question is whether the MI6, or some other agency, can help BND get the family out. In some ways I'm surprised that he asked for help, since the BND is supposed to have agents in the East. I believe he was just looking for ideas."

"Does anyone have any suggestions on how this family could be aided with their escape?" asked the colonel. "How about you chaps of MI6?"

"I suppose we could study various ways to help Herr Ebner and then get back to Franz. Ian, do you have his phone number?" queried Percival.

"Yes, I'll give it to you at the end of the meeting," replied Ian. Continuing he said, "I have an idea that might succeed in helping the scientist escape, but I'm not an engineering expert. My suggestion is for some BND agent in East Berlin to obtain, either by stealing or purchasing, a strong lorry, and then affix a special, V-shaped snow plow on the front, which could "blast" its way through the weakest border crossing. This would have to be accomplished soon, while the snow is still flying. This snow plow would not attract too much attention, until it is too late for the border guards to respond. Some border checkpoints are still not designed to stop everything. The East Germans are slowly upgrading them, but it will take time.

There's an opportunity over the next month to build this plow, and then have a BND agent drive the family to the West. Perhaps, our Corps of Royal Engineers has some skilled personnel that could help in the design of the plow. We could then provide the drawings and list of required material to BND. I believe that the plow would have to slope backwards, so as to go under the barrier, lift it up and break it. Any escape plan has to have an element of surprise, for it to be successful."

"Well lieutenant, that sounds ingenious, but whether it will work, I'm not sure," replied Colonel Thurman. "Let me talk to the CO in the 42nd Engineer Company, in order to see what they think about this idea of a snow plow. Percival, are you willing to take on the responsibility to contact the BND, with any ideas that we come up with? I believe any support, we give them, should come from your organization. The main mission of the British Army Intelligence Corps is to monitor the Soviet and Warsaw Pact troop movements."

"Yes colonel, I'll personally take on the task of coordinating any action we participate in with Franz, at BND," replied Percival

"Good. Thank you all for coming and we'll meet again next Monday."

As they all walked out of the room, Ian went over to Percival and gave him Franz's phone number.

17

Plowing Through

Three weeks later, on Thursday, the 8th of March, Ian received a call from Percival, requesting that he attend an important meeting, at 1000 hours the following day, in the MI6 offices.

The next day, he went up to the fourth floor, flashed his badge at the MPs on guard and went to the main conference room, near the entrance to the facility. There he found Percival, John, Chetwyn and an engineer from the 42nd Engineering Company, waiting for him.

"Glad you could make it, Ian," Percival said. "We're expecting two more people, and then we can proceed."

Just then there was a knock at the door. Percival went and opened it, to find his secretary standing there.

"Sir, there are two men at the main door that need to be checked in."

"Thank you, Doris."

Percival left the room and, in a few minutes, returned with two gentlemen in tow. One was Franz and the other, Ian didn't recognize, but assumed he was also from BND.

Percival introduced everyone to each other by their codenames, and it turned out the other BND chap's name was Niko. Ian was introduced as Kurt also for secrecy's sake.

"Okay, I'm glad you could all make it and, since Franz requested this meeting, I'll turn it over to him."

"Thank you all for coming and a special thanks to Percival, for organizing this get together. First, I want to point out for safety reasons, none of what you hear today must never be communicated to anyone outside this room. As you're all aware, we have an East German rocket scientist who wants to defect to the West. Since the Wall was built last August, it's been very difficult to get people out of the East. Kurt here came up with an idea about a snow plow, affixed to the front of a lorry, which could possible blast its way through the border checkpoints. These checkpoints are slowing being reinforced, and we have to act immediately, before it becomes impossible to get this scientist out. The least developed border crossing, at this point in time, is the Bornholmer Strasse checkpoint at the Bösebrücke (bridge), which leads into the French sector.

Thanks to the efforts of the 42nd Engineer Company, they have come up with a simple, and somewhat crude, design for a V-shaped plow, which can be installed on the front of an East German IFA G5, six wheel, extended cab lorry. Our people, in the East, managed to commandeer a G5 two weeks ago and parked it in an abandoned garage, near some railway tracks, south of Bornholmer Strasse. Trains going by will mask any noise coming from the garage. As we speak, this G5 is being modified with the plow, and bullet proof plates surrounding the cab.

According to the latest forecasts from our weather personnel, they are expecting a major snow storm, to pass through Berlin next weekend. Based on this expected storm and the stationing of security personnel at the border crossing, the ideal date and time for the crossing attempt will be 2300 hours, on Sunday, the 18th of March. Niko here has volunteered to drive the G5 and, in effect, place his life on the line, if something should go wrong.

181

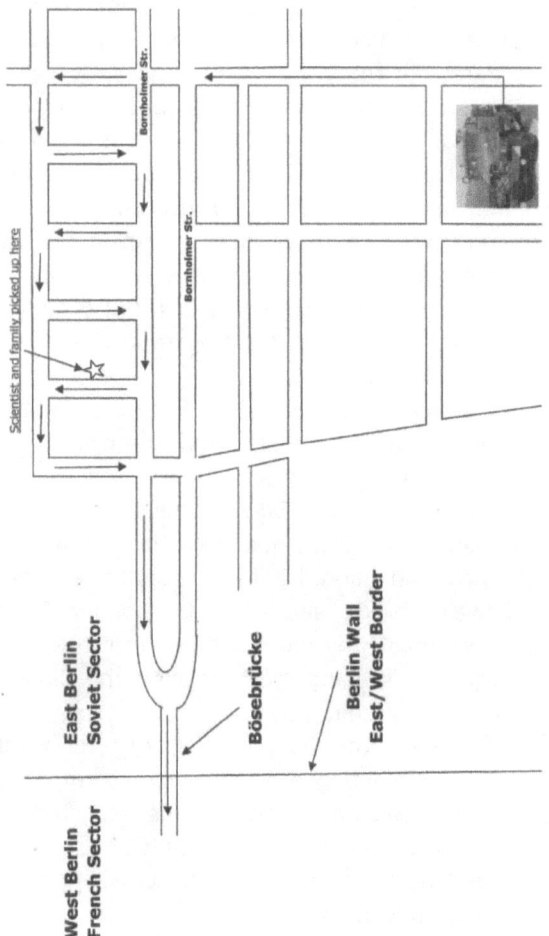

Snow Plow Escape Route

I am passing round a map of the expected route and, for obvious reasons, we cannot give you a copy. At around 2230 hours, the G5 will pull out of the garage and proceed north up Schonfließer Strasse. As it crosses over Bornholmer, Nico will look west down the street to see if there is any unusual activity. He will then drive up to Ibsenstrasse and go one block, before heading south down Aalesunder Strasse. Again, as he drives westward down Bornholmer, he will look for any unforeseen activity in the distance, at the checkpoint."

Continuing Franz asked, "Any questions so far?"

"You haven't mentioned the scientist and his family. When and where do they get into the lorry?" asked Kurt.

"I'll get to that in a minute," answered Franz. "Niko will continue driving the lorry back and forth down the streets, as though he is plowing the roads. Hopefully, this action will "disarm" the border guards and make them believe this vehicle is no threat. When the driver reaches Andersenstrasse, he will stop in the middle of the block and the scientist, with his family, will quickly climb into the lorry.

After the family is safely on board and hunkered down on the floor boards, the lorry will proceed up to Ibsenstrasse and down Malmöer to Bornholmer. At this point, Niko will determine if the escape route is safe or not. If it's a go, he will turn right onto Bornholmer Strasse, "floor" the lorry and head at maximum speed for Bösebrücke. He will have nearly two hundred meters of road, before he hits the first of two barriers. The momentum of the lorry, with its V-shaped and slanted plow, should carry them through onto the bridge and into the French sector. If the guards fire their weapons, which it can be assumed they will, the steel plate, which has been installed, will protect the occupants."

"How do you know this is the best time and day to attempt this breakout?" asked John.

"We have conducted a couple of test runs. As West Germans, we're permitted to cross the border with proper paperwork. Late at night, the number of guards is reduced, as there are few travelers to check out. In addition, on Sunday evening, most workers are home in bed and are not travelling from East to West."

"Is there a potential that the narks will have cars cruising near the border, looking for possible escapees?" asked Kurt.

"Yes, that's a potential threat to the plan. We'd like someone in the British military to run interference to draw off any narks, from the border checkpoint. As agreed to by the Soviets, the British, French and American military are allowed to visit East Berlin, as long as they don't actually help East Germans to flee."

"Well, I guess I could drive into East Berlin with our Russian speaking officer and help draw off any narks, in the area of Bornholmer Strasse. We would enter through Checkpoint Charlie at Friedrichstrasse, so as not to be aiming directly for the Bornholmer checkpoint. We could stop now and again, so as to be very visible. I'm sure the narks will want to follow us, to see what we're up to," commented Kurt.

"If you'd do that, I'm sure it would help draw off some East German forces."

"What happens if there isn't a snow storm that weekend? Will the escape attempt be called off?" queried Chetwyn.

"Of course, it would ultimately depend on the scientist and his family. However, every day or week we wait, the harder it'll be for them to escape. The East Germans are continually fortifying the Wall and making it more difficult to escape to the West."

"I have three basic questions, Franz. First, what's so important about this rocket scientist? Second, will we have a chance to talk with him, once he's in the West? Finally, what can we do to help in this matter, other, than Kurt here, to run interference?" asked Percival.

"Manfred Ebner worked on the V-2 rocket, under Wernher von Braun, during World War Two and, when the war ended, he was picked up by the Russians, before he could escape with most of the other team members. The Russians forced him to help them with the "R" rocket program, including the R-7. He can provide the West a great insight into the Russian missile capability.

In answer to your second question, once Herr Ebner has been debriefed by BND, the British and Americans will be given an opportunity to talk with him.

Lastly, besides Kurt and his Russian speaking officer running interference, we would appreciate it if, in some way, you could provide disinformation to the East Germans, about a breakout, at a southern border crossing. One suggestion is to plant a story about several East Germans planning to get on a bus and crash through the border at the Heinrich-Heine-Strasse/Prinzenstrasse crossing (checkpoint Delta) in the American sector. Hopefully, this will draw many Stasi and East German troops down to the south; away from the Bornholmer border crossing point."

"We can certainly spread some disinformation, can't we, John?" queried Percival.

"I'll work on it," replied John.

"Thank you all for coming. This is an important person for BND and the German Government, and his escape will be beneficial to the West." Franz said. "If there's a change in plans for any reason, I'll certainly let you all know."

Kurt shook hands with Franz, departed the MI6 facility and returned to his office on the lower floor. There he contacted Captain Swiderski and confirmed that he was available on Sunday evening, the 18th of March, to take a drive into East Berlin, around 2000 hours. Ian then contacted Colonel Thurman and informed him of the plan. His only comment was for the two of them not to break regulations, and observe the agreement between the

Western powers and the Soviets, concerning military visits to East Berlin.

****

On Sunday, the 18th of March, at 1945 hours, Ian met Captain Alex Swiderski at the motor pool where they checked out a Land Rover, with all-wheel drive and a canvas top. It was important that the license plate, and other labels, indicated that the vehicle belonged to the British Army. The snow had been falling since Saturday morning, and there was no doubt that they were going to need the all-wheel drive capability.

They drove out of the Olympic Stadium area and headed for Checkpoint Charlie, at Friedrichstrasse. As they left the American zone and entered East Berlin, an East German guard came to the window and asked to see their documents, and the purpose for their visit. Ian got out of the driver's seat and faced the guard, as he slapped his swagger stick against his thigh.

"You have no right to ask for our papers. Only the Soviets are entitled to see them, under the four power agreement," Ian said sternly in German, as he stared the guard in the eyes. All the while, he was slapping his swagger stick.

"Then, my orders say that I can't let you pass into East Berlin."

"Unterfeldwebel (sergeant). I'm a British Officer and, as such, you'll address me as sir. You'd better get an officer here fast or I'll report you to the Soviets."

The Unterfeldwebel hurried to the guard shack and came back with an East German oberleutnant (first lieutenant).

The East German officer inquired, "What's going on here?"

"Oberleutnant, we're here for entry into East Berlin. The captain and I are both in uniform and driving a British Army vehicle, with correct identification. Under the terms of the four power agreement, the British military have the right to enter East Berlin, at any time," Ian replied in perfect German, still slapping his swagger stick.

Oberleutnant Baumbach, after glancing at Ian, decided to moderate his tone.

"Lieutenant Black, there's no Russian officer on duty at the moment, and it wouldn't be wise to take him away from his dinner. As long as you confirm your visit is peaceful, I will permit you to pass. How long do you plan to visit East Berlin?"

"Our visit is for sightseeing in this beautiful snow, and we should be passing back through here, at around midnight."

"Very well, you may go lieutenant," Oberleutnant Baumbach said, as he indicated to the guard holding the crossing gate to raise it.

Ian jumped back into the Land Rover and drove on into East Berlin.

"You know, Alex, a swagger stick comes in useful now and again," Ian said with a grin.

He drove away slowly from the border crossing and noticed a black Wartburg-311, containing two Stasi men, had started to follow them.

"We've picked up a tail, as planned and I won't try to lose them, as we normally do," Ian continued.

"Well done, Ian. You're right, we don't want to lose them," replied Alex. "Let's stop at various points along the way, as we proceed toward the Bösebrücke on Bornholmer Strasse. This way we'll attract attention of the Stasi and the Russians."

Ian drove in the direction of the Brandenburg Gate area and, on the way, stopped at an Opera House. They both got out of the vehicle and stood in the snow, looking at the building for a few minutes. The traffic was light due to the weather, and no one stopped to ask what they were doing, or if they needed help. The Stasi car following them also stopped some distance away from them, but the occupants did not get out.

They then drove on to the Gate and stopped again to take pictures of the famous facility in the snow.

"This will make a great souvenir photo," Alex said to Ian. "Oops, there's a Russian army UAZ-69 pulling up behind us. Leave this up to me."

A Russian captain got out of the vehicle, leaving his driver behind the wheel, and approached Alex and Ian.

"What are you doing here?" the Russian asked. "I've been following you all the way, since you entered East Berlin through the Friedrichstrasse crossing point. Our East German comrades stated that you refused to show them your documents."

Alex replied, speaking in perfect Russian, "Under the four power agreement, we're only required to show our papers to Russian officers, not East German soldiers or border guards."

The Russian was taken aback by Alex's command of his native language.

"Well, let me see your papers, please," he asked politely. "Also, would you mind telling me the purpose for your visit to East Berlin."

Alex handed the Russian officer their papers saying, "This is our first opportunity to visit East Berlin in the snow. It's beautiful and we're taking a few photos of non military sights, as souvenirs."

As they were talking, Ian was standing to the side, trying to look very military like and slapping his swagger stick on his thigh. The Russian captain saw this and was somewhat taken aback, by a first lieutenant who seemed to be more senior that the captain he was conversing with.

"Okay, you may proceed," said the Russian. "Just make sure you don't take any photos of military targets. By the way, I hope you'll not be involved with this bus that supposedly is going to take some East Germans, and attempt to crash through the Heinrich-Heine-Strasse/Prinzenstrasse crossing point, into West Berlin."

"You can be sure we're not involved with the escape attempt that you're describing. It would be against the agreement worked out between the four powers that allows for military patrols, throughout Berlin," replied Alex.

The Russian returned to his vehicle and drove off to the south, toward the Heinrich-Heine-Strasse/Prinzenstrasse border post.

Ian and Alex got back into their Land Rover and proceeded in the direction of the Bösebrücke crossing point. They noticed they were now being followed by two black Wartburg-311s. Obviously, the Russian wanted to make sure they weren't breaking the four power agreement.

They drove to the Bornholmer Strasse, stopping along the way to look at a Russian War memorial and an old palace. The snow was still coming down, so the vehicle's four wheel drive came in very useful.

Ian thought to himself, as he drove, *"This weather is ideal for the snow plow escape plan to work. Let's hope it goes off without a hitch."*

As they approached the Bornholmer Strasse at 2200 hours, Ian noticed the Stasi cars, that were following them, had vanished.

"Alex, we've lost our tails. Perhaps the disinformation about a bus crashing through the border is working."

"It sure seems that way. Let's approach the bridge and see the level of security there. We could stop short, park and attract attention of any Stasi men in their cars."

"Good idea, Alex."

Ian drove down the one-way street, parked near the area where one could turn around and go back down the street, on the other side of the medium.

There appeared to be very little traffic crossing from East to West Berlin, through this border point. There was one Stasi type car parked by the guard house, with two men in it. There were two soldiers standing in the snow at the barrier, stomping their feet. Obviously, it was cold for them, standing in the snow that was still coming down.

At 2210 hours, Alex said to Ian, "Let's go and head back toward Checkpoint Charlie via a circuitous route and see if that Stasi car follows."

Ian started up the Land Rover and slowly drove down Bornholmer Strasse in an easterly direction. As they continued down the street, Ian noticed that the black Wartburg was following them.

"It worked," Ian exclaimed to Alex. "They took the bait. This should make it easier for the snow plow to transport the scientist and his family to the West; it should be leaving the garage in about fifteen minutes. Let's get out of here, with the Stasi in tow."

As they drove south, a few Russian and East German trucks loaded with soldiers passed them at great speed. Their drivers were obviously used to driving on snow.

"I wonder if they're heading for Checkpoint Delta."

"It certainly looks like the disinformation plan is working," replied Alex.

At the same time, as they were driving toward Checkpoint Charlie, the snow plow pulled out of the garage, where it had been modified, and headed north on the scheduled route. Everything went according to plan, and, at close to 2300 hours, the G5 broke the two barrier posts, crossed the bridge and ended up in the French sector of West Berlin. The few East German border guards on duty opened fire on the vehicle as it raced past, but the bullets bounced off the steel plates that were shielding the occupants. The French soldiers and the West Berlin police, at the western end of the bridge, were flabbergasted to see this strange snow plow, racing toward them. The two BND agents, also at the French border post, weren't obviously surprised, at all.

The occupants were quickly ushered into the border guardhouse for safety, and then escorted by the BND officers to a secret location, in West Berlin.

In the meantime, Ian and Alex made their way back to Checkpoint Charlie. At around 2315 hours, some East German lorries loaded with soldiers raced northward toward Bornholmer Strasse. They had evidently received word of the G5 crashing through the barriers at Bornholmer border crossing and clearly would arrive too late.

Ian and Alex arrived at the Friedrichstrasse crossing point at almost midnight and the Russian captain, whom they had met earlier, came out with an East German guard.

Alex got out of the Land Rover to talk with the Russian.

"What's going on, captain? We've seen Russian and East German lorries loaded with troops, going in all directions."

"Nothing much, we've had a few spies trying to break in to this socialist paradise. However, we stopped them. Do you mind if I look in the back of your vehicle?"

"Not at all, as I mentioned earlier, we abide by the four power agreement."

At this point, Ian got out of the vehicle and stood staring at the Russian, as he slapped his swagger stick on his thigh.

The Russian officer saw this and said to Alex, "You may proceed. I'm sure you're not smuggling anyone in the back, as it would break the agreement. By the way, who's that other officer?"

"Oh, he's just a nervous first lieutenant who speaks fluent German. That's why he's always using his swagger stick. He likes to impress people."

"I need to get one of those sticks," the Russian replied.

Ian and Alex returned to their vehicle and drove through the border to the American Checkpoint Charlie. They were safely back in the West.

18

Czechoslovakian Skater

On a Sunday, in the middle of April 1962, Ian travelled to the northern part of West Berlin to visit a friend, who lived right at the end of the U6 line. When it came time to return to his flat in the south, his friend advised him to leave at 2030 hours, since he thought the next train going south was at 2045 hours.

After a five minute walk, Ian arrived at the U-Bahn station and found the train waiting for the trip south. The doors were closed to keep the compartments warm and he had to wait for about nine more minutes, before the doors automatically opened. As it turned out, he was the only passenger waiting to board the train. Ian thought that the reason for this was that it was a Sunday, and kind of late for people going to work the next day. As soon as the doors opened, Ian entered the car, sat down on a seat close to the doors, and opened up a book he was reading.

It wasn't long before the doors closed, and the U6 train commenced its journey to the south. As Ian was reading, the train went through five stations, stopping at all of them for fifteen to thirty seconds, before proceeding to the next one. At all the stops, the platforms were deserted and no one entered Ian's carriage. The next station was

Afrikanische Strasse, and the doors again automatically opened.

Ian looked up as an attractive girl entered the carriage, although he noticed that she was half dragged onto the train, by two tough, goon-looking men. She sat down across from Ian, and the two goons deposited their fat behinds on each side of her. The girl looked frightened as she sat down opposite Ian. Looking at her, he guessed that she was in her late teens or early twenties. She had fairly short, black hair and, by her trim body, appeared to be an athlete. Upon sitting down, she placed a suitcase and an odd looking bag, similar to a bowling ball bag, on the floor of the car, in front of her. She had carried both of them on board by herself. The two men, with her, did not lift a finger to help.

Ian eyed this strange bag and thought, "*I believe I've seen bags like that before.*" He searched his memory and finally came up with where he had seen one before. He used to go to Richmond Ice Rink, when he was on holiday from school, and saw the skaters place their skates in a similar protective bag, after they had finished practicing for the day.

He realized that this girl was probably a skater, but he didn't like the look of the large, non-smiling men on each side of her. To Ian, they appeared to be some type of enforcer. Perhaps they were from Stasi or some Eastern European secret police force.

Right on time, the doors closed and the train started toward the south of Berlin again.

The girl looked very nervous throughout the entire trip, but managed to smile at Ian, a couple of times. When the train entered the Leopoldplatz station, she then mouthed silently the German words *"Helfen Sie Mir"* (Help Me), as the goons were preoccupied looking at the line chart. Luckily for her, Ian was fluent in German and he gave a slight nod, in recognition of her plea. When he realized what she was trying to tell him, Ian tensed up, since he knew the train was fast approaching the Friedrichstrasse station, the only stop

193

in East Berlin. There were five stops between the Leopoldplatz and the East Berlin stop, four of which, the train would travel through without stopping.

As they approached the Friedrichstrasse station, Ian slowly felt for his gun inside his coat, to make sure he could reach it easily, if need be. About thirty seconds later, the train pulled into Friedrichstrasse and the doors slowly opened. The two goons on each side of the girl stood up and reached for her arms, to pull her up to a standing position. It was obvious to Ian that they were going to drag her off the train, into East Berlin. The girl shouted out *"Helfen Sie Mir"* and Ian felt he could no longer stand idly by. He quickly jumped up, pulled his Browning and aimed it at the two men, shouting in German *"Lassen sie gehen, oder ich werde schießen"* (Let her go, or I'll shoot).

The men were so surprised that they let her go and ran for the train doors, shouting for the DDR soldier patrolling the station. As they jumped off the train onto the platform, Ian quickly took his gun and using the butt end, knocked out the lights in the compartment. He could have shot them out but, as a British Army officer, he would have had a lot of explaining to do, for discharging his weapon on the U-Bahn.

"Get down on the floor," he yelled at the girl, in German.

He quickly grabbed her and pushed her down, onto the floor of the carriage. The DDR guard on the Friedrichstrasse platform fired a couple of shots from his PPsh-41 into the car, but he didn't hit either Ian or the girl. The doors closed and the train started to gather speed, travelling out of the station, toward West Berlin. They went through two more East Berlin stations, without stopping, before reaching the first one in the West, named Kochstrasse. It was close to the American Checkpoint Charlie.

As the train went through the last two East Berlin stations, Ian told the girl that they had to get off the train at the first station in West Berlin. This was a precaution just in case the East Germans called ahead to one of their agents in the West, or the West Berlin police came on board to investigate the shooting.

As soon as the train pulled into the Kochstrasse station, Ian picked up the girl's suitcase and told her to follow him. They quickly got off the train and went down the stairs to the street below. They were in luck, as there was a taxi waiting right outside the station. Ian and the girl got in, and he told the driver to take them to the junction of Mariendorfor Damm and Eisenacher Strasse, in the south of Berlin. He didn't want to give his exact address, in case the taxi driver could be traced and was forced to disclose where he dropped them off.

As the taxi started to drive to their destination, Ian said to the girl in German.

"My name's Kurt and I am a Western government agent here in Berlin." He knew he had to tell her something, since he had a concealed weapon on him. However, at this point, he didn't want her to know his real name or his organization, in case she was a plant.

At that moment, Kurt looked out the rear window of the taxi and noticed that there was a possible tail, following the cab.

"Driver, I believe we may be followed. Lose them and I'll give you an extra tip."

"Okay, sir, I'll get rid of them. Hold on, because I'm going to do some sharp cornering, turning down side streets."

In about a minute, Kurt looked back up the street and didn't see the car any more.

"I think you lost them," he said to the driver.

Turning to the girl, Kurt asked her, "What's your name?"

"My name is Alena Svrček and I'm from Czechoslovakia where I was born in 1944, during the War. Thank you for saving me from the Czech secret police. They want to take me back to Prague, but I don't desire to return to that communist dictatorship. I'm here in Berlin, in order to skate in an international competition, so I'm lucky to get out for a few days. My parents told me not to come back, if I'm able to find a way to stay in the West."

"I'm glad that I can be of help. If my superiors or the West Berlin authorities are able to identify me, I could be in trouble for using a concealed weapon, to knock out the train lights. That was the reason why I insisted we get off at Kochstrasse. If it's okay with you, we're going to my place, until we can decide what we need to do with you."

"Thank you for saving me. Ultimately, I'd like to be able to go to England and train with Arnold Gerschwiler, the famous ice skating trainer at Richmond Ice Rink. He helped a former Czech skater, Alena (Ája) Vrzáñová, after she defected in 1949. She is very famous in the Czechoslovakian skating world and I've tried to emulate her style of skating."

"Tomorrow, I have to go to work and, while there, I'll contact some government acquaintances to determine if the British Consulate here in Berlin can help in getting you to England, on a political refugee status. In addition, I'll place some calls to Richmond Ice Rink and attempt to make contact with this Arnold Gerschwiler. While I'm gone, I suggest you don't go out, answer the door or open the drapes, just in case they trace us to my flat."

The taxi soon pulled up at the junction of Mariendorfor Damm and Eisenacher Strasse. After paying the driver and giving him a large tip for losing the tail, Kurt helped Alena out of the taxi. He picked up both of her bags and led her across the main street, toward his flat, on Machonstrasse.

After walking for a couple of minutes, Kurt opened the door to his flat and ushered Alena inside.

"It's not very large," Kurt said apologetically, as he showed her the small, second bedroom. "It doesn't get much use, but it's clean."

"This will be fine. I appreciate all you have done for me today," Alena replied.

"I'll bet you're hungry. I'll fix us both a sandwich, before we go to bed and get some sleep."

"That would be great. I haven't eaten since lunchtime, so I am kind of starving."

Kurt fixed them both a ham sandwich and, after they had eaten it, he bid her goodnight.

Kurt got into bed around 2300 and had trouble going to sleep, going over in his mind what had happened that evening.

He was still half awake at 2330, when his bedroom door slowly opened and Alena snuck into his room. She reached the bed, climbed in quietly and snuggled up close to him.

"I heard a noise outside the window and I'm afraid that the Czech secret police will come in to kidnap me," she whispered to Kurt. "Ája Vrzáňová had the same problem; she was almost spirited away in England. I hope you don't mind if I share your double bed, since it will make me feel much safer in here with you."

Kurt quickly thought, *"Well, at least she is eighteen years old. However, I have my reputation to uphold, so I had better be careful."*

"Perhaps the wind is blowing outside and it caused the noise you heard. I guess that will be okay, if it makes you feel more secure."

Soon, it wasn't long before she was soundly asleep. It took Kurt a little longer, before he drifted off into a fitful slumber.

****

At 0600 hours, Kurt's alarm clock sounded, waking him from a deep sleep. Alena, who had a youthful look about her, was still asleep in his bed. Kurt got up, shaved, showered and got ready to take the U-Bahn to the Olympic Stadium. He dressed in his civvies, so as not to attract attention from local inhabitants and he planned to change into his uniform at the office.

He had a quick breakfast of corn flakes, cup of coffee and a piece of toast with marmalade. Right before he left the flat for the station, he woke Alena up to tell her he was leaving.

"Don't forget that you must not open the door to anyone, answer the phone or open the curtains. There is food in the kitchen and I'll be back this afternoon at around 1700. Hopefully, I'll have good news about your ability to obtain political asylum in Great Britain. I need some particulars about you, such as full name, age, address in Prague, parents' names, etc."

"If you have pen and paper, I'll write it down for you immediately," she answered.

Kurt rounded them up, and she quickly scribbled down all the information he had requested.

Kurt then exited the flat and took the U-Bahn to the Olympic Stadium, where he changed, as planned, into his uniform. At 0845, Helga called to say that Colonel Thurman had to cancel the week's staff meeting.

Ian called Percival up at the MI6 facility and asked for a meeting, as soon as possible.

"How about at 1000 hours?" Percival asked.

"That will be great," Ian answered.

"May I ask what it's concerning?"

"It's a personal matter. I need to ask a favour of you,"

"Okay, I'll see you at 1000," replied Percival.

At the appointed time, Ian entered the MI6 facility and immediately went to Percival's office.

"What is it that's so important, Ian?" he asked.

"I have a female friend who's a Czechoslovakian ice skater. She has defected and wants to obtain entry into England. Could this be done under a political asylum procedure?"

"It certainly sounds like it could."

198

"Well, as a favour to me, could you help her out? I know you're acquainted with people at the British Consulate. It's important that she get out of Berlin as soon as possible." Ian then related to Percival what happened on the U-Bahn, the previous evening.

"Ian, you always seem to get into critical situations, where you need my help. Do you remember the time in Beirut, when you wanted to raid a warehouse stored with weapons?"

"Yes, I do. You saved my "skin" with that new, transistorized pager system."

"I'll check with someone I know at the consulate and see what they can do. It'll probably be a thirty day temporary political asylum card. During that time period, your friend would have to go up to London to be interviewed and vetted for permanent asylum. Hopefully by the end of today, I can get back to you on this. By the way, one of these days you'll have to return all the favours I've done for you."

Smiling, Ian replied, "Thanks for everything. Please call me at my office, when you have any news."

"Sure will."

Ian returned to his office and placed a call to his mother in England.

"Hi Mum, how are you and Dad doing? I hope you're both well."

"We're both fine. I'm sure you're not calling all the way from Berlin, just to ask that."

"You're correct. If everything works out, I will be visiting you both shortly, and I'll be bringing a young woman with me. I won't be able to stay long, but would you be willing to put this woman up for a week or two?"

"Probably we can, as we have two spare bedrooms. Who is she and what is her relationship to you?"

"Her name is Alena Svrček and she's an ice skater from Czechoslovakia, who is defecting from that communist country. She wants to study under Arnold Gerschwiler at the Richmond Ice Rink, if it's possible. It's a long story about how I became acquainted with her. However, to answer your question, she is not my girlfriend. I just happened to run into her. Do you know anyone at the rink?"

"I've met Violet Gerschwiler at a garden party and could give her a call about this situation. All her friends call her Vi. She's Arnold Gerschwiler's wife and they were involved with the defection of Ája Vrzáňová, back in the late 1940's."

"I'd appreciate it very much if you would call her. I'll let you know more details, as soon as I have them. Bye for now. Love you."

Ian hung up the phone and went back to work, analyzing reports of Soviet troop movements. Later that afternoon, Percival called Ian back with some good news.

"I've managed to persuade a friend at the consulate to issue a thirty day asylum card. With it, there will be a list of instructions, together with a name, address and phone number of an officer, at the Foreign Ministry in London. Your friend will have to appear before this officer, to be vetted within the thirty day timeframe. If she doesn't, she'll be arrested and deported, probably back to Czechoslovakia. Is this clear?"

"Certainly, I'll explain it to her in German. As far as I know, I don't believe she speaks English."

"On Wednesday, there is a special flight out of RAF Gatow, which leaves at 1000 hours. It will be an RAF Dakota piloted by civilians and this flight, CR107, must not be mentioned to anyone. This is critical, especially until we get out of East German airspace. I'll be on the flight with some other people. You and this Alena must sit in the rear and not make contact with any of the other passengers. Is this clear?"

"Yes, Percival, I appreciate everything you have done for us."

"Meet me at the entrance to RAF Gatow at 0830 sharp and I'll give you the papers for Alena. I'll then escort you both to the special waiting room where, it should be noted, cameras are off limits. When flight CR107 is called, get up and follow the other people. Do not speak or look directly at any of them. In addition, you must wear civvies; no uniform. If you need a uniform in England, you must pack it in your suitcase."

"Okay, I'll see you on Wednesday morning at RAF Gatow. Bye."

Ian hung up and immediately called Colonel Thurman for permission to take a week's leave. He actually hadn't taken any time off in over a year.

"Colonel Thurman's office, Helga speaking, how may I help you?"

"Hello Helga, this is Lieutenant Black. May I speak with the colonel?"

"Sorry lieutenant, he is out until tomorrow."

"Helga, it's very important that I be allowed to take one week of leave, starting as of now. If he calls in, could you check with him and determine if it's okay. It is for a personal reason and I'll tell him all about it when I return."

In about an hour, Helga called Ian back.

"Lieutenant, I just talked with the colonel and he said it was okay for you to take some time off. He said that you should make sure you are back next Monday, for the usual staff meeting."

"Thanks Helga, I'm sure that I'll be back by then. I'm flying to England Wednesday morning and will be back by Saturday or Sunday, depending on the available flights."

"Have a great trip."

Since it was 1730, Ian decided to quit for the day and return to his flat. He changed back into some civvies and packed a uniform in his American style B4 bag that he had managed to obtain a few months ago. He walked to the U-Bahn station and travelled to the Westphalweg stop. From there it was only a couple of minutes walk to his flat.

As he opened the door, he discovered Alena asleep on the sofa, with the black and white television on the one local station; it must have been boring. When he entered the kitchen and made some noise, she woke up and came in to see him.

"Alena, we are going to England on Wednesday morning. It's all arranged and you'll have a temporary permit to stay there for thirty days, during which time you will have to go to London, to obtain a permanent political asylum document. It's important that you keep out of sight, until we are on the way. You never know if the Czech secret police will try to get you back. I'll be going with you on the flight and take you to a residence in Richmond, where the lady there knows Arnold Gerschwiler's wife."

"This all sounds wonderful; like a dream come true. What airline will we be flying on? Will I have an opportunity to purchase a few things before the flight?"

"First, this is not a regular airline. It is a special flight being put on by the RAF, and the rules are that you must speak to no one, unless spoken to. It would be best if you do not look directly at the people, in the front of the plane. I know this sounds all very mysterious, but those are the requirements. As far as purchasing a few items, if you give me a list, I'll go out and buy them for you tomorrow. I'm not going to work until next week, as I managed to get some time off from my boss. Now how about some dinner, I'm not the best of cooks but I can create something for us."

"Let me put something together; my mother spent hours teaching how to cook," she said, with a smile.

Alena cooked an excellent meal and later they both watched the ARD channel that was transmitting a couple of American westerns, with German audio. After the late news programme went off, Kurt and Alena decided it was time to turn in for the night. This time however Alena came straight to Kurt's bedroom and climbed into the double bed wearing her clothes.

"This is a lot more comfortable than the bed in the spare bedroom, plus I feel safer here. You don't mind do you?" she asked.

Kurt replied, with a concerned look, "Okay, but you mustn't make a habit of this. I have my reputation to uphold, you know."

It wasn't long before both of them were sound asleep and neither woke up until around 0900, the next morning. Since Kurt didn't have to go to work that day, he had not set the alarm clock.

Alena was the first to wake up, when the sunlight streamed through a crack in the drapes, and it shone on her eyes. She rose quietly and went into the kitchen, where she cooked breakfast for both of them. As soon as it was ready, she went and woke Kurt up. After breakfast, Alena made a short list of items she needed Kurt to buy for her.

"Again, as I said yesterday, please don't answer the door or telephone. I'm sorry to keep you in here like a prisoner, but I'd really be upset, if some Czech secret service kidnapped you and spirited you back behind the Iron Curtain."

"You're right, Kurt. I'm looking forward to going to England tomorrow and don't want to jeopardize it."

Kurt went out to some nearby shops to buy her necessities, and a few things for himself. Upon returning to the flat, Kurt taught Alena how to play Canasta, and they spent the afternoon trying to outfox each other.

That evening after dinner, which Alena cooked, they sat on the sofa discussing each of their hopes, dreams and backgrounds.

Alena said "My lifetime ambition is to be the best skater I can be, eventually emigrating to America and becoming an ice show star like my fellow countrywoman, Ája Vrzáňová. As I mentioned previously, I was born in 1944, during the War, and I've never enjoyed real freedom. First, it was the Nazis and then the Communists, Czechoslovakia hasn't really been free since 1938. Thanks to you, Kurt, I have the opportunity to actually live in a free country and live out my dreams."

"Alena, look me straight in the face and into my eyes, while answering a simple, but very serious, question. Are you an agent for the Czech secret police?" He had learned how to spot a liar in his classes at the Intelligence Academy.

"No, I'm not and never have been. You should know that by now."

"Well, I asked it, because I have to be careful about what I'm going to tell you. I have something to confess," Kurt responded. "You will find out tomorrow anyway, but I had a reason to hide my identity. My name is not Kurt, and I'm not a German civilian working for a West German company. My real name is Ian and I'm actually in the British Army, here in Berlin. I can't tell you what my duties are, as it is forbidden. Tomorrow, when we reach England, the couple you'll be staying with is my mother and father. He works for an aerospace company, having been in the RAF during the War."

"I suspected something when you produced that gun on the U-Bahn. A normal German civilian probably would not have access to a weapon."

"You know Alena, I had a girlfriend in Cyprus four years ago whom I was going to marry. However, she was shot and killed by a terrorist in the capital; she died in my arms. I've never really recovered from that tragedy, because the bullet was actually aimed at me. Ever since then, I've not had a serious relationship with another girl."

"I'm sorry to hear that Ian, I'm sure you loved her dearly. I hope I may call you Ian from now on."

"Yes, you may call me Ian in private and at my parent's home but, in public or around other people, please call me Kurt. I don't want my cover blown. By the way, it's nothing personal, but I'm sure there could never be anything serious between us; even though I let you sleep in my bed. I hope you understand."

"I completely understand everything now. Will it be okay if I sleep in your bed again tonight, since your room is considerably warmer than the spare bedroom? We are and will be just close friends."

"Yes, that will be okay. Remember, we need to get up early, as we have to be at RAF Gatow by 0830, to meet a colleague of mine. Please do not ask his name for, if he gave you one, it would only be an alias anyway. I'll set the alarm for 0530, which should give us plenty of time to get ready and travel to the airfield."

****

The next morning, after eight hours of sleep, they rose as soon as the clock sounded and quickly got dressed. While Alena was doing her makeup, Ian prepared a standard breakfast of cereal, toast and coffee. At 0715, they walked out of Ian's flat with their bags and soon found an empty taxi. They climbed in and Ian told the driver to take them to the main gate at RAF Gatow.

As they went northward, Ian looked through the rear window of the cab, to make sure they were not being followed. At 0820, the taxi pulled up at the Gatow airfield main gate, in plenty of time for them to meet up with Percival. After paying off the cabbie, they got out of the cab and walked to the RAF MP, standing in front of the gate. They stood there waiting for Percival to show up. Promptly at 0830, he showed up in a another taxi.

"Kurt, I'm glad you made it on time. The organization running this flight doesn't like any delays, for any reason."

"I'd like you to meet Alena, as he beckoned her to step forward."

Percival and Alena shook hands, but he did not give her his name, even though it was an alias. Percival was always very careful. Ian found out some time ago from John that Percival used to be a colonel in the Intelligence Corps and transitioned to MI6, due to the lack of any additional promotion opportunities.

"Here are her papers to get her through the gate here and into England. I hope you have told her that the transit identification card permits her to remain in the country for only thirty days," Percival said.

"Yes, I have already given her instructions on what to do, and I'll explain them again at my parent's home. I'm sure Arnold Gerschwiler is also familiar with the requirements, since he has had previous émigrés under his wing," Ian replied.

"Good, I'm glad to hear that. Let's go in and find the waiting lounge for the flight."

The RAF MP looked at their IDs and allowed them to pass. A waiting van, which Percival had ordered, drove them to the Gatow departure hall. They entered the building and went up to the flight desk, where they were directed to gate D-4. There they had to show their IDs again, before they were permitted in. When they actually entered the secure area, their bags were taken away from them for inspection and loaded on the plane. The door to the lounge was guarded by a RAF MP, and a stern looking man dressed in a suit and tie. They entered the lounge area which had frosted windows, so no one could see in. All ready seated in there were about ten men and a woman, all huddled together talking. Off in one corner was a man, a woman and two children, together with an official looking man again dressed in a dark suit and striped tie.

"Sit over there," Percival said, pointed out two chairs in another corner of the lounge. "When they call the flight, just follow the other passengers and find seats in the back of the plane. Please don't talk to anyone, except yourselves."

"Okay Percival," Ian whispered. "I've already explained the flight rules to Alena. She doesn't speak much English anyway, just Czech and German."

"Good, I'll see you at the other end at RAF Northolt." With that Percival went and joined the other ten people talking amongst themselves.

In approximately thirty minutes, flight CR107 was called by a civilian; everyone rose and lined up at the departure gate, leading to the ramp. Their IDs were again checked thoroughly and the names crossed off the passenger list. Ian and Alena were the last ones through the security. The man looked at her, the skate bag and then at her temporary transit pass, after which he crossed her name off the list.

The man looked up at her again and smiling said, in Czech, "Have a good flight, Alena. Oh, by the way, I hope you have a happy skating life."

It took her totally by surprise to hear someone speaking in her native tongue. "Thank you very much, sir. I hope I will."

Ian and Alena, who was still carrying her valuable skates in the bag, followed the other passengers out to the RAF Dakota. They boarded the plane and sat by themselves, in the rear of the Douglas aircraft. Soon the engines were started up, and the ground crew wheeled away the portable starting generator.

The captain came on the intercom, "Fasten your seatbelts please. We'll be taking off shortly for Northolt."

The one stewardess came through the cabin and checked that all passengers were strapped in. The pilot taxied the plane to the end of the runway two six right, checked the engines and took off in a westerly direction, right on time at 1000 hours. It circled the field and headed for the main access corridor toward West Germany. After about thirty minutes, Percival came down into the rear of the plane and approached the, man, his wife and two children.

"We're now over West Germany, so you can all relax. We'll soon be winging our way to England."

"Thank you sir," the man replied in broken English, looking relieved that the plane hadn't been shot down by the Russians.

It finally dawned on Ian that this was probably the rocket scientist and his family. *"I'll have to ask Percival one of these days,"* he thought.

Percival then came over to Ian and Alena, telling them that they were out of the hundred miles of East German airspace and were headed for England. After a smooth, three hour flight, the plane landed at RAF Station Northolt, where the passengers disembarked and headed for the arrival terminal. There they had to show there documents to an immigration official. Most of them were waved through, except for the man, his wife and children, together with Ian and Alena.

Their documents were studied more intently and then were stamped approved. Ian and Alena retrieved their bags and thanked Percival for the flight, when he came over to say goodbye.

Looking at Kurt, he said, "I'll see you soon, I hope."

"Thanks for the flight. Again, we appreciate your help in getting Alena here into England."

"You're welcome," he said, as he turned and walked away.

Ian, with Alena following behind him, went over to the RAF booking department to see about a flight back to Gatow. It turned out there was a flight on the Saturday, at 1100 hours, that was only half booked. The RAF corporal placed Ian's name on the passenger list.

"Will the young lady be travelling with you also, sir?" he asked.

"No, she's staying in England. It'll just be me."

"Very good, sir, have a pleasant couple of days here," the corporal replied.

Ian and Alena walked out of the arrival hall, carrying their bags and found an unoccupied cab, waiting in the taxi rank. They climbed in and Ian gave the driver his parent's address in Richmond. It took the driver about forty five minutes to drive the fourteen miles, since it was in the afternoon and some people were already getting out of work.

The taxi stopped right in front of his parent's home and, after paying the fare, Ian helped Alena out of the rear. He picked up their luggage from the platform next to the driver and walked up to the front door. Since he had forgotten to bring his key, he rang the doorbell.

It wasn't long before his mother came to the door and opened it.

"Ian, I'm so glad to see you," she said, as she gave him a big hug. "This must be Alena. Does she speak any English?"

"Very little, Mum. If you speak slowly and use simple words, she'll probably understand you."

Then looking at the girl beside him, Ian's mother took her hand in hers, and said slowly, "Alena, welcome to England. We're so glad you could come and stay with us."

Alena smiled and said, "Thank you ma'am."

Ian's mother ushered them into the house and showed Alena to a spare bedroom, where she could place her luggage.

The next two days went fairly quickly. On Thursday evening, after Alena had gone to bed, Ian related to his parents about how he had met and saved her.

On the Friday evening, Arnold and Vi Gerschwiler came over for drinks and dinner. Alena and Mr. Gerschwiler seemed to hit it off, since he spoke German. He agreed to take her on as a pupil and help her as much as he could to achieve her goals. In fact, he thought it would be best if she stayed with Vi and him, as Ája Vrzáňová had done, after she had defected.

On Saturday morning, Ian got up fairly early, dressed in his uniform and ate a quick breakfast that his mother had prepared for him. Alena was still asleep upstairs in the spare bedroom. As he said goodbye to his parents and was just about to walk out the door, Alena came down the stairs, in her nightgown and robe. She went up to Ian and gave him a big hug and a kiss on his cheek.

"Thanks for everything, Ian," she whispered in German. "I hope I'll get to see you again sometime. You look very smart and handsome in your uniform."

Replying he said, "It's been a pleasure helping you get to England and connecting you with Arnold Gerschwiler. Good luck in your skating career. I'll be watching the sports news, for anything that has to do with ice skating."

Ian picked up his B4 bag containing his civvies and walked down the front steps to the waiting cab. His flight back to Berlin was uneventful, and it gave him Sunday to recuperate, before he went back to work. He had to attend his CO's staff meeting and afterward, relate what had happened during the past eight days.

19

Ferreting Out A Mole

On Monday morning, Lieutenant Black travelled to the Berlin Brigade Headquarters from his flat, for his COs normal staff meeting. In attendance, as usual, were all of Colonel Thurman's direct reports, plus John from MI6.

After making some announcements about the need for the development of more accurate assessments on future Warsaw Pact troop movements, and what they might mean for the security of Western Europe, he opened it up for individual reports. Ian Black was the last to give an accounting of his activities, since the previous staff meeting two weeks prior.

"Colonel, first I want to thank you for letting me take a few days leave, at the spur of the moment. It was very important and I can now tell you why. Eight days ago, I was travelling on the U-Bahn, after visiting a friend in the north part of Berlin. At one of the stops, a young woman entered the carriage, which I was in, followed by two rough looking men. After a while, she mouthed "Please help me" in German. When the train reached the Friedrichstrasse station, the two goons grabbed her by the arms and started to hustle her out, onto the platform. I pulled my Browning automatic and told them to leave her alone. They were so taken aback that they let her go and ran out to obtain help from the East German guard. Not wanting to fire my weapon, I broke the lights of the compartment out with the butt of my pistol. The East German soldier got off two shots, from his weapon, before the train left the station and headed south toward West Berlin. In the meantime I had pushed the young woman down on the floorboards. When the U-Bahn reached the first station in West Berlin, we got off and took a taxi back to my flat. On the ride through the streets of Berlin, I had to pay the driver a large tip, in order for him to lose a tail.

This woman is an ice skater from Czechoslovakia and she wanted to defect to Britain. I put her up in my flat for a couple of days and managed to get her on a special flight to Britain, with her using a thirty day alien permit. Percival managed to obtain this pass from an acquaintance in the British Consulate."

The colonel interrupted Ian, "Did it ever occur to you that this woman might be a swallow?"

"Yes sir, it did. In fact the last evening, I did look her squarely into the eyes and asked her if she was a foreign agent. At the intelligence academy, they taught us how to spot liars. It appeared what she had told me was the truth."

"Mr. Black, you know you could have got into serious trouble, if you had discharged your weapon on the U-Bahn."

"Yes, I am aware of that. This is one reason why we got off at the first station in the West. I was concerned the West Berlin police would come on board and start asking questions. Also, we weren't sure if the East Germans hadn't called ahead, for an agent to pick us up. As it turned out, we were followed for a distance, in the taxi."

"So where is this young Czech woman now?" probed Colonel Thurman.

"Well sir, currently she is in England being tutored by the famous Arnold Gerschwiler. She has to appear before a Foreign Ministry official within thirty days, in order to be vetted and obtain permanent political asylum."

"Thank you Mr. Black for the account of your activities. We'll probably speak of this more in private. We don't want to take up the rest of our attendees' valuable time."

"There is one more subject I would like to raise if I may."

"Will it take long?"

"It could sir, but I believe it's important. If you remember, I brought up the subject of a mole, named Drache, in a West Berlin military organization or the mayor's office, during a previous meeting."

"You may continue Mr. Black, but please make it short."

"Well sir, I was standing in the shower this morning and came up with, what I believe, is a brilliant idea."

"Let's hope it's better than some of your other scatterbrained ideas, Mr. Black. You're lucky to have a shower in your flat; most of us don't, we only have bathtubs."

At this, everyone in the room laughed at the colonel's comment.

Ian continued, "I suggest, with the help of our Intelligence friends, that we plant three different, but similar stories, and see which one is pounced on, by the East Germans and Russians. This type of disinformation methodology has worked before, notably during the battle for Midway island.

First, we could get the British Berlin Brigade administration to spread a story among its officers that the Defence Ministry, under orders from the Prime Minister, has ordered an additional fifty Centurion Mk7 battle tanks to be sent to Berlin, within the next two months. At the same time we get the Americans to spread the word, at their Clay Headquarters compound, that the president has ordered forty M60 Patton battle tanks be sent to their sector of Berlin. Finally, we could spread a story in the West Berlin mayor's office that a request is being made of the West German Defence Ministry to send thirty US made M48 Patton battle tanks to the city. All three stories should stress that these responses are due to the East building the Wall, and raising tensions throughout the region.

After these stories have been planted, and this is the critical part, we need John, and the listening post on Teufelsberg, to listen for and decipher messages from Berlin to Moscow. We need to know which story is sent to Moscow, and then we will know where to look for this Drache."

"This is an ingenious plan, Ian. Not so scatterbrained after all. What do the rest of you think? John, is this feasible on your part, since you'll be a key player in this plot?"

"We can pick up transmissions from East Berlin to Moscow and some of them we are able to decode. Our exact capability should remain a closely guarded secret, colonel."

"I understand, but if I hear you correctly, you might be able to determine which story is relayed to Moscow. If you can, then we will know in which organization the mole is buried. We can then come up with another plan to determine who the Drache actually is."

"That's correct, colonel," John replied.

"Do the rest of you agree it is worthwhile to attempt this deception, in order to unmask this Drache?"

"Yes" they all replied in unison.

"Very well, then. Mr. Black, why don't you come to my office at 1300 and we'll discuss this plan further, as well as your escapade of the past week. That's all for today, gentlemen. I'll see you all next week, same time."

After eating lunch in the Officers' Mess, Ian went to see Colonel Thurman in the Berlin Brigade Headquarters building, at the appointed time.

He walked in and said, "Hello Helga, how are you doing?"

"Alright, I'm glad you're on time. He's been busy today," she replied. "You can go right on in lieutenant."

"Thanks, Helga," Ian replied, as he went up to the inner door office and knocked.

"Enter," the colonel said, with a clear, loud voice.

Ian opened the door, marched in and gave him a salute.

"Take a seat, Ian," he commanded, as he casually returned the salute.

"Let's talk about your plan for flushing out the mole. How specifically do you plan to spread the disinformation through the targeted organizations?"

"Well, sir, I propose selecting one senior, trusted officer that we are sure is not the mole and have him spread the rumour about the battle tank shipments, using the grapevine approach. Preferably, this officer would be the second in command, whose statements would be taken as gospel."

"Do you believe that this mole is male or female?"

"I don't think we can tell by the name Drache (Dragon). It could be of either sex, and that's probably why the Stasi selected the codename."

"You know the British and American militaries use some German staff, mainly secretaries, but my understanding is all have been carefully vetted, to insure none of them are Nazis or Communists," continued the colonel.

"Sir, I totally agree. However, the Stasi also knows that we meticulously check them out, and they train their moles, including swallows, to lie convincingly. They only select personnel whose records are clean as a whistle."

"Okay, Mr. Black, we'll proceed with your plan. I just hope it works, since having a mole amongst us could be dangerous to our security here in West Berlin, and maybe in Germany. How do you intend to go ahead with your disinformation plan?"

"First, I'll approach Brigadier Clemens of the Berlin Brigade and explain the strategy for exposing the mole to him, assuming it is embedded in the Brigade Headquarters.

I'll request that he start spreading the rumour, via the grapevine, that the Defence Ministry is thinking about sending an additional fifty Centurion Mk7 battle tanks to West Berlin. In order to fortify the British forces in the event of a Soviet attack.

May I state to him that you approve of this plan, sir? It could be slightly awkward for a lowly lieutenant to make such a request to a brigadier."

"Yes, you may. In fact I am fairly well acquainted with Brigadier Clemens and will call him ahead of your visit, to grease the skids so to speak."

"That would be very helpful, sir."

"How about the American headquarters, what is your idea there?"

"I'm acquainted with a Colonel Tracy Haga of the 513th Intelligence Corps Group, along with a Major Vass and Captain Silverman. I'll request a meeting with them and explain the disinformation plan to them. It should be of interest to them, if they believe they could have a mole in their midst. This fact has been explained to them in an earlier meeting, but no specific action, as far as I know, has been taken to ferret out this spy. I'll request that Colonel Haga explain the issue to his superior and determine if he would spread the rumour through a grapevine that the Pentagon is planning to send forty M60 Patton battle tanks to Berlin, in order to beef up their forces opposing the Soviets. I believe I can convince the colonel that it is in the best interest of the Americans to find this spy, before he or she creates problems."

"If you need my help in your conversations with the Americans, please let me know. Also, assuming I can contact him, I will call this Colonel Haga and explain the urgency of the matter. I believe that I met him once at a security conference. How do you plan to proceed spreading the disinformation throughout the West Berlin mayor's office?"

"My contact in the BND is a man with the codename "Franz" and, if you remember, we did him a favour by coming up with the snowplow idea. On top of that, Captain Swiderski and I ran interference in order to draw away some of the Stasi, from the Bornholmer crossing point into the French sector. He owes us some support in this matter of the mole. I'll contact him and ask him to work with the mayor's office, to spread the rumour that the West German Defence Ministry is planning to relocate thirty U.S. manufactured M48 Patton tanks to the West Berlin theatre. Incidentally, the snow plow plan did work, and they managed to get the rocket scientist out, together with his wife and two children."

"Yes, I was briefed on the result of the escape into the French sector, over the Bösebrücke," replied Colonel Thurman. "One part of your deception strategy you have not mentioned. Do you believe John will be able to pick up any communications by the East Germans to Moscow?"

"This is where I believe this disinformation plan is fairly simple and ingenious. John and his analysts do not have to be able to read the entire message sent to Moscow. They just have to look for the following – Centurion Mk7, Patton M60 or Patton M48. If there is only one mole, then the name and number of the battle tank will indicate which organization has the spy."

"It seems you have given this plan some thought, Ian. If you need any assistance on my part, not already mentioned, please contact me immediately. As soon as we find this mole, the better it'll be for all of us. You have not mentioned the French sector and the French armed forces. Don't you believe the mole could be located in their organization?"

"I left them out sir, as their military group in West Berlin is small and, at the moment, the Soviets view the main threat coming from the Americans or the British. If the initial disinformation plan doesn't work, then I'll consider conducting one involving the French."

"Good, now please explain what happened with this situation on the U-Bahn and your display of a weapon."

"Well, sir, as I explained in your staff meeting, I was travelling southward on the U6 train, when it stopped at the Afrikanische Strasse and this young woman entered my carriage, with two rough looking goons. She didn't look very happy, but she gave me a smile that caught my attention. As the train picked up speed, the goons studied the U-Bahn station chart close to the ceiling of the carriage. She looked at me and smiling mouthed in German "Help Me." Well, I couldn't ignore her as I've a penchant for damsels in distress, ever since my fiancé was shot by a terrorist in Cyprus. When the train pulled into the Friedrichstrasse station, the goons tried to drag her out of the compartment into East Berlin. I pulled my gun and told them to leave her alone. They ran out of the train to get help from an East German soldier, who was standing on the platform with his weapon. I knocked the lights of the carriage out with the butt of my pistol and pushed the young lady to the floor. The soldier let off a couple of rounds, before the doors closed and the train took off for West Berlin. At no time did I discharge my gun.

The rest of the story is that Percival, in MI6, managed to obtain for her a temporary permit to enter Britain. He also got us on a special plane, I believe operated by MI6, and we flew to Britain. That's why I needed the leave I asked for. Also on the plane, I saw a man, his wife and two children, whom I figured were the rocket scientist and family. Of course, I haven't mentioned that to anyone but you, sir."

"I haven't heard about your escapade on the U-Bahn from anyone else, so I have to assume the West Berlin police don't know exactly what happened. I'm sure the East Germans or the Czech Secret Service have not made any complaints to them either. I will consider the matter closed, unless somehow it is brought to my attention by some outside authority. By the way, I have heard the story about your fiancé in Cyprus, and I'm sorry you couldn't save her."

"Thank you, sir. May I now leave and put the disinformation plan into action? The sooner we catch this mole the better."

"Yes, go ahead and I'll see you next Monday at the normal staff meeting. Again, let me know if you need my assistance on this deception."

Ian left the colonel's office in the Administration Building and returned to his room in the London Block, to put into action his disinformation plan.

First, he called Franz and asked if he could meet with him, as soon as possible. They set up a meeting at a small, quiet café, not far from the Olympic Stadium complex, for 1700 hours. Next, he contacted Brigadier Clemens's office and asked the secretary if he could have a meeting with him the next morning, at 1000 hours. Finally, he phoned Captain Silverman at the American 513th Intelligence Corps Group, located at the Clay Headquarters, in the south of Berlin. He scheduled a meeting with him for 1400 hours, the next afternoon, and requested that Colonel Haga together with Major Vass attend, if they were available.

At 1645, Ian walked out of the Olympic stadium complex and headed for the small café, where he was going to meet Franz. He found a small table in a corner of the restaurant and cleared it completely off. He then checked under the table for any hidden microphones. Exactly at 1700 hours, Franz came in and found Ian seated at the corner table.

"Hello Franz, I'm glad you could make it. I've checked the table for bugs and I'm sure it's clean, so let's get down to business. We need a favour from you, to help unmask a mole that we believe exists in one of three organizations," Ian said, speaking very softly, so as not to be overheard. "We are planning a disinformation campaign and need your assistance in planting some information, in the West Berlin mayor's office."

219

"I might be able to do that. What is the plan, and what information do you want me to spread through the mayors' offices and departments? Of course, I'll have to check with the mayor to get his approval, but I'm sure he'll have no problem, when I explain that there's a possible mole in his organization."

"As I said, we don't know which organization this mole is embedded in. Therefore, we've created three different fictitious scenarios; one for each organization. The disinformation will be spread by the grapevine methodology, throughout the personnel located in the offices. By monitoring the communications traffic between East Berlin and Moscow, we hope to find which office contains the spy. We would like you to spread a rumour through the mayor's office that the West German Defence Ministry is going to move thirty M48 Patton battle tanks from West Germany to West Berlin. The purpose being that, if there is trouble over the wall, the West will be in a better position to blunt the Soviets potential attack."

"I think I can spread that rumour. Do you want me to initiate the disinformation, by telling people not to spread it? This generally means that they will spread it and tell the next person not to pass it on."

"That's the whole idea. We want the mole to think that they're lucky to obtain this information and hopefully they'll pass it on to their controller, in the Stasi. Whichever tale is sent on to Moscow will indicate the organization that has the mole, who is in all probability a Raven or a Swallow."

"Okay, I'll do what you ask. To make sure I have it correct, you want me to spread around the mayor's office that the West German Defence Ministry is moving thirty U.S. manufactured M48 tanks to West Berlin."

"You've got it correct. Franz, we appreciate what you're doing for us."

"Well, we're all on the same side. Just one thing more though. When do you want me to start the rumour?"

"Two days from now. That'll give me time to get the other two organizations on board."

"Great, I'll see you later. I'd better go now," Franz said, as he rose from the table, shook Ian's hand and left the café.

The next morning, at 1000 hours, Lieutenant Black went to see Brigadier Charles Clemens, who was the second in command of the Berlin Brigade. He, in turn, reported to the GOC, a major general, of the British Berlin Brigade. As usual, Ian went into the outer office where there was a "gate keeper" by the name of Giselle Schmitt. She was fairly young with auburn hair and a great figure. Ian guessed she was in her early thirties.

"May I help you, lieutenant?" she asked in English.

"I have an appointment to see Brigadier Clemens at 1000 hours."

"Yes, you're on his schedule. Your CO, Colonel Thurman called yesterday afternoon to discuss your visit with the brigadier. Let me inform him that you're here."

Giselle pressed a lever on the intercom and said, "Sir, Lieutenant Black is here to see you."

"Ah, yes, send him in," the brigadier replied.

"You may go in," Giselle said to Ian.

Ian walked up to the door, entered the inner office and closed it behind him. He marched up, stood in front of the brigadier and gave him one of his best salutes.

"Lieutenant Ian Black reporting, sir."

"Take a seat Mr. Black. What can I do for you? Colonel Thurman called me yesterday and gave me a quick outline of your plan."

"Sir, I've come to ask for your help in unmasking a Stasi mole that we have been made aware of by a shot Stasi agent, who unfortunately died before we got the full name. The only thing he told me before he died was the codename Drache, or Dragon, and the beginning of the word "Bri". It could be the start of a first or last name for a country or organization, like Britain. We believe this spy is in one of three organizations; either in the British Brigade Headquarters here at the Stadium, the American Brigade Clay Headquarters or the West Berlin mayor's office."

"Obviously Mr. Black, if the mole is in this Administration Building or the Stadium complex, we need to expose him or her, as soon as possible. How can I specifically assist you in this matter?"

"Well sir, we're asking each of the three possible organizations to spread a rumour and, in fact, encourage the spread of it through the grapevine, so to speak. Perhaps you could call a meeting of all your senior officers and inform them that the Defence Ministry has decided to move fifty Centurion battle tanks into West Berlin, to face the aggressive posture of the Soviets. You can tell them this information can be given to those personnel that they feel appropriate. The whole purpose of this plan is to spread the word, without telling anyone it's a hoax. As long as the mole believes it, he or she will get word to the Stasi, who in turn will communicate the information to Moscow. We should be able to determine in which organization the spy works, from the communication that will be picked up by MI6 at the Teufelsberg listening post."

"You know Mr. Black, I could get hell for spreading a rumour, such as this, from the GOC or the Prime Minister himself. It could create a situation where the Ruskies believe we are going to attack them. By the way do you know when the name, Ruskie, first came into use?"

"I believe it was in the Crimea war, about one hundred years ago. As far as the risk of a clash with the Soviets, I think it's small compared to allowing the mole to remain hidden. I don't believe the Russians would do anything until they see the Centurions actually here in Berlin."

"Very well, I'll do as you ask. Let's hope it pinpoints where the mole is located. When do you want me to spread this rumour?"

"If it's convenient sir, tomorrow morning would be the ideal time, for you to hold the meeting with your officers."

"You know this request by a lieutenant to a brigadier is somewhat out of the norm, but, since Colonel Thurman discussed it with me, I will do as you ask."

"Thank you, sir." Ian rose gave a snappy salute, walked out of the office and said goodbye to Giselle, who smiled at him. Ian thought, as he returned to his office in the London Block, *"I wonder if she's the mole and a swallow? I hope not for the brigadier's sake."*

In the afternoon of the same day, he drove in a dark green, army Land Rover down to the American Clay Headquarters complex. As he pulled up at the gate, the American MP approached him and asked to see his ID, which he checked against his visitor's log.

"You may go in, sir. You are expected in conference room 12D," the MP said with an accent, Ian didn't recognize.

"Thanks, sergeant. By the way, I don't suppose you're from Tennessee, are you? My mother was originally from Tennessee."

"No, I'm from Long beach, California. It's a long way from there, about two thousand miles."

Ian drove on into the Headquarters complex thinking, *"I wonder what the population is of Tennessee. I haven't met too many American soldiers from there."*

Ian parked, walked into the Administration Building and soon found room 12D. When he entered the conference area, he found that Colonel Haga, Major Vass and Captain Silverman were already assembled around the table, talking about military matters.

"Come on in, lieutenant. We don't have much time, so please get to the issue at hand immediately. We have another meeting scheduled for 1600 hours, at another location," said Captain Silverman.

"Then I'll be brief, gentlemen. As I've mentioned in a previous meeting, based on some words from a dying Stasi

223

agent who was trying defect, there is a mole, named Drache, or Dragon in English, somewhere in West Berlin. All indications are that this spy is located in one of three organizations; the West Berlin mayor's Office, the British Berlin Brigade at the Stadium or the American Forces here at Clay Headquarters. We have a plan to determine which organization this mole is hiding in.

Specifically, we want to spread rumours through the three organizations that some battle tanks are being moved to West Berlin. So far, we have an agreement for the West Berlin mayor's office to disseminate the fact that thirty M48 Patton tanks are going to be moved into Berlin. Also, the British Berlin Brigade will announce, through an officers meeting, at the Stadium that fifty Centurion battle tanks are going to be sent from Britain to Berlin. We would like you to announce through an officers meeting here at Clay that the Pentagon is planning to send an additional forty M60 Patton battle tanks to Berlin, in anticipation of a more aggressive Soviet posture.

Obviously, all these rumours are false, but the Drache will not know that. The Teufelsberg listening post will be on alert for any communications between East Berlin and Moscow, about the transfer of these tanks. Assuming there is only one mole, and we hope that's true, then the contents of the message to Moscow will indicate which organization contains the Stasi mole. Once we know that, we can work to uncover the spy, within the government or military agency.

Can we count on you to spread this rumour about the forty M60 tanks being shipped to Berlin? It is extremely important we uncover this mole, before they can damage our defence plans, in the eventuality of a European war."

"Well lieutenant, I can agree the purpose of this plan is extremely important. However, no one in this room has the authority to spread such a rumour, even though it is a hoax. It will have to be cleared with Colonel Waple and Major General James Gavin, Commandant of the Berlin Brigade.

I'm sure you realize the possibility of starting an escalation, just by passing a rumour around through the grapevine."

"Yes colonel, but the danger of leaving a mole in place is also extremely risky, to the West's overall plan, for countering any action the Soviets might take."

"When do you want this rumour spread through the grapevine?" asked Colonel Haga.

"Tomorrow, if you can do it, or as soon as possible thereafter. The other two organizations will spread their rumours, and MI6 will start monitoring the communications, starting tomorrow. They may not be able to decode every word, but they will just be looking mainly for the name of the tank, and the mole's name."

"I'll get with the two people mentioned and obtain their approval, if I can."

"Colonel, this plan has been approved by my CO, Colonel Thurman and General Gavin can contact him, if he wants reassurance that this plan is legit and worth the effort."

"We have to go now to our other meeting. Captain Silverman or Major Vass will be in contact with you, to let you know our decision."

"Thank you for your time, colonel. I trust and hope the decision will be a positive one."

Ian shook hands with the American officers and left the Clay compound, to head back to the Olympic Stadium complex.

The next morning, Ian received a phone call from Major Vaas who confirmed that they would go ahead with the spread of the rumour, at a general officers meeting later in the afternoon. Obviously, the Commandant of the American Berlin Brigade considered the risks were worth the unmasking of the mole.

As soon as he had confirmation from the Americans that they would proceed to spread this disinformation, Ian called John at MI6, to schedule a meeting.

"John, I need to meet with you as soon as possible about the monitoring of communications traffic between Berlin and Moscow."

"I have time at 1130 hours and I'll meet you in the conference room, close to the entrance."

"That sounds great. I'll see you then."

Later that morning, Ian went to the MI6 facility to meet with John. He entered the conference room to find John in there already, waiting for him.

"I've received confirmation from the three organizations, we discussed earlier, that they will spread the rumours, starting later today or tomorrow.

The three basic rumours are:

1. Britain will send fifty Centurion MK7 tanks to Berlin.
2. America will ship forty M60 Patton tanks to Berlin.
3. FRG will move thirty M48 Patton tanks to Berlin.

If you can monitor the communications traffic from Berlin to Moscow at Teufelsberg and determine which message is sent, then we'll know where the mole is. It won't matter if you can't decode the entire message. The key words will be Drache, fifty Centurion Mk7, forty American M60 and thirty West German M48."

"How long do you want us to look for these key words?"

"I'd think that two weeks will be enough. Either by then the rumours will have been spread or they are not going to be. The other alternative would be that the mole has not heard the disinformation or has discounted it, as not being important."

"Okay, Ian, we'll monitor the communications between Berlin and Moscow, and I'll get back to you as soon as we hear or see anything, with those words."

"Thanks John, I'll await your call."

Ian went back to his office to catch up on some paperwork about Soviet troop movements that he had set aside for a few days, while working on the disinformation strategy.

20

Catching A Bird

For the next two weeks, Ian was on tenterhooks, waiting to see if the mole would take the bait, and whether a message would be sent from East Berlin to Moscow, listing the type of battle tank being moved to Berlin. After not hearing anything from John and the communications listening post on Teufelsberg for four days, Ian decided the anticipation for some news was more than he could stand and called him.

"John, do you have any news for me yet? Have you intercepted any communications from East Berlin to Moscow, containing the key words?"

"I'm sorry Ian, but we haven't intercepted anything at all."

"Thanks John, please keep listening."

Ian hung up the phone and thought, *"Maybe I was all wrong about this. If this becomes a fiasco, my military career could be at an end. How could the plan be so far off base? Perhaps the grapevine takes longer for the rumours to spread, or maybe the mole has just not heard the news, about the battle tank proposed shipments. "*

For the next few days, Ian stayed in his office trying to work on other matters, wanting to be by the phone, in case John called from Teufelsberg.

Finally, nine days after the rumours were first floated in the three organizations, the phone in Ian's office rang. He was actually outside his office talking to another officer about the Oxford-Cambridge boat race result, when he heard it. He ran into his office and picked up the phone.

"Ian, this is John. Your boat just came in. We picked up a message to Moscow stating that Drache had picked up some critical information, about a British plan to ship fifty more Centurion Mk7 battle tanks, to West Berlin."

"Thanks for the excellent news, John. I can finally breathe again. Recently, I've been thinking about what I would do for a living, when they drum me out of the service for incompetence. Now we know the mole is in the British Brigade, here at the Olympic Stadium. I can immediately go to work with a plan, to finally unmask this spy. I'll talk to you later. Thank everyone at Teufelsberg for all their hard work, deciphering the coded messages."

As soon as John hung up, Ian called Colonel Thurman to inform him of the news, from the Teufelsberg listening post.

"Colonel, I've just received some good news from John that they have picked up a message being sent to Moscow, which identifies the mole as being in the British Berlin Brigade."

"That doesn't sound like good news to me, Mr. Black. This means we have a mole in our midst. The sooner we hunt him or her down, the better."

"I have a two-fold plan to try and unmask the mole. First, I'll obtain from the Personnel Officer dossiers on all German citizens, working at the Stadium. After combing through them, I'll select those that look suspicious and plan to spread some more disinformation, to see if I can smoke him or her out."

"How do you plan to do that?" asked the colonel.

"I have an ironic plan to spread a rumour that the British have a mole in the Soviet GRU, using a different codename to be given to each suspect on our list. We can then monitor the communications channels between East Berlin and Moscow. The Stasi will not sit on the information, since it involves the GRU. My guess is that it's a woman working for a senior officer, even though they were vetted in depth. However, that is only speculation on my part and I hope I'm wrong. I'm going to keep an open mind until I have incontrovertible proof, as to who it is. You know we still don't know if the "Bri" muttered by the dying Stasi agent, referred to Britain or the actual name of the mole."

"Very well, Ian, develop your plan and keep me informed, as you progress."

"Yes sir, I'll do that" Lieutenant Black replied.

After disconnecting the telephone call to Colonel Thurman, Ian dialed Franz at the BND and Captain Silverman at the 513th Intelligence Group, to let them know that the mole was found to be somewhere in the British Berlin Brigade.

Ian then contacted the officer who handled the hiring of local Germans, as they were needed, to determine how many Germans were actually employed at the Olympic Stadium complex. It turned out there were twelve Germans working there at the Brigade facility. The officer handed Ian the dossiers on all twelve and asked him not to take them out of the office. After requesting the employment officer not to reveal that there was an investigation going on, Ian sat down at a table and started to make notes on all twelve. The last thing they wanted to do, at this point, was to scare the mole into vanishing behind the Berlin Wall. They needed to catch him or her red-handed.

1. Bryce Hofmann, male, married, age 34, born Spandau, height 5 ft. 11in. weight 11.4 stone, no known Nazi or Communist sympathies, Roman Catholic, no known relatives in East Germany, occupation – mechanic.

2. Hermann Vogel, male, single, age 29, born Munich, height 6 ft. 1 in., weight 13 stone, no known Nazi or

Communist sympathies, Lutheran, no known relatives in East Germany, occupation – Transportation Department.

3. Dieter Roth, male, single, age 25, born Berlin, height 5ft. 10 in., weight 11 stone, no known Nazi or Communist sympathies, religion none, only known relative in East Germany third cousin never met, occupation – Assists the quartermaster sergeant in the stockroom.

4. Giselle Schmitt, female, single, age 32, born Dresden, height 5 ft. 6 in., weight 9 stone, blond hair, blue eyes, no known Nazi or Communist sympathies, her father died in a concentration camp right before the war, most of her immediate family moved West after War ended, religion none, no known close relatives in East Germany, occupation - personal secretary to Brigadier Charles Clemens.

5. Helga Jergens, female, married, age 30, born Hanover, height 5 ft. 8 in., weight 9.5 stone, brown hair, hazel eyes, no known Nazi or Communist sympathies, religion Calvinist, all relatives live in West Germany, occupation – personal secretary to Colonel Thurman.

6. Brigitte Sommer, female, married, age 39, born Cologne, height 5 ft. 5 in., weight 8 .2 stone, auburn hair, green eyes, no known Nazi or Communist leanings, Roman Catholic, all known relatives live in the West, occupation – personal secretary to the CO of the Durham Light Infantry Regiment.

7. Anneke Böhm, female, single, age 24, born Leipzig – moved to Kiel at the end of the War, height 5 ft. 10 in., weight 10.1 stone, blond hair, green eyes, no religious affiliation, no known Nazi or Communist leanings, all known relatives live in the West, occupation – personal secretary to the CO of the Welsh Regiment

8. Elisa Meyer, female, single, age 26, born Düsseldorf, height 5 ft. 3 in., weight 8 1/2 stone, brown hair, blue eyes, Methodist, no known Nazi or Communist leanings, no close relatives except mother in Düsseldorf, occupation – personal secretary to the CO of the Kings Royal Rifle Corps.

9. Marie Keller, female, married, age 34, born Frankfurt, height 5 ft. 5 in., weight 9 ½ stone, black hair, black hair, brown eyes, no sympathy for Nazis or Communists, all known relatives live in Frankfurt area, occupation – personal secretary to the CO of the 1st Squadron, 4th Royal Tank Regiment.

10. Sophia Köhler, female, single, age 27, born Bremen, height 5 ft. 7 in., weight 10 stone, brown hair, hazel eyes, no religious affiliation, moved to Berlin with mother and siblings in 1948, father killed at Stalingrad, occupation – nurse assisting Royal Army Medical Corps (RAMC).

11. Hans Koch, male, age 50, born Münster, height 5 ft. 11 in., weight 13 ½ stone, black hair (balding), blue eyes, Calvinist religion, served in German Air Force during war, hated Nazis and has no Communist leanings, occupation – general handy man (part time) always supervised by member of British Army.

12. Wolfgang Scharbert, male, age 52, born Nuremberg, height 5 ft. 9 in., weight 11.5 stone, drafted into the Wehrmacht against his will, served on Eastern Front, Roman Catholic, no Nazi or Communist sympathies, only close relative brother who lives in Hamburg, occupation – janitor (part time) always under a British Army supervisor.

Ian studied all the files closely and started to eliminate a few of them, due to the improbability that they would have access to sensitive information. First, he set aside the files on Sophia Köhler, Hans Koch and Wolfgang Scharbert since generally they were under constant supervision by British Army personnel and would have no opportunity to obtain secret documents or information. He then eliminated the other three men Bryce Hofmann, Hermann Vogel and Dieter Roth, since in Ian's opinion they were employed at too low a level, to be of much use to Stasi, the KGB or GRU.

This left six suspects, all of whom were female, and thus the mole had to be a swallow, to use the spy industry classification. Ian looked at the files of the six again and didn't notice anything that stood out or pointed at one particular person. This left him only one alternative; put into motion the unmasking plan.

He called Colonel Thurman's office and immediately his secretary answered.

"Helga, this is Lieutenant Black and I'd like to make an appointment to see the colonel."

"Let me see," she answered, as she looked at her boss's schedule. "How about tomorrow morning at 0900, will that be okay?"

"That will be great. Put me down," Ian replied, as he started to think more about which of the six people might be the mole.

"I sure hope it isn't Helga," he thought, *"but who knows? If it is her, it'll be devastating to the colonel for him to realize that he's been harboring a spy. I wonder who did the vetting and the hiring of these Germans. Did they miss something in their background?"*

The next morning, Ian turned up at Colonel Thurman's office and, as usual, found Helga sitting behind her desk, guarding the inner office door.

"Good morning Helga, may I go in?"

"Certainly lieutenant, he's been expecting you." she replied.

Ian knocked on the door and, after hearing the colonel reply "Enter", he went in, closing the door behind him.

He saluted and then sat down in the empty chair, located in front of his CO's desk.

"What can I do for you, Mr. Black?" he asked.

"It has to do with the mole, sir. I believe I have narrowed the search down to six possible people. The other six, I eliminated due to their lack of exposure to any critical information, reports, etc. The remaining six are: Brigitte Sommer, Anneke Böhm, Elisa Meyer, Marie Keller, Giselle Schmitt and Helga Jergens."

The colonel gasped when Ian mentioned his secretary's name. "Are you sure about this?" he asked.

"As sure as I can ever be unless, of course, there just isn't a mole in our midst. However, the phony tank report, we put out, indicated that there is one."

"Let's assume you're correct. What do you propose that we do to expose this spy?"

"My plan is to create six pseudo intelligence reports concerning Soviet troop movements, all the same, except for one word; the codename for a British mole in the GRU, the Soviet military intelligence. The six codenames will be as follows; Unicorn, Tiger, Rhino, Lion, Cheetah and Leopard. Each of the six officers, with the secretaries under suspicion, will receive the report with one of the names.

This report will be sent to the six officers to whom these secretaries report. I will then again have the Teufelsberg listening post monitor the communications traffic, between East Berlin and Moscow and, assuming the traitor gets to see the report, the specific codename of the mole in the GRU, will appear in the message. To accomplish this, sir, I do need your support, since I am just a first lieutenant and the senior officers are lieutenant colonels or above."

"What do you specifically want me to do?" the colonel asked.

"Well, sir, it would be extremely helpful if you would contact each officer individually, including Brigadier

Clemens, and explain the situation to them about the mole. In addition, inform them that they will be receiving this secret intelligence report, with which they are to do nothing, except ask their secretary to file it away in a locked safe. The secretary, who is the mole, will assuredly read the report, before filing it. She will then contact her handler in the Stasi and he, in turn, will forward the codename, of the British mole in the GRU, to Moscow."

"Obviously, I need to see this pseudo Intelligence Report, before you send it out to these six senior officers. It's my duty to insure that there's nothing in it, which could be construed as really secret or confidential, other than the codename of the GRU mole. It should be in a sealed envelope, marked personal and confidential on the outside. This would increase the curiosity of the mole and she would be sure to read it, before filing it away as instructed."

"Sir, I believe this plan will work and we'll unmask the mole. I too hope it isn't Helga, as she appears to be an extremely, effective assistant to you."

"Before I contact these senior officers, I need you to write the Intelligence Report and show it to me. Is this understood?"

"Certainly, sir, I'll do it right away."

Ian stood up, saluted, and left the colonel's office, bidding farewell to Helga.

Back at his desk, in the London Block, he placed a call to John in MI6 and told him that, in the near future, he would want the crew at Teufelsberg listening post, to monitor the communications traffic for him again.

He started to work on the fake Intelligence Report using the IBM model C electric typewriter he obtained from the Quartermaster stores. He knew it had to look authentic, for the plan to work.

SECRET

British Army Military Intelligence Corps
Berlin Brigade Headquarters
Olympic Stadium, Berlin
4 June 1962; 1000 hours GMT+1

Notice: This document is covered under the Official Secrets Act.
Intelligence Assessment No: IC/IB/19629X8

1. MISSION
Determine Warsaw Pact troop movements, since the increase of American forces in West Germany, including West Berlin and the growing controversy over the spread of Communism to Cuba and other world trouble spots.

2. TROOP MOVEMENTS
   a. Soviets: They have increased the manpower in many units, including the Twenty Fourth Airborne Army, Third Shock Army, and the Seventh Rifle Corps by over twenty percent. The First Guards Tank Corps is being relocated from the Soviet Union to East Germany.

   b. Warsaw   Pact: Poland,   Hungary, Czechoslovakia, Bulgaria, Rumania have all increased the draft of young men and delayed the release from service for up to six months.

3. INTELLIGENCE SOURCES
   a. 15 MAY 1962. The British agent in the Soviet military intelligence, the GRU, named UNICORN

b. May to June 1962. Communications monitored at the Teufelsberg Listening Station.

c. April to June 1962. NSA and GCHQ signals intercepts at various locations around the world, including Ayios Nikolaos Station at Dhekelia, Cyprus and Ascension Island.

d. BND agents located in East Germany.

e. Continuous "tours" and intelligence reports by the British, American and French Military Liaison Missions into East Germany

f. CIA agents in Eastern Europe and around the world, including a few remaining in Cuba.

4. SITUATION ANALYSIS

The Soviet Union is intent on challenging the U.S. and the Western powers at every opportunity. Khrushchev is intent on showing the world how weak and impotent the West is. Hungary in 1956 and East Berlin in 1953 set the tone on how the Soviets will react to any challenge to their power.

5. TIMETABLE FOR POSSIBLE ACTION

a. Cuba could become a real hotspot by the fall of 1962. Reports are coming in that the Soviets may be planning to send missiles to the island.

b. Since the West did nothing about the first layer of the Berlin Wall, the East Germans, with Soviet assistance, will build a second wall one hundred meters behind the first.

c. Within the next twenty four months, the Soviets plans to sign a peace treaty with East Germany and recognize East Berlin as its capital.

6. CONCLUSION

    a. The Soviets are determined to sign a separate peace treaty with East Germany and naming East Berlin the capital within the next two years, in violation of the four power agreement.

    b. The East Germans, with Soviet help, will build a second barrier behind the first Berlin Wall starting in June 1962

    c. The Soviets might send missiles to Cuba and threaten the U.S. mainland. This action would be aimed at securing safety for Communist Cuba and also to apply pressure on America into withdrawing its missiles from Turkey and other locations.

                    INTELLIGENCE ESTIMATE prepared by

                              Lieutenant Ian Black
                              Intelligence Corps
                        British Army on the Rhine

SECRET

As soon as Ian finished typing the report, he made an appointment to take it to Colonel Thurman for review. He had requested to see it, before it was forwarded to the senior officers. Ian went to the colonel's office and Helga told him he could go straight in.

After closing the door and saluting his CO, he approached the officer, placing the Intelligence Report on his desk.

"Here's one copy of the report, sir, for your approval. All six copies will be identical, except for the codename of the mole at the GRU."

"Take a seat, while I review it," answered the colonel.

Colonel Thurman took about ten minutes to closely study the report and then looked up at Ian.

"Mr. Black, this is excellent. I see nothing in it that is really confidential or secret. All sources, and the information, are mundane but will look critical to a secretary acting as a spy. Go ahead and type up five more copies, changing the codename of the GRU mole in each one. Then place each copy in an envelope, seal it and write on the front the officers name, along with the words PERSONAL and CONFIDENTIAL. Do not place them in the Olympic Stadium mail system, until I confirm that I have received the cooperation of each officer, in this plan to unmask the mole. I will try to discuss the plan with all of them, within forty eight hours."

"Yes sir, I'll wait for your call," replied Ian, as he stood up, saluted and left his CO's office. He said goodbye to Helga as he departed, again thinking, *I really hope it isn't her, for both her sake and the colonel's.*

He returned to his office and typed out five more reports each one containing one of the different codenames; Tiger, Rhino, Lion, Cheetah and Leopard. After typing them out, he placed each one into an envelope, which he then sealed and marked PERSONAL and CONFIDENTIAL. He placed them in his bottom, right hand desk drawer, and locked it.

****

Two days later, at 1600 hours, Ian received a call from his CO, "Lieutenant, I've discussed the plan with all senior officers, including the brigadier, and each one has agreed with the plan. When they receive the sealed envelope, they will open it up, read it and call their secretary into their office. They will then ask them to file the important intelligence report in the locked, filing cabinet, designed for such communications. You can now deposit the envelopes in the secure Stadium mail system."

"Yes sir, I'll do it immediately and also contact John, at the Teufelsberg Listening Station, to be on the lookout for a message from East Berlin to Moscow, containing one of the six codenames."

"I hope this plan works. We need to unmask this mole as soon as possible. Let me know when you receive a call from John."

When Ian hung up the phone, he unlocked his desk drawer and retrieved the six envelopes. He took them to the mail room and placed each one in the pigeon hole assigned for mail addressed to the individual senior officers, including his CO and the brigadier.

He then decided it was time for a beer. He returned to his office, changed into his civvies and left the Olympic Stadium. He walked to a British style pub he knew about, located about a quarter of a mile from the complex. He entered it, sat down and ordered a large glass of his favorite beer - Paulaner Salvator.

As he sat at the bar, he glanced around the pub and noticed a small man with a moustache sitting in the corner. He wore a typical German soft cap, which hid most of his black hair. He was also slightly obese and did not look like a pleasant person to know.

After Ian had drunk his first glass of beer, he ordered another one, but this time only half a liter. He didn't want to get drunk, as he still had to make it back to his flat in the south of Berlin. As he took his first sip of the second beer, he noticed the pub door opened and a woman walked in. Since it was somewhat dark in the room, Ian couldn't see the female that well. As she approached the bar, she saw the man in the corner, who gave a slight nod toward her. When she got closer to Ian, he recognized her. It was Brigadier Clemens's secretary, Giselle Schmitt. At that moment, she saw him and walked toward the empty stool next to him.

"How are you doing lieutenant?" she asked.

"I'm off duty now, so please call me Ian," he replied. "Would you like a drink?"

"Yes please, I'll have one of those greyhounds. It supposed to be good and I've never had one."

After her drink arrived, Ian and Giselle started to talk about the Berlin Wall, and how it had split families apart. In addition, they discussed the weather and other non important matters. The British Army or work at the Stadium complex never came up. While they were talking, the man in the corner rose and walked out of the pub. As he did so, he gave another slight nod to Giselle, which Ian didn't see, since his back was to the man.

After about two hours, Giselle said, "Have you eaten dinner yet?"

"No, I haven't and I'm getting hungry."

"How about if we go to my place, it's not far from here and I'll rustle up something to eat?" she asked.

Ian thought for a few moments before answering, *"This could get touchy. She's a potential mole and also the brigadier's secretary; on top of that she could be a swallow. However, she is pretty, sensuous and seems to be interesting to talk to. Maybe I'll have her feed me and then leave, before I get carried away by my male hormones."*

He then said, "That sounds great, since you said your flat is fairly close."

They walked out of the pub and Ian hailed a taxi. Giselle told the driver the address and it wasn't long before they were there. Her flat was located about two blocks from the Turmstrasse U-Bahn station, in an attractive part of Berlin. As they climbed the stairs to the first floor, Ian started to wonder how she could afford such a place on her secretary's salary. Upon entering her flat, Ian's uneasiness increased, as he saw her expensive furnishings. He couldn't furnish his flat anywhere close to this one, on his lieutenant's pay.

"Take a seat on the couch Ian, while I quickly fix something for us to eat. Would you like another beer?"

"Just a small one, I think I've drunk too much already."

She smiled to herself, as she opened up a bottle and poured it into a glass for him.

"Maybe I can get him drunk and take advantage of him. He seems like a fairly nice chap and he's very handsome," she thought.

In about fifteen minutes, she carried into the living room something for both of them to eat. It wasn't fancy, but it filled them up.

After they finished, Giselle cleaned up the plates and placed them in the kitchen sink. She then went and sat down close to Ian. They talked some more about sports, mainly soccer, as she was a football fan. The West Berlin team, she supported, was doing fairly well. She thought she was getting somewhere with Ian and might get him into her bedroom.

Suddenly, there was a knock at her flat door.

Startled, Giselle asked, "Who's there?"

"Me, Chuck!" the man responded.

Giselle turned to Ian, shook him a little and whispered, "You'd better leave. There's a short drain pipe off the veranda. You can shinny down it, to the ground floor."

Ian awoke from his minor alcoholic stupor, rose from the sofa, and went out the veranda doors. He shut them quietly behind him, while Giselle closed the drapes.

Before he left the veranda, Ian peered back into the flat, through a small gap in the curtains. To his astonishment, he saw Brigadier Clemens enter the flat, after Giselle had opened the door for him.

He thought, *"The brigadier is having an affair with his secretary, a potential swallow at that, and he's married. I guess nothing should surprise me in this man's army."*

He shinnied down the drainpipe from the first floor to the ground and hurried down the street, so as not to be seen by the brigadier. Ian went to the U-Bahn station at

Turmstrasse on the U2 line and went to back to his flat, after having to change lines a couple of times.

Three days later at 1100 hours, Ian received a call from John, at Teufelsberg.

"About two hours ago, we monitored a communication from the head of Stasi to the KGB in Moscow that mentioned the words Unicorn and GRU. It took a while decipher it, but we did decode some of the message. Is this what you wanted to know?"

"Yes John, thanks a million. I believe that I now know who the mole is in the British Berlin Brigade. The question I have is, how did all the vetting miss something in her background?"

"Oh, the mole is a swallow, huh."

"Yes, I'm afraid so. Thanks again for the input. I'll talk to you about it later," Ian responded.

He scheduled a meeting with Colonel Thurman, through Helga, for 1400 hours the same day. However, first he wanted to go through Giselle Schmitt's personnel file again, to see if there was anything he missed.

He went to see the Personnel Officer and asked for the file on the brigadier's secretary. As he sat down and started pouring through the documentation, the officer asked, "Is there something I can help you with?"

"I don't know yet. Somehow, I believe whoever vetted her, missed an important detail." Ian replied. "It says here that her father was sent to a concentration camp before the war, and he died there. Why was he sent there? It doesn't say."

The personnel officer replied, "Here's a faded newspaper clipping from a Dresden newspaper that was stuck between two other pieces of paper. It may have been overlooked. Anyway, it states: *a Mannfred Schmitt has been sent to the Dachau camp for reeducation, because he's a communist.* I guess this was Giselle's father. It also mentions that his half brother Klaus Schmitt was under suspicion for being a

242

communist, but no action had yet been taken. I wonder what happened to his family, if he had one."

"Let me call a contact I have at BND, and determine if he has any information or sources that can help us out."

Ian picked up the phone and dialed Franz's number.

"Who's there?" a voice in German said, after picking up the headset.

"Franz, this is Kurt. I need your help."

"Hello Kurt, it's great to talk with you again. What can I do for you?"

"We have a problem. I believe that I've unmasked the mole at the Olympic Stadium, and I'm trying to get more information on her. Her name is Giselle Schmitt and originally she's from Dresden. According to a newspaper clipping from the 1930's, it appears her father was killed at Dachau, for being a communist. His name was Mannfred Schmitt, and he had a half brother Klaus Schmitt, who was under suspicion, but never arrested by the Gestapo. Can you look in your files or contact anyone who might have more information, on the Schmitts from Dresden? I hate to ask this, but it's urgent that I get any available information by 1345 hours today."

"I'll do the best I can for you, Kurt."

At 1330, Franz called him back.

"Kurt, we managed to find out two bits of information about the Schmitt family in Dresden. First, Giselle Schmitt has an older brother named Max, twelve years her senior, who is involved in communist party politics in the city. Second, Klaus Schmitt, her father's half brother is still alive and is a dedicated communist in the police department. That's the best we could find out in this short a time."

"Thanks Franz, that's more than enough at this point. I appreciate your assistance in this matter. I've got to run now, to see my CO."

Ian went to the Administration Building and entered the office, where Helga kept watch for her boss.

"Hello Helga, may I go in?" Ian asked with a smile. He liked her and she seemed very efficient and protective of the colonel.

Helga looked at him with a somewhat puzzled face and replied, "He's expecting you, lieutenant. You look happy today."

"Well I'm happy to see you, in more ways than one," Ian said, as he entered Colonel Thurman's office.

Helga watched him go in and wondered what that was all about.

"Maybe I'll find out one of these days." she thought.

Ian saluted the colonel and then sat down in front of his desk.

He then started to make his report.

"Sir, at 1100 hours today, I received a call from John at Teufelsberg, confirming that they had detected a communication from East Berlin to Moscow, about a mole named Unicorn, in the Soviet Military Intelligence GRU. It appears that Giselle Schmitt is the Stasi mole in our midst.

At the personnel office, the officer in charge and I discovered an old 1934 Dresden newspaper clipping stating that Giselle Schmitt's father, Mannfred Schmitt, had been arrested and sent to Dachau, for being a communist. He died in captivity a few weeks later. Her father had a half brother named Klaus Schmitt who was also suspected of being a communist, but the Gestapo never arrested him.

I also contacted Franz in the BND and he found out, in the short time I gave him, that Giselle has a brother still living in Dresden and is active in the communist party. Her father's half brother is in the police department at Dresden and is an active communist."

"Well, it seems your plan worked out. It's going to be hard to tell Brigadier Clemens that his secretary is a spy."

"I have one other point to bring up, which is somewhat touchy, but I feel I must tell you."

"What is it, Ian?"

"Last night, before I knew all this information, I met Giselle at a pub, and she invited me to dinner at her flat. I behaved myself very well, although I must admit I was tempted. Anyway, after we had eaten and were sitting on the sofa conversing, there was a knock at her front door. It was a man named Chuck. She told me I had to leave, so I went out on her veranda and slid down the drainpipe to the ground floor. Before I did so, I managed to look through a crack in the curtains, and into her flat walked Brigadier Clemens."

"I'm glad you told me all this. You are not to repeat the last part of your story to anyone. That's an order, you understand."

"Yes sir."

"Good, I will take care of the matter in due time. Now we must take care of Giselle. I want you to go round up two MPs, each with a sidearm, and the four of us will go to the brigadier's office to arrest Giselle Schmitt."

"I'll do it right away, sir."

Ian left the colonel's office and went to the guard room, to enlist the help of two MPs. He led them back to the colonel's office and Helga, when she saw them, became scared.

"Don't worry, Helga, they haven't come for you," Ian told her, as they walked into the colonel's office.

Colonel Thurman, Lieutenant Black and the two MPs walked down the hallway and up the stairs to the brigadier's office. They walked in, and Colonel Thurman told Giselle that he wanted to see the brigadier immediately. She pressed a button on the intercom.

"Sir, Colonel Thurman is here to see you."

"Send him right in."

The colonel turned to Ian, as he started to enter the inner office and said, "Lieutenant, you know your duty."

As the colonel went in and shut the door, Ian turned and said to Giselle, "Fräulein Schmitt, you are under arrest for espionage."

At which point the MPs, after placing handcuffs on her wrists, went and stood on each side of her.

"Let's go," Ian commanded the military policemen.

Lieutenant Black and the two MPs marched Giselle Schmitt out of the office and down to the guard room on the ground floor, where she was placed in a holding cell. A week later, she would be transferred to a British Army (BAOR) Detention Centre

Giselle looked terrible but, by the look on her face, Ian thought she suspected that somehow this day would come.

Ian filled out some paper work at the guard room and then returned to his office in the London Block.

He called Major Phillips, who was in charge of the Interrogation Group, under Colonel Thurman, and asked him to have Giselle interrogated. It would be wise to know what information she had given the East Germans, in case any war strategy had to be revised. During the interviews conducted by the major's personnel, Giselle Schmitt told the investigators that the main reason, she agreed to provide Stasi with information, was to protect her brother in Dresden. In addition, she blamed the Nazis and some Germans for causing the death of her father at Dachau.

Ian never brought up the subject of Brigadier Clemens and his visit to Giselle's flat. However, he did find out, a few weeks later, that the brigadier had returned to England and had been quietly forced to retire.

21

Teufelsberg Communications Intercept Station

After all the attendees exited the following Monday staff meeting, Ian went over to John to discuss the mole issue and the way the Teufelsberg Listening Post helped in the effort to unmask the spy.

"John, I really appreciate what you and your team did for us."

"We're all on the same side, so we were glad to be of assistance."

"Would it be possible for me to visit Teufelsberg and see for myself, how you monitor communications there?" asked Ian.

"I don't know. Let me check with security and see what we can do. This station is only temporary at the moment; mostly consisting of trailers connected together. Since the Station is shared with the Americans, I would need their approval also. I'll get back to you in the next couple of days."

Two days later, on cue, John called him.

"Ian, I have permission from security to allow you to see some of the Teufelsberg facility, so you can obtain a perspective, as to how we intercept messages and record them for later decoding. You must wear your uniform, and you'll be given a large yellow badge to wear around your neck, with the word VISITOR in bold letters. You'll not be able to enter some areas that have a sign stating they are off limits to visitors. Most of them are the Americans' monitoring rooms, and they are very security conscious."

"That sounds great, John. When and where shall I meet you?"

"At 0900 tomorrow, I'll be parked outside the Administration Building, in a green Ford Zephyr. We'll drive to the Grunewald Forest and then climb up the winding road, to the top of Devil's Mountain. It's about 394 feet high above sea level, and I'll tell you all about it on the way up to the Station."

"I'll be there sharp at 0900 hours. I'm looking forward to seeing the operation," Ian replied.

The next morning he walked over to the Administration Building and, in one of the parking spots, he found John sitting in a dark green Ford.

"Good morning, John," he said, as he climbed into the passenger seat. "It looks like a great day for a trip through the forest and up to the top of the mountain."

The sun was shining and there wasn't a cloud in the sky. "We should have a good view of Berlin from the mountain. By the way, why is it nicknamed Devil's Mountain?" he asked.

"Teufelsberg is basically German for Devil's Mountain. You're correct, Ian, the view should be magnificent since there isn't much haze today. Oh, by the way, I guess congratulations are in order on your capture of the mole."

"Thanks, in some ways, I hated to arrest her. Giselle seemed quite a nice person. I think she was threatened somewhat by what could happen to her relatives in the East, if she didn't cooperate."

John back out of the parking spot and then put the vehicle into first gear. Soon they exited the Olympic Stadium complex and headed for Teufelsberg. As the crow flies, the distance to mountain top was only about one mile, due south of the Stadium. However, since the road to the top wound around, it ended up to be more like a two to three mile trip. As they drove south, they entered what was called the Grunewald Forest. The mountain itself actually was made of debris from buildings bombed during the war, and lorry loads were brought up there each day, where the rubble was dumped on what used to be a military-technical college, designed by the Nazi Albert Speer. At 7,400 acres, it was the largest park in Berlin and contained much wildlife and trees.

As they approached the Station, they had to stop at a guard post, where a British MP stood guard, armed with a Sterling submachine gun. Since the Listening Post was in the British sector, the Americans using the area were there as guests of the British Government, together with the GCHQ and MI6. John flashed his ID and they were waved in by the guard, who immediately recognized him. The whole area was sealed off with barbed wire, and there were guards patrolling the perimeter, with Alsatian dogs.

The Listening Station consisted of a system of antennas and about twenty mobile homes, most of which were interconnected. There was a plan to construct some permanent buildings in 1963; however, since July 1961, the site only consisted of these temporary buildings.

John led Ian to the first building that functioned as an administration and coordination center. Half of the Station was for use by the NSA and the other half by the British BCHQ, together with MI6.

John introduced Ian to the site manager.

"Henry, this is Lieutenant Ian Black, also known as Kurt, in some circles. He has come to see where we helped identify the mole, in the British Berlin Brigade."

"It's a pleasure to meet you, Ian. I've heard a lot about you, including how you can fly a four-engine plane."

"I trust what you've heard wasn't all bad. Sometimes, John tends to exaggerate," Ian replied, smiling at John.

"No, to the contrary it was extremely complimentary. Here's your visitor's badge, which you must wear prominently at all times, and it must be turned in before you leave. John will give you the actual tour, since he knows a lot more about some of the equipment and techniques we use to obtain information. Obviously, I'm sure I don't have to tell you that anything you see here cannot be discussed, outside this facility."

"I completely understand, Henry."

"Well then, I hope you have a good visit and I'll see you before you leave."

John then explained to Ian, what he was going to see.

"The basic operation is as follows, and if you have any questions ask them at the end of each explanation.

We have special antennas that pick up the Soviet and Warsaw Pact signals. These signals are fed into a large bank of receivers, where each one is tuned to a different frequency."

"What happens if the frequencies change or a new one is detected?"

"We are constantly monitoring the radio waves for a new frequency being used. If we find one, then a new receiver is added to the bank and tuned to that frequency."

"Where does the output of these receivers go?" Ian asked.

"All the receivers are linked to three additional rooms. In one of them, there is a group of Russian and German speaking individuals, who monitor the transmissions live and make notes of any important points that they pick up. Another room is loaded with AN/TNH-11 reel to reel tape recorders, where the signals are recorded for future analysis. Finally, there is a room that contains teletype machines, which type out the gibberish they are fed, and which is later decoded, if possible."

"What happens if there is a power failure?"

"The site is normally powered with electricity provide from Berlin. If there is a power failure, we have diesel generators that automatically kick in, to provide essential power."

Teufelsberg
Listening
Station
Berlin
1962

"Finally there are vans that contain the Decoding Room, the Tape Storage Room and a Shredding Room. In addition there is equipment where we can send by code any information to GCHQ in London for additional analysis."

"That gives me an idea of what goes on here and the purpose for all the equipment I'll be seeing," Ian responded.

"One other matter, I'd like to point out," said John. "The American section of this facility is off limits to us, but my understanding is that their lay out and equipment is very similar to ours. There is some cooperation between us, but they are very protective of their secrets."

"Maybe at some future date, some contacts I have at the 513th can make arrangements for me to see the NSA operation," Ian replied.

John then led him through each of the mobile vans, pointing out the various type of equipment in each of them and explaining the purpose for all of it. When they entered the monitoring room, where Russian and German speaking personnel were listening live to any communication, a young man came up behind Ian and tapped him on the shoulder.

He turned around and was facing a young Englishman of about the same age.

"Ian, how are you doing? It's been ages since we saw each other."

Ian finally recognized the young man. He was a school mate from Harrow, who had taken German in the same classes, as he had.

"Ralph, it's great to see you again, after about five years."

"Ian, my name here is Austin, in this facility."

"Well Austin, my name is Kurt in official circles. What are you doing here?"

"I went to work for the GCHQ and they sent me here, because of my fluency in German. How about you, what are you doing here in Berlin?"

"A few years ago, I was drafted into the British Army and served a couple of years in Cyprus. Here in West Berlin, I'm in the Intelligence Corps with the Berlin Brigade, located in the Olympic Stadium. John is showing me around the place, since this operation helped expose a mole in our organization."

"Oh, so it was for you that we had to listen or look for the word Unicorn."

"Yes, that's correct. We're glad that you assisted us in that matter."

"You're welcome, any time. I'd better get back to work now, before I miss an important transmission," Austin said, as he placed his headset back on and plugged the cord into a receiver.

John continued showing Ian around the British part of the Station.

"What brand of receiver do you use for monitoring the individual frequencies?" Ian asked.

"We don't normally use a receiver from just one manufacturer. We purchase the WJ-8617B HF/VHF/UHF receiver from Watkins-Johnson, and also receivers from companies such as Marconi, Radiation Inc., Harris Corporation, Pye Ltd. and Sanders Associates."

"How about the tape recorders, do you use any particular brand?"

"We normally use Ampex S-3160A and a model T-1500 from 3M/Wollensak," John replied. "In addition, we use Hewlett Packard and Tektronix test equipment for maintaining all the gear."

"Since the Station is on a hill almost four hundred feet high, how far away can you pick up a signal?"

"Generally, depending on the weather, we can detect and monitor a signal as far away as one hundred and eighty miles," John responded. Continuing he said, "I believe we should rap up this tour. As far as I know, I've shown you the Listening Post, how it's operated and we should now return to the Stadium. I have a report I need to write."

"I certainly appreciate the opportunity to see the Teufelsberg Station, as I've heard so much about it."

They stopped at the Administration van and bid farewell to Henry, the site manager, before climbing into the Ford Zephyr, for the drive back to the Olympic Stadium.

As they drove, John told Ian how the Station got started in July 1961, about one month before the Berlin Wall was built. He pointed out that the use of mobile vans was not ideal and explained the plan was to install permanent buildings in 1963.

"That should provide a better work environment for the personnel and make them more productive, I would think," Ian said to John.

Soon they were back at the Stadium where Ian thanked John again, for the orientation and the visit to the Station.

They then parted and Ian returned to the London Block, to work on another report for his CO.

22

Promotion And The Devil's Labyrinth

At the end of Colonel Thurman's weekly staff meeting, held on Monday, the 1st of April, 1963, he asked Ian to come to his office for a private meeting, at 1100 hours.

As Lieutenant Black went back to his office, he thought, *"I wonder what this is all about? Have I done something wrong? Well, I guess I'll find out soon enough."*

He arrived at the colonel's office early and entered the outer area.

"Hello Helga, how are you today?" he said to the colonel's secretary, with a smile.

She replied with a nervous voice, "I'm okay, since I still have a job." She had been an acquaintance of Giselle and was afraid that she might be implicated in the spy scandal. In addition, she knew that Lieutenant Black was somehow involved with the uncovering and arrest of the mole.

"You have nothing to worry about, Helga," Ian replied. "The affair has been over for ten months. As long as you want this job, I'm sure the colonel will be pleased to have you, as his assistant. You can now start smiling again."

"Thank you, lieutenant," she said, finally smiling at him.

At that moment, the buzzer on her desk sounded and she triggered the intercom into the colonel's office.

"Is Lieutenant Black there, Helga?"

"Yes sir, he's been here for about ten minutes."

"Well, show him in. I need to talk to him."

Ian rose from the chair by Helga's desk, knocked on the colonel's door and entered the office. He had been here many times before and it seemed routine, as he gave his CO a British military salute.

"Come on in Mr. Black and take a seat."

"Yes sir, am I in trouble or something? he asked.

"No, of course not, I want you to pack your bag for a month's stay at the Joint Army/Air Force Headquarters, located at Rheindahlen, West Germany, close to the Dutch border. You are due to attend a Junior Officer Leadership Programme and Joint Officer Tactical Awareness Course, so you can be considered for promotion to captain."

"When do I get to start this programme, sir?"

"You're scheduled to be there next Monday, from the 8th of April to the 3rd of May. You've been a lieutenant now for five years which means, under Army rules and regulations, you can be considered for a promotion to a higher rank. You also have to take a self study course called "Military Knowledge 1" and pass the captain's exam. Another requirement is that you have to serve two and one half years at RD (Regimental Duties), however in your position in the Intelligence Corps, I'm sure this will be waived."

"Thank you for your faith in me, sir, and I won't let you or our unit down. I'll do my best for Queen and country."

"Thank you Mr. Black. I expect nothing less. Unless something else comes up in the next few days, I'll see you at the staff meeting, on the 6th of May. Helga will give you your orders and travel voucher to get you to JHQ Rheindalhen. Good day."

Ian saluted his CO and left the colonel's office. In the outer office, Helga handed him his orders and a travel voucher for the train, through East and West Germany to Mönchengladbach, the closest town to the JHQ Rheindahlen.

"I hope you have a productive course, and we'll see you back in a month," she said, with the best smile she had given him, since before the unmasking of the mole.

"Thank you Helga. Take care and I'll see you in four weeks. Keep smiling," he replied in German.

She grinned, when he spoke to her in her native language, and said, "For you, I'll do just about anything. Oops, for a second there, I forgot I'm married."

Ian left the Administration Building and returned to his office in the London Block, where he started to plan for his trip to the Rheindahlen military base. He had to prepare his uniforms and equipment, so he could present a polished image, to the officers running the courses. He knew he would be competing with some junior officers, who had graduated from a university or from the Royal Military Academy at Sandhurst.

****

On the next Saturday, Ian took the train from Berlin to Dusseldorf, where he had to change for the leg to Mönchengladbach. It was about a five hour trip in total and when he arrived at Mönchengladbach, he had to wait for a military transport, to take him to the JHQ. There he checked into the Administration Building and presented his orders to the duty officer.

"Welcome lieutenant, you are assigned to the Exeter building on Queen Anne Street, room 4B. The classes start promptly at 0830 tomorrow morning, in the St. George block. If you require anything, please let us know. The Officers' Mess is in the building next to yours and the meals are served, per the notice in your room. Welcome to the JHQ."

The next day Ian started the Joint Officer Tactical Awareness Course, which lasted two weeks, and after that he was scheduled to take the Junior Officer Leadership

Programme, for the next two weeks. The work was very intensive, and Ian had to study late into the night, to make sure he passed all the required tests.

At the end of the third week, the instructor told Ian he was wanted in the Administration Building by Colonel Armstrong, who was in charge of the Officer Training Course.

Ian walked over to the colonel's office wondering, *"What have I done wrong now? Are they going to kick me out for insubordination? I can't think of anything I did wrong. I've passed all the tests so far."*

He entered the Administration Building and found the colonel's office on the second floor. He knocked on the door and entered the room, after hearing a gruff "ENTER". He marched in and saluted, saying, "Lieutenant Black reporting as ordered, sir."

"Ah, come on in and take a seat," he replied, as he returned the salute, with almost a wave. The colonel was a balding man in his late forties, and Ian had heard he was well respected in the service. He had served in the North African campaign, under Field Marshal Montgomery, during the war.

"Lieutenant, I had a call from a Colonel Thurman this morning. I understand he is your CO in Berlin."

"That's correct, sir. He's a great officer to serve under and he requires a lot from you."

"Well, that's good. This Army needs good officers, and I understand he rates you highly. In fact, he thinks so much of you, he wants you to return to Berlin immediately. So, I'm afraid you won't be able to finish this course."

"Does that mean sir that I won't be qualified to be considered for promotion to captain?"

"Not necessarily, since exceptions can be made. It all depends on your CO and what pull he has with higher ups."

"I suppose I have no choice but to return to West Berlin, right sir?"

257

"I'm afraid so. We've been happy to have you here. I understand from the instructors that you have excelled in everything demanded of you. I'll report this to Colonel Thurman. Now, as far as getting you back to Berlin, there is a RAF plane flying from here to Gatow tomorrow morning, at 1100 hours, and you have been booked on it. There'll be transportation outside this building at 1000, to take you to the airfield. Good luck, lieutenant."

"Thank you sir," he replied, as he saluted Colonel Armstrong and left his office. As he walked back to his room in the Exeter building, he wondered, *Why has Colonel Thurman called me back, since he is the person who encouraged me to come here. Something must be up, but what? Well, I guess I'll find out on Monday."*

The next day he flew back to Berlin, in a RAF transport, landing at RAF Gatow at a little after noon. He took the U-Bahn back to his flat and arrived there around 1400 hours. Since it was only Saturday, he anticipated spending a quiet weekend, in preparation for the Monday staff meeting, when he would find out why he was recalled from Rheindahlen.

****

On Monday morning, the 29th of April, Lieutenant Black, dressed in his civvies, left his flat, in south Berlin and travelled by U-Bahn to the Olympia Stadion station. From there, he walked to his room in the London Block and changed into his uniform. He arrived at the conference room, for the Monday morning staff meeting, at 0850 and found a few attendees already there, chatting about the latest issues involving Berlin. The last few strolled in at two minutes to nine, and then, punctually, Colonel Thurman arrived exactly at 0900, followed by Brigadier James Croxford, also known as Rex.

"Gentlemen, the Director of the Intelligence Corps has a few words to say, before we start our normal staff meeting."

258

Rex stepped forward and said, "Now and again, senior officers have the opportunity and honor of rewarding British Army junior officers, for the hard work they have done in an exemplary manner. In addition, there has been a tradition, in wartime, to promote officers and enlisted men, without all the rules and regulations coming into play. I don't know if all of you are aware that Bernard Baruch, an advisor to the U.S. President Truman, coined the phrase "Cold War" in a speech to the South Carolina House of Representatives, on the 16th of April, 1947. Today, I have the privilege of rewarding a lieutenant among you, with a wartime promotion.

"Lieutenant Ian Black, will you please step forward?"

Ian slowly rose from his chair, sheepishly walked to the front of the room and stood by Rex. Colonel Thurman handed Rex a black box containing two Bath stars, also known as PIPS.

"Lieutenant Ian Black, under authority granted to me as Director of the Intelligence Corps in wartime, I hereby promote you to the rank of captain; in addition, you are now a regular army officer. Congratulations Ian, you are now a captain and here are two additional PIPS for your uniform." Rex said, as he handed him the black box.

"Thank you sir, I'm deeply honored and will do my best to bring honor to our Queen, Country and the British Army."

Ian then returned to his chair, as he was congratulated by the other attendees.

"Okay, let's get down to business," said Colonel Thurman, as he began the staff meeting. The meeting lasted about an hour and, after everyone had given their report, the colonel ended the meeting.

As the attendees started to leave the conference room, Colonel Thurman came up to Captain Ian Black and asked him to come to his office at 1300 hours.

After eating lunch in the Officers' Mess, where he was congratulated on his promotion, by officers that knew him, Ian went to the colonel's office.

As he entered the outer office, Helga smiled at him and said, "Congratulations, captain, how does it feel?"

"I'm not sure yet, but I'll let you know in due course."

"You may go in immediately. By the way, Brigadier Croxford is in there, for the meeting."

"Thanks for the warning, Helga," Ian replied.

Captain Black tapped on the colonel's door and entered the office, after hearing him command "COME IN".

Ian found the colonel seated behind his desk, and the brigadier was in a chair to one side.

"Ah, captain, come on in and take a seat. How does it feel not to be called Mr. Black anymore?"

"To be honest, sir, I'd kind of got used to it. It had a certain ring, and I always knew you were serious when you addressed me as Mr. Black, instead of lieutenant."

At this both men laughed, and the colonel said, "We pulled you out of the course at Rheindahlen and asked you to come here, for a very, serious reason. What we are about to discuss must not be divulged to the press or any inquiring people. You understand?"

"Yes sir."

"Good, as you are aware, Giselle Schmitt is sitting in a BAOR detention centre in West Germany, still awaiting trial for espionage. She will never go to trial, as we plan to exchange her, if all goes well, for a prisoner being held by the East Germans. This man in question is named Peter Lange and he was born in Germany, at about the time Hitler became Chancellor.

After the war, his parents received refugee status and moved to England, where he excelled in school and attended the Imperial College in London. After graduating with honours, he was hired by the Plessey Company and worked at the West Drayton plant, designing cryptographic systems. There he obtained an exemption from conscription, since he was designing systems for the Government. He went on a trip to East Germany in 1962, in order to meet some of his relatives who live in Chemnitz. However, he never returned from this vacation, and later we heard that he had been arrested by the Stasi for spying. There's no record of him ever being asked to spy by any intelligence organization, but that's immaterial.

We need to get him back, and the only way we can see forward is to exchange Fräulein Schmitt, for this Peter Lange. We sent word through backdoor channels to the East Germans, to determine if they are interested, and the answer has come back in the affirmative.

So, this is where you come in, Captain Black. We want you to negotiate, with Stasi, the terms of the exchange; given your command of the German language, you are the best officer to carry this out. Your contact within Stasi is Berndt Scholz, who reports to Markus Wolf, head of the Main Directorate for Reconnaissance, and the number two man under Erich Mielke.

A meeting has been arranged at the Stasi headquarters, on Ruschestrasse, for next Thursday, the 2nd of May, to discuss the terms and manner of the exchange. There are two basic conditions that must be considered in the exchange. First, it should be conducted at night time, preferably on a Sunday night, so there'll be no press around at the border crossing, picked as the exchange point. No publicity about this transfer of prisoners is critical.

Second, before the exchange actually takes place, we need to insure that the man, they are giving us, is actually Peter Lange and that he is in good condition.

Have I left anything out, Rex?" Colonel Thurman asked Brigadier Croxford.

"No, I don't think so. Can you handle this operation with tact and diplomacy, but also firmness, captain?" Rex answered, as he looked askance at Ian.

"Yes sir," Ian replied.

"Very well, captain, keep the colonel informed as you proceed with the discussions at Stasi and the actual prisoner exchange."

"That'll be all Ian," the colonel said, as he looked toward the door, as a hint that he should leave.

Ian saluted both officers, as he left the room, and said goodbye to Helga, as he returned to his office in the London Block.

****

Three days later, at 1000 hours, two Land Rovers left the Olympic Stadium area for East Berlin. The clear sky was an azure blue in colour, and it was fairly warm for an early May day in Germany. Sitting in the front of the first vehicle was a sergeant, who was driving, and Ian; in the rear were two husky looking MPs, holding Sterling machine guns. The driver, an army corporal, Captain Swiderski and two more MPs sat in the second army Land Rover. Both vehicles were dark, army green in colour, and the bonnets held a spare tyre. In addition, the Land Rovers sported a Union Jack flag, mounted on a fender post, and a special, military license plate, which was mounted in the appropriate location.

They entered East Berlin, at the Friedrichstrasse Checkpoint Charlie entry point. As they came up to the East German border crossing, an East German soldier came out of the guard house.

"Let me see your papers," he commanded, in German.

Pointing his swagger stick at the German, Ian replied, "Under the four power agreement, we are only required to show them to a Soviet army official."

The East German went back to the guard house and picked up the phone. In a few minutes a Russian officer exited a hut about seventy-five feet away and walked toward the British vehicles. Captain Swiderski got out of the second Land Rover and met the Soviet soldier. He conversed with him for a short time, in Russian, after which the officer glanced at the papers and asked, "What is your destination in East Berlin?"

Captain Swiderski replied, "We're going to the Stasi Headquarters on Ruschestrasse for a meeting."

The Russian was taken aback by this response and said, "Okay, you may proceed."

He waved to the men manning the control arms, to lift them up, and let the British vehicles go through. As he did, the East German guard who was nearby went and called Stasi headquarters to tell them that two British vehicles were on their way there.

The approximate five mile drive through the streets of East Berlin, took them a good hour, since the traffic was heavy, consisting of buses, lorries and East German designed Trabant automobiles.

Finally, they arrived at the Stasi headquarters on Ruschestrasse and parked close to the main entrance. Captain Black got out of the lead vehicle, telling the British soldiers to stay alert and to remain inside. He then walked to the other vehicle, where Captain Alex Swiderski had already climbed out, telling the driver and military policemen to remain in it.

Ian and Alex walked up the steps and entered the Stasi building; neither Captain Black nor Swiderski were armed. However, Ian carried his swagger stick, which he had kept with him, since his first day in Cyprus. They both had an eerie feeling, as though they were entering the devil's hangout. Stasi agents in the main hall, upon spotting the two British officers, started to whisper among themselves.

They approached the main desk and Ian asked for Berndt Scholz, telling the man behind the desk, that they had a scheduled meeting.

As he looked at a list of names, the man asked, "Who are you?"

"We are both from the British Army and we are here for a meeting with Berndt Scholz," Ian repeated in perfect German. "I'm Captain Ian Black and this is Captain Alex Swiderski."

The German guard found their names on the list and made a check mark by them.

He then said, "I'll have to search you for weapons, cameras, tape devices, etc."

Ian lifted his swagger stick and pointed it at the East German, saying, "My dear man, we are both British officers and, as such, our word is our bond. I tell you we have no weapons on us nor cameras and recording devices. We certainly don't allow British soldiers to search us and we're not about to let a German or Soviet soldier do it either. Again, we are officers and gentlemen on Her Majesty the Queen's mission."

The East German picked up the phone and called somewhere into the labyrinth of the Stasi building to enquire what to do. Finally, he obviously reached the right person who told him to have a soldier escort the visitors, to the second floor conference room. As Ian entered the room, he noticed it contained a large oak table and around it were seated three Germans, while in a corner chair sat a Soviet military officer. There was one large window that looked down on the street below. He assumed it was Ruschestrasse, but wasn't positive.

"Come on in, gentlemen, and take a seat," said a middle aged man, with brown hair and a moustache.

Ian assumed he was Berndt Scholz, the man under Markus Wolf.

"Mr. Scholz, I presume. Thank you for agreeing to meet with us, about the exchange of prisoners," Ian replied.

"Captain, you speak perfect German. Where did you learn it?" Scholz asked.

"I went to a school in Harrow, where they drilled German into you, especially emphasizing the accent."

"They seemed to have an excellent language curriculum. Now, with the pleasantries out of the way, let's get down to business. When, how and where do you propose that we conclude the exchange of prisoners?"

"This is the British Army proposal:

1. Date: 19 May 1963
2. Day: Sunday
3. Time: 2200 hours local Berlin time
4. Where: Heerstrasse border crossing point between West Berlin and East Germany.
5. Personnel: Four in total – A person fluent in German and English, a doctor, a person who knows the prisoner and can confirm the identity and of course the exchange prisoner. Any other people at the border must remain at least seventy-five feet (twenty-five metres) back from the border line.
6. Prisoners under exchange are: Fräulein Giselle Schmitt and Herr Peter Lange.
7. No weapons, cameras or recording devices will be allowed at the actual exchange. Any armed troops must stay at least the seventy-five feet behind the border line.
8. No press or publicity people will be allowed to witness the exchange.
9. Any traffic attempting to cross the border will be held up one mile from the border, at least one hour before and after the exchange time.
10. The actual exchange will proceed as follows: The four people listed in #5 from each side will approach the border line, at exactly 2200 hours. The doctors will have one minute to examine the prisoner, if required, to determine they are not dead or dying. Then, the identifier will have five minutes to verify the prisoner's identity. At this point, if both sides are in agreement, the

265

prisoners will cross the line at the same time and be received by their comrades. The teams will then go back the seventy-five feet, where the other people are waiting to greet the ex-prisoners.

11. End of exchange.

For our part, Captain Swiderski here will be in attendance at the thirty foot point, in case the Soviets need to converse about any issue. In general, this exchange is between the British Army and the East German authorities. The lack of press coverage is required by us. As you are well aware, the British Army does not normally deal with the East German military, but rather with the Soviets, under the four power agreement. The British diplomats in Berlin are leaving this exchange up to the military, since we are the ones that uncovered the East German spy.

Captain Swiderski here, who speaks Russian fluently, will be handy in case you bring along a Soviet who wants to be involved with the swap."

The Soviet major, who was sitting in the corner as an observer to the negotiations, nodded his head and said in Russian, "Yes, we might have to become involved and that would be extremely useful."

"Let us discuss your proposal among ourselves. In the meantime, please help yourself to some coffee in the urn on the table in the corner. We'll be back in five minutes," said Herr Scholz, as the three East Germans left the room, leaving just the Soviet major, to keep an eye on Ian and Alex.

Ian poured some coffee for himself and Alex went over to talk with the Soviet major, who seemed pleased that he had met an British officer, who spoke his language.

After ten minutes, the Germans returned to the room and sat down at the table, where Ian and Alex were already sitting.

"We've discussed your proposal and, in principle, we agree with the details." said Scholz. "However, we suggest that an unarmed MP or soldier accompany the prisoner to the border line, just in case the prisoner attempts to cross the line, before being examined."

"We can agree to that suggestion," replied Ian. "Is there anything else, you wish to propose or change?"

"No. The date, time, location and procedure you outlined are acceptable to us."

"Good, then we'll see you on Sunday, the 19th of May at 2200 hours. If something comes up, please contact me at this phone number." Ian said, as he handed him a card.

Ian and Alex stood up and politely shook hands with the East Germans and the Russian. Ian thought, as he did so, *"I have to wash my right hand, as soon as I get back to the Olympic Stadium."*

As Scholz opened the conference room door, he said, "I'll get a soldier to escort you downstairs and out of the building." He looked outside the door and beckoned to the soldier who had been standing there all the time, during the discussions.

The soldier escorted Ian and Alex down the large central staircase, toward the main door. As they left the building, the East German soldier wheeled around and reentered the devil's labyrinth, the Stasi Headquarters.

Ian and Alex returned to their respective Land Rovers where they found the drivers and MPs waiting; looking somewhat bored. They climbed in the vehicles and the drivers drove out onto Ruschestrasse. They headed toward Friedrichstrasse, where Checkpoint Charlie was located. As they left the Stasi building, Ian looked back and noticed a black car following them. He thought, *"They want to make sure we leave East Berlin."*

At Checkpoint Charlie, they were waived through by the American MP on duty and returned to the British Berlin

Brigade headquarters. There Ian prepared a report on the negotiations for Colonel Thurman.

He also placed a call to Franz of the BND and asked him if he had or could obtain any information from BND's agents, concerning the imprisonment of Peter Lange. In addition, he requested any details on the whereabouts of Giselle Schmitt's brother Gerhard, in Dresden. Franz agreed he would look into the matter, but couldn't promise anything definite.

23

The Exchange

On Friday morning, Ian finished writing up his report on the prisoner swap discussions with Stasi and made an appointment to take it to Colonel Thurman, at 1400 hours that afternoon.

The remainder of the morning, he made plans to bring Giselle Schmitt back, with a female MP, from the detention centre in West Germany, and have her confined in a holding cell, at the Olympic Stadium. In addition, he planned to talk with the management at the Plessey Company and ask them to send someone who knew Peter Lange, for the identification process.

However, all morning something nagged him about the discussions with Stasi; they agreed too easily to his proposal. Something didn't seem to smell right.

After lunch, he went to Colonel Thurman's office to turn in his report, on the prisoner exchange discussions, and talk with him about the entire situation.

"Sir, I'm making plans to bring Giselle Schmitt back here from the detention centre at the Rheindahlen military base and confine her in a holding cell here, at the Stadium. In addition, I've called the Plessey Company and I'm waiting for a return call. I need to find a manager or engineer who knows Peter Lange extremely well, so we can determine that

269

the person, being exchanged by the East Germans, is really him. I don't trust the Stasi, and they could well try to pull a fast one over on us naïve, British soldiers. I guess I've read too many spy novels."

"That's good, Ian. One can never be too careful, especially when it concerns the Communists or the Stasi. How do you propose to vet the man who they claim is Peter Lange?"

"First, I need to find someone at Plessey that knows him very well, such as a fellow engineer, manager or better yet, a family member who also works there. Then, we need to come up with questions to ask this "Peter Lange" and see if he can answer them, without hesitation or a mistake; no matter how minor. We'll only have five minutes to make sure that he is the real person.

One thing I learned at the intelligence academy, in 1960, was how to spot someone lying; all the small clues, such as facial expressions, twitching, etc. The main problem we will have is that it will be somewhat dim at the exchange point; no bright lights."

"Let me know if you need any support. It sounds like you have everything under control. I'll forward your report to Brigadier Croxford."

"There are two items that I will need your signature for, sir. First, I'll require a plane to fly Giselle Schmitt back to Gatow from the airfield at Rheindahlen, and second, I'll need a voucher to get the Plessey contact here, for the vetting process."

"Very well, get Helga to make out the necessary paperwork and I'll sign them."

"Thank you sir, I'll keep you informed as this affair progresses."

Ian walked into the outer office, after saluting his CO, and asked Helga to prepare the travel papers for the colonel to sign. He then returned to his office and placed another call to the Plessey plant in West Drayton, because no one had called him back. Since it was Friday afternoon, he hoped that all of them hadn't left work early.

"This is the Plessey Company in West Drayton. May I be of assistance?" the main operator asked.

"Yes, this is Captain Ian Black, with the British Army in West Berlin. I'd like to speak with the Division manager."

"That would be Mr. Thomas Edwards, sir. I'll see if he's in."

In about five seconds, a man came on the line.

"This is Thomas Edwards, may I help you?"

"Yes, Mr. Edwards, this is Captain Ian Black of the British Army in Berlin, and I'm calling about an employee of yours, named Peter Lange. We understand he went missing approximately a year ago, after he went on a vacation to East Germany, to visit some distant relatives. Currently, we are in negotiation with the East German authorities and hope to have a prisoner swap on the 19th of May. If all goes well, we'll be exchanging an East German spy for Mr. Lange. This exchange is, of course, extremely confidential and must not be leaked to the press."

"Peter Lange was an employee of ours but, when he didn't return from his vacation, he was finally terminated six months, after his absence, as is our normal policy. I grasp the need for secrecy, but how can I help you in this matter?"

"Before we exchange the spy for Mr. Lange, we need to be sure that he is well and is actually Peter Lange. Do you have a manager or a fellow engineer, who know him well enough, that they could verify it is him? We will have a doctor, available at the prisoner swap, to do a quick one minute check up, to ascertain his mental and physical condition."

"Let me check into this and I'll call you back on Monday, if that's okay captain. The plant is about to shut down for the weekend."

"Certainly, I'll wait for your call," Ian replied, and then gave Edwards his Berlin phone number.

271

At 1130 hours on the next Monday, after attending his CO's normal staff meeting, Ian received a phone call from Thomas Edwards at Plessey in England.

"This is Captain Black speaking."

"Good morning captain, I've found a manager, by the name of Trevor Ackerman, who was very close to Peter Lange; in fact Peter reported to him on some projects."

"That's great to hear. Could you spare this manager for a few days around the 19th of May? As I mentioned last Friday, it's very important that we make sure the prisoner, we are swapping for, is indeed Peter Lange."

"I think that can be arranged, and I assume the Army will pay for his travel and hotel," replied Edwards.

"Yes, of course. We would need him to arrive here on Thursday, the 16th, and he would return to England on Monday, the 20th. This will give us time here to discuss with him the exchange and to acquaint him with what we want him to do."

"Good, it's settled then. I'll have Trevor call you tomorrow and you can give him the travel arrangements, such as date and time of flight, airline, etc."

"Thank you very much Mr. Edwards for your cooperation, and I'll look forward to Trevor's call tomorrow."

In the afternoon, Ian walked over to the Administration Building to see Helga, in Colonel Thurman's office.

"I need to book a round trip flight on BEA from London Heathrow to Tempelhof, for a passenger named Trevor Ackerman. I believe there's a flight BE618 that is scheduled to depart London at around 0940, and arrives in Berlin at 1250, on Thursday the 16th, with a stop in Dusseldorf. Also book the return flight for Monday, the 20th. The ticket is to be picked up at the BEA counter, on the day of the flight."

"I'll work on it, captain. Is there anything else you want me to do?"

"Yes, book a room at the Grande Hotel located on Kurfürstendamm, with a check in for the 16th and a check

272

out Monday morning on the 20th. This should also be in the name of Trevor Ackerman."

"I'll get to work on it right away, captain. Anything else?" she asked.

"We need to get Giselle Schmitt back here on Saturday the 18th, on a special security flight from Rheindahlen to Gatow. Make sure they understand at the detention centre that we need her brought here, under guard by a female MP. When she arrives at the Stadium, we need to have her held in a guard room cell, until the exchange on Sunday night."

"I understand, and I'll arrange the transfer immediately. I know this sounds strange, considering what she did, but I actually feel sorry for her, in some way."

"I know what you mean," Ian replied, with a sad tone to his voice. "Anyway, let's get on it Helga. The sooner we get this exchange over, the better it'll be for all of us."

On Tuesday morning, Ian was sitting in his office writing another report about the upcoming exchange, when the phone rang.

"Captain Black here, with whom am I speaking?"

"This is Trevor Ackerman at Plessey in England. Thomas Edwards, the Managing Director at the plant here, asked that I give you a call. He led me to believe that it has something to do with Peter Lange."

"That's correct, Trevor. It's my understanding that you are well acquainted with Peter. We need you here in Berlin to identify him, when we exchange a spy for him. According to our information, he has been in an East German prison since the middle of 1962, and he may not be in the best of health. Are you willing to come here to Berlin and accompany me and some other people, at the exchange? Of course, we will pay your expenses here and back, plus the hotel and food. One last point, this operation is secret and you must tell no one what you are doing, now or in the future. Is this clearly understood?"

"Yes captain, I am willing to do this, since I believe I'm the person, who knows Peter the best. He's been to my home for dinner several times, and he worked for me on a few projects. The desire for secrecy will be observed."

"Excellent, I hoped you would give me a positive reply. One major and critical point, do you happen to have a current British passport?"

"Yes, I do. When will you want me to be there in Berlin?"

"We've booked a BEA flight for you out of Heathrow Terminal One, at 0940 on Thursday, the 16th, and it lands in Berlin at 1250, after a stop in Dusseldorf. I believe you'll be flying on a Vickers Viscount aircraft; I hope that's not a problem, since it has a good safety record. You can pick your ticket up at the BEA counter, when you check in. Unless there is a last minute change, you will be returning on Monday, the 20th, so you'll need to bring clothes to last four days. I'll meet you at the Berlin Tempelhof airport with transportation and take you to the Grande Hotel on Kurfürstendamm. Do you have any issue with this itinerary?"

"No, I don't think so."

"Good, if something comes up between now, and when you arrive here, please let me know. We will discuss the plan for the entire exchange on Friday, the day after you arrive. We'll need to be sure about what you will be doing at the prisoner exchange, and discuss any anticipated problems that could come up. I'll see you on Thursday, the 16th, at the Berlin Airport. Have a good trip."

"Thank you Captain Black, I'll see you then. If something unexpected does crop up, I'll certainly call you immediately. Good bye."

Ian hung up his phone, relaxing a little now that everything was falling into place. He started to think about various scenarios to do with the exchange.

"How are they going to be sure that this Peter Lange is the engineer from the Plessey Company? Since he had been in jail for some time, he could be in bad shape. Did Stasi torture him to get some information concerning the projects he was working on at Plessey? What questions could they ask him to be sure that only the real Peter Lange could answer? There are so many issues to be tackled," he thought.

Ian went back to work finishing his latest report to Colonel Thurman about the exchange planning. When he had completed it, he called Helga for an appointment to present the report to the colonel, and also discuss a major issue. Helga booked Ian on his CO's calendar, for the next Wednesday morning at 1000 hours.

At the appointed day and time, he entered the colonel's office and gave him his report.

"I'll read it later, Ian. I understand you want to discuss with me an important issue, concerning this exchange."

"That's correct, sir. The conundrum that I've been going over in my mind is, what do we do if the Peter Lange, the Stasi bring to the prisoner exchange, is an imposter who looks and acts like him. Will it be acceptable to you and the brigadier if, upon verifying he is not the real Peter Lange, I cancel the exchange?"

"Captain, we picked you to be our main emissary in this exchange and therefore, if you determine that we're not swapping Giselle Schmitt for the real Peter Lange, you have the authority to cancel the deal."

"Thank you sir, I understand our position and will act accordingly. By the way, is it too much to ask that you contact the CO of the Durham Light Infantry Regiment and ask him to schedule a lorry, full of twenty armed soldiers, to be at the Heerstrasse border crossing at 2100 hours. A show of force will prevent the East Germans from causing any trouble."

"Yes, Ian, I'll do that for you. I agree it's better for a colonel to ask that, than a captain," he said smiling. "As usual keep me up to date on your planning."

For the next nine days, Ian refined the exchange plan to make sure that he didn't fail in this first major task, as a captain in the British Army. If he did fail, he might have to quit the Army or be shipped off to some remote site in the Atlantic or Africa.

****

On Thursday, the 16th of May, Ian checked out an Army sedan from the motor pool and drove down to the Berlin Tempelhof Airport, to meet Trevor Ackerman's flight, which was originally scheduled to land at 1250 hours. The latest time was 1305 hours. As he waited for the plane to arrive, Ian, dressed in his British Army uniform, found a seat in the arrival hall and started to read a German newspaper. He looked up one time and noticed a small, obese man, with black hair and a moustache, who was looking around, at all the new arrivals. Ian thought, *"I think I've seen this man before, but I can't remember where. Oh well, it may come to me one of these days."*

Soon, Trevor Ackerman's flight arrived and Ian rose to meet it. As the passengers exited the immigration area, Ian spotted someone he thought was Trevor, since he looked as though he was lost and expecting someone.

"Trevor Ackerman?" Ian asked, the tall, slender young man, with light brown hair. He guessed he was in his early thirties.

"Yes, that's me. Are you Captain Black?"

"You're correct. Thank you for coming here to Berlin. Your presence at the exchange will be important. Let's get your bags and go to the car, which I have parked outside."

As they walked to the baggage area, the small, obese man rose from his seat and followed them from a distance.

276

Trevor went and stood by the carousel, searching for his bags. Finally, his baggage arrived in the hall; he picked it up and followed Ian out of the terminal, to the army sedan. Ian drove him to the Grande Hotel on Kurfürstendamm.

As they pulled up at the hotel, Ian said to Trevor, "I have some work to do at the office, so I'll leave you here for the rest of today. It's a good hotel and we've taken care of the bill in advance. You may also charge your meals in the hotel restaurant, to the room. If you want to go for a walk, this street contains plenty of stores for window shopping."

"That will be fine, captain. I'll need to stretch my legs anyway, after sitting in the plane for a few hours."

"Excellent, I hope you find Berlin interesting. Have you ever been here before?"

"No, I've never been out of England actually, so it'll be quite an adventure."

"Tomorrow morning, I'll pick you up at nine o'clock and take you to my office, in the Berlin Olympic Stadium. There we can discuss the procedure for the prisoner exchange, and the best way for you to check that Peter Lange is who we think he is."

"Sounds great, I'll see you tomorrow at nine."

The next morning, as promised, Ian drove to the Grande Hotel and found Trevor coming out of the lift, on the ground floor.

"I hope you had a restful evening," Ian asked.

"Yes, I did, thank you very much. This is a good hotel and the food in the restaurant is excellent, although with somewhat of a German flavour."

"We'll drive to the Olympic Stadium and meet in my office. Hopefully, sometime during the day, you can get to meet my CO, Colonel Thurman."

"I look forward to it."

Ian drove to the Stadium complex and they both entered his London Block office, to discuss the procedure for the exchange of prisoners. He went through basically the proposal that he had presented to the Stasi a few days before, but added their suggestion that an MP or soldier be present, with the spy being swapped.

"First, we'll have a doctor from the Royal Army Medical Corps (RAMC) conduct a medical and mental check up of Peter Lange. As agreed to, he's only allowed one minute to decide if Peter is dead or alive, and mentally alert to answer questions. Then, you'll have five minutes to talk with Peter and decide if he is an imposter or genuine. Your conversation with him, and any questions, must be planned out ahead, so as to obtain the optimum identification that we can, within the time limit."

"Where and when will the swap take place?" asked Trevor.

"It's scheduled for 2200 hours this Sunday, at the Heerstrasse border crossing point, between West Berlin and East Germany. It's about five miles from here and shouldn't take long to drive there from this complex. The actual border is a white line painted across the road, and on one side of it is a building controlled by the British, while the East Germans have an inspection facility in East Berlin."

"Will there be any traffic flowing through the crossing point, while we're there?"

"No, all traffic will be stopped between 2100 to 2300 hours however, since it will be Sunday, we expect the traffic to be light."

"Who will actually walk to the white line for the exchange?"

"I'll be there in civilian clothes, a British Army doctor, you, the spy named Giselle Schmitt and an unarmed MP. Standing back, at least seventy-five feet from the line, will be around twenty armed soldiers from the Durham Light Infantry Regiment, Russian speaking Captain Alex Swiderski and probably my CO Colonel Thurman."

"Why will the soldiers be there, and will anyone from the press be observing the transfer?"

"The soldiers will be as a show of force, in case the East Germans try to pull a fast one. No press is allowed from either side."

"Since it'll be late in the evening, will there be plenty of artificial light, at this crossing point? Why I ask is the fact that it may be hard to determine, if this person is really Peter in the dim light environment."

"I'm sorry to say the lighting will be dim at the actual white line area. Further back, at the buildings, there are some strong lights for the border patrol to look into cars that cross over at night. This is why the discussion you'll have with Peter, and any questions you'll ask him, will be critical in determining his identity."

Ian then went through with Trevor some of the discussion points, which he should have with Peter, and together they came up with some trick statements and questions, which might expose an imposter. When they had a break in the deliberations, Ian called Helga and made arrangement for the two of them to meet with Colonel Thurman that afternoon.

After lunch at the Officers' Mess, Ian and Trevor went to see the colonel in the Administration Building. There the three of them sat down and reviewed the exchange procedure, that would be followed. The colonel approved what Trevor would discuss with Peter, and the questions he would pose. It was agreed that if for any reason the transfer of spies fell through, they should hurry back to the safety of the seventy-five foot point, where the infantrymen would be located.

The meeting ended up with a clear understanding by all three, exactly was going to happen at the exchange. Colonel Thurman stated that he would attend and be positioned back with the infantrymen. Ian explained that he would be dressed in civvies, just in case some press person did appear and take a picture. At least the spy swap would appear to be a diplomatic mission, rather than a military one. The colonel concurred with this idea.

At the end of the day, Ian took Trevor back to the Grande and dropped him at the main entrance.

"I'll pick you up at six o'clock on Sunday evening and we'll quickly review on what you plan to say and ask, in your five minute time allotment. I hope you have a good time tomorrow enjoying the sights and sounds of West Berlin. By the way, on Monday, I'll drive you back to Tempelhof for your 1400 BEA flight back to Dusseldorf and Heathrow. I trust that's okay with you."

"Certainly, I'll see you at six on Sunday evening."

"Oh, by the way, as far as Peter Lange is concerned, he'll be checked into a hospital for evaluation and then flown to England a few days later."

"I'll tell the Division Manager that, when I return to Plessey on Tuesday."

Ian left him at the hotel and went back to the Stadium to think about the transfer, and to make sure he hadn't forgotten anything.

On Saturday, Captain Ian Black went to the RAF Gatow airfield to meet the plane, carrying Giselle Schmitt and the MP from the Detention Centre at Rheindahlen, in West Germany. The special flight taxied up to the arrival hall and Giselle Schmitt, in handcuffs, accompanied by a female MP, walked into the hall. She looked absolutely miserable and melancholy; nothing like the cheerful woman Ian met at the British pub, close to the Stadium complex several months before.

Ian walked up to the MP and said, "You can take those handcuffs off her, corporal. She won't be running away."

"Sir, my orders were to keep her handcuffed, until we are safely inside the holding cell at the Olympic Stadium."

"I'm countermanding that order, and I take full responsibility for anything that happens. She is now under my protection, until the exchange tomorrow night."

Giselle looked at Captain Black puzzled, since she had not heard of any exchange. *"What did it mean?"* she thought. *"Are they going to swap me with somebody? I really don't want to return to East Germany, where you have no protection from the communist government."*

"I have a car right outside," Ian said to the MP, "It will take us direct to the Stadium complex."

They walked outside to where Ian had left the car, with the driver keeping guard. The three of them climbed into the rear seat, with Giselle in the middle, and Ian told the driver to return to the Stadium.

Upon arriving at the complex, Ian led Giselle and the MP into the Administration guard room, where he had her placed in the holding cell. Ian went into the cell to talk with her.

"Why have I been brought to Berlin?" she asked, trying to wipe away a few tears.

"We have an offer from the East Germans to trade you for an Englishman, being held by them for spying, and the exchange is scheduled for tomorrow evening at 2200 hours."

"But I don't want to go back to East Germany. The country is run by a vain, egotistical Walter Ulbricht, who doesn't give a damn about the common citizen."

"Why did you spy on us for the East Germans?"

"It's very simple. They threatened to harm my brother who lives in Dresden, if I didn't cooperate. That's how the government operates. I gave them as little information, as I felt I could get away with, and they wouldn't hurt him."

"I'm sorry Giselle, but it's out of my hands. The British Army has decreed that you are to be swapped for this Englishman, who worked for a defence company. They need to find out how many secrets he may have given away, under pressure during imprisonment."

"Is there anyone I can talk with, who has the authority to cancel this exchange?"

"Regretfully there isn't, Giselle. This trade was initiated by my superiors and there is nothing you could say to them that would change their decision."

Giselle Schmitt then started to cry, and Ian felt sorry for her. She was acting like someone who had been sentenced to death and saw the hangman in front of her.

"I'm sure this won't make you feel any better, but I will be at the exchange. A doctor, a man to verify the spy being traded is real, the MP and myself."

Still crying, she asked, "What happens if the man doing the verifying comes to the conclusion that the spy is an imposter?"

"At this point, we have no contingency plan for this outcome of the vetting process. That is an issue we still have to consider. Right now, I have to leave. Is there any special food you would like? I can probably get some delivered from the Officers' Mess."

"I'm not that hungry considering the situation I'm in. I'll try and eat anything you have delivered here. Is there any way I can call my mother in Cologne and let her know what is happening?"

"I'm sorry, but that will not be possible. I'll come by here tomorrow at 2000 hours and we'll prepare to go to the exchange point on Heerstrasse."

Ian then called for the guard who opened the cell door and let him out. He then went to his office and changed clothes into his civvies, for the train ride back to his flat, in the south of Berlin.

****

The next day, Sunday, the 19th of May, Ian rose late and ate a hearty breakfast, as he might not have time to eat much during the rest of the day. He was slightly nervous about the schedule for the prisoner transfer, and the possibility that he had forgotten something. As it was, he had not anticipated a change in the fine weather; it had been great during the first part of May.

He turned on the wireless to get the latest forecast and heard that there was a good probability of light rain, starting at 1700 hours, and continuing through midnight. Ian thought, *"I have to obtain some umbrellas just in case we need them. It could be a disaster if it pours, when we are trying to conduct the exchange."*

Most stores were closed on Sunday, but he did manage to find one down an alley, that was open. Luckily, they sold umbrellas, and he purchased all three black ones, the store had remaining in stock. At 1500 hours, after he had dressed in a black suit, white shirt and his traditional Harrow, navy blue and white striped tie, he left the flat for the Stadium, carrying a raincoat and the umbrellas. He took the usual U-Bahn ride to the Olympic Stadium, and arrived there around 1530 hours. He walked to the complex and entered the London Block, where he had his office.

For the next two hours, he went over the plans for the exchange, to make sure he hadn't forgotten anything. In addition, he gave some thought to what would happen, if the vetting of Peter Lange turned out to prove, that he wasn't who they said he was. The Stasi over the years had turned out to be untrustworthy, to the West. He also monitored the latest weather on his office wireless and heard that a cold front was coming through, as previously forecast. The evening was going to be cool, with a light drizzle.

At 1730, Ian drove to the Grande hotel to pick up Trevor Ackerman, who was waiting in the lobby.

"How was your weekend, Trevor?" he asked. "I hope you had a good time looking in the store windows and visiting the museum. Since the war, Berlin reconstruction has been tremendous, compared to the East sector."

"Yes, I had a great time. It was interesting to see Berlin, as I've never been to a foreign country before. I'm now ready to get this show on the road, meet Peter Lange again, and return to England tomorrow."

After Trevor got into the car, Ian drove to the Olympic Stadium, arriving there at around 1830. The traffic was light, because it was Sunday evening and it was starting to drizzle. In fact, Ian had to use the windscreen wipers a couple of times, to deflect the raindrops to the side.

At the Stadium, Ian and Trevor went over the schedule for the exchange, especially what Trevor's role was going to be. He had to find out if Peter Lange was real or fake, before he was swapped for the Stasi spy Giselle. Ian explained exactly what the procedure would be for the doctors and the identity examiners to check out the spies. If all went well, the spies would have their handcuffs removed by the MP or East German soldier, and they would cross the line. Ian, Trevor, the doctor, Peter Lange and the MP would walk back to the West Berlin border building. There they would climb into the waiting cars and return to the Stadium.

At 2000 hours, twenty soldiers from the Durham Light Infantry Regiment and an officer started to assemble, near a waiting lorry. At the same time, Colonel Thurman came to Ian's office to discuss last minute details with him and Trevor.

At 2030, Ian went to the guard room and found the female MP waiting for him. Together, they entered the holding cell, and the MP hand cuffed herself to Giselle. She was still looking pitiful and shaking, as though she was going to her execution. This was the first time the colonel had met Giselle, and he was somewhat taken aback by her condition. He thought that she would be happy returning to the East and discovered this was not the case.

At 2100 hours, they all left the guard house in the Administration Building and climbed into two waiting army sedans. They then exited the complex and drove the five miles to the Heerstrasse crossing point, followed by the lorry loaded with the infantry.

They arrived at the West Berlin border crossing building at around 2130. The traffic on the way was light and they noticed that the West Berlin police had already stopped traffic trying to enter East Germany one mile back, as they had been requested to do.

The occupants, of the two sedans, got out of the vehicles and entered the building, while the infantry remained in the covered lorry, out of the drizzle. In the border building, Ian again went over the procedure one last time, to make sure there would be no slip ups. His army reputation hung on a smooth exchange of the spies. He handed out the three black umbrellas to the group, which was going to accompany him to the border, while he donned his raincoat and a hat. It was still drizzling, but looked like it might let up.

At 2158, Ian, the RAMC doctor, Trevor Ackerman, the MP and Giselle left the building, to walk the seventy-five feet toward the actual border line. At the same time, the officer in charge of the infantry ordered the soldiers out of the lorry and to line up just behind the raised gate poles, on each side of the building. Colonel Thurman joined the officer in charge of the soldiers, to watch what happened at the white line.

As Ian and the other four people approached the demarcation line, he noticed that four East Germans were also coming to the border, as agreed to in the meeting two weeks ago. It appeared to Ian that Peter Lange was being helped along to the border, as if he was having trouble walking and was in a daze.

At exactly 2200 hours, the two groups met at the border standing about six feet apart from each other, with the white line, in between them.

Berndt Scholz, from the Stasi, was the leader of the group, and he shook hands with Ian, remarking, "I see you've changed your uniform for some civvies."

"Yes, I didn't want to show you up," he said smiling. "Let's get this over with, shall we?"

First, the East German doctor stepped forward to the line, as the MP led Giselle up to it. Using a stethoscope and talking to her, he seemed content that she was in good physical shape and mentally fair. As he stepped back, the identity examiner walked forward to talk with her, for the five minute allotted time. Ian thought he recognized the man, and it finally dawned on him, that it was the same obese man he had seen at the pub months before, and also at the Tempelhof airport, when Trevor flew in. He then realized it must be her handler, to whom she had given classified information. At the end of the five minutes, the man stepped back and nodded to Scholz, as if everything was okay.

Scholz then held out his open hand, with the palm up, to Ian and said, "It's your turn."

The RAMC doctor stepped forward and examined Peter Lange. After his minute was up, he stepped back and told Ian, "He's still alive, but his heart is racing. In addition he seems to be only half coherent."

"Thanks doctor, I'll keep that in mind."

Trevor Ackerman then stepped forward toward Peter for his identity examination.

"Peter, it's great to see you again. We all wondered what had happened to you."

"Trevor, I'm glad you came to get me out of this fix," he replied with a slurring voice, as though he couldn't speak well.

Trevor then went on talking with him, trying to get him to relax, before he came out with the key points that he and Ian had decided upon.

"You remember the Tekline project, where we had trouble getting it to work."

"Yes, I certainly do. That was a bear to get up and running."

"Well, we finally got it to work, and it's doing a great job, monitoring undersea cables, without breaking into them."

"Hey, that's smashing. I'm glad to hear Tekline is what we designed it to be."

Trevor then went on to talk with Peter, about other ventures at Plessey, on which Peter seemed to be well versed.

Finally, Trevor reached the end of the five minute discussion with, "You remember that evening dinner at my place, right before you went on vacation to Germany."

"I think so. My mind has been foggy, due to my imprisonment."

"Well, since you were going on vacation, my wife's sister volunteered to take care of your cat, until you came back. She still has *Mister* and she can hardly wait until you return, so she can give him back to you."

"Yes, I've sure missed that cat over the past year. What is the name of your wife's sister? I don't remember it."

"It's Margaret, and she lives just down the road from us."

"Oh, yes. Margaret, she's a pretty woman, and I was glad when she offered to take *Mister*."

Trevor looked at his watch and said, "Well, my five minutes are up. I'll be glad when you get back to Plessey and start work again, Peter."

"Me too!" Peter Lange replied, still with a slurring voice.

During the entire time, Peter spoke in English, with a slight accent, just like Trevor remembered.

Trevor stepped back and whispered to Ian, "He's phony. Peter Lange hated cats and my wife doesn't have a sister. She's an only child. On top of that, we never had a project at Plessey named Tekline."

Ian signaled back to the border building, by raising his hat a couple of inches off his head. The infantry locked and loaded their weapons, in unison, and stepped forward ten paces. The East Germans heard the bolt action of the rifles, and some of their troops stepped forward.

287

Ian sent Trevor, the RAMC doctor, the MP and Giselle scampering back, to the safety of the border building and the infantry. He then stepped forward to the line to talk with Berndt Scholz.

"Herr Scholz, we're not prepared to go forward, with the transfer of the prisoners. It appears that the person you've put forward, to be swapped with Giselle Schmitt, is not the real Peter Lange. What's happened to him I don't know, but we'll find out sooner or later?"

"Captain Black, we came here in good conscious and are dismayed that you'll go back on your word. You know this will be detrimental to any future prisoner swap, between our two sides."

"So be it! You wanted to exchange prisoners, as much as we did. But, we wanted Peter Lange back, not someone who is pretending to be him. Good night."

Ian turned and walked away from the border; hoping one of the East Germans did not decide to shoot him. After walking, what seemed to be a long seventy-five feet, back to the building, he was relieved that he was still alive. Colonel Thurman came to meet him and said, "Trevor Ackerman has told me all about it. You made the right decision to call this off. Let's get out of here and go back to the Stadium."

They all climbed into the vehicles and drove back the five miles to the complex, followed by the lorry loaded with soldiers.

At the Stadium, Ian took Giselle back to the holding cell, where she asked, "What happens to me now?"

"That hasn't been decided yet. I will discuss the issue first thing in the morning with Colonel Thurman, and let you know."

"Well, I'm relieved that you did not turn me over to the East Germans. I might be able to sleep a little better tonight."

"I have to take Trevor Ackerman to the Tempelhof, first thing in the morning. Then, I'll meet with the colonel, to talk

288

about your situation and, hopefully tomorrow afternoon, I can let you know the outcome."

Ian left her looking a little cheerier than earlier, and took Trevor back to his hotel, using an unmarked army sedan. From there, he drove to his flat where it took a while for him to go to sleep, as he had to unwind his brain from the evening's events.

24

Dilemma Resolved

The next morning, Ian's alarm clock went off at 0630, after only a six hour fitful sleep; dreaming about the exchange and gunshots that he thought rang out, after they walked back to the border building. He jumped out of bed, shaved and showered. After drying off, he donned his uniform which he normally didn't wear around his flat, but today he had to pick up his Plessey guest at the hotel and take him to the airport. Finally, he fixed himself a bowl of corn flakes, together with a piece of toast and a cup of coffee.

He left the flat and drove the unmarked army sedan to the Grande Hotel, on Kurfürstendamm, to pick up Trevor. Exactly at 0900, he pulled up at the main entrance and Trevor came out with his luggage. After he placed it in the boot, he climbed in and Ian headed for Tempelhof Airport.

"I'm glad you could make it, Trevor," Ian said. "You saved the British Army from making a major, embarrassing mistake."

"I'm glad I could help out. In my mind last night, I reviewed his responses to my statements and questions, and I have no doubt that was not the Peter Lange, I know."

"If I ever find out what happened to the real Peter, I'll let you know for sure."

Soon they arrived at Tempelhof and they both got out of the car. Ian went around and shook Trevor's hand saying, "Thanks again for coming. You saved the day."

"You're welcome. When you come back to England, stop by at Plessey and look me up."

"I certainly will. Don't forget your bags in the boot."

Trevor retrieved his luggage, waved at Ian and entered the departure terminal, for his flight back to Heathrow.

Ian drove straight to the Olympic Stadium and entered his London Block office, to call the colonel's office. Helga made an appointment for him to meet with Colonel Thurman at 1100 hours.

As Ian hung up the phone, after talking with Helga, it rang almost immediately.

"Captain Black here, with whom am I speaking."

"Kurt, this is Franz. I have some news for you that isn't too pleasant."

"That's all I need right now. Last evening didn't go too well either. We cancelled a prisoner swap with the East Germans, after they tried to pull a fast one. Anyway what's your news, Franz?"

"You remember two weeks ago you asked me to look into the whereabouts of two people in East Germany; Peter Lange and Gerhard Schmitt. Well, I have news on both of them."

"That's great, spill it out, Franz."

"First, Peter Lange was arrested soon after he arrived in East Germany, on the charge of spying. It appears he had been asked by the CIA to visit an East German electronics company and find out about the special receiver, they were working on for a Soviet missile. He languished in a Stasi prison and, after several interrogations, he had medical complications and died; probably from heart failure.

Second, one of our agents in Dresden checked into the whereabouts of Gerhard Schmitt, Giselle Schmitt's older brother. It turns out he was arrested, for unspecified crimes against the state, right after you picked up Giselle, for spying at the British Berlin Brigade. Gerhard Schmitt has not been seen since, and all indications are that he was executed, three months after his arrest."

"I'm sorry to hear this news and I'll have to tell my CO, since it may affect what we do with Giselle. One good point is that we made the correct decision last night; cancelling the exchange of spies. Thanks for all the information and your effort in this matter. I owe you one."

"You sure do, Kurt. Talk to you later."

After he hung up the phone, he walked over to the Administration Building, first to see Giselle Schmitt and then to meet with the colonel.

He entered the guard room and had the MP on duty take him to the holding cell, where he let him in. He entered the cell as the MP locked the door behind him. Giselle was reading a book when he entered and her face lit up somewhat, when she saw who it was. Ian went over to the bunk and sat down beside her.

"Giselle, I have some news to give you. It's nothing to do with your situation here; it has to do with your brother Gerhard."

"Is he okay? I haven't seen or talked with him, since the Wall went up, almost two years ago."

"I have just received reliable news that he was arrested for crimes against the state, right after you were arrested. All indications are that three months later, he was executed for these crimes. There is no record of a trial being held. I'm sorry."

Giselle started to break down, sobbing. "The only reason I gave classified information to my handler was that he promised me my brother would not be in any danger, if I cooperated. I did it all for nothing. Does my mother know?"

"I doubt that your mother knows yet. This information just recently came from a reliable source that I can't reveal."

"I have to leave now and discuss with my CO, what we're going to do with you. Personally, I believe you have been punished enough, but that is just my opinion. I'll let you know what the decision is,"

"Thank you, captain. I know some of this must be hard on you also."

Ian rose and called for the MP, who came to let him out of the cell, after which Ian then went upstairs to see his CO.

As he entered the outer office, Helga told him, "The colonel will see you in a few minutes. He's discussing an issue with another visitor at the moment."

"Thanks Helga, how are you doing today?"

"Probably better than you," she replied smiling. "I hear that the exchange didn't go as planned."

"Yes, you might say that we had a slight hitch. Hopefully all's well that ends well, to quote William Shakespeare."

"How is Giselle doing by the way? I know she was a spy, but I still liked her as a person."

"She's really down. I just had to tell her that her brother was probably dead; executed. You know that's why she did what she did; they promised not to harm him, if she provided information. I'd better not say any more."

At that moment, the CO of the Durham Light Infantry Regiment came out of the colonel's office.

Ian saluted him, saying, "Thank you for your support last night, sir."

"Ah, Captain Ian Black, I've heard all about you," he said with a smile, as he returned the salute. "Good luck in there."

Ian wondered what he meant by that, but he had no time to think, as the buzzer on Helga's desk sounded and she told him he could go in immediately. Ian went into the colonel's office and saluted, as normal.

"Take a seat, Ian," he said, as he returned the salute, with a wave of his hand.

"Sir, before we start into a critique of last night, I have some news that was relayed to me from Franz of BND."

"What did he have to say?"

"A couple of weeks ago, I asked him to find out anything he could about the condition and location of Peter Lange and Gerhard Schmitt. He called me this morning and gave me the following information.

First, Peter Lange was arrested soon after he arrived in East Germany on his vacation. It turns out he was caught at an electronics company, trying to obtain information for the CIA. After he was arrested, he was interrogated thoroughly and that is when the Stasi probably obtained all the information they needed, to create a phony Peter Lange. Peter subsequently died in prison some time ago.

Second, according to a BND agent in Dresden, Gerhard Schmitt, Giselle's brother, was arrested in the city on unspecified charges, right after we arrested her here. All indications are that he was executed for treason, a few months after his arrest. Giselle told me about an hour ago that she only gave information her Stasi handler, after he promised her that her brother would be safe, as long as she cooperated."

"Well, that does shed some light on what has happened. The question now is what do we propose to do with Giselle Schmitt?"

"Well sir, as you probably already know, I have one failing and that is a soft spot for attractive women."

"Yes, that has come to my attention. Let me ask you captain, what would you do, in my position, to Giselle?"

"I figure that we have three alternatives. One: Have her mother fly in, take custody of her here, with the promise that she will take her back to Cologne. Two: Take her to the main refugee centre at Marienfelde and have them process her. They would probably send her to her mother in

Cologne.   Three: Turn her over to the German State Attorney for prosecution.

The major concern I have is to keep the British Army out of the papers. If the press found out we had a spy in our midst, it wouldn't look good for public relations. I figure that she has been punished enough, considering the situation with her brother. From what I can gather, the information she leaked to Stasi was inconsequential in most cases, even though she did pass on the name of the pseudo mole in the GRU. Major Phillips's Interrogation Group did interview her right after her arrest, to determine what information she had given the East Germans. Since she's a German citizen, my preference would be to call her mother in order to see if she is willing to travel to Berlin, and take her daughter back to Cologne.

Before we let her go, I believe I would have the Interrogation Group again interview her and find out as much as they can about what information she passed on. This second screening would tell us if she told the truth in the first interrogation.   Also, I would have her sign a statement that she was well treated here, and at the detention centre in Rheindahlen.

Of course, this is a recommendation from a British Army captain who has had a drink and dinner with the offender, as I mentioned previously about a year ago. However, I want it clear, sir, that in no way am I condoning what she did."

"Ian, I have actually been thinking along the same lines, even before you told me about her brother. With this additional information, I can more easily go to Brigadier Croxford and get his okay. If I can reach him today, hopefully I will have his response immediately. By the way, I believe you conducted the exchange in a professional manner and I will tell Rex so. That's all for now, I'll let you know what the decision is."

Ian saluted and, as he turned, said, "Thank you for your confidence in me, sir."

The colonel returned the salute saying, "You're welcome Ian."

Ian walked out of his office, waved at Helga and went to the guard room on the ground floor. He entered the area, where the holding cells were, and told Giselle that he hoped to have some positive news, by the end of the day.

"Give me your mother's phone number in Cologne, just in case I need to call her."

"This is the last number I had," she said, as she wrote it down on a piece of paper. "I haven't been able to talk with her, since I was arrested last year."

"I'm sorry about that. Do you have a good relationship with her?"

"Yes. When she left Dresden years ago, I was the only known relative who came with her."

"Thanks for the number. As I said a few minutes ago, I'll let you know the decision as soon as I receive it."

He then returned to his office in the London Block, to wait for a call from the colonel.

At about 1600, the phone rang and Ian picked up the handset saying, "Captain Ian Black speaking."

"Ian, this is Colonel Thurman. Rex has agreed that the first alternative is the best one, if the mother is agreeable."

"I'll call her right away sir. I have her number in Cologne and I'll let her know the situation."

"Very good, Ian; just keep me informed."

He picked up the phone and dialed the Cologne number, Giselle had given him. After three rings a woman answered.

"Hilda Schmitt?" Ian asked.

"Yes, I am Hilda. To whom am I speaking?"

"This is a Captain Black of the British Army in Berlin, and I'm calling about your daughter Giselle."

"Is she in trouble? I haven't heard from her in over a year. The last time I heard from her, she was working for the British Army at the Olympic Stadium."

"Yes, she was working for us, but a year ago she was arrested for espionage."

"Oh no, my Giselle a spy, there must be some mistake."

"It's no mistake Frau Schmitt, and she has admitted to the charge. It appears she was trying to protect her brother, Gerhard, in Dresden."

"She always looked up to him, who is ten years older than she is."

"The reason I'm calling you is to see if you're willing to fly to Berlin, and then take your daughter back to Cologne with you. You would have to pay your own way here and Giselle's back to Cologne. One other condition is that you do not mention any of this to the press. It must be kept confidential. If you can agree to this, Giselle will be freed. However, she will never be able to work for the British forces again, as she will be placed on a *Do Not Hire* list."

"Yes, I can afford to travel to Berlin and bring her home. When would you like me to come?"

"Are you able to come tomorrow? She's in a holding cell at the Olympic Stadium, and once she signs a release form, she'll be free to go. I'll meet your plane and also take you back to the airport, just to insure she leaves Berlin safely."

"Let me call the airline for flights and I'll call you back within the hour. What is your number?"

Ian gave her his phone number and then went to talk briefly with Giselle, in the Administration Building guard room.

"Giselle, I have good news. Your mother has agreed to fly to Berlin and take you home back to Cologne. She is checking the airline schedule and seat availability for tomorrow, as we speak."

"You mean that I'll be free to go."

"Yes, we feel your one year in jail is enough. However, there are three conditions for your freedom. First, you must sign a statement that you've been well treated during your captivity. Second, you may never work again for the British forces worldwide. You'll be placed on a *Do Not Hire* list. Third, and lastly, you must never talk to the press about this entire affair, including the failed prisoner exchange. If you agree to all three terms, you'll be able to leave with your mother. One final point, I will take you to the airport and make sure you leave Berlin."

"I agree to your terms. Bring me the statement of how I've been treated, and I'll sign it immediately. Actually, considering the charges, I have been treated very fairly here, and at the Rheindalhen detention centre."

"Very well then, right now I have to get back to my office, to receive your mother's call. If all goes well, I'll pick her up at the Tempelhof tomorrow and bring her straight here. Sleep well tonight. Hopefully, it'll be your last night in captivity."

Ian left and went back to his office. As he walked in, the phone rang.

"This is Hilda Schmitt in Cologne."

"Yes, Frau Schmitt, this is Captain Black.

"I've booked a seat on the BEA flight BE718 from Cologne to Tempelhof and two seats on BE721 back to Cologne. Both are for tomorrow. The flight arrives in Berlin at 1045 and the return flight departs at 1800."

"Very good Frau Schmitt, I'll meet you tomorrow at 1045. I'll be in my British Army uniform. Goodbye for now."

The next day Ian went to the Stadium from his flat and exchanged his civvies for a uniform. At 1000 hours, he checked a car out of the motor pool and headed for the Tempelhof airport, to meet Hilda Schmitt's flight due in at 1045. Actually, her flight arrived five minutes early but Ian made it in time to greet her at the gate. He recognized her almost immediately, since she looked just like Giselle, except twenty-eight years older.

"Hilda Schmitt?" Ian asked the woman, as she came through the arrival gate.

"Yes, that's me. Are you Captain Black?"

"Yes, Frau Schmitt."

"Please call me Hilda. I'm glad you called me yesterday. I was so worried about Giselle, because I hadn't heard from her for over a year."

"Follow me, I have a car outside."

They walked outside and climbed into the unmarked army vehicle. Ian drove Hilda to the Olympic Stadium, as he chatted with her about what she did in Cologne.

While Ian was picking up Frau Schmitt, the Interrogation Group was interviewing Giselle one last time in her cell, to be sure what she told them in the first interview, a year ago, was the truth; in other words she didn't change her story.

At around 1100, Ian entered her cell with her mother and Giselle fell into her arms, crying. After they both had recovered, Giselle signed the statement of fair treatment, which Ian placed in front of her.

The three of them had lunch in the Officers' Mess where they were met by Colonel Thurman who stressed, on both of them, the requirement that there was to be no mention about the whole affair and failed exchange, to the press.

Later that afternoon, Ian drove her and her mother back to the Tempelhof airport, in time to catch the BEA flight back to Cologne. They got out of the car at the Departure Hall and all three entered the building where they checked in for the flight. As they waited in the departure lounge, Giselle turned to Ian to thank him for his help.

"I know it must have been tough for you, but I really appreciate what you did for me. The last year for me has been terrible, not knowing what was going to happen. Then that proposed exchange really threw me for a loop. The last thing I wanted to do was to go back to East Germany. They would have hounded me, until I died. I would give you a kiss, but it wouldn't look good, so I'll just shake your hand."

She held out her hand, Ian shook it and then gave her hand a slight kiss. "It's been nice knowing you and please stay out of trouble. Also, be kind to your mother when you tell her about the probable fate of her son Gerhard. I didn't have the heart to give her the news."

At last, flight BE721 was called and the passengers entered the gate. Giselle and Hilda turned and waved goodbye; Giselle mouthed the words "Auf Weidersehen and Danke". The two women walked out to the BEA Viscount, climbed up the stairs and entered the cabin. The plane's turboprop engines started up and it taxied out to the main runway. In a few minutes, they received clearance from the tower; the aircraft rolled down the runway and rose into the clear blue sky.

Ian breathed a sigh of relief, as the matter of the mole had finally come to a just and fair finish.

25

Visitor Preparation

About ten days later, Ian received a call from Captain Silverman of the United States Army 513th Intelligence Group, at Clay Headquarters complex in the American Sector. The purpose of the call was to invite him down for an important meeting, to discuss the upcoming visit of a famous United States politician.

"When and what time is the conference scheduled?" Ian asked.

"It's slated for next Monday, the 3rd of June, at 1400 hours. Will you be able to make it? It's a matter that will affect security throughout West Berlin."

"I'll be there," Ian replied.

"Good, we'll see you then. By the way, there will be about twenty people attending this meeting, including Brigadier General Gross, who is in charge of all U.S. Army intelligence in West Germany and Berlin. It will be held in the small auditorium, on the ground floor of the main building."

At the colonel's Monday morning staff meeting, Ian mentioned that he was going down to the Clay complex for a crucial meeting.

"Captain, what is the subject matter for this conclave?" Colonel Thurman asked.

"I don't know for sure. Captain Silverman did say it was a major intelligence meeting and involved a visit by a prominent American official."

"I've heard rumours about such a visit, but we'll wait for you to report back, after the meeting," replied the colonel.

At the end of the staff meeting, Ian returned to his office to prepare for the visit to the Clay Headquarters. He called the motor pool and reserved an Army Land Rover, with which to drive down into South Berlin.

After lunch, he picked up the vehicle and drove to the American headquarters. As he approached the main gate, he was stopped, as usual, by an MP, asked for his ID and the purpose of his visit.

After the MP checked his name on a list he held on a clipboard, he said, "Welcome captain. If you drive straight ahead and park near the far door, the auditorium is right inside."

"Thank you, sergeant," Ian replied, as he put the Land Rover in gear and drove forward, after the gate was raised.

Ian found a vacant spot near a large door that obviously led into the auditorium area. As he walked in, he was greeted by Captain Silverman.

"Ian, I see you made captain. Congratulations."

"Yes and there is one advantage, I don't have to call you "sir" anymore. Which do you prefer Patrick or Bob?"

"Call me Patrick, unless we meet off the complex, in which case it will be Bob. Come on in and we'll find a seat together. This meeting should be very interesting."

Right at 1400, the meeting was called together by Colonel Haga and he introduced Brigadier General James Gross, who had more ribbons than Ian had ever seen, up to then, on one military officer.

General Gross approached the microphone and started speaking, "Gentlemen, I have asked you all here today, in order to bring you up to date on the visit by our Commander in Chief. Yes, for those of you who have not already heard

302

the news, President Kennedy will be visiting German and Berlin during the latter part of this month, June 23 to June 26.

His first stop will be in the Cologne/Bonn area for the first two days. On the third day, he will travel to Hanau to visit the 3rd Armored Division V Corps, after which he will go on to Frankfurt. Finally, on the 26th, he will fly to Berlin and, together with Chancellor Konrad Adenauer and Mayor Willy Brandt, will drive in a motorcade to a viewing stand, near the Brandenburg Gate. From atop this raised platform, he'll be able to obtain a view of East Berlin and its divisive Wall. Afterwards he will visit Checkpoint Charlie and end up at the Berlin City Hall, called the Schöneberger Rathaus, where he will make a speech.

Security for this visit will be tight and will be provided by the West Berlin police, together with the U.S. Secret Service. What I want all intelligence service members to do, whether you're from the United States, Britain or France, is to keep your eyes and ears open to any potential threat that could ruin this visit. If your authorities allow it, I would suggest that on the day of the visit, you dress in civilian clothes so you can blend into the crowd. I want to stress that any support the British and French intelligence services can provide will be extremely welcome. This is why representatives, from these two organizations, were invited here today.

Thank you and now I'll turn the podium over to Colonel Haga so he can outline, in complete detail, the schedule for the Berlin visit by the president."

For the next hour, the colonel went over the itinerary, almost minute by minute, of the president's visit, including the route of the motorcade and the stops along the way. At the end he opened it up for questions, of which there were several, mainly from the American attendees.

He finished up the presentation, by thanking all for coming and expressing a desire, that if any further questions do crop up, to give him a call.

As they were filing out of the auditorium, Colonel Haga came over to Ian and said, "Congratulations on making captain. I believe you deserved it from what I've heard through the grapevine. I'd like you to meet somebody."

He took Ian by the arm and led him over to Brigadier General Gross, who was talking to some American officers. When he saw the colonel leading Ian over in his direction, he stopped chatting with these men and turned to face Colonel Haga, accompanied by Ian.

"Sir, I'd like you to meet Captain Ian Black of the British Intelligence Corps, here in Berlin."

"It's a pleasure to meet you, captain. I've heard a few things about you, especially the way you tracked down the mole in your organization. You should go far in the British Army. It's a pity you aren't in the American forces, but it can't be helped, I guess," he said with a smile.

"Thank you for the complement, sir, but I'm not sure I deserve it."

"Well anyway, it's a pleasure to meet you."

Ian saluted the general and walked away with Colonel Haga, telling him that he would relay the contents of the presentation to his CO.

As Ian left the building to go to his Land Rover, Major Vass, who also attended the meeting, came up to him and congratulated him on the well deserved promotion. Upon sitting down in his vehicle, he noticed a couple of men dressed in civilian clothes, climbing into a 1963 black Chevrolet Impala. He assumed they were from the CIA, but wasn't sure, and he certainly wasn't going to inquire.

He drove back to the Olympic Stadium, changed into his civvies and caught the U-Bahn back to his flat.

The next day he returned to the Stadium complex and went to see Colonel Thurman, after he had dressed in his uniform. He scheduled an appointment, through Helga, to meet with him at 1030.

When he entered the outer office for his meeting with his CO, Helga commented, "I'm kind of glad that Giselle is out of Berlin and with her mother. Hopefully, she can regain her optimism and find a good job. Maybe, some rich American company will pick her up, since she speaks fluently both English and German; and some Dutch, I believe."

"I agree," Ian replied. "I believe one year in jail taught her a powerful lesson and I too hope she gets her life together. She's young enough that I think she might. Her mother seemed very level headed and she'll help her, I'm sure."

Helga's buzzer on her desk intercom sounded and she said, "You can go in now, captain."

Ian entered the colonel's office, saluted as usual and sat in a chair close to his desk.

"What can I do for you, captain?" he asked.

"Yesterday, I went to a meeting at the Clay Headquarters complex that was held by the Americans and it was announced that President Kennedy would be coming to Berlin, at the end of a three day tour of Germany. Specifically, he will be here on the 26th of this month; arriving in the morning and leaving in late afternoon for Ireland. A General James Gross and Colonel Haga held the meeting consisting of about twenty intelligence professionals.

The president will be arriving at Tegel, because the runways at Tempelhof are too short for the Boeing 707. He will then be driven, from this airport in the French sector, to a stand that will be built close to the Brandenburg Gate. From there, he'll be able to look into East Berlin and also view the Wall, close at hand. Then, he will visit Checkpoint Charlie and end up at the West Berlin city hall, where he will make a speech. Later, he'll be driven back to Tegel through the British and French sectors of Berlin. On the visit, he will be accompanied by the Chancellor Konrad Adenauer and Mayor Willy Brandt.

In general, the West Berlin police will provide security along the route and in front of the motorcade. As usual in visits like this, the president will also be guarded by the America Secret Service. However, one factor that bothers me is that they will be travelling in a convertible, with the result that the president could be a sitting target, so to speak.

General Gross asked that we support this visit as much as we can, by going in among the crowd in civilian clothes and watch for anything unforeseen."

"The idea seems to make sense. We, of course, have some responsibility while he is in the British sector and I certainly wouldn't want anything to happen to him, while he's here. Why don't you bring this subject up at the next staff meeting on the 10th, and we can discuss what resources we can apply."

"I'll do that sir."

"Good. Is that all for now? I have another important meeting I have to go to," replied the colonel.

"Thank you for your time, sir," Ian said, as he rose and left the colonel's office.

He bade good bye to Helga and returned to his office in the London Block, to read the latest assessments on the Russian troop movements in East Germany.

26

Ich Bin Ein Berliner

On the morning of the 26th of June, 1963, President Kennedy flew from Frankfurt, after visiting the American 3rd Armored Division at Hanau, to the Berlin Tegel airport in the French sector on Air Force One, a Boeing 707 specially equipped aircraft. His plane couldn't land at Berlin Tempelhof airport, because the runways were too short for a 707 aircraft.

As Air Force One was in the air, Captains Ian Black and Alex Swiderski, his Russian speaking fellow officer, made their way to just west of the Brandenburg Gate, in the British sector. They were dressed in mufti, so they would not stand out to anyone meaning to do harm to the president. They were both armed with their weapons hidden beneath their loose shirts, and they had with them a British Army document showing they were allowed to be armed. They walked among the crowd of people who were waiting for Kennedy, Adenhauer and Brandt to arrive.

The president drove in an open 1963 Lincoln convertible, with suicide doors, from the Tegel airport to the Brandenburg Gate area. In the car with him were the Chancellor of West Germany, Konrad Adenhauer, and the West Berlin Mayor, Willy Brandt. In front of the Lincoln were several West Berlin policemen riding on motorcycles, and

307

behind it was a Cadillac loaded with Secret Servicemen. They were standing on special running boards and holding onto unique handrails, attached to the president's automobile. Following the Cadillac, there was another vehicle filled with the press and official photographers.

Ian was amazed at the reception for the three men, especially when they exited the Lincoln and started to walk toward the viewing stand that had been set up, very close to the now famous Berlin Wall. The crowd of many thousands of people was cheering them, without stopping, and Ian wished he had some ear plugs.

This noise, to Ian, all but vanished when he noticed a suspicious, rough looking man, dressed in a dark suit, working his way toward the famous politicians.

"Look at that man over there," Ian said to Alex as he nudged him. "He looks dangerous to me. What do you think?"

"Yes, I believe you're correct. He has his right hand in his pocket, as though he's hiding something. Let's get a West Berlin policeman over here. There is one about thirty feet away."

"I'll go get him, while you keep track of this man," Ian replied. They had been given orders not to use or show their weapons, except in a dire emergency.

Ian worked his way through the dense crowd to where the policeman was standing and finally reached him.

After showing him his ID, Ian said to the security official, "We've seen a sinister man over there about ten metres away. Can you come and check him out?"

"Of course, I'll come immediately. That's what I'm here for. Lead the way."

Ian pushed his way, through the crowd, back to where he had left Alex. The policeman followed as best he could, since the crowd was pushing toward the Gate.

The problem was Alex had moved forward toward the Gate, as the suspicious man had worked his way in the direction of President Kennedy. Ian finally caught sight of Alex and reached him, followed by the West Berlin security man.

The policeman went over to the shady looking man, took him by the arm and led him away. Ian and Alex later found out that the man did not have a weapon, but a pocket full of rotten tomatoes that he was going to throw at Kennedy.

When Ian heard that, he thought, *"Well you never know, it could have been a weapon and it would have been extremely bad PR, if JFK had been shot in the British sector."*

The three leaders walked onto the stand and looked over the Wall into East Berlin. As they did so, a few East German soldiers took pictures of them and looked through binoculars at all the guests on the stand. After standing there for some time, the guests left the platform and entered the convertible, for the drive south to Checkpoint Charlie.

There they went off to the large hut, which was very close to the border crossing into East Berlin. President Kennedy, who was saluted by the American MPs as he approached, peered at the East German checkpoint on Friedrichstrasse, a few metres north of the American position. He then talked with the America soldiers for a few minutes before reentering the convertible for the ride to the West Berlin City Hall; known as the Schöneberger Rathaus to Berliners.

All along the way enthusiastic West Berliners lined the route and cheered the three leaders, who smiled and waved at the crowd. They gathered not only along the streets, but on top of signposts, on balconies and on rooftops to try to catch a glimpse of the American leader. People, who were unable to get off work and join the crowd, watched the live broadcast on television or listened to the RIAS station on the wireless.

Even some East Berliners, who were brave enough, listened to the broadcast or watched it illegally on their television. If caught, they would have been severely punished, since Walter Ulbricht, the East German leader, had decreed that it was illegal to tune into a West Berlin radio or television transmission.

At the West Berlin City Hall, Kennedy gave a speech that was broadcast live throughout West Germany and West Berlin. He started his speech with:

"I am proud to come to this city as the guest of your distinguished mayor, who has symbolized throughout the world the fighting spirit of West Berlin. And I am proud to visit the Federal Republic with your distinguished Chancellor, who for so many years, has committed Germany to democracy and freedom and progress, and to come here in the company of my fellow American, General Clay, who has been in this city during its great moments of crisis and will come again, if ever needed."

Continuing on, a few minutes later, he added:

"There are many people in the world who really don't understand, or say they don't, what is the great issue between the free world and the Communist world.
   Let them come to Berlin.
There are some who say that communism is the wave of the future.
   Let them come to Berlin.
And there are some who say in Europe and elsewhere we can work with the Communists.
   Let them come to Berlin.
And there even a few who say that it is true that communism is an evil system, but it permits us to make economic progress.
   Lass'sic nach Berlin kommen.
   Let them come to Berlin."

Later, in the speech, Kennedy went on to say:

"Freedom is indivisible, and when one man is enslaved, all are not free. When all are free, then we can look forward to that day when this city will be joined as one and this country and this great Continent of Europe in a peaceful and hopeful globe. When that day finally comes, as it will, the people of West Berlin can take sober satisfaction in the fact that they were in the front lines for almost two decades.

All free men, wherever they may live, are citizens of Berlin, and, therefore, as a free man, I take pride in the words **"Ich bin ein Berliner!"**

Later, as the leaders were driven from the West Berlin City Hall back to the Tegel airport, they were scheduled to stop by the Siegessäule, located in the Große Tiergarten, so President Kennedy could view it for a few minutes. This Victory Column commemorated the Prussian victory in the Danish-Prussian war that took place in 1864. The Berliners nickname for the column was Goldelse or Golden Lizzy.

Since the Siegessäule was in the British sector of Berlin, Ian and Alex again worked the crowd, looking for any threat against the three major leaders of the United States, Germany and West Berlin.

When the Lincoln convertible left the Victory Column, Ian turned to Alex and said, "I guess we can soon retire to a pub and get a beer. President Kennedy will shortly be out of our jurisdiction and into the French sector, which means we will no longer be needed. What do you think?"

"That's a wonderful idea, Ian. Let's go find our car and head back to the Stadium, where there's a pub close by," replied Alex.

Ian didn't tell him that was where he had a drink with Giselle Schmitt a little over a year ago.

27

In Memoriam

Ian woke up with a start, as the phone rang in his West Berlin flat. *"Who could be calling this early in the morning?"* he thought. It was only 0600, and normally his alarm clock didn't go off until 0630. It was the 14th of August, 1963.

He picked up the handset and heard his mother, in England, say sobbing, "Your father died early this morning from a heart attack."

It was the blackest day in Ian's life up till then. His father, James Black, had always seemed full of life and appeared invincible. Ian had thought that he would live forever.

"I'll come home as soon as I can get a ride, mother," he responded, with his voice cracking.

"Hurry home dear. I need you," replied his mother, as she hung up her phone.

Ian quickly shaved, showered and got dressed. He then called Colonel Thurman at his house.

"Sir, my father just died and I need to get home and help my mother. I would like to take some leave."

"I'm sorry to hear that, Ian. Take as long as you need. Just keep me informed. How do you plan to get home?"

"Thank you, sir. I'll certainly call you and keep you up to date. I'm going immediately to RAF Gatow and hopefully

312

there is a flight out today to RAF Northolt that has a vacancy."

"Good luck on your flight. If you need my help, don't hesitate to call. Again, I'm sorry to hear the bad news."

Ian packed a bag, went outside his flat and found a taxi to take him to RAF Gatow, in the British sector. The cab dropped him off at the front gate and he walked into the airfield, after showing his ID to the RAFP MPs guarding the gate. He entered the main facility and walked up to the information desk, to check if there were any flights going out that day to RAF Northolt.

A RAF officer walked up behind him and said, "Ian, is that you. I haven't seen you since January 1961. Where've you been, all this time?"

Ian turned and was face to face with Chris Mullins, who was now a Squadron Leader.

"I've been giving the Ruskies and the East Germans hell, for the past two years," Ian replied, with a smile.

"I see you've made captain. What are you doing here?"

"My father died early this morning. I'm trying to get a flight back to England, so I can take care of my mother and make arrangements for her."

"I'm sorry to hear about your father. There's a flight leaving here at noon and should be at Northolt by 1500 hours. Let me go and see if I can get you on the plane. If not, I'll give you my seat. I'm just a passenger today."

Mullins walked away and came back a few minutes later, with a smile on his face.

"I've managed to get you on the flight. There was one seat left that some RAF chap was trying to take. I outranked him and got you on board."

"Thanks a lot, I appreciate it. How about if I buy you a cup of coffee?"

"That sounds great. The NAAFI is just down the hallway. We have plenty of time before the flight is called."

RICHARD AND BARBARA OSBORN

In thirty minutes, their RAF flight was called and they both walked to the gate, where a corporal checked their names on the roster. They walked out of the terminal onto the tarmac and boarded the Dakota. There were no assigned seats, so Ian and Chris were able to get seats together. During the uneventful flight, they reminisced about their times in Cyprus, including the time when Ian had to pilot the Shackleton.

They landed at three o'clock and Ian bade farewell to Chris.

"Thanks again, Chris, for getting me on the flight. It'll mean everything to my mother, for me to be home today."

"You're welcome, Ian. Hopefully we'll meet again sometime soon."

Ian grabbed his bags and left the terminal to find a taxi. Soon he was at his parents' home in Richmond and he realized he had left Berlin, in such a hurry, that he forgot to bring a key. He rang the doorbell and soon the door was opened by a friend of his mother.

"Come on in, Ian. You will find her upstairs in her bedroom. Now that you're home, I'll leave, unless you think she'll need me."

"Thanks for staying with her. You can leave now and I'll go upstairs to comfort her."

He went up to the second story of the home, bounding two steps at a time. He came to her bedroom door and knocked.

"Come in," said a voice, crying and sobbing.

Ian entered his mother's bedroom and found her on the bed, crying. He went over and solaced her, saying, "I'm home now, to take care of you." He stayed there all night, comforting her. She finally fell asleep.

The next morning, Ian fixed breakfast and his mother finally came downstairs to the kitchen. After eating, they discussed the final arrangements and what his father wanted. He had laid it out in his will, which took some worry

314

off his mother. Ian went into his father's study and found an address book of all his friends, old buddies in the RAF and current business executives. He called everybody in the book, to tell them of the sad news.

Ian made arrangements with a local funeral home to have his father's body taken down to the Kent County Crematorium, where his father's parents were cremated. Their ashes were scattered among the trees and plants. It was a beautiful setting. He scheduled it for two days later and ordered a limousine to take them behind the hearse.

On the appointed day, they drove down to Charing and, in a private service, said goodbye to his mother's husband and his father. It was very poignant and Ian finally broke down crying. He didn't do it very often, as he was very reserved in matters such as this. After the ashes were scattered in the same area as James Black's parents, Ian and his mother were driven back to Richmond.

The next day, the phone rang and Ian answered it, since his mother was still not in the mood to accept calls.

"Hello, this is Ian Black."

"Ian, this is Air Commodore Terrance Braddock of the RAF. Do you happen to be a relative of Wing Commander James Black?"

"Yes, I'm his son."

"I'm sorry to bother you in your family's time of sorrow. We've heard about the passing of your father Wing Commander James Black and the RAF, together with some members of the United States Air Force, would like to pay a tribute to him. Would Mrs. Black and you be willing to come to a memorial service in the RAF Lakenheath Chapel on the Station, near Cambridge, next Wednesday?"

"I believe it would be okay. I'm sure my father would be greatly honored, to know that his service to our country, and the cause of freedom, is recognized. However, I'll have to check with my mother and then call you back."

"That will be fine. Please call me back as soon as possible, so arrangements can be made for the service."

Air Commodore Braddock gave Ian his phone number, who quickly scribbled it down.

Ian then went to see his mother, who was upstairs taking a rest. He knocked on the door softly and entered. His mother was wide awake looking at a photo of her late husband.

"Mum, we just received a call from an Air Commodore who wants to know if we are up to going to a memorial service at RAF Lakenheath next Wednesday. A group of RAF and US Air Force personnel want to pay tribute to Dad. What do you think?"

"I think your father would be proud to know he is still remembered by the service and country that he fought for. Let's do it for him."

"Okay Mum, I'll call him back and give him the go ahead."

Ian went to the phone and dialed the number Braddock had given him. A sergeant answered and said he would transfer the call.

"This is Air Commodore Braddock. To whom am I speaking?"

"This is Ian Black, sir. I talked with my mother about the memorial service, and she said she would make it, in order to honor my father. We'll have to arrange a car to get us there. At what time will the service take place?"

"The service is scheduled to start at 1400 hours, but don't worry about transportation. I will make arrangements with the RAF to pick you up at 0900 next Wednesday and bring you straight to the station. The RAF automobile will then return you to Richmond, in the evening. What is your exact address, so the driver can find your residence?"

"We'll certainly appreciate the lift. Thank you." Ian said, after giving him the address.

ON HER MAJESTY'S BERLIN MISSION

****

The following Wednesday, at nine o'clock sharp, a large blue sedan pulled up outside their home. A RAF corporal got out, came to the door and knocked. Captain Ian Black, already dressed in his best Army uniform, opened the door.

The corporal saluted Ian and said, "Air Commodore Braddock sent me to pick you up and take you to Lakenheath, sir."

"My mother will be ready in a minute. Would you like to come in?"

"I'd prefer to wait out here sir, if it's okay with you."

"Certainly, we'll be out shortly," Ian said, as the corporal returned to the RAF staff car. Ian shouted to his mother upstairs, "The sedan is here, Mum."

"I'll be down in a moment," she replied.

In a minute his mother came downstairs, dressed in a black suit and a pearl necklace that her husband had given her many years ago.

"Let's go, Ian" she said. He opened the front door and they went down the steps to the waiting car. The corporal jumped out and opened the rear door for them.

They arrived at the main gate to RAF Lakenheath at just before noon and the driver showed his pass to the RAFP MP. The guard had been expecting them and he directed the corporal to drive to the Officers' Mess, where Air Commodore Braddock would greet his guests.

They pulled up outside the building and the driver jumped out of the car, to open their doors. Ian stepped out onto the pavement and helped his mother out of the rear. As he did so, Air Commodore Braddock walked up to greet them. Ian turned and gave him a salute, saying, "It's an honor sir. I'd like you to meet my mother, Mrs. James Black."

He returned Ian's salute and said, "Thank you both for coming to such an occasion, since we have a special guest coming for the memorial. First, though I'd like to invite you to a small lunch, before we go to the Station Chapel."

He ushered them into the Officers' Mess, where they were guided to a small private dining room. There they had lunch and had a fairly enjoyable conversation, considering the purpose of their visit. When they had finished, Commodore Braddock suggested they take a short walk to the Chapel.

As they walked the few blocks to the Chapel, there was suddenly a huge roar as a four engine jet flew overhead. Ian looked up and saw a huge plane that he did not recognize. It was marked with "Military Air Transport Command" on top of the fuselage and toward the front "U S Air Force" was painted on the side. Ian found out later, it was a Boeing 137-B that was often used as a transport plane for senior brass.

"That's our VIP guest, the United States Air Force Chief of Staff, arriving from Washington." Braddock said loudly to Ian, so he could hear over the jet's noise.

The large plane circled the base and landed, into a light northeasterly wind, on runway 06. Two dark blue Cadillacs, with USAF on the doors, drove up to it, after the plane had taxied close to a small flight operations building. The six occupants of the plane entered the cars and they headed for the Chapel.

In the meantime, Ian, his mother and the Air Commodore had reached the Chapel, where they walked in and sat down in a front row of chairs. The chapel appeared to be filled with RAF officers and men, and a few United States Air Force personnel. Ian didn't remember seeing so much brass in an enclosed area before. After they were seated, waiting for the service to begin, they heard whispering by the men and women behind them. In a moment, up walked a USAF officer with lots of braid, followed by five other similar men, with a little less glitter on the hats they were carrying.

The officer in front nodded slightly to Mrs. Black and then sat down in the other front row, followed by the other five senior officers. Ian thought he had seen the man before but couldn't place him.

The resident chaplain conducted the service, with the usual hymns and prayers for such an occasion. Toward the end, a few RAF officers, current and retired, went up to the lectern to expound on their memories of Wing Commander James Black. They told stories, some funny and others about his courage in adversity. When they had finished, the USAF officer who was obviously the VIP from Washington, went up and gave a few words.

"In case some of you don't know me, my name is General Curtis LeMay, and I was honored to serve with the Eighth Air Force, during the war. It was during that long campaign that I met Wing Commander James Black, who with his brave pilots, protected our bombers, as we went into the enemy's heartland, to bomb their factories and cities. If it hadn't been for Commander Black, we would have lost many more men and bombers. Initially, they flew the Spitfire, and then later the P-51 Mustang, with its extended range tanks.

Mrs. Black, I came here all the way from Washington today, to pay homage to one of the bravest and patriotic men, I have ever known. I know he's been received up above, in the way all men like him are welcomed."

The general then descended from the lectern, walked over to Mrs. Black, shook her hand and said softly, "I share your grief. He was a great friend in those dark days, twenty years ago."

"Thank you for those kind words, general. If he was here today, he would be humbled by your presence."

The chaplain finished the memorial with the Station choir singing James Black's favorite hymn "Onward Christian Soldiers" and followed it up with the benediction.

When it was over, General LeMay came over, took Mrs. Black's arm and escorted her out of the chapel, followed by the other five senior officers, Commodore Braddock and Ian.

They drove over to the flight line where a reviewing stand had been set up, with the Union Jack and the Stars and Stripes on poles. They walked up the stairs and sat down on the chairs, lined up in the front. The remainder of the guests came over in blue Air Force buses and joined them at the base of the stand.

When everyone was assembled, the RAF band played both the US and British national anthems. Then they started to play the RAF March Past, as a group of RAF men and women marched past the reviewing stand. General LeMay, Mrs. Black and Ian stood to the front and saluted as the men marched by. Then an American Air Force honor guard marched by as the band played The Stars and Stripes Forever. It was all very patriotic and Mrs. Black had to use her handkerchief a few times, to wipe some tears away.

As the band stopped playing, Ian heard a very faint rumble, coming from the west. The noise got louder and louder, and soon he saw what was causing it. Into view came a B-17 bomber, with a Spitfire on one wing tip and a P-51 Mustang on the other side. They had flown out of the Duxford airfield, where James Black had flown from during the war. It was a magnificent sight as they flew right over the reviewing stand. The noise was deafening and Ian's mother held his hand, to steady herself. She knew her husband would have been proud, if he had been there.

After the old war birds had past, they heard another noise coming in from the same direction. The planes finally appeared overhead and Ian saw four F-100 Super Sabres in a "Missing Man" formation. They were a beautiful sight, but very noisy. They were stationed at Lakenheath, in support of NATO.

After the review was over and the planes had flown by, General LeMay turned to Mrs. Black to speak to her.

"It's been a pleasure meeting you at last, but I'm sorry it is under such a sad occasion. Please accept my heartfelt condolences. Is this your son here in a British Army uniform?"

"Yes general, this is my son Captain Ian Black."

"It's a pleasure to meet you son. Do you happen to be the same Ian Black I read about in a report, one on my aides gave me five years ago? This Ian Black was a soldier who was in Cyprus, and he had to fly a Shackleton four engine aircraft, after the two pilots became incapacitated. He managed to land it without crashing it into the ground."

"Yes sir. I'm afraid it was me. I took the only action possible, and I must admit I was slightly scared, while I'll was at the controls."

"Well Ian, it sounds as if you're a chip off the old block. I'd like you to meet General Jonathan Carter of Air Force Intelligence, whose office is located at the Pentagon in Washington."

General Carter stepped forward and shook Ian's hand saying, "It's a pleasure to meet you, captain."

"Likewise, general."

General Lemay looked Ian straight in the eyes, and then proposed, "If you ever get bored with British Army life and want to come to the States, we could do with men like you in the Air Force. Since you're a dual citizen, it should be simple for you to enter America. If you do, contact General Carter and he'll see what he can do for you; your experience in Army intelligence should be extremely useful. Correct, Jonathan?"

"Sure thing general."

"Again, it's been a pleasure Mrs. Black. If you happen to ever make it to Washington, please look me up."

"Thank you, general for coming to the memorial service. It's meant a lot to me and my son."

"Well, I have to leave know. Our group has to get back to Washington. Duty calls."

General LeMay and the other officers left the parade ground, walked over to their Boeing C-137B Stratoliner and climbed up the stairs to enter the plane.

Commodore Braddock escorted Ian and his mother to the waiting Royal Air Force car. Ian helped his mother into the rear and Ian turned to salute the commodore.

"Thank you, sir, for arranging this memorial for my father. It has meant a lot to my mother and me."

"You're welcome captain. By the way, for your information, this whole memoriam was actually planned By General LeMay and his staff."

Ian climbed into the rear and sat beside his mother, as they were driven back to Richmond. Mrs. Black slept most of the way as she was exhausted.

****

Back in East Berlin at 1800 that evening, Monika turned on her television and tuned it in to the West Berlin station ADR. Even though it was illegal for East Germans to do this, Monika figured that if she kept the volume down, no one would know. The news was on and most of it was about events of the day in West Germany.

Toward the end of the broadcast, there was a short news report about an event that took place at RAF Lakenheath Airfield in England. The newsreel showed pictures of a General Curtis Lemay attending a memorial for a British war hero, named Wing Commander James Black. It included pictures of the general, with a Mrs. Black and her son, Captain Ian Black of the British Army. The commentator named the people in the pictures, and as Monika looked at the screen, she gasped in amazement. The young British Army officer looked just like a man she knew as Kurt Beck.

After a few seconds, it finally dawned on her that Kurt Beck was actually Captain Ian Black of the British Army.

28

Going Home

About six months after his father's death, Ian received a sweet, poignant letter from his mother, who was still living in the Richmond home, which she shared with her husband and idol. In it, she described the reasons why she was leaving England and returning to the United States. His mother stated she missed her husband terribly and she was very lonely. In addition, now her son was in the Army and appeared to be making it a career, she realized she would not see him very often. She had therefore decided to sell the house and move back to Franklin, Tennessee, where she had relatives living in the greater Nashville area.

Ian remembered that his mother had a sister and a brother, who still lived in Franklin. He met her brother, his uncle, one time when he came to visit his parents in England. Ian was only eight when Uncle Charlie came and stayed for two weeks, fairly soon after the war. The only thing he remembered about his uncle was that he spoke with an accent that was similar to his mother's. She had never totally lost hers.

After reading the following letter, Ian decided he had to take some leave to assist his mother in packing up her personal belongings, mementoes and sell off what she didn't want.

85, Hillcrest Lane
Richmond
Surrey

4 February 1964

My Darling Son Ian,

Since the death of your father, the last few months have been terrible, as he was the love of my life. Lately, I've been extremely despondent. The only way I believe that I can recover is move to a different environment. Therefore, I have decided to sell the house here in Richmond and move back to Tennessee, where I still have relatives in the Nashville area.

You are now a grown man, of whom I am very proud, and seem to be settled into the British Army life. One of these days, you will meet a young lady whom you can love and cherish, as your father and I did each other. You will then understand how I felt about your father and why the burden of his memory, here in Richmond, is too much to bear. I need people around me that I know and who understand me.

I trust you will comprehend my decision, to move back to the country of my birth. I am not in any way deserting you.

With Much Love,

Your Mother

He telephoned Helga Jergens, Colonel Thurman's personal assistant and secretary, to ask for five minutes of his time. She told him that the colonel was out that day but that his schedule had an opening the following day at 1000 hours.

After finishing his telephone conversation with Helga, Ian called his mother in England to determine what her schedule was in closing up the house.

"Hello, Mum," Ian said, when she answered. "I received your letter and I've decided to take some leave, assuming the colonel will permit it. This will give me some time to come to England, assist you in cleaning out the house and putting it on the market."

"It's great to hear from you Ian. Yes, I would like your help very much."

"I can probably get off ten days to a fortnight. What time period would be the best for you, mother?"

"Right now, I'm looking at starting the packing process in two weeks and hopefully put the house on the market by the middle of March. Perhaps, if you could come for two weeks starting the 29th of February, until the 15th of March that would be great."

"Let me talk to my CO tomorrow and see if he'll let me take two weeks leave, around those dates. I'll let you know if I can make it then."

"Thanks Ian. Anything you can do to assist me will certainly make the move easier. Talk to you soon."

The next day Ian went to the colonel's office to discuss with him the possibility of getting some leave.

"Take a seat, Ian," his CO said, as he entered the office. "What can I do for you?"

"Well sir, my mother has been taking it very hard, since my father died last August, and has decided to move back to Tennessee, where she originally came from, back in the 1930's. I herewith request two weeks leave, starting the

29th of February, so I can go home, help her pack and get the house ready for placing it on the market."

"I think that can be arranged.   Will two weeks be enough?"

"She has a house keeper also who can probably help. Hopefully two weeks will be sufficient."

"When you're there, and if you find out you require more time, give me a call and I'll see what I can do."

"Thank you sir," Ian responded, as he rose from the chair and left the colonel's office.

As he walked past Helga's desk, he mentioned to her he would be gone for two weeks, starting the 29th of February. Ian returned to his office and called his mother to tell her the good news.

He then called RAF Gatow to find out if they had a flight scheduled to Northolt on the last day of February and whether there was a vacancy.   It turned out there was no flight that day, so he dialed BEA in Berlin and booked a commercial flight from Tempelhof to Heathrow.

On Saturday morning, the 29th of February, Ian went to Tempelhof airport from his Berlin flat to catch the 0730 flight that stopped off in Dusseldorf, on the way to Heathrow.   He arrived at the London airport around noon and took the Underground to Richmond station, from where he walked to his mother's home, on Hillcrest lane.

She came to the door and hugging him said, "I'm glad you could make it, dear.   It has been terribly lonely these last six months and I've had many sleepless nights.   Come on in to the kitchen.   I have lunch ready, since I knew you would probably get here a little after one o'clock."

For the next two weeks, Ian helped his mother go through each room and decide what to keep for shipment to Tennessee, or to discard by giving it to a charity shop.   As his mother went through some of the drawers, she would stop and start to cry, after discovering an item her husband had cherished.   It was very hard for her to decide what to keep and what to get rid of. What she did opt to keep, Ian started to wrap and place in boxes, for shipment to the USA.

One week later, Ian said to his mother, "I'll think I'll go to the Richmond Ice Rink, for a couple of hours, to see Alena, if she's still there. I've never seen her skate."

"That's a great idea, Ian. I'm sure she'll be pleased to see you."

Ian left the house, walked over Richmond Bridge and turned left, once he reached the East Twickenham side. He then went along Clevedon Road until he came to the famous London area ice rink. He wandered inside and went to the barrier that surrounded the ice surface. Looking out into the middle, he spotted Alena Svrček.

"Alena," he shouted.

She looked up from the figure she was practicing and raced over to him.

"Ian, what are you doing here?" she exclaimed.

"It's great to see you Alena. I came home for two weeks to help my mother pack up. She's moving back to Tennessee, since my father died last year."

"Oh, I'm sorry to hear about your father."

"It's been tough on her and we both miss him a lot. How are you doing? Do you like Arnold Gerschwiler and is he a good skating instructor?"

"I'm doing great and I'm learning a lot from Mr. Gerschwiler. His wife Vi is also very supportive and they have put me up for a while, while I'm looking for a place I can afford. Let's go to the Arosa rink in the back and I'll show you how I can skate."

They walked into the rear of the large building and there was another ice surface called the Arosa. Alena went out on the ice and gave Ian a short exhibition, doing some spins and jumps.

"You're very good Alena," Ian said, as she came over to him breathless. "Have you had any trouble with Czech security people, like Ája Vrzáňová did fifteen years ago?"

"If they're around, I haven't seen them, but I'm careful when I go out at night. I make sure I'm always with someone else for protection."

"Well it's great to see you again and to know you are doing well. I better get back to my mother's place to help her. Bye'"

Alena gave him a short kiss on his cheek and then skated off to the centre of the ice rink.

Ian returned to the home on Hillcrest Lane, to help his mother continue packing. At the end of the second week, he accompanied his mother to a real estate agency, to talk with them about listing the house. She decided to offer it for sale on the 16th of March, at the price the estate agent recommended. The agent thought it was a fair price, since the house was in excellent condition.

On Friday the 13th, Ian called RAF Northolt to see if they had any vacancies on flights going to Berlin, on the weekend. The sergeant, who worked at the reservation desk and answered his call, stated that there was a plane leaving Sunday morning at 0900, going to RAF Gatow. Ian booked a seat and, for the next couple of days, helped his mother wrap up most of the remaining items to be packed.

On Sunday morning, they both got up early and had a good English breakfast, after which he quickly threw his clothes in a suitcase and called a taxi. It soon arrived and it was time to say goodbye to his mother.

"Mum, if you need me before you leave for the States, I'll try and make it back. Also don't worry, I'll come and see you in the U.S one day and surprise you."

He then gave her a long hug and a kiss, saying "I love you, Mum."

"I love you too, son. Try and get over to Nashville, before too long. At least, phone calls are not hard to make nowadays, across the Atlantic."

ON HER MAJESTY'S BERLIN MISSION

Ian jumped into the taxi and headed for RAF Northolt where he boarded a Dakota for the flight back to Gatow, in the British sector of Berlin.

His mother sold the house in less than a month, since it was in a prime location in Richmond, and close to the park. She packed up what remained in the house and had it shipped to her sister's house in Franklin, Tennessee. A few days later, Reba Ann Black took a direct BOAC 707 flight from Heathrow to Atlanta, and from there she drove to Franklin.

29

Auf Weidersehen Berlin

As Ian flew back to RAF Gatow from helping his mother pack up her home, he reminisced about his life, since being drafted into the British Army. His mind drifted back to the time he ended up in Cyprus, searching for Colonel Grivas, the EOKA terrorist, flying a Shackleton aircraft and saving the crew, after the pilots became incapacitated. Then, after attending the Intelligence Academy, he was posted to Berlin, just in time to see the Wall go up.

Being a young man, he also thought about the women in his life. First, there was the love of his life, Aphrodite Palas, while he served in Cyprus, and they were engaged to be married. This all came to a tragic end, when a bullet aimed for him, ended her life in error. Then, in Berlin, he met Monika, who ended up being trapped behind the newly constructed Wall, and he could no longer see her. Later, he saved this skater Alena from the Czech secret police, but she went to England in order to study figure skating. Finally, he became acquainted with a Giselle Schmitt who turned out to be a swallow, buried within the British Berlin Brigade.

He thought, *"So far my love life hasn't turned out so well. How am I going to get married and make my mother happy? She's probably looking forward to a grandchild, before she gets too old. Oh well, we'll see what happens."*

Finally, the Dakota landed at Gatow where he walked down the portable stair ramp onto the tarmac and into the arrival hall. There, he retrieved his two bags and headed for the exit to find a taxi, which drove him back to his flat.

The next day, he attended the normal Monday morning staff meeting, to let Colonel Thurman know that he had returned from England and was ready to get back to work. For the next two weeks, Ian applied himself to the analysis of Soviet and Warsaw Pact troop movements, and what effect they had on the potential for a ground war in central Europe.

Toward the end of March, Ian made an appointment, through Helga, to have a private meeting with Colonel Thurman on Tuesday, the 31st, at 1400 hours. He wanted this meeting because, since he had returned from England, he felt he wanted a change in his life; it was a difficult decision to make. Before going to see his CO, Ian sat at the typewriter in his office and wrote a one page request, to present to him.

Ian walked over, feeling some angst, to the Administration Building of the Stadium complex at the appointed time and entered the outer office, where Helga sat guarding the CO's door.

"Hello, captain, I hope you had a smooth flight back from the UK," she said, smiling. "He'll see you in a moment."

"Yes, it was and on time, for a change. I'm glad see you appear to be happy, Helga."

"Yes, I am. Thank you."

In a moment, Major Phillips, Ian's acquaintance from the old Cyprus days and head of the Counter Intelligence Unit, came out of the colonel's office. He saw Ian sitting against the wall and waved at him, as he walked past.

Helga told Ian he could now go in to see the colonel. He rose and walked to the door, knocked and then entered. He saluted the colonel, who returned it and told him to take a seat.

"What can I do for you, Ian?" he asked.

331

"Well sir, it's like this. The last six months have been an emotional burden on me, since my father's death. I have tried to shake it off and pick myself up. Now my mother has sold her home and returned to the United States where she has friends and relatives. This, of course, leaves me with no close kin in Britain, except for a few distant cousins. I have given all of this a lot of thought, during the past few weeks, and have decided that I want to resign my commission with the British Army. This will permit me to move permanently to the United States. Since my mother is American, I am automatically an American citizen and will have no problem entering the country."

"I had an idea you might decide to resign from the army, ever since your father died. I trust you have given it a lot of thought."

"Yes sir, I have and my mind is made up."

"If I thought I could make you change your mind, I would try, however knowing your situation, I can appreciate your decision. When are you planning to leave? I trust you will give me some time to find a replacement, since it's going to be hard to find someone of your caliber."

Ian handed him the piece of paper that he had typed in his office earlier that day and said, "This is my letter of resignation. I would like to leave by the 26th of June, if that is acceptable. I have investigated the requirements for resigning a commission and understand them to be as follows:

- Serve a minimum period of three years.
- Give a notice period of six months.
- No money is required except for special kit supplied.
- Under personal pressing matters, all the above may be waived by the Commanding Officer.

Since I don't meet the six month notice, I hereby request that you grant me just a three month notice period."

"Let me look into that time period and I'll get back to you. I hate to lose you, but I understand why you are doing it. What career plans do you have once you reach America?"

"At this point, I haven't given it too much thought. My mother and her relatives are fairly well connected with the power brokers in the State of Tennessee, and hopefully I can start a career in one of their companies that they own."

"Again Ian, I'm sorry to see you leave. Please make sure you wrap up any lose ends and write me a final report. I suggest you make your decision known to your contacts in MI6 and the 513th down at Clay, telling them that in due time I will send them the name of the new coordination contact."

"I'll do that, sir."

The colonel rose, came around his desk and shook Ian's hand. "I'll let you know about the three month notice period. I'm sure it will be approved."

Ian saluted the colonel and said, "It's been a pleasure serving under you sir, and I have learned a lot from you, during these past three years."

The colonel saluted back and said, "I'll see you later."

Ian turned and exited his CO's office. As he walked past Helga, she asked, "May I ask what your meeting was about?"

Ian replied, "Normally I couldn't tell you, but in this case I will, since you will soon find out. I have handed in my resignation, effective the end of June."

Helga sighed and said, "That's a disappointment and I hate to see you leave. Make sure you come and see me before you take off."

"I'll be here for three more months, so I'm sure I'll see you a few times, before my last day."

Ian returned to his office in the London Block, sketched out a plan to finish his assignments and inform his contacts in the other organizations. In April, he went to the MI6 facility on the top floor and told Percival, John and Chetwyn of his decision. In May, he drove down to the Clay Headquarters complex and informed Captain Silverman, Major Vass and Colonel Haga of the 513th that he was leaving and going to America. Finally he called Franz in the BND and told him. Franz wanted to know who his replacement was going to be, and Ian informed him that the new liaison hadn't been selected yet. As soon as he was on board, he was sure that he would be contacting him.

In his last month of serving the army, Ian finished up his assignments and wrote his last report for the colonel. His CO had already informed him, at least a month before, that the six month time period would be waived, and he could leave on his planned date of the 26th of June, 1964.

****

On the first Saturday in June, Ian was sitting in his flat, around 1300, watching a soccer match between Frankfurt and Munich when the phone rang.

He picked up the handset and a woman's voice, at the other end, said, "Ian?"

"Yes," he answered. "Who is this?"

"This is Giselle Schmitt."

"How did you get my number?" he asked.

"The company I work for has its ways. I didn't call you at work because, for obvious reasons, I didn't want you to get into trouble."

"Well, it wouldn't matter much anyway now, since I'm resigning my commission at the end of this month and moving to Nashville, Tennessee."

"For your information Ian, since I left and went to Cologne, I've managed to obtain an excellent job with IBM in Sindelfingen. The reason I called was to see if you wanted to have dinner tonight. I'm staying at the Hilton and hate to eat alone. I can tell you all about my job and how I obtained it, over the meal."

"To be honest Giselle, I would hesitate to take you up on your offer, if I wasn't getting out. However, since I'll no longer be in the British Army three weeks from now, I could do with a good meal."

"Great Ian, can you be here by 1900? I'll make a reservation in the restaurant, which I've heard has pretty good food."

"Okay Giselle, I'll see you at 1900 hours."

Ian watched the rest of the soccer match on the television and then took a shower. Afterward, he got dressed in some civvies and left his flat at 1815 to find a taxi. He told the driver to take him to the Hilton Hotel, on Kurfürstendamm. When the cab pulled up, Ian paid the driver and got out of the taxi, after the doorman of the hotel had opened the vehicle door. He walked into the elegant main lobby and asked the concierge where the restaurant was located. The man pointed down a hallway and said, "It's on the right, sir."

Ian walked in the direction he pointed out and soon found the large ornate restaurant, which he assumed was where Giselle wanted to meet him. He walked in and the manager asked, "Do you have a reservation, sir?"

"I'm here to meet a lady."

"Would her name happen to be Giselle Schmitt?"

"Yes, it would."

"Please follow me," the manager said, as he led Ian to a quiet corner table, where Giselle was already sitting. She stood up, shook Ian's hand and gave him a kiss on his cheek.

"I'm glad you could make it. I assume that I may now call you Ian."

"Of course you may, Giselle."

They both sat down and the waiter came over to take their cocktail order. After they had given him their choices, they struck up a conversation.

Ian asked her, "So what have you been doing since you went to Cologne, with your mother? It's been about a year, I believe."

"My mother had some good contacts and I was able to get a position with IBM; probably because of my language skills. Anyway, I've worked there for nine months, as Business Development Manager, for all of Germany. We are just introducing the IBM System 360, and that's why I'm here in Berlin. I drove here yesterday in the company car I have assigned to me. This Monday, I'm calling on the West Berlin mayor's office, to talk with them about the product. I want to thank you again for everything you did for me. It could have been a lot worse, if you hadn't handed me over to my mother. When I told her about her son, my brother, she took it very hard but has since recovered. She was depressed for quite a few months and under a doctor's care. So what are you doing, if I may ask?"

Just as she asked that, the waiter reappeared to take their meal order. "It'll be here soon," he said, as he walked away.

After he left, Ian answered Giselle's question. "Since the last time I saw you, my father died in August and my mother decided to move back to Tennessee, earlier this year. Recently, I resigned my commission with the Army and will be out at the end of this month. I'll be flying to England for a couple of weeks to see some old school friends, and then go to America."

"I'm sorry to hear about your father. What are you going to be doing over there?"

"I'm not sure, but I believe I can get a job in one of my cousin's companies. I'll see when I get there."

"Perhaps we can get together some day in America, as the IBM corporate headquarters is in Armonk, New York. I'm sure I'll be going there now and again, on business."

"Yes, that would be smashing, if we could." Ian replied, thinking *"She's pretty and smart; the mole affair would have*

336

no effect, once I'm out of the army. She only did what she had to do to save her brother, he was sure."

"If you don't mind me asking, how did you get involved with the Stasi?"

"Actually, it was quite simple and I was totally naïve. I worked for Brigadier Clemens for three years before the Wall was built, and then one Friday after work, I went to the pub for a drink. As I sat there, this attractive young man, probably thirty years old, came in and sat on the next stool, beside me. We started to talk and, before I knew it, I was telling him about my family and where I was from. He then asked me where I was working, and I told him that I was a secretary at the British Berlin Brigade. Soon, he was asking me questions about my work, and I told him something that was not public knowledge. He said he had to go and asked if we can meet again next Friday.

The following Friday I met him again and he told me that my brother, in Dresden, was in trouble, but he could help if I would assist him. He wanted more details which I had access to at work and pointed out that I had given him some information last time. He had his hooks into me. It went downhill from there and he turned me over to a handler; the obese man you saw in here a year ago."

"You must have felt terrible and scared, after you realized you had been duped."

"Yes, I was and in some ways I was relieved, when you came and arrested me."

At this point, the waiter reappeared with their meals and they ate it, while continuing their conversation. When they finished, and she had charged the meal to her room, she said, "Ian, why don't you come up to my room for a nightcap? The room mini bar is stocked with everything imaginable."

"That sounds like a great idea. We could talk some more, where it 's not so noisy."

They stood up, walked out of the restaurant and headed for the lift. As they stood waiting for it, Giselle looked at Ian and smiling said, "I'm in room 407." When it finally arrived, they took it up to the fourth floor and walked down the hallway to her room.

They entered and she closed the door behind them, making sure it was bolted.

Whereupon Giselle asked, "Ian, will you unzip my dress and unclasp my bra please. I want to get into something more comfortable. While I do that, will you pour us a drink?

"Sure thing," Ian replied, as he went behind her to comply with her initial request.

"How about a glass of champagne, I believe there's a bottle in the mini bar?" she suggested.

"That sounds wonderful," he answered, as she walked into the bedroom to change.

Ian went to the bar and found the champagne, which he immediately poured into two glasses. In a few minutes, Giselle came out of the bedroom dressed in a loose fitting, terry robe, tied with a belt of similar material.

When Ian saw her, he thought, *"She's a stunning woman, even if she is a few years older than me."*

They sat on the sofa sipping the champagne and talking about their backgrounds. Later, Giselle asked Ian a question which brought back sad memories to him.

"Ian, have you ever been in love? I mean real love."

He looked at her and replied, with eyes welling up, "I had this girlfriend in Cyprus, Aphrodite was her name, and we were engaged to be married. One day, we were in Nicosia, the capital, for the purpose of planning our wedding, when a terrorist tried to shoot me, on one of the main streets. He was a poor shot and hit Aphrodite instead, who ultimately died in my arms. I felt terrible, since he was trying to kill me, not her."

"You must have been devastated. How dreadful it must have been for you."

"Yes, it took me a long time to get over it."

She leaned over and gave him a long, soft kiss. At the same time, her robe opened up a little and he could see parts her bountiful breasts, with their hard nipples. He felt himself rising.

"Why don't we go into the bedroom and lie on the bed, while we talk. It will be a lot more pleasant than sitting on this sofa," she queried.

"That's sounds like a good idea," Ian said, as his male hormones started to perk up.

They walked into the bedroom and lay on the large, soft bed, talking about events in their past.

After a while, she reached over and started to rub his chest. Soon her hand went down to his stomach and it finally found what she was looking for. At this point, he was lost. It wasn't long before she sat naked astride of him and moving up and down in a slow methodical way. She wanted to control the situation, because she figured he hadn't made love in quite a while and would be in a hurry. At the same time, he held her breasts in his hands, manipulating them, which made her even more eager to reach a climax.

Finally, after a few minutes, she felt his semen shoot into her vagina, as she reached a glorious orgasm.

"Was it okay for you?" she whispered to him softly.

"It was smashing," he answered quietly. "I've never felt like this before in my life. How about you, was it good for you too?"

"It was exquisite, Ian. Thank you for letting me ride you bareback into heaven."

They lay there holding each other and they slowly drifted off to sleep. The next morning, Giselle was the first to wake up and she softly padded out of the bedroom, to go to the bathroom. There she got dressed in some slacks and a blouse, and went to the phone to call room service. She ordered breakfast for two, to be delivered in one hour.

She went back into the bedroom, sat in a chair and watched him sleeping. She thought to herself, *"He's a good looking man and I wish he was staying in Germany. Maybe I'll go to the States one of these days and reconnect with him."*

Half an hour later, Ian stirred and opened his eyes. He looked up and saw her eyeing him.

"Is everything okay?" he asked quizzically.

"Most certainly it is," she answered, with a grinning smile. "I've ordered breakfast and it should be here shortly."

As she sat in the chair, he rose from the bed naked and walked past her toward the bathroom. She thought to herself, as he ambled frontal view to the WC, *"Boy, he is well endowed."*

After they ate breakfast, Ian said, "I have to leave now and return to my flat."

"Do you want me to drive you?" she asked.

"No, don't bother, it will be just as easy for me to grab a taxi."

He went over to her, gave her a kiss and handed her a piece of paper, saying, "Thank you, I enjoyed it. Maybe we can do it again sometime in the States. Here's my mother's phone number in the Nashville area, just in case you want to reach me."

"I would love that Ian. I'm sorry you will be so far away, because I'm getting to like you."

He left the Hilton and found a taxi that took him back to his flat.

****

Three weeks later, he left the army and Berlin behind, after turning in his Browning automatic. He flew from Tempelhof on BEA into London Heathrow. On the way, he thought, *"I wonder if I'll ever see Giselle again. I could probably fall for her, if we saw each other a lot."*

In London, he spent two weeks visiting old school mates from Harrow, in order to say goodbye before he left for the States. He also went to see Alena at the Ice Rink, where he told her he was going to America.

"If you ever get to the United States, please call me Alena. Here is my mother's phone number, which will be the best way to reach me."

"I'll do that if I get over there. Maybe one of these days, I'll be in an American ice show, like the Ice Capades."

He booked a flight on BOAC for Monday, the 13th of July, 1964, that landed at JFK in New York. As soon as he arrived in the terminal, he called his mother and told her which flight he would be on, for Nashville.

When he landed at the Country Music City, his mother was at the gate to greet him.

She gave him a big hug and a kiss, saying, "Ian, I'm so glad you decided to come to the States. Even though I have friends and relatives here, it will be so much better now you're here."

He returned her warm welcome, and they walked to the baggage area to pick up his bags.

Two weeks later, one of his mother's cousins offered him a job at his music company, as Marketing Manager. In this capacity, he met many famous musicians, mainly country western, and talked with several of the major record companies. However, he felt that something was missing in his life; maybe it was the excitement of danger and analyzing the unknown.

Finally, he decided to check out an offer that he received a little over a year ago, at Lakenheath.

30

New Commission

On a warm September Monday morning in Nashville, Tennessee, Ian went to a local armed forces recruiting office to talk with the Air Force representative there. He entered and walked up to a USAF sergeant, sitting behind a desk.

"Sergeant, my name is Ian Black and I'd like to obtain a phone number for the Pentagon, in Washington, DC."

"Normally, we'll only give out the general switchboard number. Will that suffice, sir?"

"Well no, I was hoping you could give me the number and extension for a General Jonathan Carter, who is head of the Air Force intelligence organization, under Air Force Chief of Staff, General Curtis LeMay."

"May I ask why you want to talk with General Carter, sir?"

"Last year, I met both generals at Lakenheath in England, and General LeMay told me that, if I was ever bored with the British Army, I should look General Carter up."

"Well sir, I can't give you the number, but what I'll do is ring the Pentagon and see if I can get General Carter's department. I could then hand you the phone and you can discuss your matter with someone, in the general's office. Would that help?"

"If you would do that, I'd be extremely grateful."

"Please take a seat while I call the Pentagon, it may take a few minutes."

Ian walked over and sat down in a chair, along the recruiter's office wall. As he did so, the sergeant picked up the phone and dialed a Pentagon number. After being placed on hold and talking to several people at the defense facility, he finally reached a captain in General Carter's office. The sergeant then signaled for Ian to come and talk to a Captain Carroll.

"Captain, my name is Ian Black and until recently I was a captain in the British Army Intelligence Corps, stationed in Berlin. In August of 1963, I met General Carter and General LeMay at a memorial service, at Lakenheath in England, and was told, if I ever got bored with Army life, to look General Carter up."

"Can you hold while I go check with the general? What did you say your name was?"

"Captain Ian Black, the son of RAF Wing Commander James Black and I met the general at Lakenheath a year ago. Yes, I can hold."

In a few minutes, Captain Carroll came back on the line.

"General Carter will be glad to meet with you two days from now, on Wednesday, September 16 at 1000 hours. If you can make it, I'll place you on his calendar."

"Yes, I'm free on that date. I'll fly in the night before and stay at a hotel close to the Pentagon. Can you recommend one?"

"I'm not supposed to recommend any hotel, but I've heard the Twin Bridges Marriott Motor Hotel is very good and is close by the Pentagon."

"Thank you Captain Carroll, I'll see you in a couple of days."

After placing the handset back on the cradle, Ian thanked the sergeant and left the recruiting office. Later that day, he booked a flight on American Airlines from

343

Nashville to Washington National Airport, for September 15. He then booked a room at the Twin Bridges Hotel for two nights, just in case he had to stay over.

The next day he flew to Washington and stayed at the Marriott hotel in Arlington, Virginia. The following morning, he took a cab to the Pentagon, entered the main door and approached the visitors' reception desk.

"My name is Ian Black and I'm here to see General Jonathon Carter at 1000 hours. The appointment was made through a Captain Carroll, his aide I believe."

The receptionist looked at her list and didn't find his name. She looked up Captain Carroll on her phone list and called him.

"Captain, there's an Ian Black here to see General Carter."

Ian couldn't hear the response but, in a few seconds, the receptionist replied, "Yes sir." and hung up the phone.

She looked at Ian and said, "The captain will be down here in a few minutes to take you up. You can have a seat over there, if you would like."

"Thank you, ma'am," Ian replied.

In a few minutes, Captain Carroll dressed in a blue air force uniform, came up to the receptionist, who pointed Ian out to him. He came over to where Ian was seated.

"Ian Black?"

"Ian stood up and replied, "Yes. Captain Carroll, I presume."

They shook hands and the captain told Ian to follow him. They walked down what seemed miles of corridors and went up one floor, in an elevator full of military personnel. Finally, they reached a door that had the initials USAFSS on it. The captain opened the door and they walked into an outer office. On one wall was a door that had a sign with "General Jonathon Carter" written on it in bold, black letters.

"Wait here," the captain said, as he knocked on the door, entered and closed the door after him. In a moment the

344

captain came out, followed by a man Ian recognized. It was General Carter.

"Welcome to America, Ian," he said, as he held out his hand and shook Ian's. "Come on in to my office and let's talk."

Ian followed him into his office and Captain Carroll closed the door after them.

"Last time we met was at a sad occasion for you and your mother. What can I do for you?"

"Last year, I was a captain in the British Army Intelligence Corps, stationed with the Berlin Brigade. When we met at Lakenheath, General Le May told me if I was ever bored with the British Army and came to America, to look you up. My mother came back to live in Tennessee and I followed her a few months later."

"Yes, I remember that brief conversation."

"At the moment, I have a good job in Nashville that pays very well, but, to be honest, I'm bored and would like to get back into military life. I'm hoping that it will be possible for me to join the Air Force and work in the intelligence field again."

"What kind of rank were you envisioning, if you could join us?"

"I'm hoping that I can join at the same rank I left the British Army; that is the rank of captain. I could learn the American salute very quickly," he replied with a smile.

"Well, I'll tell you what Ian. Something came up this morning and I'm sorry that I can't spend any more time with you today. Can you stay the night and come back to see me tomorrow, at the same time? I'll make sure that we won't be disturbed, until we talk it through."

"Yes, I can do that. Actually I booked a room for two nights, in anticipation that I might have to stay."

"Very good, in the meantime I'll have Captain Carroll look into any regulations that prohibit bringing someone, with your experience, in at a higher rank than lieutenant."

345

The general rang the buzzer on his intercom and asked Captain Carroll to come in.

"Captain, Ian is going to stay overnight and will come back tomorrow, at the same time, for an in depth discussion with me. Make sure that two hours are blocked out on my schedule. Also, I want you to look into regulations and past exceptions made about bringing someone in from a foreign military service; this should include rank, age, etc."

"Yes sir, I'll do that right away."

"Good. Since you're not married captain, would you be available to take Ian to dinner tonight. Of course, you'll be reimbursed for the expense."

"Yes, I'll be glad to do that."

"I'll see you tomorrow Ian and have a good dinner tonight, with Austin here. I have to run."

Austin ushered Ian out of the general's office and took him down to the main lobby.

"I'll see you tonight Ian at 6:30 pm and I'll take you to dinner, where we can compare military experiences. You're staying at the Marriott, correct?"

"Yes, that's right. See you later and thanks for your help, Austin."

Ian took a taxi back to his hotel and, in the afternoon after lunch, he toured the Washington area, as much as he could by walking.

That night Austin took him to dinner at the Orleans House in Rosslyn, where they compared life between the American Air Force and the British Army. This restaurant, which was not far from the Pentagon, was famous for its prime rib. As they ate the delicious beef and drank some red wine that Austin selected, they compared notes about military life.

"So Ian, what did you exactly do in Cyprus and Berlin, for the British Army Intelligence Corps?" Austin asked.

"In Cyprus, our main job was to track down the EOKA terrorists and, in particular, the leader of the group, Colonel

Grivas. We eventually managed to corner him at a house in Limassol but, at the last minute, the British Government signed a treaty and we were ordered to stand down."

"It must have been very frustrating," Austin commented.

"It certainly was. We spent months tracking him down, all for naught."

"What were your major duties in Berlin?"

Ian responded, "Our major task was to keep track of the Soviet and Warsaw troop movements and to anticipate new developments. This involved "touring" East Germany, looking for weapons and convoys. As far as the Berlin Wall is concerned, I did warn my superiors about it being built, in advance, but no action was taken. It seemed that everyone was waiting for President Kennedy to move, but nothing happened. Even the Americans I knew in the U.S. Army were frustrated. I also met a Colonel Tracy Haga, of U.S. Air Force intelligence, who had also come up with some information about the potential of a Wall being built.

One other interesting task I had, while in Berlin, was to develop a strategy for unmasking a mole in the British Berlin Brigade. It turned out to be a swallow."

"What is a swallow? I haven't heard that term except for a type of bird."

"A swallow, in spy language, is a female who will use anything, including sex, to get information. How about you, Austin? How long have you been in the Air Force?"

"I joined the Air Force after graduating from Penn State ROTC in 1958, as a second lieutenant, and managed to get into Air Force Intelligence, mainly because I took languages at the University. My first major task was to analyze the Cuban Air Force capability, after Castro took over in early 1959. In 1960, I went to a hush-hush listening post and monitored Russian and Chinese communications traffic. Finally, by a stroke of luck, I met General Carter who selected me to become his aide. His previous assistant had been promoted and reassigned to other duties."

"Do you think you will ever go to Vietnam?" Ian asked.

"No, I don't think so, as long as General Carter needs me and thinks I'm doing a good job."

"Well, this has been an interesting evening. The food and wine was excellent. Thanks very much. I guess I'll see you tomorrow at ten o'clock, in the lobby," Ian responded.

"I'll drive you back to the Marriott. How do you like that hotel?"

"It's very good. I appreciate the recommendation and it's close to the Pentagon."

Austin drove Ian to the hotel, said goodnight and dropped him off.

The next day, Ian went back to the Pentagon and had the receptionist call Captain Austin Carroll. He came down and ushered Ian back up to General Carter's office, where he was waiting for him.

"Come on in Ian and close the door." At the same time he told Austin not to disturb them, except in a dire emergency.

For the next hour, Ian related to the general what he had done for the British Amy in Cyprus and Berlin. Now and again, the general asked a few questions to get some clarification. After finishing a recap of his British Army experience, Ian explained that he wanted to get back into military life, and he believed his experience would be of great value to the Air Force. In addition, he explained that his background did not seem to fit too well in the Nashville music industry.

When Ian finished, General Carter said, "I glad you came to us and not the U.S. Army. I can understand why you wish to join the Air Force, and we certainly need people like you; especially with your experience in Berlin and Cyprus. However, I can assure you that you will not be required to ever fly a four-engine Shackleton," he said, with a grin.

The general continued, "As you're probably aware, the Vietnam area is heating up, since the Gulf of Tonkin resolution was passed by Congress on August 7, just a month ago. We're going to need every experienced person that we can get our hands on. I managed to contact your previous CO, Colonel Thurman in Berlin, and he highly recommended you. He explained he was sorry to see you leave the British Army, since you carried out every assigned task in an exemplary manner. I also managed to contact Colonel Tracy Haga, Air Force Intelligence in Berlin, and he thought you would be an excellent fit in the United States Air Force Security Service. I believe you know him.

Also, Captain Carroll checked into any problems with bringing experienced people on board, such as you, with an officer's commission. Its turns out, there is no regulation that prohibits it and therefore, if you're willing to join the USAFSS, I can get you the rank of captain. It would be a reserve commission but, at some point, I'm sure you'll be given a regular commission. The only major difference is that it's easier to obtain a promotion, if you're a regular officer."

"I gladly accept the offer, general. When can I start?"

"I'll have a letter drawn up offering you the rank of captain and, included in the envelope, will be orders for you to report to Maxwell AFB in Montgomery Alabama, where you will be sworn in and attend the Air Force College for three months, for indoctrination about the Air Force ways. In addition, you will take an introductory class in the Vietnamese language. It will probably come in useful. I'm not sure exactly, but I believe you'll be required to report to Maxwell on Monday, the 5th of October. This gives you about two weeks to get your affairs in order.

Welcome on board, Ian. I hope you will not be disappointed in the Air Force. I can assure you that the food is better than the British Army," he said, with a smile.

Ian flew back to Nashville and told his mother, who was not surprised. Ever since he had arrived in Tennessee, he had seemed restless.

His mother drove him down to Montgomery and dropped him off at the main gate of Maxwell Air Force Base. He presented his orders and was assigned a room, where he deposited his bags. A mentor, by the name of Captain McCarthy, had been assigned to him for one month, to assist him in the transition from the British Army way of doing things, to the American Air Force standards.

He was sworn in by the commandant of the Air Force College and outfitted with uniforms.

"I, Ian Black, having been appointed a captain in the United States Air Force, do solemnly swear that I will support and defend the Constitution of the United States against all enemies, foreign or domestic, that I will bear true faith and allegiance to the same; that I take this obligation freely, without any mental reservations or purpose of evasion; and that I will well and faithfully discharge the duties of the office upon which I am about to enter; So help me God."

He was on his way; Captain Ian Black, United States Air Force. Vietnam might be calling him in the near future.

EPILOGUE

Captain Ian Black departed West Berlin, in June 1964, and headed back to England, where he visited some old school mates. From the UK, he flew on to the USA to join his mother in Tennessee, and there he worked for one of her cousins. However, he missed military life and became bored with the marketing job. He decided to travel to Washington for a discussion with General Jonathan Carter, whom he had met at the Lakenheath memorial service for his father. Through this General Carter, he managed to obtain a commission in the USAF and ultimately was shipped to Vietnam, to serve as an intelligence officer.

When he flew from Germany, he left behind the Berlin Wall that remained in place for another twenty-five years, before it was finally breached on the 9th of November, 1989. It was ultimately torn down and Germany became reunified on the 3rd of October, 1990. How many people were killed trying to escape through, over or under the Wall is not known for sure? The estimate is that anywhere from 136 - 250 East Berliners died, trying to flee their Communist masters.

During the next few years, leaders in the East came and went. Nikita Khrushchev, the Soviet leader in favour of the wall, was ousted on the 14th of October, 1964, and was replaced by Leonid Brezhnev. The East German leader Walter Ulbricht was forced to resign in 1971, because of DDR economic problems and disagreements with Brezhnev over détente policies, together with PR problems caused by the Wall itself. Erich Honecker took over as General Secretary of the German Socialist Unity Party.

Citizens of East Berlin, trying to flee, came up with some ingenious escape methods, including sliding down a Zip Line, using a Munich Playboy membership card that looked like a passport, riding in a hot air balloon, digging tunnels, swimming the Spree River, using a handmade miniature submarine, flying an ultra light aircraft with Soviet markings and stealing a Soviet car, with the three occupants dressed as Soviet soldiers. The last one made it past the checkpoint, because the East German guard just waved them through.

In 1964, a British business man, Greville Maynard, and a Soviet spy by the name of Konon Trofimovich were exchanged at the Heerstrasse border crossing. However, Captain Black had nothing to do with this exchange. It was conducted through diplomatic channels.

In 1969, Willy Brandt, former Berlin mayor, became the chancellor of the Federal Republic of Germany but was forced to resign in 1974, when it came to light that he had an aide, Günter Guillaume, who was a Stasi spy.

Since his mother was an American citizen and he was registered at birth, Ian was a dual citizen and therefore had no problem moving to the States.

He was an American citizen, and, with his background in the British Army Intelligence Corps, he became a valuable resource for the United States Air Force, which was headed up by General Curtis LeMay.

GLOSSARY

AYIOS NIKOLAOS	Cyprus CIA/NSA/MI6/GCHQ Listening Post
BAOR	British Army on the Rhine
BEA	British European Airways
BFO	Blinding Flash of the Obvious
BND	West German Bundesnachrichtendienst
BOAC	British Overseas Airways Corporation
BRIXMIS	British CIC Mission to Soviet
CHECKPT. CHARLIE	Major Crossing Point into East Berlin
CIA	United States Central Intelligence Agency
CLAY COMPOUND	Main U.S. Military Complex in West Berlin
CLOBBER	Arrest or detention by Soviets / East Germans
DDR	East Germans Initials for East Germany
DGSE	French Security Agency
FLAT	British word for Apartment or Wohnung
FRG	Federal Republic of Germany (West Germany)
GCHQ	British Government Communications HQ
GDR	West Germans Initials for East Germany
GRU	USSR Military Intelligence
HUMINT	Human Intelligence
KGB	USSR Intelligence & Internal Security
KOMENDATURA	Soviet Military Police Station
LORRY	British word for Truck
MI5	Protects UK national security from espionage
MI6	UK Secret Intelligence Service (SIS)
MLM	Military Liaison Mission

GLOSSARY (CONT.)

MfS	Ministerium für Staatssicherheit (aka Stasi)
MOLE	Spy embedded deep into an organization
MUFTI/CIVVIES	Military slang for civilian clothes
NARK	Slang for East German Secret Police (Stasi)
NSA	National Security Agency
OLYMPIASTADIUM	Berlin Olympic Stadium – British Brigade HQ.
OPERATION GOLD	Known as Operation Stopwatch to the British
OPERATION ROSE	Plan to build the Berlin Wall
PRA	Permanent Restricted Area
RAF	Royal Air Force (British Air Force)
RAF DAKOTA	Douglas DC-3, US Military C-47 Skytrain
RAF GATOW	Main RAF airfield - British Sector West Berlin
RAF NORTHOLT	RAF Transport Command airfield near London
RAVEN	Male Spy for Seducing Target
SIEGESSÄULE	Prussian Victory Column
SIGINT	Signal Intelligence
STASI	East German Secret Police (aka MfS)
SWALLOW	Female Spy for Seducing Target
TEUFELSBERG	Field Station Berlin – NSA, MI6 Listening Post
TOUR	Trip by a MLM into East Germany
TRA	Temporary Restricted Area
U-BAHN	Berlin Underground Train System
U6	North-South U-Bahn Line
USAFSS	United States Air Force Security Service
USMLM	United States Military Liaison Mission

REAL HISTORICAL CHARACTERS

East German GDR President..............................Walter Ulbricht (1907-1990)

Security Secretary, Central Committee............Erich Honecker (1912-1994)

GDR Chief of Foreign Intelligence.........Markus Johannes Wolf (1923-2006)

1st Secretary Berlin Socialist Unity Party (SED).....Paul Verner (1911-1986)

West Berlin Mayor...Willy Brandt (1913-1992)

West German Chancellor ....Konrad Adenauer (1876-1967

U.S. President ....John F. Kennedy (1917-1963)

British Prime Minister ....Maurice Harold MacMillan (1894-1986)

Richmond Ice Skating Trainer ....Arnold Gerschwiler (1914-2003)

General Secretary of USSR............................Nikita Khrushchev (1894-1971)

USAF Chief of Staff.....................................General Curtis LeMay (1906-1990)

US Commandant, West Berlin.......Major General James Gavin (1907-1990)

U.S. Army G-2 Intelligence............Lt. Colonel Laurence Waple

FICTIONAL CHARACTERS

Lieutenant Ian Black (Kurt).............................Intelligence Corps
Captain Alex Swiderski......................................Intelligence Corps
Major Clifford Phillips (Martin)..................... Intelligence Corps
Colonel David Thurman (Jack)...................... Intelligence Corps
Brigadier James Croxford (Rex)............Dir. Intelligence Corps
Brigadier Charles Clemens.......................British Berlin Brigade
Capt. Patrick Silverman (Bob)...513th USA Military Intel. Grp.
Major Vass......................................513th USA Military Intel. Grp.
Alena Svrček ....Czechoslovakian Ice Skater
Andrew Dinglefoot (John).....................................MI6 Teufelsberg
Peter Ford (Percival)..MI6 Berlin
Walter Briggs (Chetwyn)....................................MI6 Berlin
Jack Rowe (Wally)...CIA Berlin
Colonel Tracy Haga................................USAF Intelligence Berlin
General Jonathan Carter............USAF Intelligence Washington
Captain Austin Carroll................USAF Intelligence Washington
Ingrid Meyer (Monika)......................Erich Honecker's girlfriend
Hans Schubart (Franz) ....BND Intelligence Agent
Giselle Schmitt.....................................Stasi Mole (Swallow)
Hilda Schmitt...Giselle Schmitt's Mother
Trevor Ackerman..Plessey Company plc
Brigadier General James Gross ....US Intelligence, Germany

BERLIN U-BAHN MAP

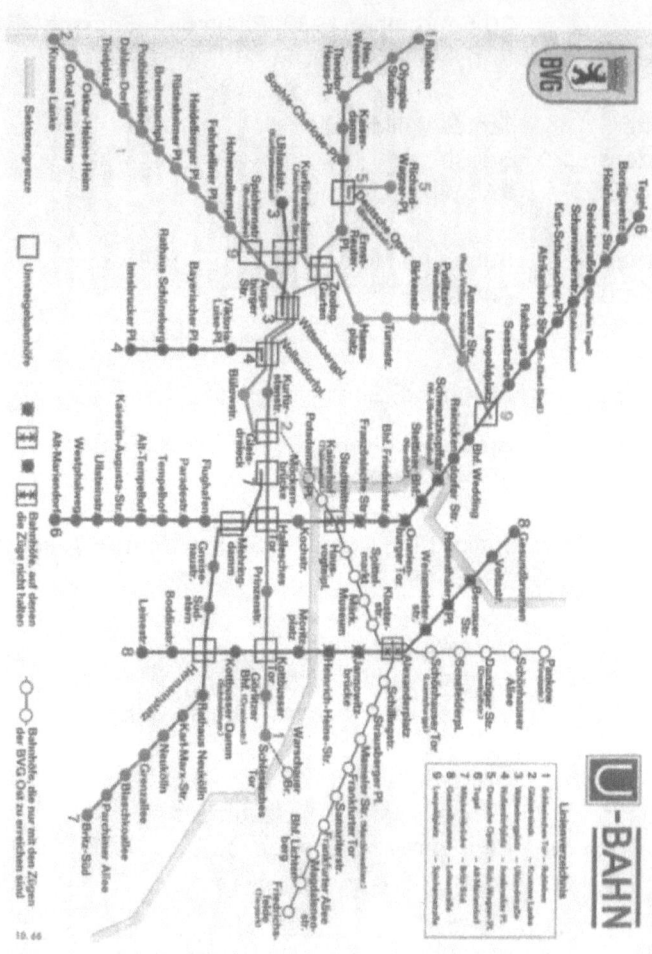

IAN BLACK'S BIOGRAPHY

Born:	30 September 1939, Richmond, England
Citizenship:	British and American
Father:	James William Black
Citizenship:	British
Wartime:	RAF Wing Commander
Mother:	Reba Ann Miles
Citizenship:	American
Hometown:	Franklin, Tennessee
Domicile:	Richmond, Surrey England
Education:	Broomfield House School, Kew, England 1944 – 1946
	Junior King's School, Sturry, Kent, England 1947 -1952
	Harrow, England 1953-1957 English "Public" School Studied – Languages: Greek, German
British Army:	Drafted 1957
Rank:	2nd Lieutenant, 1st Lieutenant
Assignment:	Cyprus during Emergency 1958-1960
Height:	Seventy-three inches (6' 1")
Weight:	Thirteen Stone (182 pounds)
Hair:	Brown
Eyes:	Hazel

THE AUTHORS

Richard Osborn

He was born and raised in England, and educated at King's School, Canterbury. He is a veteran of the British Army Royal Artillery and the United States Air Force. He is a graduate of California State University at Los Angeles and of the Thunderbird Graduate School of International Management. Later, he worked at General Dynamics, Aeronutronic Ford, Hughes Aircraft and Tektronix. He is a licensed pilot and has conducted numerous seminars for Tektronix Inc. in the Far East and Europe. Now he is writing fiction and non-fiction in Knoxville, Tennessee.

Barbara Osborn

She was born and raised in Virginia. She attended art classes at the University of Georgia and studied art history at the University of Tennessee. She has travelled extensively in Europe and the Mediterranean. After living in England for awhile, she came back to Knoxville, Tennessee remarried and retired. Currently, she and her husband are co-writing fiction novels.

RICHARD AND BARBARA OSBORN

AVAILABLE NOW

The Osborns' novel is about a young British lieutenant, Ian Black, who arrives in Cyprus and soon comes face-to-face with EOKA terrorists. He falls in love with a nurse at the hospital and saves the Cyprus governor from assassination. Ian survives an attempt on his life, but to his horror faces a tragedy. He returns to England after helping to save the Cyprus peace treaty.

BRITANNIA-AMERICAN PUBLISHING

ISBN-13: 978-0692294246

AVAILABLE NOW

After resigning his commission in the British Army and going to the United States, Ian Black meets with General Carter in Washington. He is offered a commission in the USAF and works in the Air Force ISR Agency as a captain. Due to his experience in Berlin, he is transferred to the USAFSS Section H during the Vietnam War.

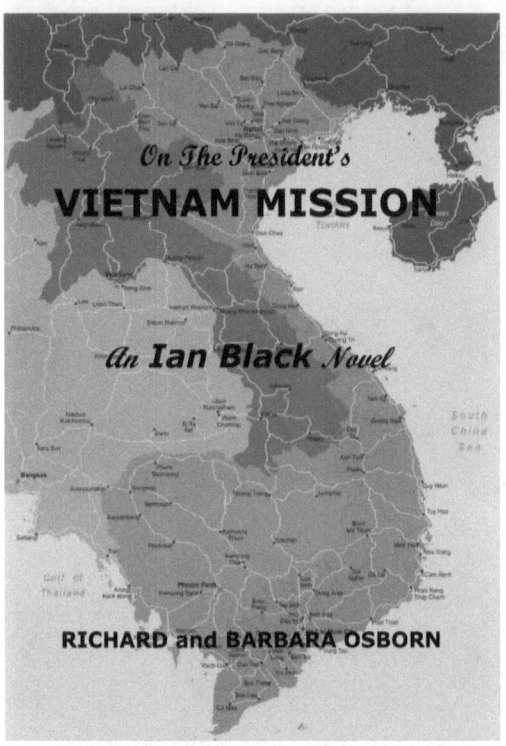

On The President's
VIETNAM MISSION

An **Ian Black** *Novel*

RICHARD and BARBARA OSBORN

BRITANNIA-AMERICAN BOOKS
ISBN-13: 978-1981773022

RICHARD AND BARBARA OSBORN

AVAILABLE NOW

The Osborns' explosive novel delves into whether the President, Edward Tuckwell, is able to remain in office after two terms, using a false flag operation. The climax shocks the nation and calm finally returns to Washington, after the tanks knock down the White House gates.

BRITANNIA-AMERICAN PUBLISHING
ISBN-13: 978-0692503379

AVAILABLE NOW

The Osborn's book delves into the blunders and
appeasements that occurred during the years 1914-2014.
It gives some historical background in each chapter and
analyzes the blunders. In the final chapter the author lists
the most important blunder(s) and the selection criteria.

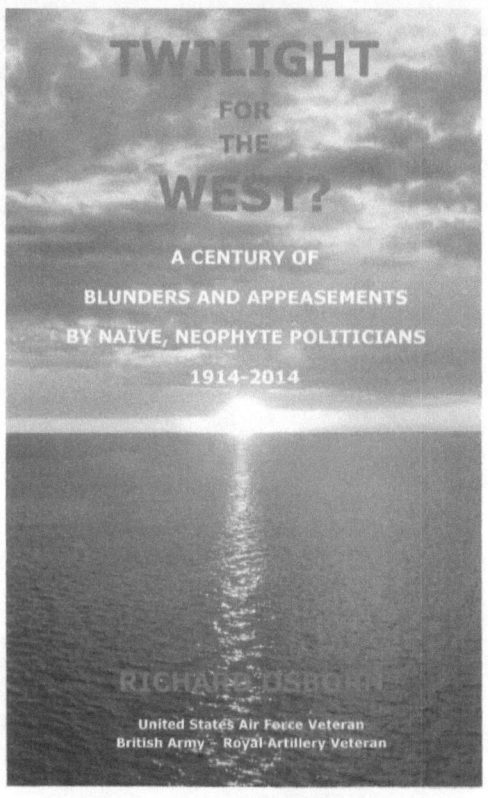

BRITANNIA-AMERICAN PUBLISHING
ISBN-13: 978-0692418413

RICHARD AND BARBARA OSBORN

AVAILABLE NOW

This Ian Black Trilogy covers his actions, adventures and romance through the years 1958 to 1968. He starts out in the British Army being assigned first to Cyprus and then Berlin. Upon the death of his father, he moves to the United States and serves in the U.S. Air Force in Vietnam battling the North Vietnamese.

TRUE
PATRIOTISM

An **Ian Black** *Novel*

RICHARD and BARBARA OSBORN

BRITANNIA-AMERICAN BOOKS
ISBN-13:978-1719086462